OXFORD WORLD'S CLASSICS

THE SATYRICON

ALMOST all scholars today identify the author of the *Satyricon* with the Petronius whom Tacitus describes as 'the arbiter of elegance' of the emperor Nero. This Petronius had earlier been a competent administrator as governor of the province of Bithynia, and he subsequently attained the honour of the consulship (?AD 62). He then retired into a private life of refined luxury, from which he was advanced by Nero to enliven the cultural life of the court. But his close relations with the emperor Nero attracted the vindictive envy of the praetorian prefect Tigellinus, who succeeded in alienating him from Nero's affections and in engineering his downfall. He was forced to commit suicide in AD 66. His ribald novel dates to the closing years of his life.

P. G. WALSH is Emeritus Professor of Humanity at the University of Glasgow. His translations for Oxford World's Classics include Apuleius, *The Golden Ass*; Boethius, *The Consolation of Philosophy*; Pliny, *Complete Letters*; and Cicero, *The Nature of the Gods*, *On Obligations*, and *Selected Letters*. He has also published extensively on Livy, on the Roman novel, and on patristic and medieval Latin.

OXFORD WORLD'S CLASSICS

*For over 100 years Oxford World's Classics have brought
readers closer to the world's great literature. Now with over 700
titles—from the 4,000-year-old myths of Mesopotamia to the
twentieth century's greatest novels—the series makes available
lesser-known as well as celebrated writing.*

*The pocket-sized hardbacks of the early years contained
introductions by Virginia Woolf, T. S. Eliot, Graham Greene,
and other literary figures which enriched the experience of reading.
Today the series is recognized for its fine scholarship and
reliability in texts that span world literature, drama and poetry,
religion, philosophy and politics. Each edition includes perceptive
commentary and essential background information to meet the
changing needs of readers.*

OXFORD WORLD'S CLASSICS

PETRONIUS

The Satyricon

Translated with an Introduction and Notes by
P. G. WALSH

OXFORD
UNIVERSITY PRESS

OXFORD

UNIVERSITY PRESS

Great Clarendon Street, Oxford OX2 6DP

Oxford University Press is a department of the University of Oxford.
It furthers the University's objective of excellence in research, scholarship,
and education by publishing worldwide in

Oxford New York

Auckland Bangkok Buenos Aires Cape Town Chennai
Dar es Salaam Delhi Hong Kong Istanbul Karachi Kolkata
Kuala Lumpur Madrid Melbourne Mexico City Mumbai Nairobi
São Paulo Shanghai Taipei Tokyo Toronto

Oxford is a registered trade mark of Oxford University Press
in the UK and in certain other countries

Published in the United States
by Oxford University Press Inc., New York

Translation, Introduction, and Notes © P. G. Walsh 1997

The moral rights of the author have been asserted

Database right Oxford University Press (maker)

First published as a World's Classics paperback 1997
Reissued as an Oxford World's Classics paperback 1999
Reissued 2009

All rights reserved. No part of this publication may be reproduced,
stored in a retrieval system, or transmitted, in any form or by any means,
without the prior permission in writing of Oxford University Press,
or as expressly permitted by law, or under terms agreed with the appropriate
reprographics rights organizations. Enquiries concerning reproduction
outside the scope of the above should be sent to the Rights Department,
Oxford University Press, at the address above

You must not circulate this book in any other binding or cover
and you must impose this same condition on any acquirer

British Library Cataloguing in Publication Data

Data available

Library of Congress Cataloging in Publication Data

Petronius Arbiter. [Satyricon. English].
The Satyricon / Petronius ; translated with an introduction
and notes by P. G. Walsh
(Oxford world's classics)
Includes bibliographical references.
1. Satire, Latin—Translations into English. 2. Rome—Fiction.
I. Walsh, P. G. (Patrick Gerard) II. Title. III. Series.
PA6558.E5W3 1997 873'.01—dc21 96–40165

ISBN 978-0-19-953921-5

6

Printed in Great Britain by
Clays Ltd, St Ives plc

In Memoriam
M. S. S.

Preface and Acknowledgements

Few readers of Petronius can be spared the feelings of ambivalence which have dogged the reception of the *Satyricon* for close on two thousand years. Even in our more permissive age (perhaps especially in our more permissive age), it is difficult not to share the distaste earlier expressed by a Fielding or a Cowper, as we review the occasional episodes which jauntily recommend paedophilia and scopophilia among the diversions presented for our entertainment. On the positive side, we share with T. S. Eliot and Anthony Powell an appreciative exploration of the underside of the Roman imperial society as it really existed, in the company of a guide of devastating wit and devil-may-care gaiety, qualities which mark him off so decisively from the sober *grauitas* of much of the surviving Roman literature.

Following the publication of *The Roman Novel* in 1970, my approaches to the *Satyricon* were confined to occasional reviews in the journals until 1990, when the arrival of Costas Panayotakis from the University of Crete to undertake doctoral studies at Glasgow revived my waning enthusiasm. As often happens in these circumstances, the supervisor became the learner, and the publication of Dr Panayotakis's dissertation, *Theatrum Arbitri* (Brill, 1995), will be heralded as an important contribution to Petronian studies. He has put me further in his debt by compiling the Select Bibliography which follows the Introduction to this translation. I must express warm thanks also to Professor Ted Kenney and Professor Bryan Reardon for helpful criticism of an early draft of the translation of the first episodes; and to

John Betts of the Bristol Classical Press for agreeing to reissue *The Roman Novel* (1995), which can be consulted as a companion volume to this translation and to that of Apuleius' *The Golden Ass*, now published in *The World's Classics* series by Oxford University Press.

P. G. W.

Contents

Abbreviations

AJP	American Journal of Philology
ANRW	Aufstieg und Niedergang der römischen Welt
Ant. Class.	L'Antiquité Classique
AUMLA	Journal of the Australasian Universities' Language and Literature Association
Balsdon	J. P. V. D. Balsdon, Life and Leisure in Ancient Rome (London, 1969)
BICS	Bulletin of the Institute of Classical Studies
BSA	Annual of the British School at Athens
B. Stud. Lat.	Bolletino di Studi Latini (Naples)
CB	Classical Bulletin
CHCL	Cambridge History of Classical Literature
CJ	Classical Journal
C&M	Classica et Mediaevalia
CP	Classical Philology
CQ	Classical Quarterly
CR	Classical Review
G&R	Greece and Rome
JHS	Journal of Hellenic Studies
JRS	Journal of Roman Studies
MCSN	Materiali e Contributi per la storia della narrativa greco-latina (Perugia)
MD	Materiali e Discussioni per l'analisi dei testi classici (Pisa)
Mnem.	Mnemosyne
Mus. Helv.	Museum Helveticum
OCD	Oxford Classical Dictionary
OLD	Oxford Latin Dictionary
PCPS	Proceedings of the Cambridge Philological Society

PMLA	*Proceedings of the Modern Languages Association of America*
PSN	*Petronian Society Newsletter*
RE	Pauly-Wissowa, *Real-Encyclopädie*
REL	*Revue des Études Latines*
RhM	*Rheinisches Museum*
RSC	*Rivista di Studi Classici*
Smith	M. S. Smith, *Petronii Arbitri Cena Trimalchionis* (Oxford, 1975)
TAPA	*Transactions and Proceedings of the American Philological Association*
WS	*Wiener Studien*
ŽAnt	*Živa Antika* (Skopje)

Introduction

Proconsul of Bithynia,
Who loved to turn the night to day,
Yet for your ease had more to show
Than others for their push and go,
Teach us to save the Spirit's expense,
And win to Fame through indolence.

(Oliver St John Gogarty, *An Offering of Swans*
(Dublin, 1923), 17)

I

Though the date at which the *Satyricon* was composed has
been hotly debated since the Renaissance, virtually all modern critics have now concluded that its author is identical
with the Petronius of the Neronian age, unforgettably portrayed in a thumbnail sketch by Tacitus. The references to
contemporary figures, the economic and social indications
offered by the novel, the legal arguments, and above all the
literary connections with the younger Seneca and with Lucan,
have combined to make this Neronian date highly prob-
able. Moreover, the sobriquet Arbiter appended to the novelist's name in the manuscripts corresponds with the title
of *elegantiae arbiter* accorded him by Tacitus. Once this
identification of the author with the Petronius in Tacitus is
accepted, it is possible to date the *Satyricon* closely. Tacitus'
Petronius died by his own hand in early AD 66; and there
are manifest connections between Petronius' poem on the
Civil War with its preliminary observations (§§ 118–24) and
the epic of Lucan, which was still incomplete when its
author committed suicide in 65. Even if the *Satyricon* was

written in part before publication of Lucan's epic, a date for
the *Satyricon* of 63–5 cannot be far out; this would square
also with possible allusions in the novel to Seneca's *Moral
Epistles*, which are to be attributed to the last three years of
Seneca's life in 62–5. If, as I believe, the *Satyricon* was a *jeu
d'esprit* rapidly completed, the year 65 could have marked its
beginning and its end.[1]

   This identification of the author with the Petronius in Tacitus is of some importance for a proper assessment of the
novel. The historian emphasizes that in his earlier career
as proconsul of Bithynia and later as consul (he was probably suffect consul in 62) he was a vigorous and competent official; it should not surprise us to find that the most
detailed characterization in the novel is devoted to an Asian
ex-slave turned millionaire, Trimalchio, and that this portrait reflects a close awareness of the social and economic
changes in Italian society.[2] Subsequently, Tacitus tells us,
Petronius became celebrated at Rome for an indolent life
of refined luxury, out of which Nero summoned him to be
his arbiter of elegance ('the emperor in his life of luxury considered nothing as agreeable and degenerately pleasurable
except what Petronius recommended to him for approval').
But subsequently the machinations of the praetorian prefect Tigellinus caused him to be alienated from the emperor, at the cost of his life. Tacitus had earlier[3] described
the recent suicide of Seneca evoking the end of Socrates;
his account of the last hours of Petronius offers a studied
contrast. Our author listened to his friends 'not discoursing

---

[1] The point of departure for modern reconsiderations of the date of composition is K. F. C. Rose, *The Date and Author of the Satyricon* (Leiden, 1971); Rose also
contributed an amusing sketch of the earlier controversies in *Arion* (1966), 275 ff.
For the social and economic factors, see J. H. D'Arms, *Commerce and Social Standing
in Ancient Rome* (Ann Arbor, 1981); for the literary connections, J. P. Sullivan,
Literature and Politics in the Age of Nero (Ithaca, NY, 1985). Residual doubts about
a Neronian date are well formulated in M. S. Smith's edition of *Cena Trimalchionis*
(Oxford, 1975), App. 1; cf. R. Martin, *REL* (1975), 182 ff. For the thumbnail sketch
in Tacitus, see *Annals* 16. 17–19. The single MS of Tacitus refers to him as Gaius
Petronius, but the Elder Pliny (NH 37. 20) and Plutarch (*Moralia* 60D) both refer
to him as Titus; there is no *praenomen* in Petronian MSS.
   [2] See especially §§ 75–7.   [3] *Annals* 15. 64.

on the immortality of the soul, or on the precepts of the philosophers, but reciting light lyrics and impromptu verses'. In his will, so far from following the convention of flattering the emperor to ensure the safety of his kin, Petronius documented Nero's immoralities, citing the names of his male and female partners and the novel forms of lust which he had practised with each one. Having sealed the will with his own ring, he had it dispatched directly to the court.

This account makes compulsive reading, and inevitably affects our outlook on the novel; cries of 'biographical fallacy' do little to remove the Tacitean spectacles. We inevitably visualize Petronius as a cynical successor to the worthy Seneca at court, where as *arbiter elegantiae* he is surrounded by a circle of political opportunists whom Tacitus depicts with icy contempt. The period of his cultural dominance coincides with some of Nero's worst excesses. We are hardly surprised on reading the novel to find this gifted cynic of profoundly literary tastes exploiting his status to denigrate the writings of Seneca and Lucan, former intimates of Nero now discarded and disgraced; he even has the nerve to poke fun at the emperor himself.[4] Any lingering temptation to regard the *Satyricon* as a moral diatribe meets its first impenetrable obstacle in Tacitus' devastating sketch of the author, which encourages us to adhere to the traditional view that the book is a comic romance, 'seeking solely pleasure for people's ears'.[5]

II

This traditional interpretation is supported by the title of the novel, whether cited as *Satyricon* (a genitive plural with *libri* understood) or as *Satyrica* (a neuter plural). The heading means 'A recital of lecherous happenings'. There is

[4] Here I contend that the long poems, *The Capture of Troy* and *The Civil War* are presented in parody of Seneca, Lucan, *et hoc genus omne*; and that the portrayal of Trimalchio comically incorporates attributes of Nero. See further pp. xxxiii f., xxx below.   [5] Macrobius, *In Somn. Scip.* 1. 2. 8.

probably also a punning reference to the Latin *satura*.
Though there is no etymological connection, a Roman ear
would have been cocked in that direction, inferring that the
novel was to be a narrative of lascivious behaviour infused
with satirical elements.

Reconstruction of the length and content of the whole
work is hazardous, since the evidence offered by the manuscripts and the surviving sections of the work is tenuous. From
the combined information offered by the manuscripts and
one external source we learn that all the surviving portions are from Books XIV–XVI, which on a simple calcu-
lation would imply that in the original they were preceded
by a narrative five times as long. Emboldened by these
figures, some critics suggest that Petronius modelled his
book on the length of the *Odyssey*, and composed a work
of twenty-four books. If this view were accepted, we should
have to reconcile ourselves to the loss of seven-eighths of
the original, and to visualize a work as long as all the extant
Greek romances combined.[6]

Evidence gathered from references in the surviving text
and in the fragments suggests that the story may have begun
in Marseilles, where the hero is betrothed to a lady called
Doris. After scabrous experiences in which he incurs the
wrath of Priapus, he quits the city. In his travels he encounters Lichas (the captain of the ship which later bears him
to Croton) and his wife Hedyle; he robs the husband and
seduces the wife. He becomes involved also in a sexual
adventure with Tryphaena, a friend of Lichas and later a
fellow passenger on the sea-journey to Croton; from her
entourage he steals her comely slave Giton, who becomes
his companion throughout the extant sections of the novel.
Whether at Marseilles or 'in the portico of Hercules' (? at
Baiae) he is prosecuted by Euscius, a formidable advocate,
and anticipates condemnation by flight. On his departure,

---

[6] *Collected Ancient Greek Novels* in translation, ed. B. P. Reardon (Berkeley and
Los Angeles, 1989) has 827 pages. For a review of the problem of the length of
the *Satyricon*, see P. G. Walsh, *The Roman Novel* (Cambridge, 1970), 73 ff.; H. Van
Thiel, *Petron* (Leiden, 1971), who tentatively argues for twenty-four books.

he leaves for dead the man at whose house he had been detained; the heroes plunder the house of this aptly named agent of the law, Lycurgus. They move on, striking up an acquaintance *en route* with Ascyltus, who becomes Encolpius' rival for the affections of Giton in the first half of the extant novel. In a town on the Bay of Naples, they gain acquaintance with Quartilla, a priestess of Priapus, whose shrine they desecrate. During or shortly after this episode, they steal an expensive cloak, and leave behind a shirt containing gold coins (perhaps stolen from the house of Lycurgus). This is virtually all we can glean of the action of the earlier lost portions of the novel.[7]

There is one fragment[8] which may point to a lost episode towards the end of the romance. This makes reference to the religious ceremonial at Memphis in Egypt, which has encouraged speculation that the dissolute heroes extended their travels eastward. But the Isiac worship with which Memphis is associated was a familiar feature of life in Puteoli, Pompeii and other Campanian towns as early as the second century BC,[9] so that evidence for an episode in Egypt is hardly compelling.

Since all these indications of the action in the lost sections of the novel could be fitted comfortably into half-a-dozen episodes, the notion of a monster *Satyricon* many times longer than any other work of ancient fiction can reasonably be viewed with some scepticism. Hope of glimpsing an intelligible structure rests on close attention to the parts which survive.

Analysis of these sections reveals the alternation of 'internal' and 'external' episodes. The 'internal' episodes centre on the uneasy relationship between the hero Encolpius and his boyfriend Giton (the names throughout the novel denote the role-playing; Encolpius means literally 'On the

---

[7] For the episode at Marseilles, see fragments 1 and 4; for Doris, § 126; for the earlier encounter with Lichas, Hedyle and Tryphaena, §§ 105, 107, 113. For Euscius, fr. 8; Lycurgus § 117; the earlier meeting with Quartilla, § 17; the cloak and shirt, §§ 12–13. There may have been a further episode centring on Albucia, a lady of easy virtue (fr. 6).   [8] fr. 19.

[9] See Roeder, *RE* s.v. Isis, 2103, 2107.

Bosom', and Giton 'Neighbour' in the sexual sense). With
the appearance of Ascyltus ('Unwearied', again a name with
sexual overtones) as a rival for the affections of Giton, we
are presented with a series of variations on the 'jealous lover'
theme, idyllic bliss being followed by rampant jealousy.
Eventually Encolpius shakes off Ascyltus, only to find him
replaced as rival by Eumolpus ('Bon Chanteur'), who thus
provokes further jealousy.

This obsessive attachment of the hero to Giton as the
pervasive theme of the extant portions of the novel allows
more pragmatic speculation on the structure and length of
the whole. Closely relevant here is the motif of the anger of
Priapus. The precise circumstances in which Encolpius initially attracts the god's wrath remain obscure, but Priapus
hovers over both the Quartilla and the Circe episodes,[10] in
which the hero suffers sexual enervation. When in the final
extant section Encolpius gives thanks to Mercury, god of
thieves, for the restoration of his sexual powers,[11] it is
tempting to regard this as the climax in which the hero
finally emerges from his nightmare. The denouement would
then be comically analogous to the close of the sentimental
Greek romances, in which the lovers are conventionally
delivered from their tribulations by the kindness of a deity
to whom they render pious thanks. But this can be no more
than a speculative suggestion.

The 'external' episodes with which these internal scenes
alternate parade a range of contemporary figures and attitudes which Petronius is concerned to satirize; thus the
Saturika, the satyr-like behaviour, merges with the *satura*, the
satirical element. The heroes are initially seen at the school
of rhetoric, allowing Petronius to present barbed observations on the nature of Roman higher education and
the venality of its teachers. From there they move on to
encounter Quartilla, who offers a double target for satirical
treatment as libidinous female and hypocritical priestess.
Third in the parade of Petronius' contemporary targets is

[10] See §§ 17, 21; 139. Priapus also reveals to Lichas the presence of Encolpius
on board his ship (§ 104).   [11] § 140.

Trimalchio, the centre-piece of the surviving novel, who is here presented as the boorish host. He is followed on the narrative stage by the manic poet Eumolpus, Petronius' richest creation after Trimalchio. In his company the heroes embark on ship to confront the next satirical targets, Lichas and Tryphaena; their earlier roles in the lost sections of the novel are obscure, but here they represent the derisory face of superstition. When the heroes secure their escape from the sinking ship and make their way to Croton, they confront a second libidinous lady in Circe, and a further satirical portrayal in the legacy-hunters. All these figures, it must be stressed, are types prominent in Roman satire.

III

How are we to interpret Petronius' purposes in writing the *Satyricon*? Hopes of guidance from Greek fiction which might set the novel within a recognizable genre have as yet proved largely illusory. Recent discoveries of papyri have established that Greek novels with bawdy content, set out in the Menippean *mélange* of prose and verse favoured by Petronius, did exist.[12] The fragments indicate that there may have been Greek comic romances which are mirrored by the 'internal' sequences in the *Satyricon*. What makes Petronius' novel distinctively different is the injection of the Roman satirical element, with its parade of contemporary Italian figures derisively presented.

Thus the combination of *Saturika* and *satura* establishes an original form of fiction independent of its predecessors. Since it is impossible to categorize the novel in terms of genre,

[12] For the jejune evidence offered by the fragments of Lollianus' romance, see A. Henrichs, *Die Phoenikika des Lollianos* (Bonn, 1982); the fragments of *Iolaus* (which contain an address in the Sotadean metre, also found in Petronius) are edited by P. J. Parsons, *P.Oxy.* 3010 (1974), 34–41. These papyri both date to the second century AD; there are translations of them by G. A. Sandy in *Collected Ancient Greek Novels*, ed. Reardon. Henrich's attempt to impose a religious interpretation on the Lollianus fragments is vigorously disputed by J. J. Winkler, *JHS* (1980), 155 ff., among others.

scholars have been compelled to scrutinize the novel itself
to define its nature and purpose. Manful attempts have been
made to establish Epicurean credentials for Petronius.[13] It is
certainly true that several poetic pieces among the fragments
reflect an attraction towards Epicurean theory, especially
in relation to epistemology.[14] But the novel itself scarcely
reflects the ethos of austere Epicureanism. Epicurus himself
lauded religious worship, on the grounds that the gods offer mankind models of the life we should lead, but no hint
of such an attitude emerges from the novel's sardonic tone.
It is hardly necessary to add that the characters in their
behaviour are far from reflecting the ethical teachings of
the master. It is much truer to claim that the novel reflects
the debased Epicureanism which Roman critics like Cicero
presented as a caricature of the teachings of the Garden.

None the less, spirited but short-lived attempts to interpret the novel as a serious analysis of the sicknesses of Roman
imperial society, based on Epicurean premises, have been
advanced. This approach may have been initially inspired
by T. S. Eliot's *The Waste Land*. Eliot attended classes on
Petronius at Harvard; he prefaces *The Waste Land* with a
quotation from Trimalchio's remark at the dinner-table: 'As
for the Sibyl, I saw her with my own eyes at Cumae, suspended in a bottle, and when boys asked her "Sibyl, what is
your wish?", she would reply "I want to die." ' Eliot exploits
the anecdote to crystallize the sense that life is stale, flat and
unprofitable. In parts IV–V of *The Waste Land*, a sequence
of images evokes scenes in the *Satyricon* immediately prior
to the episode at Croton. Just as in Petronius the corpse of
Lichas, the puritanical ship's captain, is washed ashore from
the shipwreck, so in Eliot's poem

> Phlebas the Phoenician, a fortnight dead,
> Forgot the cry of gulls and the deep sea swell . . .

Eliot's next section has a physical description of the deso-
late mountain-terrain ('There is not even silence in the

---

[13] O. Raith, *Petronius, ein Epikureer* (Nuremberg, 1963); G. Highet, *TAPA* (1941),
176 ff.   [14] See especially frr. 25, 27, 29, 30 with the appended annotations.

mountains . . .'), which recalls Petronius' description of Croton as 'a plague-ridden expanse, populated by nothing but corpses being pecked to pieces, and the crows at work pecking them'.[15] This exploitation by Eliot of the *Satyricon* for his bleak vision of spiritual desolation sent modern critics back to Petronius in search of similar cries of despair. One critic entitles her article 'The Sibyl in the Bottle', and summarizes like this:

The *Satyricon*, like *The Waste Land*, contains a series of rapes, seductions, intrigues, and esoteric sexual adventures in high and low life. And here too is sensuality without joy, satiety without fulfilment, degradation without grief and horror . . . Real laughter is rare in Petronius. There is little joy. The characters lack just what Eliot's characters lack—the feeling of being alive, the sense of good and evil.[16]

Another influential critic[17] accepts that Petronius is consciously criticizing his corrupt society, but protests that the novel has a fundamental gaiety foreign to Eliot's poem. Yet beneath the gaiety lies 'a deep, searching analysis of the death-throes of Classical Romanitas', for Petronius is the last Classical author 'in whom we can feel the firmness of moral control that underlies the Greek tragedians', a writer 'squarely in the Latin moralist and satirical tradition, and the greatest moralist of them all'.

This thesis argues that Petronius is preaching from an Epicurean platform, with the message that luxury spells death. An earlier writer of similar views[18] visualizes the novel as a sort of documentary, 'a gigantic imaginative record of the night-life of Rome as visited by Petronius and Nero together'. Petronius, it is claimed, wrote the book 'to show the repulsiveness of the manner of life, and the danger and guilt that it brings'. Without explicitly condemning the squalid mores of the characters and the society which breeds

[15] § 116. For a general account of the influence of Petronius on Eliot, see G. L. Schmeling and D. R. Rebmann, *Comparative Literature Studies* (1975), 393 ff.

[16] Helen Bacon, *Virginia Quarterly Review* (1958), 276 ff.

[17] William Arrowsmith, *Arion* (1966), 304 ff. = *Essays on Classical Literature*, ed. Niall Rudd (Cambridge, 1972), 122 ff.　　[18] G. Highet, *TAPA* (1941), 176 ff.

them, the author preaches his message dispassionately. The description of their behaviour sufficiently indicates the manner of life which sane Epicureans will eschew.

But the arguments against this interpretation of Petronius as Epicurean moralist are overwhelming,[19] and more recent critics have largely rejected it. One critical response which is especially worthy of consideration argues that the disorganized plot, and the bewildering incongruities, are deliberately assembled to depict the author's sense of a world which is irrational, confused and illusory. The inconsequentiality of the plot, reinforced by the inner contradictions of the protean characters, conveys the impression that confusion and anarchy reign over the world. Such a view of life may not attract us, but it is clear and comprehensible. 'Petronius is surely no neo-Epicurean, no neo-satirist in the old tradition . . . The *Satyricon* sees only a disorderly world unsupported by the rational guidance of gods or their substitutes.'[20]

As an analysis of Petronius' outlook on the world, this seems to me to come close to the truth. The question which it leaves unanswered is whether his novel was written as a serious exploration of such an anarchic world, or whether it was composed as a light-hearted *jeu d'esprit*. The Tacitean portrayal of the author, and the title which he gave to his work, both support strongly the notion that the work has no serious intention, and is to be envisaged merely as relaxation for an audience at play. In short, it is a comic romance. Perhaps the clearest statement of the aim of such compositions is provided by Lucian's programme at the outset of his *True History*.[21] He promises a story which will incorporate strange, elegant and mendacious themes adorned by subtle and witty evocations of earlier literature; he thus seeks to provide pleasurable reading at two levels, the narrative of low adventure relieved by the sophisticated literary texture imposing a more intellectual dimension of entertainment for his highly educated audience.

[19] The counter-arguments that follow are summarized from my paper in *G&R* (1974), 181 ff.   [20] F. Zeitlin, *TAPA* (1971), 676 f.
[21] *Vera Historia* 1. 1.

This purely comic intention is underlined by Petronius' sustained comparison of his romance with the world of the mime.[22] This popular entertainment usually presented three actors on stage performing bawdy plots developed with stilted dialogue combined with slapstick and other crude effects. The characters in Petronius so often compare themselves to actors on the low stage, and the action so often mirrors mimic situations that the twelfth-century humanist John of Salisbury aptly remarks[23] that Petronius seems to regard the whole world as acting out a mime. The Quartilla scene, the dinner of Trimalchio, the episode aboard ship, the scene at Croton when Eumolpus devises his scheme to deceive the legacy-hunters, are all studded with explicit references to the action of the mime. Above all, the 'internal' sequences, in which Encolpius and Giton constantly react to events with extravagant bouts of indignation, jealousy or despair, are deliberately compared with the melodramas of the low stage. Well may Encolpius murmur

> A company mounts the stage, presents a play,
>   Taking the roles of rich man, father, son;
> But once these comic parts have had their say,
>   Our true selves reappear; the roles are gone.[24]

IV

This claim, that the *Satyricon* is to be visualized predominantly as the narrative equivalent of the action of the low stage, especially in its 'internal' scenes, does not exclude the possibility that Petronius incorporates into his delineation of the troubled homosexual relationship between Encolpius and Giton a sustained skit on the Greek sentimental romances. These stories, as represented by the half-dozen surviving examples from Chariton to Heliodorus, enact the

[22] This approach to the novel is comprehensively explored by C. Panayotakis, *Theatrum Arbitri* (Leiden, 1995), with full documentation of earlier studies.

[23] *Policraticus* 3. 8.

[24] § 80. For other references to the mime, see §§ 19, 94, 106, 117; and A. Collignon, *Étude sur Pétrone* (Paris, 1892), 275 ff. (The Latin in the verse-quotation here has *agit . . . mimum.*)

trials and tribulations of a pious pair of lovers who struggle
to overcome the obstacles to their union set up by malevolent Fortune. After undergoing the hazards of shipwreck,
piracy, enslavement, and attempted seduction, they are
eventually rewarded for their piety and fidelity when a kindly
deity intervenes to rescue and unite them.[25]

This suggestion, that the central thread of the homosexual relationship in Petronius makes deliberate sport of
the conventional piety of the heterosexual lovers of Greek
romance, can be supported in two ways. First, the *Satyricon*
presents standard situations found in the romances: the motif of cruel Fortune is prominent,[26] as Encolpius and Giton
experience separation through the intervention of lustful
rivals, and undergo the hazards of shipwreck and other
ordeals. Secondly, in the history of later European literature it is almost a rule of thumb that the comic romance is
composed in reaction to sentimental and strait-laced predecessors. Since Cervantes in *Don Quixote* burlesques such
romances as *Amadis the Gaul*, since Sorel and Scarron in
seventeenth-century France likewise poke fun at the popular French romances, and since Fielding's *Shamela* was
written in irritated reaction to the best-selling *Pamela* of
Richardson, it would not be surprising if Petronius sharpened his claws on the Greek romances known to have existed long before the age of Nero.[27] It would certainly not
be the last occasion in European literature when such exploitation of sentimental predecessors was to be observed.

V

The literary texture, designed to amuse the sophisticated
graduates of the Roman system of mandarin education and

[25] On the characteristic themes of the sentimental Greek romances, see now
B. P. Reardon, *The Form of Greek Romance* (Princeton, 1991); T. Hägg, *The Novel in Antiquity* (Oxford, 1983), both with extensive bibliographies.

[26] See §§ 101, 114, 125.

[27] The thesis, earlier proposed by R. Heinze and R. Reitzenstein among others,
is less favoured nowadays; cf. J. P. Sullivan, *The Satyricon of Petronius* (London, 1968), 93 ff.

simultaneously to soften the crudities of the narrative of low life, is pervasive in both the 'internal' and the 'external' episodes. There is a sense in which the genre of romance develops out of that of epic,[28] so that the general theme of the *Satyricon* can be visualized as the hilarious extension of the great Greek and Roman epics. The anger of Priapus, which overhangs the hero throughout the extant novel, is clearly a comic evocation of the wrath of Poseidon against Odysseus in Homer's *Odyssey*, and of the malice of Juno against Aeneas in Virgil's *Aeneid*. Petronius' anti-hero Encolpius is presented successively as a second Achilles, a second Aeneas, a second Odysseus: an Achilles when he broods morosely by the shore when robbed of Giton by Ascyltus, just as the Greek hero acts when robbed by Agamemnon of the slave-girl Briseis; an Aeneas as he stalks impotently round the colonnades like the Virgilian hero in fallen Troy; an Odysseus at Croton, when he assumes as pseudonym the name which associates him with that Homeric hero as he seeks to satisfy the sexual appetites of Circe, whose name further recalls the connection with the *Odyssey*.[29]

The entire scene of the storm, shipwreck, and exploration of the terrain around Croton is clearly modelled on the episode at the outset of the *Aeneid*, in which Aeneas is shipwrecked after the storm raised by Juno, and makes his way to Carthage as the prelude to the celebrated love-affair with Dido; it is no coincidence that Encolpius after his arrival at Croton becomes similarly involved in the love-encounter with Circe.[30]

In the 'external' scenes, in which Petronius focuses the reader's attention on the figures encountered by Encolpius and Giton, his chief quarry is inevitably Roman satire, supported by satirical contributions from writers of other

[28] This evolution of genres is well sketched by B. E. Perry, *The Ancient Romances* (Berkeley and Los Angeles, 1967), 45 ff.

[29] Encolpius as reincarnation of Achilles, § 81 and *Iliad* 1. 348 ff.; of Aeneas, § 82 and *Aen.* 2. 314 ff., 671 ff.; of Odysseus, §§ 126 ff. and *Od.* 12. 184 ff.

[30] For the numerous verbal echoes of *Aen.* I in the sequence in the *Satyricon*, see Walsh, *Roman Novel*, 37 ff.

genres. The scathing portrayal of Agamemnon, and the exposé of the deficiencies of the Roman rhetorical education, may be indebted to Varro's criticisms in his Menippean satires (such an assumption can be made independently of the question whether Petronius' adoption of the formal *mélange* of prose and verse sets the *Satyricon* within the tradition of Menippean satire).[31] The Quartilla episode, and the characterization of the Priapic priestess, draw much of their inspiration from performances on the Roman stage.[32] Many of the characterizing touches in the portrayal of the disgusting host Trimalchio are evocations of Horace's equally boorish dinner-host Nasidienus, as we shall see. The manic poet Eumolpus bears a close resemblance to the literary circle scathingly described in the first satire of Persius, who targeted the poets of his day for particular censure.[33] Tryphaena, the handsome lady whom the heroes encounter again aboard ship, bears an uncanny resemblance to the mistress of the famous Oxyrhynchus mime, who is in love with her slave and claims to be attentive to the gods' will; Tryphaena shares with the captain Lichas a superstitious outlook on life, an attitude repeatedly condemned by the satirists.[34] Finally, the legacy-hunters at Croton mirror the behaviour repeatedly excoriated by Horace and later by Juvenal.[35] It should be emphasized that since the satirists berate contemporary manners, the inspiration for these derisive portrayals stems from Petronius' own observation as well as from his reading, but almost every scene in the *Satyricon* is seen to have a literary point of reference.

This deployment of satirical models raises the general question: how far is the work to be interpreted as a satire?[36]

[31] R. Astbury, *CP* (1977), 22 ff. is sceptical of the suggestion that the *Satyricon* is in the tradition of Menippean satire.

[32] See now C. Panayotakis, *Mnem.* (1994), 319 ff.

[33] See Suetonius, *Life of Persius.*

[34] Varro, fr. 181, Horace, *Sat.* 2. 3. 281 ff.; cf. Niall Rudd, *The Satires of Horace* (Cambridge, 1966), 180 ff.

[35] See Horace, *Sat.* 2. 5 (with Rudd, *Satires of Horace,* 224 ff.); Juvenal 5. 98, 12. 93 ff.

[36] Of the voluminous literature, I particularly recommend G. N. Sandy, *AJP* (1969), 293 ff.; R. Beck, *Mus. Helv.* (1982), 206 ff.

There is no doubt that in the choice of targets for satirical observation, Petronius is striking heavily at the features which offend him most in his contemporary society. These elements cluster most conspicuously round the centrally placed character of Trimalchio; they form a trinity of vulgar abuse of wealth, pretentious claims to learning, and debilitating religious superstition. These criticisms ripple outward through the other scenes of the *Satyricon*, so that it is possible to affirm that Petronius proclaims a trinity of values: social refinement, literary taste, and a rational attitude towards life and death. These values do not dominate the novel throughout, but subordinate themselves to the literary entertainment, so that we are reminded of Smollett's programmatic preface to *Roderick Random*: 'Of all kinds of satire, there is none so entertaining and universally improving as that which is introduced occasionally, as it were, in the course of an interesting story.' In short, Petronius' standards of social decorum, literary purism, and contempt for popular religion subserve rather than dominate the literary entertainment.

This becomes clear as we observe how Petronius invests almost every scene with its literary evocation. There are reminiscences or burlesques of every imaginable genre of literature—oratory, historiography, epic, tragedy, satire, elegy, mime—constantly providing a second more intellectual level of entertainment beyond the narrative of lubricious adventures. The *Satyricon* is not a closely articulated work of art in which these reminiscences are assembled to present an integrated vision of the world. Such evocations are a form of literary sport with no ulterior purpose.

VI

Trimalchio at the centre of the extant novel offers the clearest picture of how Petronius' creative imagination is shaped by the two kinds of experience. First, the observation of his own eyes. (Authors who preface their novels with the

statement that their characters 'bear no resemblance to any
living person' are usually being economical with the truth;
among present-day novelists Anthony Powell and Graham
Greene are obvious examples of writers who have exploited
the foibles of their contemporaries in this way.)[37] Secondly,
literary reminiscence. Edinburgh University's motto in Greek,
διπλῶς ὁρῶσιν οἱ μαθόντες γράμματα, meaning 'Those who
have learned letters have two sets of eyes', underlines the
truth that literature provides a second world of experience.

The characters in Charles Dickens's novels present a useful analogue of this combination of the literary and the
observed. Some of his characters are taken wholly from
life. In his Preface to *Nicholas Nickleby*, Dickens states that
the Cheeryble brothers were based on merchants from
Ramsbottom in Lancashire called William and Daniel Grant.
When he created Mr Fang, the ferocious magistrate in *Oliver
Twist*, Dickens took the trouble to watch an aggressive character at work at Hatton Garden; his name was Laing, which
has been nicely turned to Fang. In other instances, a character is partly built on a real person. Squeers, the tyrannical
schoolmaster in *Nicholas Nickleby*, is said by Dickens himself
to be 'the representative of a class, not an individual' (a
phrase which recalls Fielding's description of his hero Joseph
Andrews, 'not an individual, but a species'), yet Dickens
is known to have visited the school at Barnard Castle in
Yorkshire to watch the chilling performance of a one-eyed
teacher called William Shaw. A more general instance of
a character drawn from life is Mr Pickwick; Chapman (of
Chapman & Hall, Dickens's publishers) claimed that he was
modelled on his fat friend John Foster, but the name
Pickwick was derived from the proprietor of the White Hart
hotel at Bath.

Petronius' Trimalchio is likewise based in part on *nouveau-
riche* hosts whom he encountered in the flesh. It has been
suggested that he was modelled on an old family dependant

---

    [37] See for example Greene's comments in *In Search of a Character* and in his
Introduction to *A Burnt-Out Case* in the new collected edition of the novels (London, 1974).

on the estate of Petronius at Herculaneum,[38] but this is
speculation plucked from the air. More down to earth are
parallels to be observed in Seneca's *Letters*; as we read there
the animadversions on individuals who lead a life of shallow
luxury, we repeatedly gasp at the Trimalchio-like figures
walking the streets of Neronian Rome.[39] Calvisius Sabinus
is a striking example: 'He had the inherited wealth of
a freedman,' writes Seneca, 'and a freedman's mentality; I
never saw a man use his wealth more disgustingly.' Sabinus
aspires like Trimalchio to be a *littérateur*, but cannot bring
to mind such recondite names as Priam and Ulysses. There
is a rich householder who keeps a slave merely for carving
meat, as Trimalchio keeps Carpus ('Carver'); another rich
man in Seneca who is keen on exercise keeps slaves who
'divide their time between oiling and drinking', just as
Trimalchio's masseurs swill and spill the expensive Falernian
wine. When half-way through Trimalchio's dinner the ceiling panels part and a huge tray descends bearing gifts for
the guests to take away, this is no flight of imagination on
Petronius' part; Seneca documents a similar instance from
his own experience. The crowning parallel in Seneca's letters is Pacuvius, who morbidly celebrates his own death and
funeral in a manner close to Trimalchio's lachrymose performance at the close of the dinner.[40]

Archaeology and other contemporary writers provide further evidence that features of Trimalchio's establishment
closely reflect the real world around him. The huge dog
which discomfits Encolpius on his arrival at Trimalchio's
door, and which turns out to be a mere mosaic with the
subscription *Cave canem*, has its counterparts revealed by
excavation at Pompeii. The skeleton with flexible joints with
which Trimalchio juggles at table can be likewise paralleled,
bearing the subscription 'Know thyself'; the sick humour

---

[38] So G. Bagnani, *Phoenix* (1954), 77 ff.

[39] The parallels are well assembled in Sullivan, *Satyricon of Petronius*, 129 ff.

[40] For Calvisius Sabinus, Seneca, *Ep.* 27. The meat carvers, *Ep.* 47. 6 and *Sat.* 36;
the masseurs, *Ep.* 15. 3 and *Sat.* 28; gifts from the ceiling, *Ep.* 90. 15 and *Sat.* 60;
Pacuvius, *Ep.* 12.

doubtless inspired Petronius to develop the morbid strand
in Trimalchio's characterization. At the door of Trimalchio's
house a magpie in a cage greets the visitors; the Elder Pliny
notes this as a popular feature outside Neronian residences.[41]
Petronius incorporates such touches in implicit criticism
of the lack of refinement in his neighbours, the equivalent
of the gnomes which litter the gardens of our suburban
dwellings.

Other characterizing touches from life appear to guy the
emperor Nero and his predecessors, for Suetonius' *Lives of
the Emperors* reveal amusing parallels. Trimalchio, like Nero,
wears a golden bracelet on his right arm, and takes his place
at table with a napkin round his neck, as Nero did. Nero
kept his first shaving-hairs in a golden casket; so does
Trimalchio. Both keep bemedalled runners in their establishment, and both own a slave called Carpus. But the fat
old freedman is not being presented as a comic reincarnation of the youthful Nero, but more generally as the posturing lord of all that he surveys, a would-be *princeps* in
miniature; hence Petronius incorporates notorious habits
of previous emperors as well. Claudius is said to have contemplated an edict permitting guests to belch and to break
wind at table, and Trimalchio urges the same licence.
Augustus' dinner parties were notorious for the mean gifts,
adorned with punning labels, which were bestowed on the
guests; Trimalchio's carrying-away gifts are similarly mean
and similarly inscribed.[42]

These characterizing touches from life are integrated with
literary reminiscences. The first figure to spring naturally
to Petronius' mind was Horace's boorish host Nasidienus,
who sets before his guests the most oppressive courses
imaginable from the hour of midday: boar, fowl, lamprey,
crane and hare, blackbirds and pigeons—at which point the
guests flee; a similar flight ensues from Trimalchio's table
after seven or eight weighty courses. Nasidienus retires in
the course of the meal to relieve himself, allowing the

---

[41] See §§ 28, 29, 34 with Smith's Commentary.
[42] For these and other suggestive parallels, Walsh, *Roman Novel*, 138 f.

guests free gossip; Trimalchio and his guests follow suit. At Nasidienus' meal an awning falls over the table and ruins the food; the weeping host is consoled by a guest, who tongue in cheek inveighs against the cruelty of Fortune; when in Petronius an acrobat falls from a ladder on to Trimalchio, similar comments on life's unpredictability follow from the guests.[43]

The range of learning which Petronius calls up includes Greek as well as Roman animadversions on unrefined behaviour. It is clear that the *Characters* of Theophrastus, Aristotle's successor as head of the Lyceum, was a rewarding quarry. The boor in Theophrastus summons his dog before his guests, lays hold of its muzzle, and exclaims: 'This is the guardian of my home and household'; Trimalchio has his hulking beast Scylax (the word means 'puppy') brought to the table, and delivers himself of the identical phrase. The boor in Theophrastus also sings in his bath; Trimalchio, enticed by the acoustics, 'began to murder the lyrics of Menecrates'. The shameless man in Theophrastus when drunk performs the Syrian belly-dance; Trimalchio likewise takes the floor until his wife Fortunata tactfully dissuades him. The garrulous man in Theophrastus praises his wife before strangers; Trimalchio similarly praises Fortunata—till the drink gets the better of him! The disgusting man in Theophrastus recounts the cure for his constipation; Trimalchio goes one better than the doctors by prescribing for himself as a laxative pomegranate rind and pinewood dipped in vinegar.[44]

From this synthesis of the literary and the observed, Petronius created his superb portrait of Trimalchio, underlining the four features which particularly offended him in the mores of the emergent capitalists with freedman status:

[43] For Nasidienus, Horace, *Sat.* 2. 8; for these and other parallels, Sullivan, *Satyricon of Petronius*, 126 ff.

[44] These and other parallels (see Walsh, *Roman Novel*, 134 f.) are so close that the scepticism of Sullivan and others is hard to understand. Philodemus, the Epicurean of the first century BC, whose philosophical stance may have recommended him to Petronius, provides in his *Peri Kakiōn* further parallels critical of the arrogance and ignorance of the boorish host; see Walsh, *Roman Novel*, 135.

the boorish behaviour of the dinner host, the arrogance of the master shown in the contemptuous treatment of his slaves (Trimalchio means 'thrice the master' or 'the lord *par excellence*'), the pretence to learning which he does not possess, and the superstition and morbidity which dominate his thoughts and his life in spite of, or in consequence of, his fabulous wealth.

VII

The second major figure of the novel on whom Petronius bestows loving attention is Eumolpus,[45] who dominates the second half of the extant work. Horace, in his *Ars Poetica*, dwells briefly but memorably on figures who cultivate an appearance of eccentricity to obtain the esteem and reputation of poet; Persius, contemporary with Petronius in the age of Nero, waxes sarcastic against the versifiers of his day; and Juvenal opens his programmatic first satire with a withering onslaught on the horde of mediocre poets infesting his society.[46] Petronius' creation fits snugly into this company of self-inflated, manic figures. We are left in no doubt from his first appearance that we are to regard him as such; his verses are branded by Encolpius as inept and a disease, and he is labelled a lunatic, a lowing poet. He is pelted with stones by bystanders as he declaims his lines, and he complains that this is his experience wherever he goes.

In this role of self-styled poetic genius and aggrieved *littérateur*, Eumolpus utters sententious laments on the decline of the arts, which he associates with a national decline in morals. Two clearly derisive strands in the characterization emerge here. First, Eumolpus' glorification of earlier

---

[45] There are excellent studies by K. Beck in *Phoenix* (1979), 239 ff., and by J. Elsner, *PCPS* (1993), 30 ff. (with particular reference to the episode in the picture gallery, suggesting that Petronius subverts and satirizes 'the pretensions of contemporary aesthetics').

[46] See Horace, *AP* 295 ff. (also Crispinus in Horace, *Sat.* 1. 4. 14); Persius, 1. 13 f., 5. 5 ff.; Juvenal 1. 13 f.

figures in the realms of natural philosophy and of art is marked by ignorance of their true significance and achievements; he is depicted as the poseur whose opinionated confidence masks a fundamental pretentiousness. Secondly, the hypocrisy of his cliché-ridden nostalgia for the golden days of sound morality, which we associate with the ritual laments of Seneca and earlier worthies, is exposed by his dissolute behaviour in his personal life, as reflected in his anecdote of the boy from Pergamum and his later role as moral guardian of the girl at Croton—not to mention his attempts to wean Giton away from the over-possessive Encolpius.

It is within this derisive characterization of Eumolpus that we are to evaluate the point of the two long poems on the capture of Troy and the Civil War. The manic poet, after meeting Encolpius in a picture gallery, attempts to impress his new acquaintance with an impromptu declamation in iambics on the subject of one of the pictures, the fall of Troy. The poem is the stock type of messenger speech which is a familiar feature in tragedy. Though Virgilian touches appear in the diction, differences of content point to some other mythological version as source. The metre and tricks of style recall Seneca's contemporary plays, notably in the tedious repetition of diction in line-beginnings and line-endings. The reader encounters precisely what he should have expected from such an unrehearsed performance; the similarities to Senecan tragedy convey the hint that it is all too easy to compose such iambic verses on well-worn themes, and in this sense the composition is clearly part of the literary entertainment.

A similar judgment must be passed on the longer poem on the Civil War, which Eumolpus declaims in hexameters while the heroes are *en route* to Croton. The pompous poet precedes his poetic outburst with theoretical observations on how epic should be written. There is clearly implicit criticism here of Lucan's quasi-historical approach, which had dispensed with divine machinery, and based itself largely on Livy's historical narrative of the struggle between Julius

Caesar and Pompey, though this is supplemented by many
speeches and fictitious, highly imaginative scenes which lend
themselves to rhetorical treatment. When Eumolpus delivers his verses, they reflect his traditionalist views on what
epic should be like, being more mythological in content
than Lucan's, and more Virgilian in diction. The style, however, including certain irritating metrical mannerisms, recalls Lucan's treatment. Again it must be stressed that this
composition is presented by Petronius as an impromptu
declamation, not as a carefully crafted poem.

Surprisingly enough, many critics have taken these compositions seriously. It has even been suggested that they
represent Petronius' best efforts, discreetly hidden within
the comic romance to avoid arousing the jealousy of the
emperor Nero.[47] More illogical still is the suggestion that
the *Halosis Troiae* is parody but the *Bellum Ciuile* a poem
seriously intended.[48] Yet there has been no shortage of
demonstrations that the *Halosis Troiae* contains conscious
echoes of Seneca, that the *Bellum Ciuile* closely approx-
imates to the presentation of Lucan at many points, and
that both are lack-lustre productions.[49] The solution seems
inescapable that Petronius dashed them off at speed to
demonstrate how fatally easy it was to compose the hackneyed verses masquerading in his day as serious poetry. (My
translations have the same modest ambition; the medium of
the iambic pentameter seems more suited for rendering the
traditionalist verses than Sullivan's imitations of Ezra Pound.)
In this sense the long poems form an integral part of the
literary entertainment.

[47] So Perry, *Ancient Romances*, 197; cf. F. Zeitlin, *Latomus* (1971), 56 ff.

[48] So Sullivan, *Satyricon of Petronius*, 170 ff., a view apparently retracted later; see
'On Translating Petronius' in *Neronians and Flavians*, ed. D. R. Dudley (London,
1972), 172.

[49] See H. Stubbe, *Die Verseinlagen im Petron* (Leipzig, 1933); on the *Halosis Troiae*,
Sullivan, *Satyricon of Petronius*, 186 ff. (with references). On the *Bellum Ciuile*, F.
Baldwin's competent edition (New York, 1911); Heitland's Preface to Haskins's
edition of the *Pharsalia* (Cambridge, 1887); G. Guido, *Il Bellum Civile* (Bologna,
1976). P. A. George, *CQ* (1974), 119 ff., is sceptical about Lucan as target, whilst
agreeing on the mediocrity of the poem within the derisive characterization of
Eumolpus. See also my own paper in *CP* (1968), 208 ff.

VIII

In spite of its lubricious content, the *Satyricon* appears to have enjoyed a wide circulation in late antiquity among both pagan and Christian readers. Terentianus Maurus in the second century, Servius the fourth-century commentator on Virgil, and Macrobius, roughly his contemporary, all reveal a knowledge of the work; among Christian writers who cite him are St Jerome in the fourth century, Sidonius Apollinaris who was to become bishop of Auvergne in 469, Boethius (whose *Consolation of Philosophy* composed shortly before his execution in 524 is written, like the *Satyricon*, in the Menippean medley of prose and verses), Fulgentius, the sixth-century bishop of Ruspe in North Africa who repeatedly quotes from the novel, and Isidore of Seville in the seventh century. These citations are from lost sections of the novel, suggesting that for many centuries fuller versions circulated widely in Italy and Africa, Gaul and Spain.[50]

Thereafter the novel goes underground largely, though fragmentary versions survive in French monastic libraries between the ninth and the eleventh centuries. It was in France that John of Salisbury in the mid-twelfth century was able to lay his hands on manuscripts of the *Cena Trimalchionis* and of the families O and L, which contain narrative sections from the rest of the novel.[51] He probably returned to Canterbury with his personal copy; John's citation of the poem *Grex agit in scaena* ('A company mounts the stage', § 80) inspired the motto for the Globe theatre, and indirectly the speech of Jacques in *As You Like It*, 'All the world's a stage . . .'.

Poggio Bracciolini was the key figure in restoring the fortunes of Petronius in the Italian Renaissance, when he discovered one manuscript in Britain in 1420, and another (the sole manuscript of the *Cena Trimalchionis*) at Cologne

---

[50]. For these citations, see below, pp. 149 ff.

[51] For the Carolingian MSS, see M. D. Reeve in *Texts and Transmission* (ed. L. D. Reynolds, Oxford, 1983), 297 ff. For John of Salisbury, Janet Martin in *The World of John of Salisbury*, ed. M. Wilks (Oxford, 1984), 185 f., with further references.

in 1423. At this time the *Satyricon* was totally unknown in Italy; the manuscript of the *Cena* was sent to Poggio's friend Niccolo Niccolini, but for reasons which are obscure it disappeared for more than two centuries. Meanwhile the manuscript from England fathered more than a dozen fifteenth-century manuscripts in Italy, and with the invention of printing, successive editions appeared at Milan (*c.* 1482), Venice (1489), and Paris (1520). Further discoveries of fragments enabled an enlarged edition to be published at Lyon in 1575, though still without the *Cena*.

There is strong evidence that through these editions the *Satyricon* (without the *Cena*) was known to Spanish humanists, and played a modest role in the rise of the picaresque novel towards the close of the sixteenth century.[52] From this time on, Petronius enjoyed an increasing vogue in France; a striking example of this is the *Euphormionis Satyricon* of John Barclay, a Scot reared in France, who published his novel in 1603 in the hope of winning the patronage of James I at the London court. This satirical entertainment adopts the Menippean medley of prose and verses, and like the *Satyricon* alternates mimic scenes with derisive vignettes of contemporary figures and manners. A pompous lecturer in Roman law is a latter-day Agamemnon; there is a Lucretius who delivers tirades against modern trends in literature and education in the manner of Eumolpus.[53]

Following the reappearance of the manuscript containing the *Cena Trimalchionis* at Trogir in Dalmatia in 1650, a full edition of all that we possess of the *Satyricon* today became possible, and duly appeared in 1669.[54] This prompted the

---

[52] I draw attention to the likely influence of Petronius on Aleman's *Guzmán* (1599–1604) in Walsh, *Roman Novel*, 235. R. J. C. Boroughs in his (unpublished) Cambridge 1993 PhD dissertation on Eumolpus provides more detailed evidence of Petronian influence on the Spanish picaresque. But Apuleius is far more influential.

[53] For Petronius' popularity in France, A. Collignon, *Pétrone en France* (Paris, 1905). There is an English translation of Barclay's novel by Paul Turner (London, 1954), and an edition by Iulia Desjardins of selections (Avignon, 1969).

[54] For details, Reeve in Reynolds (ed.), *Texts and Transmission*, and the successive editions of K. Müller, most recently his Tusculum edition (1978). A further Müller edition is published in the Teubner series. See also A. C. De la Mare in *Studies*

first English translation by William Burnaby, a London law-
yer, in 1694 ('The Satyr of Titus Petronius Arbiter . . . Made
English by Mr Burnaby of the Middle-Temple and Another
Hand'), which was to hold the field virtually unchallenged
as a translation for more than two centuries. Following the
restoration of the Stuarts with the return of Charles II to
London in 1660, the popularity of the novel spread from
France to the cultural circle of the English court. Before
this date learned individuals like Ben Jonson and George
Chapman reveal their acquaintance with it; Ben Jonson's
play on the theme of avarice, *Volpone* (1605), contains several echoes, and Drummond of Hawthornden attests that
Jonson thought highly of Petronius' Latin.[55] George Chapman's *The Widowes Teares* (1612) is based on Eumolpus' tale
of the widow of Ephesus. Another influential figure earlier
in the century who exploited the *Satyricon* was Robert Burton
in his *Anatomy of Melancholy* (1621), a work which contains about seventy citations of Petronius. Even a religious
divine like Jeremy Taylor, bishop of Down and Connor, in
his *Rule and Exercises of Holy Dying* (1651) lends authority to
the novel.

But enthusiasm for Petronius becomes much more marked
in the years following the Restoration. A contributory reason for this was the rising popularity of Epicureanism, following upon publication of Walter Charleton's *Epicurus's
Morals . . . Faithfully Englished* (1656; Charleton's *Ephesian
Matron* was composed about this same time), and John
Evelyn's *Essay on the First Book of Lucretius, De rerum natura*
(1656). Petronius was naturally associated with this enthusiasm, and especially in the aristocratic circle dominated
by Saint-Evremond. This exiled French nobleman found in
Petronius his ideal of the refined hedonist and gentleman.

in Medieval Learning and Literature: Essays in Honour of R. W. Hunt, eds. J. J. G.
Alexander and M. T. Gibson (Oxford, 1976), ch. 10. T. Wade Richardson,
Reading and Variant in Petronius (Toronto, 1993) studies the sixteenth-century
French editions and the MSS on which they are based.

[55] Jonson said that 'Petronius, Plinius Secundus, Tacitus speke best Latine' (C.
Herford and P. Simpson, *The Works of Ben Jonson* (Oxford, 1925), i. 136. I owe this
reference and what follows to J. Stuckey, *RSC* (1972), 3 ff.)

Identifying the author of the novel with the Petronius
described by Tacitus, he wrote admiringly of his suicide as
'the most exemplary death of all antiquity', and he repeatedly praised the style and tone of the *Satyricon*. He would
have pooh-poohed twentieth-century attempts to canonize
Petronius as moralist: 'If Petronius would have left us an
ingenious moral of the description of sensualists, he had
endeavoured to give us some disgust, but 'tis in this, that
vice appears with all the graces of the Author; 'tis in this,
that he sets forth with more excellency the acuteness and
politeness of his spirit.'[56]

Of particular interest in this period is the attitude of John
Dryden. Earlier in his career, in his essay *Of Heroique Plays*,
he quotes with approval Eumolpus' condemnation of Lucan's
'godless' epic, ascribing the judgment to Petronius himself,
'the most elegant and one of the most judicious authors of
the Latin tongue'.[57] This is only one of many such compli-
mentary references. But following the death of Charles II
and the accession of the Catholic James II in 1685, the year
in which Dryden himself converted to Catholicism, his tone
becomes more critical of Petronius' obscenity, though he continues to respect the authority of Petronius as an 'ancient'.

With the accession of William and Mary in 1688, a more
censorious and puritanical attitude towards the vogue of
Epicureanism in general, and of Petronius in particular,
becomes the norm, a trend which continued well into the
twentieth century. There were of course distinguished exceptions. It was Alexander Pope who anticipated the epigram of St John Gogarty set at the head of this Introduction:

> Fancy and Art in gay Petronius please;
> The Scholar's learning with the Courtier's ease![58]

Indeed, amongst lettered men this was a period of qualified
approval, manifested for example in acknowledgements from
Swift, Addison and Steele.

[56] St-Evremond, *Judgment on Alexander and Caesar: and also on Seneca, Plutarch and Petronius*, trans. J. Dancer (London, 1672), 43.
[57] *Essays of John Dryden*, ed. W. P. Ker (Oxford, 1900), i. 132.
[58] *An Essay on Criticism* (London, 1711), 667 f.

But when the picaresque novel makes its way to Britain in the eighteenth century, there is little acknowledgement of Petronius as precursor. The case of Tobias Smollett is an interesting exemplar: in his Introduction to *Roderick Random* (1748), he makes no mention of Petronius, claiming that Cervantes was the originator of realistic fiction, and that Le Sage's *Gil Blas* was his direct inspiration. Yet in the course of the story, Lord Strutwell presses the *Satyricon* into Roderick's hands, saying: 'Here's a book, written with great elegance and spirit, and though the subjects may give offence to narrow-minded people, the author will always be held in esteem by every person of wit and learning.' 'So saying', adds Roderick, 'he put into my hand Petronius Arbiter . . .'. Smollett clearly felt reluctant to recommend the book directly, citing it ambivalently in a context in which Strutwell was trying to seduce Roderick. Henry Fielding knew the novel equally well; in his case we may take his criticism (he writes of 'the unjustly celebrated Petronius') at face value, since he saw the function of his fiction as 'to promote the cause of virtue' and 'to recommend virtue and innocence',[59] aims for which Petronius could scarcely be summoned as advocate.

The tendency to regard Petronius with abhorrence, or at best reticence, continued throughout the eighteenth and nineteenth centuries. So, for example, William Cowper attacks Philip Dormer Stanhope, 4th Earl of Chesterfield, as a latter-day Petronius in his *The Progress of Error* (1782):

> Thou polish'd and high finish'd foe to truth,
> Gray beard corrupter of our list'ning youth . . .[60]

But there were striking exceptions. The most notable of the independent spirits was Thomas Love Peacock, a voracious reader of the Greek and Latin authors. 'In Petronius . . . was a satirist, a versifier, and a man like himself, with antipathy towards his age. The *Satyricon*, mixing prose with verse,

[59] Walsh, *Roman Novel*, 226, 243; for Fielding's knowledge of Petronius, see J. A. K. Thomson, *Classical Influences on English Prose* (London, 1957), 89.

[60] See J. D. Baird and C. Ryscamp (eds.), *The Poems of William Cowper* (Oxford, 1980), i. 515; I take this reference from B. Baldwin's n. in *PSN* (1993), 10 ff.

... understandably became one of Peacock's favourite works.'[61] Both the poems and the novels of Peacock attest Petronius as a major influence. Of his poem *Rhododaphne*, Peacock's friend Shelley claimed that it incorporated 'the transfused essence of Lucian, Petronius and Apuleius'.[62] In Peacock's novels there are numerous citations from the *Satyricon*, and especially from 'Dinner at Trimalchio's'; *Gryll Grange* exploits as chapter headings the declaration of Eumolpus, 'Always and everywhere I have lived my life as though I were spending my last day, and would not see another,' and Trimalchio's 'So wine, sad to say, enjoys longer life than poor humans. So let us drink and be merry. Wine is life-enhancing.'[63]

The twentieth century has witnessed an astonishing reversal in Petronius' fortunes; the *literati* of our more permissive age have found the combination of good humour and advocacy of unconventional, even deviant behaviour an agreeable counterweight to the stern morality of the Victorian age. The harbinger of this changing attitude appeared in the last decade of the previous century in the person of Oscar Wilde, one of a group of Irishmen of Protestant stock, including W. B. Yeats and Oliver St John Fogarty, who greatly admired Petronius for being 'a gentleman, and incomparably aristocratic' (the phrase is Charles Whibley's). Wilde had received a good Classical education at Portora and Trinity College Dublin, where he studied under Mahaffy and Tyrrell; initially he outshone his contemporary Louis Purser with his accomplishments in Greek and Latin, which won him a scholarship to Oxford. In *The Picture of Dorian Gray* (the novel which depicted a young man who sold his soul in exchange for the promise of eternal youth), his comparison of the hero to Petronius roused reviewers to accusations of immorality and *snobbisme*. His responses to the first charge were rather muddled: 'I am quite incapable of understanding how any work of art can be criticised from a moral stand-

[61] Carl Dawson, *His Fine Wit* (London, 1970), 281.

[62] Shelley, *Letters*, i. 569, cited by Dawson, *His Fine Wit.*

[63] See §§ 99, 34, epigraphs to chs. 1 and 3 of *Gryll Grange.*

point,' he wrote in one letter; but in another, 'The real
moral of the story [i.e. *Dorian Gray*] is that all excess, as well
as all renunciation, brings its punishment.'[64] The charge of
snobbery for having introduced mention of Suetonius and
Petronius elicited a superbly Wildean reply: '*The Lives of the
Caesars*, at any rate, forms part of the curriculum at Oxford
for those who take the Honour School of *Literae Humaniores*;
and as for the *Satyricon*, it is popular even among pass-men,
though I suppose they are obliged to read it in translation.'[65] Wilde became so closely identified with Petronius
that a translation appeared under his *nom de plume* Sebastian Melmoth, though he appears not to have been the
author of it.[66]

As in Ireland, so in America the cult of Petronius was
becoming popular. F. Scott Fitzgerald's *The Great Gatsby*
(1925), which describes the false values of his generation,
had as its earlier projected title 'Trimalchio at West Egg'.
More recently Ezra Pound in his *Cantos*, Henry Miller, Gore
Vidal and others have all acknowledged their debt to
Petronius; Pound uses the same quotation which Eliot
exploited as epigraph in *The Waste Land*, and Miller, in *The
Books in my Life* (1969), states that the *Satyricon* had as much
influence upon him as any other work.[67] At a less pretentious level, and one which Petronius himself might have
appreciated more, E. Shrake's *Peter Arbiter* faithfully images
the Petronian characters to satirize the social scene in contemporary Texas.[68]

We have already made brief reference to the influence of
Petronius on T. S. Eliot; with Eliot, who migrated from
America in 1914, we can follow the *Satyricon*-trail to Eng-
land, where an even longer roll-call of Petronian devotees

---

[64] Letters to *St James's Gazette* and *Daily Chronicle* on 26 June and 2 July 1890
respectively. [65] *St James's Gazette*, 27 June 1890.

[66] Paris 1902; I take this reference from Schmeling and Rebmann, *Comparative
Literature Studies*, 397.

[67] On Petronius and Scott Fitzgerald, see P. Mackendrick, *CJ* (1950), 307 ff. For
the citation by Ezra Pound, see *Canto* 64; this and the reference to Miller I take
from Schmeling and Rebmann, *Comparative Literature Studies*, 399.

[68] Austin, Tex., 1973.

can be cited. Eliot met in England apologists for Petronius
in novelists like D. H. Lawrence and Aldous Huxley. Lawrence characteristically idealizes Petronius ('. . . straight and
above-board. Whatever he does, he doesn't try to degrade
and dirty the pure mind in him.'); Huxley repeatedly cites
Petronius in his novels, and in *Crome Yellow* (1921), his
character Sir Hercules emulates the Tacitean Petronius in
his mode of suicide. Eliot himself annotated his Latin edition of the *Satyricon* extensively with observations and with
bibliographical references, and he refers in his writings to
Petronius on at least ten occasions. Several of these are in
the course of tributes to Charles Whibley, who befriended
Eliot and helped him to obtain his publishing post with
Faber and Gwyer in 1925. Whibley had already contributed
an essay on Petronius to *Studies in Frankness* (1898), and Eliot
shared with him the conviction that Petronius' merit was to
depict the cruel realities of the Neronian world. So in his
Charles Whibley: A Memoir, he writes: 'In the essay on Petronius,
his [Whibley's] amused and Catholic delight in what he
called "the underworld of letters" is as well expressed as
anywhere.' Elsewhere Eliot contrasts Walter Pater, author of
Marius the Epicurean, unfavourably with Petronius; Pater was
'unconcerned with the realities of Roman life as we catch a
glimpse of them in Petronius'.[69]

Of recent authors of fiction, Anthony Powell presents a
striking parallel to Petronius in many respects. The hero
Nick Jenkins, a modest and moral figure, could not be more
unlike Petronius' Encolpius, and there are no scenes com-
parable to the 'internal' episodes of the *Satyricon.* But the
range of characters, benignly or cruelly drawn, the social
milieu, the highly literary texture, and the elegance of the
narrative combine to present similar satirical comedy which
induces thoughtful laughter. In his autobiographical work
To Keep the Ball Rolling (vol. II (1978), 120 f.), Powell describes
how he chanced upon Burnaby's translation of the *Satyricon*

[69] Citation from Lawrence, and a full list of references to Petronius in Eliot,
appear in Schmeling and Rebmann, *Comparative Literature Studies*, 399, 401 f. This
article also provides details of the annotations of Eliot in his Bücheler edition.

in a second-hand bookshop: 'I was captivated by the genius of Nero's more intellectual Brummell, . . . the writer of what can reasonably be called the first modern novel.' In the later volumes of the sequence *A Dance to the Music of Time*, Trimalchio repeatedly raises his head. The literary character X. Trapnell, a down-at-heel figure in some senses evocative of Eumolpus, cites only the *Satyricon* of the Greek and Latin Classics.[70]

Petronius' comic romance has extended its influence to the stage and the wide screen. Stage performances have been of a minor nature, but Fellini's film the *Satyricon* (1968) reached a wide public, finding more favour with viewers innocent of the comic romance than with the *cognoscenti*. Two reviews of the film in the *Petronian Newsletter* (December 1970) waxed particularly unenthusiastic: 'The point is made in the first five minutes, and the remaining two hours are repetitious embellishment . . . We see the spirit of Bosch, but end by muttering "bosh".' 'An incongruous pastiche of Petronius and Apuleius . . . with a little Juvenal, Tacitus, Suetonius, Plautus and Catullus thrown in . . . ponderous and boring.'[71]

IX

Translations of the *Satyricon* have multiplied since the Second World War, reflecting the attractions of its realism and the acceptability of its licentious content. The latest bibliography, covering the years 1945–1982, lists no fewer than fifty-five partial or entire translations in eighteen different languages. The thirst for new versions seems inexhaustible, especially in Spain (ten recent translations have appeared in Spanish), Italy (seven new versions) and Germany (five recent renderings).[72]

[70] On Petronius and Anthony Powell, see T. P. Wiseman, *Classical and Modern Literature* (1981), 16 f.

[71] Among stage presentations, *The Satyricon* (book and lyrics by Tom Hendry, music by Stanley Silverman) made a hit at the 1969 Stratford Ontario season. The criticisms of Fellini are by B. Baldwin and G. Sandy in *PSN* (Dec. 1970), 2–3.

[72] See M. S. Smith, *ANRW* 2/32.3 (1985), 1629–32.

As has been noted, the first translation to appear in English was that by William Burnaby in 1694; Burnaby felt the need to apologize for publishing the obscene content in the vernacular, but justified himself by appealing to Petronius' standing as an ancient. It is a measure of the dominant distaste felt for the *Satyricon* that there was only one translation in the eighteenth century, by Addison (1736), and only one in the nineteenth century, the literal version in the Bohn series by W. K. Kelly (1854). But following the translation by 'Sebastian Melmoth' (1902), a glut of new renderings has appeared, heralded by Michael Heseltine's in the Loeb series (1913; this was recently revised by E. H. Warmington in 1969). These include translations by W. C. Firebaugh (1922), Jack Lindsay (1927), Paul Dinnage (1953), William Arrowsmith (1959), and J. P. Sullivan (1965).[73]

There may seem less justification for a new version of the *Satyricon* than for my recent rendering of Apuleius' *The Golden Ass*; Arrowsmith's translation, aimed especially at an American readership, and Sullivan's excellent Penguin edition may be felt to fill the need. A new class of reader, however, has emerged in the past thirty years. Students in institutes of Higher Education are crowding into courses on Classical Civilization and Comparative Literature; they may find the additional annotations useful, as well as the attempt in this Introduction to survey the range of recent interpretations of the novel, and to set it more broadly in the frame of European literature. Though I have consciously aimed at the needs of such students, I hope that the translation is sufficiently readable and lively to cater for a more general readership.

---

[73] See J. P. Sullivan, 'On Translating Petronius' in *Neronians and Flavians*, ch. 6.

Note on the Text and Translation

This translation is based on K. Müller's magisterial Latin text (third edition, Munich 1983; a further revision by Müller (Leipzig, 1995) appeared too late to be consulted). But since the Latin abounds in Graecisms and colloquialisms, and is notoriously an open playing-field for textual critics, I have felt at liberty occasionally to depart from readings in the Müller edition. The chapter-headings (and the division into chapters) do not appear in the original; I have inserted them as a guide to the reader, for structural coherence. In the Appendix ('Fragments, Testimonies, Poems'), I have deliberately followed Müller in incorporating only those passages which throw some light on the novel and on the attitudes of Petronius as novelist.

Two major problems challenge the translator of the *Satyricon*. The first is the prosimetric texture. I do not rank Petronius as a poet of major stature. My interpretation of the novel assumes that the purpose of the shorter poems is to present a comic contrast between their worthy sentiments and the encompassing narrative which undermines their messages. I visualize the long poems, the *Capture of Troy* and the *Civil War*, as mediocre offerings subserving the satirical portrayal of Eumolpus as manic poet. The translations seek to reflect these satirical aims.

The second difficulty concerns the rendering of the language of the freedmen at Trimalchio's table. The temptation to use a variety of regional dialects has to be resisted; the participants, though of Greek origin, have lived their adult lives in their city on the Bay of Naples. Their speech is studded with colloquialisms, which can and should be attempted in English, but also with solecisms of orthography and grammar, which cannot be registered without reducing the English to a bizarre hotch-potch.

Select Bibliography
Compiled by Costas Panayotakis

The following bibliographical lists on the *Satyricon* are bound to be selective, since scholarly contributions on various aspects of Petronius' novel have increased to an overwhelming degree already from the early 1960s. For fuller bibliographies, which include references to works on Petronius before the 1940s, consult:

J. MAROUZEAU (ed.), *L'Année Philologique*, s.v. Petronius.

H. SCHNUR, 'Recent Petronian Scholarship', *CW* 50 (1957), 133–6, 141–3.

G. L. SCHMELING, 'Petronian Scholarship since 1957', *CW* 62 (1969), 157–64.

G. L. SCHMELING (ed.), *Petronian Society Newsletter* 1– (1970–).

G. N. SANDY, 'Recent Scholarship on the Prose Fiction of Classical Antiquity', *CW* 67 (1974), 355–7.

M. S. SMITH (ed.), *Petronius. Cena Trimalchionis* (Oxford, 1975), xxviii–xxxiii.

C. L. SCHMELING and J. H. STUCKEY, *A Bibliography of Petronius* (Leiden, 1977).

M. S. SMITH, 'A Bibliography of Petronius (1945–1982)', *ANRW* 2/32.3 (1985), 1624–65.

E. L. BOWIE and S. J. HARRISON, 'The Romance of the Novel', *JRS* 83 (1993), 159–78.

N. HOLZBERG, 'Petron 1965–1995' in K. Müller-W. Ehlers (eds), *Petronius: Satyrica. Schelmenszenen* 4 Auflage (Zürich 1995), 544–60.

The reader should also consult, from the 'General' list below, the bibliographies provided in Sullivan 1968, Walsh 1970, Slater 1990, Panayotakis 1995.

1. Editions and Commentaries

There is no satisfactory Commentary on the entire surviving *Satyricon* yet, though one is being prepared by G. L. Schmeling, incorporating work by the late J. P. Sullivan. The fourth edition of the text by K. Müller is now available in the Teubner Series. Among recent, easily accessible editions and commentaries see:

A. ARAGOSTI, P. COSCI, and A. COTROZZI, *Petronio: l' episodio di Quartilla (Satyricon 16–26.6)* (Bologna, 1988).

F. BÜCHELER, and G. HERAEUS (rev.), *Petronii Saturae et Liber Priapeorum* (Berlin, 1922).

E. COURTNEY, *The Poems of Petronius* (Atlanta, 1991).

A. ERNOUT, *Pétrone. Le Satiricon* (Paris, 1962).

J. C. GIARDINA, and R. C. MELLONI, *Petronii Arbitri Satyricon* (Turin, 1995).

M. HESELTINE, and E. H. WARMINGTON (rev.), *Petronius* (Loeb. edn Cambridge, Mass., 1987).

E. V. MARMORALE, *Petronii Arbitri Cena Trimalchionis* (Florence, 1947).

K. MÜLLER, *Petronii Arbitri Satyricon* (Munich, 1961; 2nd edn 1965; 3rd edn 1983; 4th edn Leipzig, 1995).

C. PELLEGRINO, *Petronii Arbitri Satyricon* (Rome, 1975).

P. PERROCHAT, *Pétrone. Le Festin de Trimalcion* (Paris, 1952).

E. T. SAGE, and B. B. GILLELAND (rev.), *Petronius. The Satiricon* (New York, 1969).

W. B. SEDGWICK, *The CENA TRIMALCHIONIS of Petronius* (Oxford, 1959).

M. S. SMITH, *Petronii Arbitri Cena Trimalchionis* (Oxford, 1975).

2. Translations

The Satyricon (either the whole surviving text or parts of it) is translated into Bulgarian, Catalan, Czech, Danish, Dutch, English, Estonian, Finnish, Flemish, French, German, Greek, Hebrew, Hungarian, Icelandic, Italian, Japanese, Norwegian, Polish, Portuguese, Romanian, Russian, Serbo-Croat, Slovene, Spanish, Swedish, Turkish, and Welsh (see Schmeling and Stuckey, *A Bibliography of Petronius*, 77–125; Smith, *ANRW* II.32.3 (1985), 1629–32; *PSN*, passim). Among the English translations see:

P. DINNAGE, *The Satyricon of Petronius* (London, 1953).

W. ARROWSMITH, *The Satyricon of Petronius* (Ann Arbor, 1959)

J. P. SULLIVAN, *Petronius. The Satyricon* (Harmondsworth, 1965).

M. HESELTINE, and E. H. WARMINGTON (rev.), *Petronius* (Loeb. edn Cambridge, Mass., 1987).

R. B. BRANHAM, and D. KINNEY, *Petronius, Satyrica* (London, 1996).

3. General

The following selective list contains works published mainly after 1970, although it does take into account books and articles which, though written much earlier, ought not to be overlooked by the student interested in Petronius.

ADAMIETZ, J., 'Zum literarischen Charakter von Petrons _Satyrica_', _RhM_ 130 (1987), 329–46.

ANDERSON, GRAHAM, _Eros Sophistes. Ancient Novelists at Play_ (Chico, Calif., 1982).

ARAGOSTI, ANDREA, 'L'episodio petroniano del _forum_ (_Sat._ 12–15): assimilazione dei codici nel racconto', _MD_ 3 (1979), 101–19.

ARROWSMITH, WILLIAM, 'Luxury and Death in the _Satyricon_', _Arion_ 5 (1966), 304–31 (reprinted in _Essays on Classical Literature_, with an introduction by Niall Rudd (Cambridge, 1972)).

ASTBURY, RAYMOND, 'Petronius, _P. Oxy._ 3010, and Menippean satire', _CP_ 72 (1977), 22–31.

BACON, HELEN H., 'The Sibyl in the bottle', _Virginia Quarterly Review_ 34 (1958), 262–76.

BALDWIN, BARRY, _Studies on Greek and Roman History and Literature_ (Amsterdam, 1985).

BARBIERI, AROLDO, _Poetica Petroniana. Satyricon 132.15. Quaderni della Rivista di cultura classica e medioevale_ 16 (Rome, 1983).

BARCHIESI, ALESSANDRO, 'Il nome di Lica e la poetica dei nomi in Petronio', _MD_ 12 (1984), 169–75.

BARCHIESI, MARINO, 'L'orologio di Trimalcione (struttura e tempo narrativo in Petronio)' in _I moderni alla ricerca di Enea_ (Rome, 1984), 109–46.

BECK, ROGER, 'Some observations on the narrative technique of Petronius', _Phoenix_ 27 (1973), 42–61.

—— 'Encolpius at the _Cena_', _Phoenix_ 29 (1975), 271–83.

—— 'Eumolpus _poeta_, Eumolpus _fabulator_: a study of characterization in the _Satyricon_', _Phoenix_ 33 (1979), 239–53.

—— 'The _Satyricon_: Satire, Narrator and Antecedents', _Mus. Helv._ 39 (1982), 206–14.

BERAN, ŽDENKA, 'The realm of sensory perception and its significance in Petronius' _Satyricon_', _ŽAnt_ 23 (1973), 227–51.

BLICKMAN, DANIEL, 'The Romance of Encolpius and Circe', _PSN_ 17/1&2 (1987), 6–9.

BOWERSOCK, G. W., _Fiction as History_ (Berkeley, 1994).

BOYCE, BRET, _The Language of the Freedmen in Petronius' Cena Trimalchionis_ (Leiden, 1991).

CALLEBAT, LOUIS, 'Structures narratives et modes de représentation dans le _Satyricon_ de Pétrone', _REL_ 52 (1967), 281–303.

CAMERON, AVERIL M., 'Myth and meaning in Petronius: some modern comparisons', _Latomus_ 29 (1970), 397–425.

CAMERON, H. D. 'The Sibyl in the _Satyricon_', _CJ_ 65 (1970), 337–9.

CANALI, LUCA, _L'erotico e il grottesco nel Satyricon_ (Bari, 1986).

CICU, L., *Donne Petroniane. Personaggi femminili e techniche di racconto nel Satyricon di Petronio* (Sassari, 1992).

COCCIA, MICHELE, *'Novae simplicitatis opus* (Petronio 132.15.2)' in *Studi di poesia latina in onore di Antonio Traglia*, 2 (Rome, 1979), 789–99.

COLLIGNON, A., *Étude sur Pétrone. La Critique littéraire, l'imitation et la parodie dans le Satiricon* (Paris, 1892).

CONNORS, C., *Petronius the Poet* (Cambridge, 1998).

CONTE, G. B., *The Hidden Author* (Berkeley, 1996).

CORBETT, P. B., *Petronius* (New York, 1970).

COSCI, PAOLA, 'Per una ricostruzione della scena iniziale del *Satyricon*', *MD* 1 (1978), 201–7.

—— 'Quartilla e l'iniziazione ai misteri di Priapo (*Satyricon* 20.4)', *MD* 4 (1980), 199–201.

COTROZZI, ANNAMARIA, 'Enotea e il fiume di pianto (Petronio 137; frg. LI Ernout)', *MD* 2 (1979), 183–9.

COURTNEY, EDWARD, 'Parody and Literary Allusion in Menippean Satire', *Philologus* 106 (1962), 86–100.

—— 'Petronius and the Underworld', *AJP* 108 (1987), 408–10.

CURRIE, H. MacL., 'Petronius and Ovid' in *Studies in Latin Literature and Roman History* V—*Collection Latomus*, vol. 206 (Brussels, 1989), 317–35.

DIMUNDO, ROSALBA, 'Da Socrate a Eumolpo. Degradazione dei personaggi e delle funzioni nella novella del fanciullo di Pergamo', *MD* 10–11 (1983), 255–65.

—— 'La novella del'efebo di Pergamo: struttura del racconto', *MCSN* 4 (1986), 83–94.

FEDELI, PAOLO, 'Il tema del labirinto nel *Satyricon* di Petronio', *MCSN* 3 (1981a), 161–74.

—— 'Petronio: il viaggio, il labirinto', *MD* 6 (1981b), 91–117.

—— 'La Matrona di Efeso. Strutture narrative e tecnica dell' inversione', *MCSN* 4 (1986), 9–35.

—— 'Petronio: Crotone o il mondo alla rovescia', *Aufidus* 1 (1987), 3–34.

—— 'Encolpio—Polieno', *MD* 20–1 (1988), 9–32.

FERRI, ROLANDO, 'Il Ciclope di Eumolpo e il Ciclope di Petronio: *Sat.* 100 ss', *MD* 20–1 (1988), 311–15.

FRÖHLKE, FRANZ M., *Petron. Struktur und Wirklichkeit* (Frankfurt, 1977).

FUCHS, H., 'Verderbnisse im Petrontext' in *Studien zur Textgeschichte und Textkritik*, ed. H. Dahlmann and R. Merkelbach (Cologne, 1959), 57–82.

GAGLIARDI, DONATO, *Il Comico in Petronio* (Palermo, 1980).

GAMBA, G. G., *Petronio Arbitro e i Christiani* (Rome, 1998).

GELLIE, G. H., 'A comment on Petronius', *AUMLA* 10 (1959), 89–100.

GEORGE, PETER, 'Style and character in the *Satyricon*', *Arion* 5 (1966), 336–58.

——— 'Petronius and Lucan *De Bello Civili*', *CQ* 24 (1974), 119–33.

GIGANTE, VALERIA, 'Stile nuovo ed etica anticonvenzionale in Petronio', *Vichiana* 9 (1980), 61–78.

GILL, CHRISTOPHER, 'The sexual episodes in the *Satyricon*', *CP* 68 (1973), 172–85.

GOODYEAR, F. R. D., 'Petronius' in *Cambridge History of Classical Literature, vol. II Latin Literature*, ed. E. J. Kenney and W. V. Clausen (Cambridge, 1982), 635–8.

GRIMAL, P., *La guerre civile de Pétrone dans ses rapports avec la Pharsale* (Paris, 1977).

GRONDONA, MARCO, *La religione e la superstizione nella Cena Trimalchionis. Collection Latomus*, vol. 171 (Brussels, 1980).

HÄGG, THOMAS, *The Novel in Antiquity* (Oxford, 1983).

HEINZE, RICHARD, 'Petron und der griechische Roman', *Hermes* 34 (1899), 494–519.

HIGHET, GILBERT, 'Petronius the Moralist' in *The Classical Papers of Gilbert Highet*, ed. Robert J. Ball (New York, 1983), 191–209. [Reprinted from *TAPA* 72 (1941), 176–94.]

HORSFALL, NICHOLAS, ' "The uses of literacy" and the *Cena Trimalchionis*', *G&R* 36 (1989), 74–89 (p. I) and 194–209 (p. II).

HOLZBERG, NIKLAS, *Der antike Roman* (Munich, 1986). English edition, *The Ancient Novel: an Introduction* (London 1995).

HUBBARD, THOMAS, 'The narrative architecture of Petronius' *Satyricon*', *Ant. Class.* 55 (1986), 190–212.

HUBER, G., *Das Motiv der 'Witwe von Ephesus' in lateinischen Texten der Antike und des Mittelalters* (Tübingen, 1990).

JONES, F., 'The narrator and the narrative of the *Satyrica*', *Latomus* 46 (1987), 810–19.

——— 'Realism in Petronius', *Groningen Colloquia on the Novel* 4 (1991), 105–20.

KENNEDY, GEORGE, 'Encolpius and Agamemnon in Petronius', *AJP* 99 (1978), 171–8.

KISSEL, WALTER, 'Petrons Kritik der Rhetorik (*Sat.* 1–5)', *RhM* 121 (1978), 311–28.

KORN, MATTHIAS, and REITZER, STEFAN, *Concordantia Petroniana. Computer Konkordanz zu den Satyrica des Petron* (Hildesheim, 1986).

KRAGELUND, PATRICK, 'Epicurus, Priapus and the dreams in Petronius', *CQ* 39 (1989), 436–50.

LABATE, MARIO, 'Di nuovo sulla poetica dei nomi in Petronio: Corax "il delatore"?', *MD* 16 (1986), 135–46.

NETHERCUT, W. R., 'Petronius, epicurean and moralist', *CB* 43 (1967), 53–5.

NISBET, R. G. M., Review of Müller, Konrad (ed.), *Petronii Arbitri Satyricon* (Munich, 1961). In *JRS* 52 (1962) 227–32.

PACCHIENI, MARINA, 'Nota Petroniana. L'Episodio di Circe e Polieno (capp. 126–131; 134)', *B. Stud. Lat.* 6 (1976), 79–90.

PACK, ROGER, 'The criminal dossier of Encolpius', *CP* 55 (1960), 31–2.

PANAYOTAKIS, COSTAS, *Theatrum Arbitri. Theatrical Elements in the Satyrica of Petronius* (Leiden, 1995).

PARSONS, PETER, 'A Greek *Satyricon*?', *BICS* 18 (1971), 53–68.

PECERE, ORONZO, *Petronio. La novella della matrona di Efeso* (Padua, 1975).

PERRY, B. E., *The Ancient Romances: A Literary-Historical Account of their Origins* (Berkeley and Los Angeles, 1967).

PERUTELLI, ALESSANDRO, 'Le chiacchiere dei liberti. Dialogo e commedia in Petronio 41–46', *Maia* 37 (1985), 103–19.

—— 'Enotea, la capanna e il rito magico: l'intreccio dei modelli in Petron. 135–136', *MD* 17 (1986), 125–43.

—— 'Il narratore nel *Satyricon*', *MD* 25 (1991), 9–25.

PETERSMANN, HUBERT, 'Umwelt, Sprachsituation und Stilschichten in Petrons "Satyrica"', *ANRW* 2/32.3 (1985), 1687–705.

PRESTON, KEITH, 'Some sources of comic effect in Petronius', *CP* 10 (1915), 260–9.

PRIULI, STEFANO, *Ascyltus. Note di onomastica petroniana. Collection Latomus*, vol. 140 (Brussels, 1975).

RAITH, OSCAR, 'Veri doctus Epicurus. Zum Text von Petron 132.15.7', *WS* NS 4 (1970), 138–51.

—— 'Unschuldsbeteuerung und Sündenbekenntnis im Gebet des Enkolp an Priap (Petr. 133.3)', *Stud. Class.* 13 (1971), 109–25.

RANKIN, H. D., 'Some themes of concealment and pretence in Petronius' *Satyricon*', *Latomus* 28 (1969), 99–119.

—— *Petronius the Artist. Essays on the Satyricon and its Author* (The Hague, 1971).

REEVE, M., 'Petronius' in *Texts and Transmission: A Survey of the Latin Classics*, ed. L. D. Reynolds (Oxford, 1983), 295–300.

RICHARDSON, T. WADE, 'The Sacred Geese of Priapus? (*Satyricon* 136.4 f.)', *Mus. Helv.* 37 (1980), 98–103.

—— 'Homosexuality in the *Satyricon*', *C&M* 35 (1984), 105–27.

RICHLIN, AMY, *The Garden of Priapus: Sexuality and Aggression in Roman Humor* (New Haven, 1983).

ROSATI, GIANPIERO, 'Trimalchione in scena', *Maia* 35 (1983), 213–27.

ROSE, K. F. C., *The Date and Author of the Satyricon*, intr. J. P. Sullivan, *Mnemosyne* Suppl. 16 (Leiden, 1971).

ROSENBLÜTH, M., *Beiträge zur Quellenkunde von Petrons Satiren* (Berlin, 1909).

SANDY, GERALD N., 'Satire in the *Satyricon*', *AJP* 90 (1969), 293–303.

—— 'Petronius and the tradition of the interpolated narrative', *TAPA* 101 (1970), 463–76.

—— 'Scaenica Petroniana', *TAPA* 104 (1974), 329–46.

SAYLOR, CHARLES, 'Funeral games: the significance of games in the *Cena Trimalchionis*', *Latomus* 46 (1987), 593–602.

SCHMELING, GARETH, 'Petronius: satirist, moralist, epicurean, artist', *CB* 45 (1969), 49–50 and 64.

—— 'The literary use of names in Petronius *Satyricon*', *RSC* 17 (1969), 5–10.

—— 'The *Satyricon*: forms in search of a genre', *CB* 47 (1971), 49–52.

—— 'The *Exclusus Amator* motif in Petronius' in *Fons Perennis. Saggi critici di Filologia Classica raccolti in onore del Prof. Vittorio D'Agostino* (Turin, 1971), 333–57.

—— 'The *Satyricon*: the sense of an ending', *RhM* 134 (1991), 352–77.

—— 'Petronius 14.3: Shekels and Lupines', *Mnem.* 45 (1992), 531–6.

SCHUSTER, MAURIZ, 'Der Werwolf und die Hexen. Zwei Schauermärchen bei Petronius', *WS* 48 (1930), 149–78.

SINCLAIR, BRENT W., 'Encolpius and Asianism (*Satyricon* 2.7)' in *Classical Texts and their traditions. Studies in honour of C. R. Trahman*, ed. David F. Bright and Edwin S. Ramage (Chico, Calif., 1984), 231–7.

SLATER, NIALL W., *Reading Petronius* (Baltimore, 1990).

SOVERINI, PAOLO, 'Il problema delle teorie retoriche e poetiche di Petronio', *ANRW* 2/32.3 (1985), 1706–79.

STUCKEY, JOHANNA H., 'Petronius the "Ancient": his reputation and influence in seventeenth century England', *RSC* 20 (1972), 145–53.

SULLIVAN, J. P., 'Satire and Realism in Petronius' in *Critical Essays on Roman Literature—Satire*, ed. J. P. Sullivan (London, 1963), 73–92.

—— *The Satyricon of Petronius. A Literary Study* (London, 1968).

—— 'Petronius, Seneca, and Lucan: A Neronian literary feud?', *TAPA* 99 (1968), 453–67.

—— 'On translating Petronius' in *Neronians and Flavians—Silver Latin I*, ed. D. R. Dudley (London, 1972), 155–83.

—— 'Petronius: artist or moralist?' in *Essays on Classical Literature*, selected from *Arion* with an introduction by Niall Rudd (Cambridge, 1972), 151–68. [Reprinted from *Arion* 6 (1967), 71–88.]

—— 'Petronius' *Satyricon* and its Neronian Context', *ANRW* 2/32.3 (1985), 1666–86.

THIEL, HELMUT VAN, *Petron. Überlieferung und Rekonstruktion. Mnem.* Suppl. 20 (Leiden, 1971).

—— 'On the order of the Petronius Excerpts', *PSN* 15.1 (1983), 5–6.

VERDIÈRE, RAOUL, 'La Tryphaena du *Satyricon* est-elle Iunia Silana?', *Latomus* 15 (1956), 551–8.

WALSH P. G., 'Eumolpus, the *Halosis Troiae*, and the *De Bello Civili*', *CP* 63 (1968), 208–12.

—— *The Roman Novel. The 'Satyricon' of Petronius and the 'Metamorphoses' of Apuleius* (Cambridge, 1970; Bristol Classical Press, 1995).

—— 'Was Petronius a moralist?', *G&R* 21 (1974), 181–90

—— 'Petronius and Apuleius' in *Aspects of Apuleius' Golden Ass: A Collection of Original Papers*, ed. B. Hijmans and R. van der Paardt (Groningen, 1978), 17–23.

ZEITLIN, FROMA, 'Romanus Petronius: a study of the *Troiae Halosis* and the *Bellum Civile*', *Latomus* 30 (1971), 56–82.

—— 'Petronius as paradox: anarchy and artistic integrity', *TAPA* 102 (1971), 631–84.

Petronius
The Satyricon

1

At the School of Rhetoric

1 [Encolpius is in full flow:] 'This, surely, is the same band of
Furies goading our teachers of rhetoric when they cry: "These
wounds have I sustained for our country's liberty, this eye
have I forfeited in your service. Give me a helping hand to
escort me to my children, for my legs are hamstrung and
cannot support my body's weight." Utterances even as bad
as this we could stomach if they advanced students on the
path to eloquence. But in reality all that they achieve with
their turgid themes and their utterly pointless and empty
crackle of epigrams is that when they set foot in court they
find themselves transported into another world. This is why
I believe that our hapless youngsters are turned into total
idiots in the schools of rhetoric, because their ears and eyes
are trained not on everyday issues, but on pirates in chains
on the sea-shore, or on tyrants signing edicts bidding sons
decapitate their fathers, or on oracular responses in time of
plague urging the sacrifice of three or more maidens. These
are nothing but verbal gob-stoppers coated in honey, every
word and every deed sprinkled with poppy-seed and sesame!

2   'Students fed on this fare can no more acquire good sense
than cooks living in the kitchen can smell of roses. Forgive
my saying so, but you teachers of rhetoric more than any
others have been the death of eloquence. Your lightweight,
empty bleatings have merely encouraged frivolity, with the
result that oratory has lost all its vigour, and has collapsed.
Young men were not as yet strait-jacketed with declamations
when Sophocles and Euripides devised the language they
needed. No professor in his ivory tower had as yet expunged
all genius when Pindar and the nine lyric poets shied from
Homeric measures in singing their songs. Not that I need
to cite the poets in evidence; so far as I am aware, neither

Plato nor Demosthenes*had recourse to this kind of exercise. Lofty and what one may call chaste eloquence is not
blotchy or turgid; its inherent beauty lends it sublimity.
But of late this flatulent, disordered garrulity of yours has
decamped from Asia to Athens.* A wind as from some baleful star has descended on the eager spirits of our youth, as
they seek to rise to greatness, and eloquence has been
stopped in its tracks and struck dumb, once its norms were
perverted. In short, who in these later days has attained the
renown of Thucydides or Hyperides?* Even poetry has not
maintained the brilliance of its complexion unimpaired; it
has all been fed on the same diet, and has not been able to
survive to grey-haired old age. Painting too came to a similar end, once the shameless Egyptians devised short cuts to
so noble a pursuit.'*

3   Agamemnon* refused to allow me to deliver in the colonnade a declamation longer than the one which had raised
sweat on him in the school. 'Young man,' he said, 'your
speech reflects no ordinary taste, and you are uniquely gifted
with love of good sense, so I shall not withhold from you the
secrets of the trade. It is hardly surprising that teachers are
at fault in these school exercises; they have to go along with
lunatics, and play the madman. Unless their speeches meet
with the approval of their young pupils, they will in Cicero's
words* be left high and dry in the schools. Our plight is like
that of flatterers on the stage who cadge dinners from the
rich; their chief preoccupation is what they think will please
their hearers most, for they will attain their aim only by
laying traps for their ears. Likewise, unless the teacher of
eloquence turns angler and baits his hook with the morsel
which he knows the fish will bite on, he stands idle on the
rock with no hope of a catch.

4   'So what is the moral? It is the parents who deserve censure
for refusing to allow stern discipline to ensure the progress
of their children. To begin with, they sacrifice their young
hopefuls, like everything else, on the altar of ambition. Then,
in their haste to achieve their goals, they bundle them into
the courts while their learning is still undigested. When their

sons are still in their cradles, they swaddle them with eloquence, believing that eloquence is the be-all and end-all.
Whereas if they allowed them to struggle step by step, making the youngsters work hard, steep themselves in serious
study, order their minds with the maxims of philosophy,
score out with ruthless pen* what they had first written, lend
patient ears to the models which they wished to imitate,
convince themselves that nothing admired by boys can be of
intrinsic worth—then the lofty utterance of old would maintain its weight and splendour. But as things stand, as boys
they fool around in school, and then as young men attract
derision in the courts; and what is more shameful than either
of these, in old age they are unwilling to acknowledge the
defects of their education. But I would not have you think
that I have been carping at the impromptu, commonplace
utterances of a Lucilius,* so like him I shall express my feelings
in verses.

5   'The man who seeks success in austere Art,
         And sets his thoughts on mighty enterprises,
         Must first refine his ways by rigid laws
         Of serious living. Let him not aspire
         To insolent palace with its lofty stare;   5
         Nor as dependant scheme to gain admission
         To dinners of intemperate hosts. Nor must he
         Attach himself to wastrels, and with wine
         Submerge his mind's hot flame, nor yet again
         Sit as a hired claqueur before the stage,*   10
         Applauding the actor's grin.
                              What *must* he do?
         Whether the smiling citadel*
         Of armed Tritonis guards him there,
         Or where the Spartan immigrant dwells,
         Or where the Sirens* have their lair.   15
         To poetry let him first commit
         His earliest years, drink at the pool
         Maeonian, to his heart's delight.
         Next have his fill of Socrates' school,

Then loose his reins, and riding free   20
Wield great Demosthenes' armoury.*

Then, Roman poets* circling round,
From Greece's measures newly freed,
Must well up in him, and transform
His taste-buds. Still must he secede   25
From lawcourts. Let his page run free,
Proclaiming Fortune in its clear, swift
    course,
Recounting feasts, and war's harsh blasts*
With lofty Ciceronian force.

Virtues like these must clothe your soul;   30
Your river of eloquence then is full,
Words will well forth at the Muse's call.'

2

Dubious Encounters in the Town

6 Through listening with close attention to Agamemnon, I
failed to notice that Ascyltus had made off from my side . . . As
I walked along, excited by this tide of words, a great crowd
of students entered the colonnade. It seemed that they were
emerging from a declamation delivered off the cuff by
someone who had followed after Agamemnon's set piece
of persuasion.* So while the youths were having fun with
his epigrams, and ridiculing the scheme of his entire speech,
I seized the chance to slip away and began to hare after
Ascyltus. But I had failed to take careful note of the route,*
and did not know the way to our lodging. So whichever
direction I took brought me back to the same place. Eventually, exhausted by the chase, and dripping with sweat, I
approached a little old lady selling farm produce.

7   'Tell me, mother,' I said, 'have you any idea where I hang
out?' She was tickled by such asinine wit, and replied: 'Yes;
no problem.' She then got up and began to lead the way.
I thought she had second sight, and followed after her.
Then, when we reached some hole-in-the-corner place, the
witty old creature drew back a patchwork curtain, and said:
'This must be where you stay.' I was just remarking that I
did not recognize the lodging when my eyes fell on some
men furtively pacing among the price-tags and naked pros-
titutes. It slowly dawned on me all too late that I'd been
brought to a brothel.* So cursing the old woman's duplicity,
I covered up my head, and began to belt through the middle of the brothel to the far end. Who should meet me at
the very entrance there but Ascyltus, just as clapped out and
half dead as myself! You'd have thought that the same old
woman had escorted him there. So I greeted him with a
grin, and asked him what he was doing in such a disreputable place.

8   He brushed off the sweat with his hands, and said: 'If you only knew what happened to me!' 'Tell me the story,' I replied. He looked all in. 'As I was wandering all over town,' he said, 'unable to locate where I'd left the lodging, a respectable gent came up to me, and very decently offered to show me the way. Then after taking me through the dingiest side-streets my guide surfaced here, took out his wallet, and began to proposition me. By then the madam had already got the money for the hire of a room, and he had his hand on my shoulder. If I hadn't proved the stronger, it would have been all up with me.'

*

In fact my impression was that the whole town had been downing aphrodisiacs. By joining forces we shrugged off the troublesome fellow . . .

3

Jealousy at the Lodging

9 Through misty eyes I caught sight of Giton* standing on the kerb in an alleyway, and I darted to the spot... When I asked my boyfriend whether he had cooked anything for our lunch, the lad sat on the bed wiping away floods of tears with his fingers. My friend's demeanour upset me, and I asked what had happened. His response was slow and reluctant, but when my pleading began to give way to irritation, he said: 'That boyfriend or companion of yours came rushing into the room a minute ago, and started trying to rape me on the bed. When I cried in protest, he drew his sword, and said: "If you are Lucretia,* you have met your Tarquin!"' On hearing this, I brandished my fist in Ascyltus' face, and said: 'So what's your excuse, you cheap tart, you easy lay? Why, even your breath is rancid!' Ascyltus pretended to bridle, but then he raised his fists more aggressively, and bawled out much more loudly than I had: 'Shut your mouth, you filthy gladiator, saved by the midday Circus crowd!* Pipe down, you assassin by night! Even on your good days you never found a decent woman to have a go at! Didn't I play partner to you in the park, just as the boy here does in the lodging?'

10 'You sidled off', I said, 'while the professor was chatting to us.'

'You crass idiot,' he replied, 'what did you expect me to do when I was dying of hunger? Listen to his banalities, I suppose, nothing but bits of broken glass and explanations of dreams! For God's sake, you're a damned sight worse than I am, praising that poet just to cadge an invitation to dinner.' So our unedifying brawl dissolved into laughter, and we resumed our unfinished business in a more comradely spirit...

But then the recollection of the insult came flooding back,

and I said: 'Ascyltus, I've come to the conclusion that we can't get on. So we'd better divide our bits of luggage, and try to keep poverty at bay by making money each on our own. We've both gone through school. I'll try some separate ploy so as not to prejudice your takings. Otherwise a thousand things will cause friction between us every day, and the whole town will be gossiping about us.' Ascyltus did not demur. 'Right,' he said. 'But let's not waste the chance of tonight, seeing that our scholarly status has won us a dinner invitation. But tomorrow, as that's what you want, I'll prospect for a different lodging and another boyfriend.'

'But our minds are made up,' I countered. 'Putting it off is mere procrastination.' It was the sexual itch that motivated this quite sudden parting; I had been keen for some time to see the back of this tiresome chaperon in order to resume my former relationship with Giton.

*

11 After a sightseeing tour of the whole town, I returned to our little room, and at last elicited Giton's kisses with true affection. I folded the boy in the closest embrace, and fulfilled my heartfelt desires to an enviable degree. But things hadn't reached their climax when Ascyltus came creeping up to the door. He burst the bolts violently, and caught me redhanded sporting with my boyfriend. The room echoed with his laughter and applause. He rolled me out from under the bedclothes, and said: 'Whatever were you up to, my clean-living friend? Are you playing at houses under the blanket?' He didn't confine himself to taunts, but took the strap from his satchel, and started to give me a thorough thrashing, punctuating it insolently with these words: 'This will teach you to share with your brother!'

4

An Episode in the Market

12 We entered the market-place just as daylight was fading.
We observed there quite a collection of goods for sale, none
of them of any value—just the sort of merchandise whose
shoddiness the darkness of evening could most readily con-
ceal. We too had brought along the stolen cloak,* so we
proceeded to exploit this most favourable opportunity, and
in a corner of the market we waggled the hem of the garment up and down, hoping that its bright colour would
attract a buyer. Almost at once a peasant, whom I seemed
to recognize, and his female companion came up and began to examine the cloak with some care. Ascyltus in turn
glanced at the peasant's shoulder, and suddenly held his
breath and fell silent. I too was somewhat shaken at the
sight of the fellow, for he looked very like the man who had
come across my shirt out in the country: he was clearly the
very man. Ascyltus could scarcely trust his eyes. Not wishing
to surrender to impulse, he first edged closer, as though he
were a prospective purchaser. He pulled the edge of the
garment from the man's shoulders, and fingered it with
some care.

13   Fortune plays some strange games. The peasant hadn't as
yet so much as run inquisitive fingers along the stitching.
There was even a hint of disdain in his sales pitch, as though
he'd filched the garment from a beggar. Once Ascyltus noted
our treasure still intact,* and the mean status of the vendor,
he took me aside a little from the crowd, and said: 'Hey,
look, dear boy! That treasure whose loss I was lamenting
is back with us! That shirt of ours seems to be bulging with
the gold coins intact. So how do we set about lawfully claiming our property?' My own spirits were soaring not merely
because I could see the loot, but also because Fortune had

cleared me of a most foul suspicion.* So I answered that we
must not act deviously, but contest the issue openly by civil
action. If the peasant refused to restore the property not his
own to its rightful owner, we should seek an injunction.

14   But Ascyltus demurred from fear of the laws. 'Who in this
place knows us, or who will believe a word we say? Now that
we have identified it, I'd much prefer to buy it, even though
it belongs to us, and to get back the hidden hoard by paying a copper or two rather than by getting involved in the
uncertain outcome of a lawsuit.

> 'What point have laws, where Mammon solely reigns,
> Where poverty no victory obtains?
> The very Cynics who scorn modern ways*
> —Bearing in wallets life's necessities—
> Perjure themselves at times for sordid gains.   5
> In lawsuits, widespread bribery obtains.
> The knights who sit empanelled* have been bought;
> The ones who grease their palms will get their vote!'

But we had no ready cash, apart from one shekel and some
counterfeit coins,* with which we had planned to make some
purchases. So to ensure that in the meantime our loot should
not vanish, we decided to reduce the price-tag on the cloak;
in this way a smaller loss would bring a greater gain. So we
laid out our merchandise. But at once the woman accompanying the peasant with her face veiled took a closer look
at the marks on the cloak, seized the hem in both hands,
and cried in a loud voice: 'Thieves!' In our anxiety not to
appear passive, our dismayed reaction was to grab in turn
the torn and filthy shirt, and in the same resentful tones
loudly to assert that the garment in their possession had
been looted from us. But the contest was wholly one-sided,
and the dealers,* who had flocked around at the brawling,
characteristically derided our lunacy, for they saw that the
one party was claiming a very expensive cloak, and the other
a ragged shirt not worth patching with good cloth.

15   At this juncture, Ascyltus suddenly broke into their laughter. This provoked silence, and he said: 'It's clear to us that

we all like our own best. So let them return the shirt to us, and get their cloak back in return.' The peasant and the woman were agreeable to the exchange, but the security men on the evening shift*were hoping to make money out of the cloak, and demanded that both garments be placed under their care so that the magistrate could investigate the dispute next day. They claimed that the case involved more than the objects before their eyes; much more serious was the fact that both parties were under suspicion of theft. The course now agreed was to deposit the garments with trustees.* One of the dealers, a bald man with a wart-covered face who doubled as a part-time court-pleader, laid hold of the cloak and undertook to produce it next day. But it was clear what the game was: once the cloak was in his hands, those thieves would keep a tight hold of it, and we would fail to turn up for the appointed case for fear of being charged. This solution clearly suited us as well. So as it turned out, both sides got what they wanted. The peasant was infuriated because we demanded that the patched shirt be produced in court, and he threw it in Ascyltus' face, telling us, now that our complaint was dealt with, to deposit the cloak, the only article now under dispute . . .

Once we had, as we thought,* recovered the treasure, we rushed pell-mell back to the lodging. Once the doors were closed, we began to laugh at the sharp conduct of the dealers and our vexatious accusers alike, because by being so terribly clever they had restored our money to us . . .

> To sate my longing I would rather wait;
> So please don't hand me victory on a plate.*

5

Enter Quartilla, the Priapic Priestess

16* No sooner had we filled our bellies with the dinner which
Giton had kindly prepared for us than there was a peremp-
tory hammering on the door . . . We blanched, and asked
who was there. 'Open up', a voice said, 'and you will soon
find out.' In the course of this exchange, the bolt gave way
of its own accord, and fell off; the door suddenly yawned
open and admitted our visitor. It was a woman, heavily veiled.
'Did you imagine', she asked, 'that you had fooled me? I am
the maid of Quartilla, the lady whose ritual you interrupted
in front of her chapel. She is coming in person to your
lodging, and begs leave to have words with you. Don't get
agitated; she is not here to condemn or to punish your sin;
on the contrary, she wonders what god has led such elegant
young men into her neighbourhood.'

17   We were still reduced to silence, saying neither yea nor
nay, when the lady herself entered, escorted by a young girl.
She seated herself on my bed in a bout of weeping. Even
then we did not offer a word, but waited in bewilderment
for this tearful demonstration of grief to end. Once the
impressive shower of tears had subsided, she unveiled her
proud head, pressing her hands hard together until the
joints cracked. 'Why have you behaved so recklessly?' she
asked. 'Where did you learn to outdo the story-books in
your thieving? I swear to heaven I'm sorry for you; no one
goes unpunished for having gazed on things forbidden. This
locality of ours in particular is so crowded with the presence
of divinities that it's easier to find a god here* than a man.

'Please don't think that I have come here bent on revenge. I'm more concerned for your tender years than for
the harm you've done me. I still think that it was thought-
lessness that made you commit that irreparable crime. That

night I myself was on edge. I got the shivers from so dangerous a chill that I even feared an attack of tertian fever. So
I sought a remedy from my dreams. In them I was bidden
to seek you out, and to relieve the onset of my illness by a
clever device that was revealed to me. But that cure is not
what bothers me most. A greater affliction seethes deep
within me, dragging me down willy-nilly to death's door: it
is the fear that youthful excess may induce you to noise
abroad what you witnessed in Priapus' shrine, and to make
the gods' designs known to the world at large. This is why
I stretch out suppliant hands to your knees, begging and
imploring you not to decide to betray the secrets of countless years which are known to barely a thousand mortals.'*

18   She followed this entreaty with a further outburst of tears.
Her body shook with protracted moaning, and she sank her
entire face and breast into my bed. Shaken simultaneously
by pity and fear, I urged her to be of good heart, and to
be reassured on both counts: none of us would divulge the
rites, and if the god had revealed to her some further cure
for the fever, we would carry through the design of divine
Providence even if it put us in danger. This promise cheered
the lady, and she rained kisses on me. Her tears were transformed into laughter, and with lingering fingers she stroked
the hair tumbling over my ears. 'I declare a truce with you',
she said, 'and discharge you from the indictment laid against
you. But if you had not consented to the remedy I seek, I
had already mustered a mob to avenge the affront to my
honour.

> 'If patronized by others, I lose face;
> It's arrogance to put me in my place.
> I like the chance to go my own sweet way.
> Why, even wise philosophers of the day,
> If treated with contempt, weave words to harm.   5
> The merciful combatant oft wins the palm.'

Then she clapped her hands, and dissolved into such par-
oxysms of laughter that we were alarmed. For her part, the

maid who had entered before her behaved likewise; so did
the young girl who had come in with her.

19   The entire place resounded with the laughter of the low
stage.* We were wholly at a loss about the meaning of this
sudden change. We stared blankly now at each other, and
now at the women . . .

*

'So I have given instructions that no mortal be allowed into
this lodging today, so that I can obtain the cure for my
tertian fever from you without interruption.' When Quartilla
said this, Ascyltus was momentarily struck dumb; I felt colder
than a Gallic winter, and could not utter a word. However,
the nature of the company reassured me against anticipating anything unpleasant. They were three mere women, their
strength puny if they tried anything on; whatever else was
said about us, at least we were male, and our clothes were
certainly hitched higher than theirs. Indeed, I had already
mentally matched up the pairs in case we had to fight it out;
I would face up to Quartilla, Ascyltus to the maid, and Giton
to the young girl.

*

At that moment of bewilderment,* our entire resolve melted
away. Certain death began to shroud our unhappy eyes.

20   'Madam, I beg you,' I said, 'whatever sinister plan you
have in mind, get it over and done with. The crime we committed was not so monstrous that we must die by torture.'
. . . The maid, whose name was Psyche, carefully spread
a blanket over the stone floor . . . She addressed herself
to my parts, already cold through suffering a thousand
deaths. Ascyltus had buried his head in his cloak; he doubtless remembered the warning that it was dangerous to witness
the secret rites of others.

The maid produced two straps from her dress; she tied
our feet together with one, and our hands with the other . . .

*

Our flow of chatter was now flagging, so Ascyltus piped up:
'Don't I merit a drink, then?' The maid, prompted by my
laughter, clapped her hands and said: 'But I did put one by
you . . . Young Encolpius, have you drunk the entire potion
yourself?'

'Good heavens!' said Quartilla. 'Has Encolpius downed
all the aphrodisiac?' Her sides shook rather fetchingly.
Finally even Giton failed to restrain his giggles, especially
when the young girl hung on his neck and deluged the
unresisting lad with countless kisses . . .

*

21 We would have cried out in our wretched state, but there
was no one at hand to lend help. On the one side Psyche
was gouging my cheeks with a hairpin as I sought to raise
a hue and cry, and on the other the young girl was dous-
ing Ascyltus with a sponge which she had soaked in the
aphrodisiac . . .

Eventually a catamite appeared on the scene, dressed in
a cloak of myrtle green hitched up with a belt. First he
wrenched our buttocks apart and forced his way in, and
then besmirched us with the foulest of stinking kisses, until
Quartilla, wielding a whalebone ferula and hitching her
skirts high, gave the order for our release from our unhappy
service . . .

We both swore an oath in the most solemn terms that so
grim a secret would never be divulged by either of us . . .

Several attendants from the gym came in, and revived us
by rubbing us down with the usual oil. So we were able to
dispel our weariness, and to resume our dress for dining.
We were escorted into the next room, in which three couches
had been laid and every other elegant preparation had been
made on a lavish scale. So when the word was given we
reclined on the couches. There was a splendid hors d'œuvre
to start with, and we were also abundantly plied with
Falernian wine. Then we were served with several main
courses as well. But when we began to doze off, Quartilla

said: 'What's this? Are you even contemplating sleep, when you are aware that a night's vigil is owed to the guiding spirit of Priapus?'

*

22 Ascyltus was wearied by the many indignities he had suffered, and he fell asleep. The maid whose approaches had been so rudely rejected coated his entire face with masses of soot, and painted his torso* and shoulders vermilion. He did not feel a thing. By now I too was exhausted by all these grisly experiences, and had savoured a quick snatch of sleep. So had the whole retinue of servants, both in the room and outside. Some were lying scattered round the feet of the reclining guests, others were propped against the walls, and others still waited at the threshold, heads supporting each other. The lamps too were running out of oil and giving off a dim and dying light. At that moment two Syrians* came into the dining-room intending to strip the place. Their greed got the better of them as they squabbled over the silver, and they pulled a decanter apart and broke it. The table with the silver on it went flying, and a drinking cup was accidentally dislodged from a high shelf, and gave the maid a bleeding head as she lay drooping over a couch. The impact made her cry out; this both exposed the thieves and roused some of the revellers. When the Syrians realized that they had been caught in the act, they simultaneously collapsed by a couch as if by a prearranged ploy, and began to snore as though they had been asleep for some time.

By now the steward had been roused, and had poured some oil into the flagging lamps. The slave-boys rubbed their eyes for a moment or two, and returned to duty. A female cymbal-player entered and roused everyone with the clash of brass.

23   So the party recommenced. Quartilla recalled us to our cups, and the cymbal-player sang to add to the jollity. Then in came a catamite,* the most repulsive character imaginable, surely a worthy representative of that household. He

wheezed as he snapped his fingers, and spouted some lines
like this:

'Assemble here, you wanton sodomites,
Drive yourselves forward, let your feet take wing.
Full speed ahead. Come now with pliant thighs,
And mincing buttocks, fingers gesturing!
Come, tender youths, and you in later life,   5
And lads castrated by the Delian's knife!'*

Having delivered his lines, he slobbered over me with the
filthiest of kisses. He then mounted the couch as well, and
stripped me with all his strength in spite of my resistance.
He laboured long and hard over my parts, but all in vain.
Streams of brilliantine poured over his forehead as he
sweated away, and so much chalk appeared in the wrinkles
of his cheeks that you would have thought that a wall was
flaking after being damaged by rain.

24   I could not restrain my tears any longer, for I was reduced
to extreme distress. 'Please, madam,' I said, 'surely what you
prescribed for me was a tumbler to have in bed?'*She clapped
her hands gently, and replied: 'What a clever fellow you are,
a positive fount of native wit! Did you not realize that a
catamite is also called a tumbler?' Then, so that things would
turn out better for my comrade, I remarked: 'For goodness'
sake, is Ascyltus the only one in the dining-room enjoying a
holiday?'

'So it seems,' said Quartilla. 'Ascyltus must get a tumbler
as well.' At these words the catamite changed mounts and
crossed over to my companion, smothering him with his
buttocks and his kisses.

Giton stood there watching this and splitting his sides
with laughter. So Quartilla cast an eye on him, and with
great interest enquired whose boy he was. I replied that
he was my friend. 'So why hasn't he given me a kiss?' she
demanded. She called him over to her, and kissed him.
Then she slipped her hand inside his clothes, and fondled
his virgin tackle. 'These will make a good starter to rouse

my appetite in tomorrow's encounter,' she said. 'As I've already had the fish course today, I don't want dry bread!'

25   As she was saying this, Psyche came close to her ear wearing a grin, and whispered some suggestion. 'Quite right,' said Quartilla. 'You did well to remind me. This is a most auspicious moment, so why shouldn't our Pannychis lose her maidenhead?' At once the girl was ushered forward. She was extremely pretty, and seemed to be no more than seven years old. One and all applauded, and demanded a wedding.* I was astounded and protested that Giton was an extremely modest lad, not up to such wanton behaviour, and the girl was not old enough to undertake the woman's role. 'What?' said Quartilla. 'Is she any younger than I was when I first submitted to a man? I don't recall ever being a virgin—Juno strike me down* if I lie! Even as a baby I played dirty games with boys of my own age, and as I grew up I associated with bigger lads till I reached womanhood. In fact I think that's how the proverb, "Carry a calf, and carry a bull", originated.'

26   I was afraid that the boy would come to greater harm if he were unaccompanied, so I got up to play my part in the ceremony. By now Psyche had draped a marriage veil over the girl's head, and the Tumbler was leading the way with a marriage torch. The drunken females formed a long line, clapping their hands; they had adorned the bridal chamber with lewd coverlets. Quartilla was roused by the lecherous behaviour of the sportive crowd. She sprang up, grabbed Giton, and dragged him into the bedroom. The boy had clearly offered no resistance, and the girl had not blanched fearfully at the mention of marriage. So they were tucked in, and they lay down; we seated ourselves at the threshold of the chamber. Quartilla took the lead in gluing an inquisitive eye to a chink she had shamelessly opened, and she viewed their youthful sport with prurient attention. Then with caressing hand she drew me to watch the spectacle as well. Our faces as we eyed the scene were close together, and whenever she took a rest from the show she would

move her lips over, and press kisses on me from time to time on the sly . . .

*

We threw ourselves on our beds, and spent the rest of the night without apprehension.

*

6

Dinner at Trimalchio's

Two days had now elapsed, and the free dinner*was in pro-spect. But we were transfixed by so many wounds that we were bent on flight rather than relaxation. So in our dejec-tion we were discussing how to avoid the storm-clouds ahead, but then one of Agamemnon's servants broke in on our anxieties, and asked: 'What's the matter with you? Don't you know your host for today? He is Trimalchio,* a man of supreme refinement. He keeps a water-clock in his dining-room, and a trumpeter at the ready, so that from time to time he can keep count of the lost hours.' So we forgot all our misfortunes, and dressed with some care. Giton was playing the role of servant with great *élan*, and we bade him follow us to the baths.

27   To pass the time we strolled about in our dinner dress. Indeed, we were laughing and joking as we approached the groups of those who were taking exercise. Suddenly we caught sight of a bald old man wearing a red shirt and playing ball with some long-haired young slaves. The boys were worth a good look, but they were not so much the attraction as was their master. He was wearing slippers, and throwing a green ball around. Any ball which came in con-tact with the ground he did not bother to retrieve; there was a bagful supervised by a slave, containing enough for the players. We noticed some other unusual features: two eunuchs stood in the circle facing Trimalchio. One was hold-ing a silver chamber-pot; the other was counting the balls, not as they sped from hand to hand as they were thrown in the course of the game,* but as they dropped to the ground. As we were admiring these refinements, Menelaus* came bustling up. 'This is the host at whose table you will rest your elbows. This in fact is the prelude to the dinner.' As

Menelaus was still speaking, Trimalchio clicked his fingers, and at this signal the eunuch supplied him with the chamber-pot as he continued playing. The host voided his bladder, demanded water for his hands, and after perfunctorily washing his fingers, wiped them on the slave's hair.

28   Reporting all the details would be tedious. So we entered the baths, and as soon as we had raised a sweat we passed through to the cold plunge.* By now Trimalchio was doused with fragrant oil, and was being rubbed down—not with linen cloths, but with bath-towels of softest wool. Meanwhile his three masseurs were drinking Falernian before his eyes. They spilt a lot of it while sparring with each other; Trimalchio claimed that they were commemorating him!*

He was then installed in a litter, wrapped in a scarlet dressing-gown. In front were four bemedalled runners,* and a go-cart in which his boy-favourite* was riding, a wizened youth with watery eyes, uglier than Trimalchio his master. As the host was borne off, a musician with miniature pipes came close to his head, and played in his ear the whole way, as if he were imparting confidential information to him.

Quite wonderstruck we walked behind, and in company with Agamemnon drew near the door. On the doorpost a notice had been fastened, bearing the inscription: 'Any slave leaving the house without his master's bidding will receive a hundred stripes.' At the very entrance stood a janitor in a green outfit hitched up with a cherry-coloured belt; he was shelling peas in a silver dish. Over the threshold hung a golden cage, in which a dappled magpie* greeted the incomers.

29   As I stood lost in amazement at all this, I nearly fell flat on my back and broke my legs. On our left as we entered, close to the janitor's office, a massive dog* fastened by a chain was painted on the wall, with an inscription above it in block letters: BEWARE OF THE DOG. My companions burst out laughing at me; I gathered my wits, and proceeded to examine the entire wall. There was the representation of a slave market, with placards bearing the names and prices of the slaves. Trimalchio himself was there, sporting long hair

and holding a herald's wand; Minerva was escorting him* on his entry into Rome. Next the painter had carefully and scrupulously depicted, with commentary below, the detail of how Trimalchio had learnt accountancy, and had then become a steward. At the end of the colonnade, Mercury had raised him by the chin, and was bearing him up on to a lofty dais. Fortune with her horn of plenty was in attendance, and the three Fates were there spinning their golden threads. I observed also in the colonnade a team of runners practising under their trainer. In a corner I noted a large sideboard enclosing a tiny shrine. In it were set the household gods in silver, a marble statue of Venus, and a golden container of some size, in which they said Trimalchio's beard was stored . . .*

So I began to question the porter about the subjects of other pictures on display. 'There is the *Iliad*,' he replied, 'and the *Odyssey*, and *Laenas' Gladiatorial Games*.'*

30   But we were unable to examine the numerous exhibits . . . We had now reached the dining-room. A steward was posted at the entrance, approving the accounts. I was particularly surprised to see a bundle of rods and axes* attached to the doorposts, supported below by what seemed to be the bronze beak of a ship, containing the inscription: 'To Gaius Pompeius Trimalchio, member of the sextet of the College of Augustus. Presented by his steward Cinnamus.' A two-branched lamp with the same inscription hung from the ceiling. There were also two panels set in the two doorposts. If my memory serves me right, one of them had this inscription: 'Our Gaius dines out on 30th and 31st December.' The other depicted the course of the moon, with representations of the seven planets.* Days of good and evil omen were marked with distinctive counters.

Sated with these delights, we attempted to make our way into the dining-room. As we did so, one of the slaves allotted to this duty cried out: 'Right feet first!'* For a moment we were in utter panic, in case one of us disobeyed the injunction in crossing the threshold. As we all as one put our right feet forward, a slave stripped for flogging* grovelled

at our feet, and proceeded to implore us to rescue him
from punishment. The cause of his predicament, he said,
was a mere peccadillo: the steward's clothes which were in
his charge at the baths had been stolen* from him, but they
would have fetched no more than ten thousand sesterces.*
So we withdrew our right feet, and implored the steward, as
he counted out gold pieces in his office, to grant the slave
a remission. That arrogant official raised his nose in the air.
'It is not so much the loss that annoys me', he said, 'as that
good-for-nothing slave's dereliction of duty. He lost my
dining-out clothes given to me by one of my dependants for
my birthday. They were Tyrian of course, but they had been
laundered once,* so the loss is of no account. I make you a
present of him.'

31   This lordly concession put us in his debt. As we entered
the dining-room, we were confronted by the same slave for
whom we had pleaded. As we stood there open-mouthed,
he thanked us for our kindness by showering us with kisses.
'I won't labour it,' he said, 'but you will soon be aware who
the recipient of your kindness was. "The master's wine is in
the butler's gift." '*

At last we were able to settle on the couches. Some
Alexandrian slave-boys* poured iced water on our hands, while
others behind them bent over our feet, and with great dex-
terity cut our toenails. Even this degrading duty did not
silence them, for they sang as they worked. I wanted to find
out if the whole entourage was composed of songbirds, so
I asked for a glass of wine. A slave was immediately at hand,
and took my order while singing in a shrill voice; so did all
the others when complying with a request. You would have
thought it was a dancer's supporting group,* and not the
service in the dining-room of a wealthy householder!

By now a most elegant hors d'œuvre had been brought
in, for all the guests had taken their places on the couches,
with the sole exception of Trimalchio, for whom contrary to
custom a top place* was being reserved. In the entrée dish
stood a donkey made of Corinthian bronze, bearing a double
pannier which contained white olives on one side, and black

on the other. Covering the donkey were two dishes, on the rims of which were engraved Trimalchio's name and their weight in silver. Little bridges which had been soldered on spanned the dishes; they contained dormice dipped in honey and sprinkled with poppy-seed. There were also hot sausages lying on a silver grill, and underneath were plums and pomegranate-seeds.

32   We were enjoying this refined fare, when to the sound of music Trimalchio himself was carried in. He was deposited between cushions piled high, and the sight of him evoked laughter from the unwary, for his shaven head protruded from a scarlet dressing-gown, and round his neck draped with a muffler he had thrust a napkin with a broad purple stripe* and fringes dangling from it all round. On the little finger of his left hand he sported a huge gilt ring, and the top joint of the next finger held a smaller one, which seemed to me to be solid gold, though it was clearly studded with iron stars.* Not content with demonstrating these marks of wealth, he bared his right arm to show that it was adorned with a golden bracelet*and an ivory bangle fastened with a shining plate of metal.

33   As he hacked at his teeth with a silver toothpick, he said: 'My friends, I did not relish coming to the dining-room so soon, but I did not wish to detain you any longer, so I have foregone all my own pleasure. Allow me, however, to finish the game.'*A slave followed behind him bearing a board of terebinth wood*and crystal dice; what struck me as the height of refinement was that in place of white and black counters, he was using gold and silver *denarii*.* In the course of the game he exhausted every hackneyed expletive.

While we were still on our starters, a large platter bearing a basket was brought in. It contained a wooden hen, sitting as hens do when hatching eggs with wings outspread. At once two slaves drew near, and to the blaring sound of music began to rummage in the straw. They promptly unearthed peahens' eggs, and distributed them among the guests. Trimalchio surveyed this tableau,* and said: 'My friends, I gave instructions for these peahens' eggs to be

hatched under the hen. Good Lord, I'm afraid the chickens
are on their way out! However, let's see if they are still soft
enough to eat.' We picked up our spoons weighing not less
than half a pound, and assaulted the eggs which were made
of flour baked in oil. I nearly discarded my helping, as it
seemed already to have hardened into a chicken, but then
I heard an experienced guest say: 'There is sure to be something good in this.' So I poked my finger through the shell,
and found inside a plump little fig-pecker, coated in peppered yolk of egg.

34   By now Trimalchio had abandoned the game, and had
demanded a helping of everything. He had just loudly
authorized* a second glass of the sweetened wine for anyone requesting it, when at a sudden musical signal the hors
d'œuvre dishes were all whisked away simultaneously by the
singing troupe. In the mêlée, however, a dish happened to
fall. As it lay there, a slave picked it up. Trimalchio noticed
this, ordered the boy to have his ears boxed, and made him
throw it down again. A servant whose job was to keep things
tidy followed behind him, and with his broom began to
sweep out the silver dish with the rest of the debris. Then
two long-haired Ethiopians* moved in carrying diminutive
wineskins, like the men who sprinkle water on the sand* in
the amphitheatre, and poured wine on our hands.* No one
in fact offered water. When our host was praised for the
refined arrangements, he remarked: 'Mars loves an equal
contest, so I gave instructions for each guest to have his own
table. So that way those stinking slaves* will not make us
sweat by crowding on top of us.'

At that moment glass winejars, carefully sealed with gypsum, were brought in. On their necks were fastened labels,
with the inscription: 'Falernian wine of Opimian vintage.*
One hundred years old.' As we scrutinized the labels, Trimalchio clapped his hands and exclaimed: 'So wine, sad to
say, enjoys longer life than poor humans! So let us drink
and be merry.* Wine is life-enhancing. This is genuine
Opimian that I'm serving. Yesterday the wine I provided was
not so good, though the company at dinner was much more

respectable.' So we got started on the wine, taking the great-est pains to express our wonder at all the elegance. A slave now brought in a skeleton of silver,* constructed in such a way that its joints and spine were loose, and could be twisted in every direction. Trimalchio threw it down on the table several times, to allow its supple joints to fall into various postures. He added in commentary:

> 'Sad creatures we! In sum, poor man is naught.
> We'll all end up like this, in Orcus' hands,
> So let's enjoy life while we can.'

35   After our praise of these lines, there followed a dish clearly not so lavish as we anticipated, but unusual enough to rivet the eyes of all of us. The circular plate had the twelve signs of the Zodiac in sequence round it, and on each of them the chef had placed foodstuffs appropriately matching the subjects. On the Ram, he had placed chickpeas shaped like a ram's head; on the Bull, a portion of beef; on the Twins, testicles and kidneys; on the Crab, a crown; on the Lion, an African fig; on the Virgin, a barren sow's womb; on the Scales, a balance with different cakes on each side; on the Scorpion, a small sea-fish; on the Archer, a crow; on the Goat, a lobster; on the Water-bearer, a goose; on the Fishes, two mullets. In the middle of the dish was a square of turf still sporting its grass, with a honeycomb on it.* An Egyptian slave was carrying bread round in a silver dish . . . and the host himself joined in, with a most scurrilous and tortured version of a mime-song from *The Silphium Gatherer.* As we rather gloomily contemplated this plebeian fare, Trimalchio said: 'Come on, let's tuck in; this is the dinner menu.'*

36   As he spoke, four servants bounded forward rhythmically in time to the music, and removed the covering of the dish. Inside we saw fowls, sows' udders, and in the centre a hare equipped with wings, a veritable Pegasus.* We also noticed four representations of Marsyas at the corners of the dish; from their wineskins a peppered gravy was pouring over fish which were swimming, so to say, in the channel.* The slaves applauded, and we all joined in, smiling appreciatively as we

attacked the choice fare. Trimalchio too was tickled by the
success of such a trick. He called out 'Carver!' At once the
carver came forward, and with extravagant motions in time
to the music, cut up the meat in such a way that you would
have thought he was a charioteer engaging to the music of
a water-organist. Trimalchio still continued repeating in the
most droning voice: 'Carve 'er, Carver!'* I suspected that
such frequent repetition of the word spelt a sophisticated
joke, so I boldly questioned the man reclining next to me.*
He had witnessed such sportive diversions quite often, and
replied: 'You see the fellow carving the meat? His name is
Carver, so whenever Trimalchio cries "Carver", he is at once
calling on him and giving him his instructions.'

37   In my desire to learn as much as possible, I could not
swallow another mouthful, so I turned to my neighbour and
began at some length to elicit all the gossip.* I enquired
about the woman scurrying to and fro. 'That's Trimalchio's
wife,' he answered. 'Her name is Fortunata. She measures
her money by the bushel. Yet what was she only a short time
ago? You will pardon my saying this, but you wouldn't have
taken a bread-roll from her hand. But now—there's no rhyme
or reason in it—she's on top of the world, and Trimalchio
thinks the world of her. To put it bluntly, if she tells him
at high noon that it's pitch dark, he'll believe her. As for
Trimalchio, he's so wealthy he doesn't know how much he's
got. But that lynx sees to everything. She turns up in the
most unlikely places. She keeps off the booze, and she's a
steady influence, offering sound advice. But what a forked
tongue! She's a real magpie of the couch.* If she likes you,
she likes you; if she doesn't, she doesn't.

'As for the boss himself, his estates are so extensive that
kites fly over them. He has oodles of money. There's more
silver coin lying in that janitor's office than the entire fortune of any of us. As for his household—good God, I don't
think a tenth of them could recognize their master. In a
word, he can box and bury* any of these smart Alecs.

38   'Don't imagine for a moment that there is any produce
that he buys; it's all grown on his property. Wool, citrus

fruit, pepper—look for cock's milk, and you'll find it. For example, the wool he was getting wasn't too good, so he bought rams from Tarentum,* and got them to have a go at his ewes. He ordered bees brought from Athens to get home-produced Attic honey; the wee Greeks incidentally will improve the native strain a bit as well. And listen to this: only a few days ago he wrote for mushroom-spawn to be dispatched from India.* As for his mules, he hasn't one which isn't sired by a wild ass. You see all these cushions; every one of them is stuffed with purple or scarlet. That's how well-endowed he is.

'As for the other freedmen sharing his table, don't write them off; they're loaded. You see the one reclining at the end of the bottom couch? Today he's worth 800,000.* He's risen from nothing; only the other day he was carting logs on his back. The story goes—I'm talking only from hear-say—that he grabbed a gnome's cap* and found a treasure. I don't begrudge anyone getting what God gives him, but he's a bit of a braggart and not slow in putting himself forward. For example, he published this advertisement the other day: "Gaius Pompeius Diogenes is letting his upper room from July 1st, and is buying a house."*

'Take a look at the one reclining in the freedman's place.* He used to be well off. I'm not blaming him. He had a million of his own to feast his eye on. But he's had a bad time; I don't think he can count his hair his own. But I swear it's not his fault. There's not a better man living. But his freedmen are real villains; they've done everything to suit themselves. You know how it is; a shared pot goes off the boil, and once things begin to slide, your friends melt away. You see him in this parlous state, yet he ran a really decent business; he was an undertaker. He used to dine like a king; boars served whole in their skins, fancy cakes, game-birds . . . cooks and confectioners. There was more wine poured under his table than any of us has in his cellar. He wasn't a man, he was a walking circus. Even when he was down on his uppers, he was anxious that his creditors shouldn't think that he was bankrupt, so he advertised an auction with this announcement: "Gaius Iulius Proculus will auction his surplus stock." '

39   Trimalchio broke into this congenial gossip. By now the first course had been cleared away. The guests were in high spirits, and had begun to concentrate on the wine and general conversation. So the host leaned back on his elbow. 'Your company', he said, 'must help us savour the wine; the fishes must swim. Did you really think that I was happy to offer you just the food which you saw on the lid of the dish? "Is this the Ulysses you know so well?"'So what was the point of it? Well, even when we're dining we must advance our learning. My patron—God rest his bones—wanted me to take my place as a man among men; what the dish showed was that there's nothing that I didn't know already.

'The sky above* is the home of twelve gods, and is transformed into as many shapes. First it becomes the Ram. So whoever is born under that sign has many flocks, and huge stocks of wool—yes, and a hard head, a shameless front, and a sharp horn. Most of those who frequent the schools, and the muttonheads, are born under this sign.' We praised our astrologer's wit, so he continued. 'Next the whole sky turns into a young bull, so at that time recalcitrant people are born, and ploughmen, and those who provide their own dinners. Under the Twins are born chariot pairs, teams of oxen, big-bollocked lechers, and those who like to have it both ways. I myself was born under the Crab, so I have several feet to support me, and a lot of possessions on both land and sea, for the Crab is equally at home on both. That's why I placed nothing over this sign earlier, to avoid putting pressure on my own natal star. Under the Lion are born those who feast gluttonously, and who boss you around; under the Virgin, woman-chasers, runaways, and slaves in chains.* Under the Scales come butchers, perfume sellers, and those whose job it is to weigh things; under the Scorpion, poisoners and assassins; under the Archer, cross-eyed people, lifting the bacon while looking at the vegetables;

under the Goat, those who have a hard time, whose worries make them sprout horns; under the Water-bearer, innkeepers and those with water on the brain; under the Fishes, chefs and teachers of rhetoric.* So the world turns on its course like a mill-stone, always bringing harm in its train, so that people are born or die. As for the turf you see in the centre, and the honeycomb on the turf, none of my arrangements is without a purpose. Mother earth is set in the middle, rounded like an egg, and containing within her like a honeycomb all that is good.'

40   As one we all cried 'How clever!' We raised our hands to the ceiling, and swore that Hipparchus and Aratus* were not in the same league as Trimalchio. Then servants came in, and placed coverlets over the couches. On them were depicted nets, and hunters lying in wait with hunting spears, and all the paraphernalia of the chase.* Our suspicions were roused, but we had not yet divined why, when a great din resounded outside the dining-room. Would you believe it, Spartan dogs* joined in, and began to bound round the table. Behind them followed a tray with a massive boar on it, wearing the cap of freedom.* From its teeth hung two small baskets woven from palm-leaves, one filled with fresh dates, and the other with the dried Egyptian variety. The boar was surrounded by tiny piglets of pastry, seemingly crowding over the teats, which indicated that the beast was a sow. The piglets were in fact gifts to take away.* The slave who came in to cut up the boar was not the carver who had mangled the poultry, but a huge bearded figure. His legs were encased in puttees, and he wore a multi-coloured hunting coat. He drew his hunting knife, and plunged it enthusiastically into the boar's flank. This incision prompted thrushes to fly out; fowlers stood at the ready with limed reeds, and speedily trapped the birds as they circled round the dining-room. Trimalchio ordered each guest to be served with his helping of pork, and then he added: 'Do also notice what refined acorns this woodland pig has devoured.' Slaves at once approached the baskets dangling from the

boar's teeth, and in time to the music shared out the fresh
and dried dates among the diners.

41   Meanwhile I withdrew into myself, and pondered the
various possibilities for the boar's having entered wearing
the cap of freedom. After exhausting every fatuous explana-
tion, I steeled myself to seek the solution to my nagging
problem from that informant of mine. He replied: 'Why,
even I your humble servant can answer that. It's no riddle,
but quite straightforward. Yesterday the main course claimed
him, but the diners set him scot-free; so today he returns to
the feast as a freedman.' I cursed my stupidity, and did not
ask a single question thereafter, in case I should give the
impression of never having dined in respectable company.

During this conversation of ours, a handsome slave wearing a wreath of vine-leaves and ivy (he was performing successively the roles of Bacchus the Thunderer, Bacchus the
Deliverer, and Bacchus God of Devotees) carried grapes
round in a basket, reciting his master's poems in a high-
pitched voice. On hearing this, Trimalchio said: 'Dionysus,
now be Liber.'* The slave snatched the cap from the boar
and put it on his head. Then Trimalchio further added:
'You won't deny that my father is Liber.' We applauded this
bon mot, and kissed the boy enthusiastically as he made his
way round.

Following this course, Trimalchio rose to go to the lav-
atory. Now that the tyrant was deposed and we had gained
our freedom, we began to entice [? the rest of the company
to speak?]. So Dama spoke up first.* After demanding larger
winecups, he said: 'Daylight's just non-existent. Turn round,
and it's nightfall. So there's no better order of the day than
to get out of bed and to make straight for the dining-room.
What a sharp spell of frosty weather we've had! Even after
my bath I've hardly warmed up. But a hot drink's as good
as a topcoat. I've had a basinful, and I'm absolutely pissed.
The wine's gone to my head.'

42   Seleucus chipped in with his bit of gossip. 'Myself, I don't
take a bath every day. Taking a bath is as bad as being sent

to the cleaner's; the water's got teeth. My blood gets thinner every day. But once I get a jug of mead inside me, I can tell the cold to bugger off. Actually I couldn't have a bath today because I attended a funeral. Good old Chrysanthus, handsome fellow that he was, has given up the ghost. He said hallo to me only the other day; I could be talking with him at this very moment. Dammit, we're nothing but walking bags of wind. Flies rank higher; they do have a bit of spark, whereas we're no more than bubbles. If only he hadn't gone on a diet! He didn't take a drop of water or a crumb of bread for five days. And yet he's away to join the majority. The doctors killed him off—or the truth is it was his bad luck, because a doctor does nothing but set your mind at rest. Still, he had a decent cortège. He was laid out on a bier, covered with good quality drapes. The mourning party was great, for he'd freed several slaves,* though his widow was grudging with her tears—and him the best of husbands! But women as women are nothing but a bunch of kites. None of us should treat them decently; it's like dropping all you've got down a well. But a love-liaison of long standing is a festering sore.'

43   He was getting us down, and Phileros burst out: 'Forget the dead, and think about the living! He had his money's worth, a good life and a good death. What's he got to grumble about? He started out with only a penny in his pocket; at that time he'd have picked up a farthing with his teeth out of the shit. Then he grew and grew just like a honeycomb. My God, I think he left a cool hundred thousand, all in ready cash. I'm a Cynic with a dog's tongue inside me, so I'll tell it straight. He had a rough tongue, and he opened his mouth too often; he was a living argument, not a man. His brother was a decent guy who would do a friend a good turn; he was open-handed, and kept a tidy table.

'Chrysanthus caught a cold when he first set up in business, but his first vintage set him up again, for he sold his wine at the high price he asked. But what really brought him up in the world was the estate he inherited, and he made off with more of it than had been left to him. And

now, just because he fell out with his brother, the loony has
left his property to some nobody. The man who runs from
his family runs many a mile. But his confidential slaves were
his undoing. You'll never prosper if you give credit* on
impulse, especially if you're in business. But it's true that
he enjoyed himself all his life; it's a matter of who lays his
hands on it, not who should have got it. He was a real child
of Fortune; put lead in his hand, and it turned to gold. It's
easy to make your way when everything goes hunky-dory. And
how many years do you think he totted up? More than seventy. He was a horny old bird, carried his age well, hair
black as a crow. I knew him years and years ago, and even
then he was one for the girls. Heavens, I don't think he left
the dog in his house unmolested. He was fond of boys as
well, a real all-rounder. Not that I blame him; it was the only
thing he took with him.'

44   After Phileros had his say, Ganymede spoke up. 'You're
all nattering on about things of no concern in heaven or
on earth, and all the time no one gives a damn about the
crippling price of corn. I swear I couldn't afford a mouthful
of bread today. The drought still continues—there's been a
shortage for a year now. To hell with the aediles,* I say, for
they're in league with the bakers. It's a case of "You look
after me, and I'll look after you." So those at the bottom of
the heap suffer, because the ones on top grind them down,
and enjoy a perpetual holiday. If only we had the lionhearts
whom I found living here when first I arrived from Asia!
Life was good in those days. If the best Sicilian flour* wasn't
as it should have been, they would give those devils such a
hiding that they knew heaven was frowning on them. Safinius
is one I remember. When I was a boy he lived down by the
old arch. He was a firebrand, not a man; wherever he put his
feet, he scorched the ground. But he was straight as a die,
utterly reliable, never let a friend down—you could happily
play *morra* with him in the dark. How he used to dress 'em
down one by one in the council chamber! He didn't use
fancy language but spoke straight out. And again, when he
pleaded in court, his voice would swell like a trumpet. He

never sweated or spat; I think the gods had blessed him with a dry inside. He would return your greeting as friendly as you like, and address everyone by name; he was just like one of the boys.

'So at that time corn was as cheap as dirt. The bread you bought for a penny was more than enough for two of you to swallow. But today I've seen bull's eyes that are bigger. Sad to say, every day things get worse.⌋ The colony's like a calf's tail, growing backwards. Why do we put up with an aedile not worth three figs, who would rather make a penny profit for himself than keep us alive? He sits at home, laughing all over his face, raking in more money by the day than the next man's entire fortune. I know quite well where he got his thousand gold pieces.* If we were men with real balls he wouldn't be so pleased with himself. But as it is, people are lions at home but foxes outside. In my own case, the rags on my back are already spoken for; if this corn shortage continues, I shall have to sell my little shack. If neither gods nor men take pity on this colony, heaven knows what will happen to it. As I hope to have the joy of my children, I really do think that the gods are visiting all these things on us. It's because no one believes in heaven, no one observes the fasts, no one gives a toss for Jupiter; they all sit with their eyes closed, but they're reckoning what they're worth. At one time the women wore long dresses, and walked barefoot up the hill with their hair unbound and their clothes washed dazzling white, praying to Jupiter for rain. At once it came down in buckets; otherwise it never rained. They would all go home looking like drowned rats. So this is why the gods wrap their feet in wool:* it's because we don't keep the faith. The fields lie fallow—'.

45   The clothes dealer Echion interrupted: 'Do look on the bright side. As the countryman said when he lost his dappled pig, it's not the same all over. What we don't have today we'll get tomorrow. That's what life's all about. You couldn't name a better town than this to live in, I'll swear, if only we had real men about. But like other places, it's depressed at the moment. Let's not be too hard to please;

it's the same weather for all of us. If you were living somewhere else, you would be saying that the streets here were
alive with roast pork.

'And remember we're due to have a marvellous show
on the holiday three days from now. There'll be a lot of
freedmen in the arena, not just the gang of gladiators from
the training school. Our friend Titus the showman is ambitious and hot-blooded. It won't be wishy-washy; there'll be
something worth watching. I'm on good terms with him;
he doesn't shilly-shally. He'll offer us some bonny fighting.
There'll be no chickening out; it'll be a butcher's shop for
the whole amphitheatre to see. And he has the wherewithal
to mount the show; he came into thirty million on the sad
death of his father. He can spend four hundred thousand
without his estate's feeling it, and he'll be a byword for ever.
He's already lined up several freaks, and a woman who fights
from a chariot, and a steward of Glyco's caught in the act
of pleasuring his mistress. You'll witness brawls breaking out
in the crowd, jealous husbands against lover-boys. Fancy that
twopenny-ha'penny Glyco throwing his steward to the beasts!
He might as well expose himself to them. What sin did the
steward commit, when he was forced to push it in? That
piss-pot of a wife deserved to be tossed by a bull. But if you
can't beat the donkey, beat the saddle. How ever could Glyco
have imagined that Hermogenes' daughter, a chip off the
old block, would turn out decent? That guy could cut the
claws of a kite in flight; vipers like him don't hatch lengths
of rope. It's Glyco, poor Glyco, who has paid the price. As
long as he lives, he'll be branded, and only death will clear
the slate. But our sins make sticks for our own backs.

'My nose tells me that Mammea is going to lay on a banquet worth two *denarii* for me and my colleagues. If it comes
off, he'll put Norbanus right out of the running; I'm sure
you'll realize that he'll win hands down. And let's be honest, what pleasure did Norbanus ever give us? He put on
some cut-price gladiators on their last legs, who would have
fallen over if you blew on them. I've seen better specimens
matched with the wild beasts. As for the mounted gladiators

that he disposed of, they came off table-lamps;* the horses
pranced about like farmyard cocks. One was thin as a rake,
another had club feet, and the reserve* was a corpse standing in for a corpse—it was hamstrung. There was one
Thracian* with a bit of spunk, but even he observed the rule-
book. In short, they all got a flogging later, for they were at
the receiving end of shouts of "Get stuck in!" from the
crowded amphitheatre; it was a total shambles. "Well, I did
put on a show for you!" claims Norbanus. Yes, and I gave
you a good hand. If you work it out, I did you a bigger
favour than you did me. One good turn deserves another.

46 'Agamemnon, am I right that you are saying "Why is this
boring man prattling on?"? I'm doing it because though
you're the expert with words, you're saying nothing. You
don't belong to our patch, so you sniff at the way we poor
buggers talk. We know you're off your head with all that
education. I tell you what: can I persuade you to come out
to our country place one day, and take a look at our little
house? We'll get a bite to eat there—some chicken, and
eggs. It'll be a pleasant outing, even if the weather this
year has turned everything upside down. We'll certainly get
enough to fill our bellies.

'My little feller is growing fast, ready to sit at your feet; he
can divide by four already. If God spares him, you'll have a
young devotee beside you soon. Whenever he has a spare
moment he never lifts his head from the slate. He's a smart
lad, made of the right stuff, though he's crazy about birds;
I've already killed three goldfinches of his and told him that
the weasel ate them.* But now he's found another hobby;
he's very fond of painting. He's begun to make a decent
start on Latin literature now that he's giving the Greek boys
the boot. Mind you, that teacher of his is cocky, always shift-
ing his pitch. He knows his stuff,* but he doesn't like hard
work. There is another teacher; he doesn't know much, but
he's got an enquiring mind, and he imparts more than he
knows. He often visits us on holidays, and is happy with
whatever food you put before him.

'I've now bought the lad some law-books; I want him to

get a smattering of the law to cope with our property. Law is where the bread is; he's had enough literature to mark him for life. If he shies at law, I've decided that he must learn a trade as a barber, or an auctioneer, or if the worst comes to the worst an advocate—some career that only death can rob him of. So every day I rail at him: "Primigenius, believe me, education's for your own benefit. Take a look at Philero the advocate. If he hadn't applied himself, today he wouldn't be able to keep the wolf from the door. It's no time since he was lugging goods for sale round on his shoulders, and now he's challenging even Norbanus. Education's a real treasure; a profession's something for life."'

47 Gossip of this sort was being bandied about when Trimalchio came in. He mopped his brow, and washed his hands with perfume. He waited only a second or two before remarking: 'Excuse me, my friends, but for some days now my stomach has not responded to nature's call. The doctors are at a loss. But in my case pomegranate-rind and pine-wood dipped in vinegar have done the trick. I now have hopes that my stomach will be regular as before. Anyhow, my inside is rumbling like a roaring bull, so if any of you want to relieve yourselves, there's no need to be ashamed. None of us was born rock-solid. I can't imagine any torture worse than having to hold it in. This is the one thing that even Jupiter can't forbid. I see you're grinning, Fortunata, but that's how you keep me awake at night. But even in the dining-room I don't forbid anyone to ease himself, and the doctors forbid us to keep the wind inside. If anything heavier is imminent, everything's ready outside—water, chamber-pots, the other bits and pieces. Believe me, the vapours attack the brain, and flood through your whole body. I know quite a few who've died that way through refusing to face the facts.' We thanked him for his generosity and consideration, and hastened to choke our laughter by taking frequent swigs of the wine.

We were blissfully unaware that we were still toiling half-way up the hill, as the saying goes. When the tables had been cleared to the sound of music, three white pigs wearing

halters and bells were led into the dining-room. The spokesman*said that one was two years old, the second three, and
the third as old as six. I thought that some circus performers had arrived, and that the pigs were going to perform
some tricks, as they commonly do in sideshows. But my
anticipation was dispelled when Trimalchio asked: 'Which
of these would you like to have served this moment for
dinner? Only country bumpkins offer a farmyard cock, or a
goulash, or miserable dishes of that kind; my cooks often
put on pot-roasted calves.'

There and then he ordered the cook to be summoned.
Without waiting for us to make our choice, he ordered the
slaughter of the oldest pig. He then questioned the cook
loudly: 'Which company do you belong to?'*The cook told
him the fortieth. 'Were you purchased,' asked the host, 'or
are you home-born?'

'Neither,' said the cook. 'I was bequeathed to you in the
will of Pansa.'*

'Be sure, then', said Trimalchio, 'to make a good job of
serving this course, or I'll order you to be demoted to the
company of messengers.' On being reminded of the master's power over his destiny, the cook was led into the kitchen
by our next course.

48   Trimalchio then adopted a meek demeanour, and turned
his eyes on us. 'If the wine is not to your taste', he said, 'I'll
have it changed. Your presence must make it acceptable.
The gods' kindness saves me from having to buy it. All the
fare that now makes your mouth water is produced on an
out-of-town estate that I haven't yet seen. They tell me that
it's bounded by Tarracina and Tarentum.* At the moment
I'm trying to join Sicily to my little estates, so that if I take
a fancy to go to Africa, I can sail there by way of my own
territory.

'But tell me, Agamemnon, what legal dispute was the
subject of your declamation today? I don't practise in the
courts, but I've educated myself to run the household. Don't
think that I despise learning; I've got two libraries, one Greek
and one Latin. So be good enough to tell me the topic of

your declamation.' When Agamemnon began 'A poor man
and a rich man were enemies', Trimalchio asked: 'What is
a poor man?' Agamemnon acknowledged the witticism, and
then recounted some legal argument. Trimalchio at once
observed: 'If this happened, there is no disputing it; if it
didn't happen, it's a non-starter.' We greeted these and other
comments with the most extravagant praises. Trimalchio then
proceeded: 'Tell me, Agamemnon my dearest friend; have
you any recollection of the twelve labours of Hercules, or
that story of how Ulysses had his thumb twisted off by the
Cyclops with his pincers?* I used to read these stories in
Homer when I was a boy. And as for the Sibyl, I saw her with
my own eyes at Cumae, suspended in a bottle,* and when
boys asked her, "Sibyl, what is your wish?", she would reply,
"I want to die."'

49   He had not finished all his blethering when a dish bearing an enormous pig took over the table. We began to express surprise at the speed of the cooking, swearing that not
even a farmyard cock could have been thoroughly roasted
so quickly. Our surprise was all the greater because the pig
seemed to be far bigger than the boar had been a little
earlier. Then Trimalchio looked closer and closer at it, and
said: 'What's this? Has this pig not been gutted? By heaven,
it hasn't. Get the cook, call the cook into us.' The cook took
his stand by the table with downcast face, and admitted that
he had forgotten to gut the pig. 'What's that? You forgot?'
Trimalchio shouted. 'You would think he'd merely omitted
to season it with pepper and cumin. Off with his shirt!' The
cook's shirt was at once ripped off, and he stood there
unhappily between two torturers. Then everyone began
to plead for him in these words: 'This often happens. Do
let him off, we beg you, and if he does it again, none of us
will speak up for him.' But I myself am the hardest of task-
masters, and I could not contain myself. I leaned over to
Agamemnon's ear, and said: 'He must obviously be the most
slovenly of slaves. Could anyone forget to gut a pig? I swear
to God that I would not let him off for omitting to gut even
a fish!' But Trimalchio did not share my indignation. His

face softened to a smile, and he said: 'Well, then, since you are so forgetful you must gut it while we watch.' The cook got back his shirt, and seized a knife. Then with shaking hand he slit the pig's belly on each side. At once the slits widened with the pressure of the weight inside, and sausages and black puddings came tumbling out.

50   The slaves clapped their hands at this trick, and cried in unison: 'Three cheers for Gaius!' The cook too was rewarded with a drink and a silver crown; he was handed a goblet on a tray of Corinthian ware. Agamemnon took a closer look at the tray, whereupon Trimalchio remarked: 'I am the only person to possess genuine Corinthian ware.' I anticipated that his words would match his general extravagance, and that he would claim that he imported vessels from Corinth. But he went one better. 'Perhaps', he said, 'you are wondering why I am the sole possessor of genuine Corinthian. It's because the bronze-smith from whom I purchase is called Corinthus. How can any ware be Corinthian, if one doesn't have a Corinthus to supply it? But in case you think I am an ignoramus, I'm perfectly aware how Corinthian bronze originated. At the capture of Troy, that rascally slimy lizard Hannibal*piled all the statues of bronze, gold and silver on a pyre, and set fire to them; all the various elements merged into an alloy of bronze. Craftsmen then removed lumps of this amalgam and made plates, dishes and statuettes out of them. This is how Corinthian ware originated, from this *mélange* of metal which is neither one thing nor the other. Pardon me for saying so, but I myself prefer glassware; at any rate no smell comes off it.* I'd prefer it to gold if it didn't get broken, but as things are it's cheap stuff.

51   'There was a craftsman who made a glass goblet which was unbreakable.* He was accordingly ushered with his gift into Caesar's presence. He got Caesar to hand it back to him, and he let it drop on the paved floor. Caesar could not have been more startled. However, the craftsman picked up the goblet from the ground; it was dented like a bronze vessel. He then produced a little hammer from his clothing, and without fuss restored the goblet good as new. After this

demonstration he thought that he was on top of the world, especially when the emperor asked: "Does anyone else know about this technique of glass-making?" Now hear the outcome. When the craftsman said no, Caesar ordered him to be beheaded, for of course if the secret had leaked out, gold would be as cheap as dirt.

52   'I'm quite keen on silver. I have something like a hundred* three-gallon bumpers . . . with the motif of Cassandra killing her sons; the boys are lying there so vividly dead that you'd think they were alive! I have a bowl which king Minos bequeathed to my patron; on it Daedalus* is enclosing Niobe in the Trojan horse. I've also got in relief on goblets all of solid silver the fights of Hermeros and Petraites.* I wouldn't sell these evidences of my learning at any price.'

Just as he was recounting this, a slave dropped a goblet. Trimalchio eyed him, and said: 'Off you go, and kill yourself for being such a fool.' The boy's lips trembled, and at once he began to beg for mercy. Trimalchio responded: 'Why address me? I'm not hounding you. I suggest that you prevail upon yourself not to be a fool.' But eventually we pleaded successfully with him, and he let the slave off. The boy celebrated his acquittal by prancing round the table . . .

Trimalchio called out: 'Out with the water, down with the wine!' We hailed his witty quip, led by Agamemnon who knew how to earn a further invitation to dinner. This praise roused Trimalchio to more genial drinking. He was now very nearly drunk. 'Will none of you ask my dear Fortunata to dance? Believe me, nobody does the cordax* better.' He himself then placed his hands over his brow, and began to ape the actor Syrus, while the whole ménage sang in chorus: 'Madeia, perimadeia'.* He would have advanced to the centre of the floor, if Fortunata had not whispered in his ear; I suspect that she told him that such degrading tomfoolery detracted from his high dignity. But he was the personification of vacillation supreme, for at one moment he would respectfully heed Fortunata, and at the next would revert to his natural self.

53 This dissolute dancing was rudely interrupted by the accountant, who read out the equivalent of the city gazette:*

'July 26: on our estate at Cumae were born thirty boys and forty girls. Five hundred thousand pecks of wheat were lifted from the threshing-floor and stored in the barn. Five hundred oxen were broken in.

The same day: the slave Mithridates was crucified for blaspheming against the guardian spirit of our master Gaius.

The same day: ten million sesterces were stored in the chest because they could not be invested.

The same day: fire broke out in our gardens at Pompeii, originating in the house of the steward Nasta.'

'What's that?' asked Trimalchio. 'When were gardens at Pompeii purchased for me?'

'Last year,' said the accountant, 'so they haven't as yet been entered into the books.' Trimalchio grew hot with rage. 'Unless', he said, 'I am informed within six months of any estates bought on my behalf, I forbid them to be included in my accounts.'

Next followed a recital of the aediles' edicts,* and wills of foresters containing a codicil disinheriting Trimalchio;* stewards' accounts; a patrolman's divorce from a freedwoman caught red-handed when shacked up with a bathman; a hall porter exiled to Baiae;* the prosecution of a steward; and a court action between chamberlains.

At last the acrobats made their entrance. A most ungainly brute took up his position with a ladder, and ordered a boy to mount it, to perform a song and dance routine on the top, then to jump through burning hoops, and to pick up a winejar with his teeth. Trimalchio alone appreciated this turn. He kept saying that it was a thankless occupation, but that there were two kinds of human activity which he enjoyed watching most, acrobats and horn-players; all other entertainments were rubbish. 'I did buy some comic performers,' he said, 'but I preferred them to put on Atellane farces, and I told my flute-player to perform in Latin.'*

54   Just as Trimalchio was explaining this, the boy tumbled
down* [on top of him]. The slave-boys cried out in unison,
and the guests too, just as vehemently. They were not so
much anxious for the welfare of so contemptible an individual, for they would gladly have seen him even break his
neck, but they feared that an inauspicious end to the dinner
might compel them to lament the death of one they did not
know. Trimalchio himself let out a howl of pain, and nursed
his arm as if it were fractured. The doctors charged forward,
with Fortunata in the van, her hair flying, cup in hand,
proclaiming her wretched and hapless lot. As for the slave
who had tumbled, he was already doing the rounds of our
feet, pleading to be let off. I was considerably exercised that
by these entreaties some trick was being engineered by comic
means, for I had not yet put out of my mind the cook who
had forgotten to gut the pig. So I began to cast an eye all
round the dining-room, in case a surprise packet should
issue from the wall, especially when a slave began to get the
belt for having bandaged his master's bruised arm with white
wool instead of purple. My suspicions were not far off the
mark, for Trimalchio, instead of having the young acrobat
punished, issued a decree declaring him free, to ensure that
no one could claim that a man of such eminence had been
wounded by a slave.

55   We expressed our approval of this, and with a range of
sentiments prattled on about how our human lives lie on a
knife's edge. 'That's so,' said Trimalchio. 'We must not let
this event pass without recording it.' At once he called for
his notebook, and after racking his brains for a moment or
two declaimed this effort:

'Just when you're off your guard,* you get a sideways blow.
Lady Fortune above directs our affairs below.
    So come, boy, the Falernian to us bring.'

This epigram gave rise to discussion of poets, and for some
time the poetic crown was set on the head of Mopsus of
Thrace.* Then Trimalchio said: 'Tell us, master, how do you

think Cicero differs from Publilius? I myself think that Cicero
was the more eloquent, but that Publilius had more probity,
for what could be better than these lines of his?

> ''Neath Luxury's grin the walls of War soon fold.
> Peacocks from Babylon clothed in feathered gold
> To please your palate in their cages feed;
> Numidian fowl and capons serve your need.
> The very stork, loved guest from foreign creek,   5
> With matchstick legs and loudly rattling beak,
> Tending its young 'neath fond maternal wing,
> Fleeing from winter, signalling soft spring,
> In your foul cooking-pot has laid its nest.
>
> Why purchase 'Indian berries', pearls so blest?   10
> To let your wife in sea-spoils rest her head
> Writhing in passion on a stranger's bed?
> Why seek those emeralds green, that glass so dear,
> Rubies from Carthage, glowing red like fire,
> Unless those jewels reflect an honest life?   15
> It surely ill-befits a modest wife
> Garments as thin as wind or cloud to don,
> Offering her goods for sale with little on?'

56   'What profession', he went on, 'do we consider most difficult after that of letters? I myself imagine it is that of the
doctor, or of the bank teller; the doctor, because he's an
expert on what we poor mortals have beneath the skin, and
he knows when a fever's on the way—mind you, I utterly
loathe the profession, because they keep prescribing a diet
of duck for me—, and the teller because he spots the copper lurking beneath the silver. As for dumb beasts, the ones
that work hardest are cattle and sheep. It's thanks to cattle
that we get bread to eat, and sheep help us to preen ourselves with their wool. It's a disgrace that people eat poor
sheep and then wear woollen shirts. I take the view too that
bees are creatures from heaven, for they spew out honey,
though some say they fetch it from Jupiter. The reason why
they sting is because you will find that everywhere the sweet
lies side by side with the bitter.'

By now he was putting even the philosophers out of business, when inscribed slips began to be carried round in a goblet, and a slave appointed to the task read out a list of gifts to be taken away:*

'Accursed silver'—a ham-shank topped with a vinegar bottle was brought in.

'A neck-rest'—a scrag of neck was the present.

'Taste learnt late, and given the stick'—a dry salt-biscuit and a toffee-apple.

'Leeks and peaches'—the recipient got a whip and a knife.

'Sparrows and fly-paper'—raisins and honey.

'Quarry and footwear'—a hare and a slipper were brought in.

'Dinner-things and lawcourt-wear'—the guest received a chop and writing tablets.

'Lamprey and letter'—a mouse and frog tied together, and a bundle of beet.

We laughed and laughed; there were countless labels like this which have now slipped from my mind.

57 Ascyltus, unruly and ill-behaved as ever, kept throwing his hands up and scoffing at each announcement, laughing till the tears came. The fellow-freedman of Trimalchio reclining next to me flushed with anger. 'What are you laughing at, muttonhead?' he asked. 'Are my host's elegant jokes not to your taste? I suppose you're higher up the scale and used to better dinners. So may the guardian spirit of this place preserve me, if I were reclining next to him I'd have made him bleat for mercy. He's a fine specimen to be laughing at others—a runaway fly-by-night, not worth his own piss. In a word, if I peed all round him, he wouldn't know where to take cover. I'm not one to get hot under the collar, but worms breed in the softest flesh. He's laughing, but what's he got to laugh at? Did his father pay good money for him when he was born? What, you're a Roman knight? Well, and I'm a king's son.* "Why, then, were you a slave?" It was because I voluntarily embraced slavery, preferring to be a Roman citizen* rather than a taxpayer. So now my hope is to live a life at which no one can scoff. I'm a man among men;

I walk about with my head uncovered; I owe no one a penny-piece; I've never been in debt; no one has ever accosted me in the centre of town, saying "Pay what you owe". I've bought a plot or two, and laid aside a few coppers; I feed twenty bellies and a dog; I purchased my partner's freedom to ensure that no one used her hair as a towel; I bought my own freedom for a thousand *denarii*; I was elected without subscription as one of the six priests;* my expectation is that at death I'll have nothing to be ashamed of.

'But what about you? Is your nose so close to the grindstone that you don't look behind you? You see the lice on your neighbour, but don't notice the fleas on yourself. You're the only one who regards us as comic. Take a look at your teacher, an older man than you; we pass muster with him. But you're still sucking your mother's milk and can't yet gurgle mu or ma. You're an earthenware pot, a wash-leather in water, too soft to be serviceable. If you are better off, then eat two lunches and two dinners. I'd rather keep my reputation than have loads of money. Let me say just this: nobody has had to ask me twice to pay up. I was a slave for forty years, but no one knew whether I was slave or free. I came to the colony as a long-haired slave before the town hall was built. I made a point of pleasing my master, a worthy, respectable man; your whole person doesn't measure up to his fingernail. There were some in the household who tried to trip me up one way or another, but—God bless the master's soul!—I managed to steer clear. These are the real struggles in life; being born free is as easy as answering a come-hither. Why are you now gaping at me like a goat in a vetch-field?'

58   At these words Giton, who was standing at my feet and had been repressing his laughter for some time, burst out into a quite shameless giggle. When Ascyltus' critic heard this, he switched his abuse to the boy, and said: 'What? Are you laughing as well, you curly-topped onion? What is this, the Saturnalia,* the month of December? So when did you pay your five per cent?* [The boy doesn't know] what he's about; he's nothing but gallows-meat, crows' pickings. I'll

see to it that Jupiter falls on you like a ton of bricks, and on that master of yours who doesn't keep you in order. As I hope to get my daily bread, I'll let this matter go, out of respect for my fellow freedman; otherwise I'd let you have it here and now. There's nothing wrong with us, but as for these good-for-nothings—it's clearly like master, like slave. I can barely restrain myself. I'm not normally hotheaded, but once get me started, and I don't give a toss for my own mother. So right, I'll deal with you outside, you rat, you excrescence. I won't swell or shrink by an inch until I make your master eat humble pie, and by God, I'll not let you away scot-free even if you call on Olympian Jupiter for help. I'll see to it that those cheap curls of yours and your twopenny-ha'penny master don't rescue you. Make no mistake, you'll feel my teeth. If I know Hermeros, you'll not go on sneering, even if you grow a golden beard.* I'll see to it that Athena bears down heavily on you, and on the one who first made you his come-hither.

'I know no geometry or fancy criticism or any such meaningless rubbish, but I do know my capital letters, and I can work out percentages in weights and measures and currency. If you're game, let's have a wee wager between the two of us. Come on, I'm putting my money down. You'll soon realize that your father wasted his funds on your fees, even if you do know rhetoric. Here you are then: "Something belonging to us that comes from far and wide; what am I?"*I'll ask you: "What part of us runs yet stays put?" And "What grows yet becomes less?" I see you're on the run, you're bewildered, you're racking your brains; you're like a mouse in a piss-pot. So either shut up, or don't annoy your betters when they don't know you exist. Don't think I'm impressed by your boxwood rings* which you've pinched from your girlfriend. Let's play Opportunity Knocks and go into the market and borrow some money—you'll soon realize that this iron ring of mine commands credit. Huh, a drowned fox is a pretty sight. As sure as I hope to make a fortune and die content, or have folk swear by my death, I'll haunt you everywhere with my black cap on.* What a fine figure this fellow here

cuts, who teaches you to behave like this; he's a muttonhead,
not a master. When I was young we were taught differently.
The master would say to us: "All your belongings safe and
sound? Straight home now. Look ahead. No cheek to your
elders." But these days it's sheer anarchy. Nobody ends up
worth twopence. I just thank the gods for giving me the
occupation which made me what you see me.'

59   Ascyltus had begun to counter this abuse, but Trimalchio,
delighted with his fellow freedman's eloquence, said: 'Come
on, now, that's enough wrangling. Better for us to keep our
tempers. Hermeros, don't be hard on the lad. He's got hot
blood in him, so be more indulgent. The victor in these
cases is always the one who gives way. When you were a
young cock, you used to crow; like him, you hadn't any
sense. So it's better for us to be cheerful, as we were at
the outset. Let's watch these actors reciting Homer.'

The company at once entered, rattling their spears on
their shields. Trimalchio himself was perched upright on a
cushion, and when the Homeric players addressed each other
in Greek verses, he would recite the text in Latin in a tune-
ful voice. Then he requested silence, and said: 'Do you know
the story they're dealing with?* Diomedes and Ganymede
were two brothers. Their sister was Helen. Agamemnon bore
her off and substituted a hind as an offering to Diana. So
now Homer is describing how the Trojans and Tarentines
are at war with each other. Of course Agamemnon was victorious, and gave his daughter in marriage to Achilles. This
causes Ajax to go mad, and he will now complete the story.'
At these words of Trimalchio, the Homeric performers raised
a shout, and as the slaves scurried back on each side, a
boiled calf wearing a helmet was borne in on a dish weighing two hundred pounds. Ajax followed behind, and playing the madman with drawn sword he finished off the beast;*
with forehand and backhand sweeps, he lifted the slices on
his sword-point, and shared them out among the startled
guests.

60   We were not given much time to admire such sophisticated
turns, for suddenly the ceiling panels began to rumble, and

the entire dining-room shook. In my agitation I leapt up,
apprehensive that some acrobat might come down through
the roof. The other guests were equally startled, and trained
their eyes upwards, waiting to see what strange augury was
being announced from heaven. Then suddenly the panels
parted,* and a huge hoop, probably prised from a giant cask,
was let down. All round its circumference hung golden
crowns and alabaster jars of perfume. While we were being
bidden to take these as departing-presents, I glanced at the
table . . . A dish with several cakes on it had been set there.
A figure of Priapus, fashioned by the chef, occupied the
centre, and in his expansive paunch he held fruit of every
kind, and grapes in the conventional mode. With some
eagerness we stretched out our hands towards this display,
whereupon a fresh round of trickery renewed our merri-
ment, for all the cakes and all the fruit, when disturbed by
the slightest touch, began to squirt out saffron; the juice
shot disconcertingly even into our faces. So under the impression that this was a sacred dish, since it was steeped in
such a sacred preparation,* we shot to our feet and declaimed
'Health to Augustus,* father of the fatherland'. When even
after this obeisance some of the guests grabbed the fruit, we
too filled our napkins; I took the lead in this, for I thought
no gift too generous to load into Giton's lap.

While this was going on, three lads came in, with their
white shirts tucked high. Two of them placed on the table
statues of the Lares with medals round their necks,* while
the third carried round a wine-bowl, shouting out 'Gods,
have mercy!'*

*

He said that one was Gain, the second Luck, and the third
Profit. There was a living likeness of Trimalchio* himself;
since everyone else was kissing it, we had not the gall to give
it a miss.

61   So once all had invoked good sense and good health
upon themselves, Trimalchio turned to Niceros, and said:
'You used to be quite affable at table. I can't understand

why you're keeping mum; there's not a sound out of you. Do tell us of that experience of yours, and you'll see my face light up.' Niceros was gratified by his friend's overture, and he said: 'All this time I've been cock-a-hoop at seeing you in such good form; I swear it if I lose every penny I've got. So let's have a good laugh, though I'm afraid these schoolmen are going to scoff at me. Well, they can please themselves; I'm going to tell my story. It's no skin off my nose if someone laughs at me. Better to be laughed at than jeered at.'

So 'these were the words he uttered';* then he embarked upon this tale:* 'When I was still in service, we lived in an alley-way in the house now owned by Gavilla. There I fell in love—the gods arranged it that way—with the wife of the innkeeper Terentius; you knew the lady—quite a fetching bit of goods from Tarentum called Melissa. But I swear that for me the attraction wasn't physical or sexual; it was her good nature that I liked. She never refused me anything I asked of her; any penny or ha'penny I'd got I lodged with her, and she never rooked me. This girl's partner died*out on the country estate, so I schemed and planned to get to her by hook or by crook. You know how it is; a friend in need is a friend indeed.

62   'It so chanced that my master had gone off to Capua to attend to some odds and ends, so I seized my chance, and persuaded a chap staying with us to accompany me as far as the fifth milestone. He was a soldier, as brave as the devil. We buggered off about cockcrow. The moon was shining so brightly it was as light as midday. We passed between the tombs;* when your man began to piss against the monuments, I walked on, singing away and counting the gravestones. But then when I looked back at my companion, he stripped off and laid all his clothes by the side of the road. My heart was in my mouth, and I stood there, rigid as a corpse. He pissed round his garments, and suddenly changed into a wolf. Don't think I'm having you on; the offer of no man's fortune would induce me to lie. As I was saying, he turned into a wolf, and then he began to howl, and he disappeared into the woods. To begin with, I couldn't recall

where I was. Then I drew near to pick up his clothes, but they had turned into stone. No one has ever been more frightened to death than I was then. But I drew my sword and slashed away at the early-morning shadows* till I could reach the country estate where my girlfriend was. I walked in looking like a ghost, panting my heart out; the sweat was dripping down my legs, and my eyes were glazed. I could scarcely pull myself round.

'My girl Melissa started in surprise that I was walking in at that late moment. "If you'd arrived earlier", she said, "you could at any rate have given us a hand. A wolf invaded the estate and worried all the sheep; it drained their blood like a butcher. But it didn't get away with a grin on its face, because one of our slaves shoved a spear through its neck." On hearing this I couldn't relax with my eyes closed for a minute longer. As soon as it was properly light, I rushed back home like a man who's had his inn burgled. When I reached the spot where the clothes had been petrified, I found nothing but blood. And when I got home, my friend the soldier was lying on his bed like a felled ox, and a doctor was treating his neck. I realized that he was a werewolf, and after that day I could never have shared a loaf of bread with him, not even if you killed me. Others can decide for themselves what they think about this, but I challenge your guardian spirits to come down heavily on me if I'm telling lies.'

63   We were all dumbfounded. Trimalchio said: 'Saving the presence of your story, you can take my word for it that my hair stood on end. I know that Niceros doesn't deal in trifles, but comes straight to the point without wasting words. But I too will tell you a hair-raising incident,* as scary as "the donkey on the roof".*

'When I was still a long-haired lad (even from my early years I lived as the Chians do),* our master's favourite died. Honestly, he was a real gem, a pretty boy, quite the bee's knees. Anyhow, when his poor mother was crying over him, and a number of us were joining in the wake, suddenly some witches started up. You'd have thought it was a

dog chasing a hare. At that time we had living with us a
Cappadocian, a massive chap with plenty of spunk and brute
strength—he could lift a mad bull. He fearlessly drew his
sword, and charged out of the gate with his left hand carefully covered. He ran one of the women through the belly,
just where I'm pointing—heaven preserve the mark!—, and
we heard a groan. Without a word of a lie the witches just
disappeared. That strapping fellow of ours came in and threw
himself on his bed. His whole body was black and blue, as
if he'd been flogged. We closed the gate, and returned to
our wake. But when the mother took her son's body into
her arms and fondled it, she realized that it had become a
bundle of straw; no heart, no innards, no nothing. I suppose
the witches just at that moment had carried off the boy and
put a straw doll in his place. You've got to believe what I
tell you: there are women about with superhuman powers,
who flit around by night and bring down the firmament
from above. As for that tall, hefty fellow, he never looked
the same again after that incident; in fact a few days later he
went off his head and died.'

64   We one and all expressed our astonishment and belief.
We kissed the table, and begged those witches of the night
to keep their own company till we got back from dinner. By
now the flaming lamps seemed to me to have swollen in
number, and the entire dining-room looked totally transformed. Then Trimalchio said: 'Now then, Plocamus, haven't
you anything to relate to us? Won't you give us a treat? You
used to charm us, reciting verses and adding in the lyrics.
Hey ho, farewell to those sweet treats of old!' Plocamus
responded: 'Nowadays my chariot's completed the circuit,
ever since I got the gout. It was different when I was a
youngster; I sang so much I almost got consumption.
Dancing, recitations, barber's-shop stories—I did the lot.
When did I have anyone to match me, except Apelles'alone?'
He then put his hand in front of his mouth, and made a
foul whistling noise, later claiming that it was Greek.

Trimalchio himself also joined in, doing an imitation of
trumpeters. He then looked over at his boy-favourite, whom

he called Croesus, a lad endowed with watery eyes and hideously rotting teeth. He was fastening a green jacket round
a repulsively fat black puppy. He set a loaf weighing half a
pound on the couch, and proceeded to cram it into the dog,
which threw it up. Trimalchio, on observing this devoted
service, took the hint, and commanded that Scylax, 'the
guardian of home and household',* be brought in. Immediately a hulking dog was led in on a lead, and on being
prompted to lie down by the heel of the janitor, settled in
front of the table. Then Trimalchio threw it some white
bread, and said: 'No one in my household loves me more.'
The boy Croesus, fuming at this extravagant praise of Scylax,
set his puppy on the floor, and incited it to get into a fight.
Scylax, doubtless exploiting his dog-sense, filled the dining-
room with the most cacophonous barking, and almost tore
Croesus' Pearl to bits. The disturbance was not confined to
the dog-fight; a lampstand was overturned on the table,
shattering all the crystal glassware, and spraying some of
the guests with hot oil.

  Trimalchio did not wish to appear irritated by the damage, so he kissed the boy, and told him to mount his back.
Croesus promptly played the jockey, and kept striking
Trimalchio's shoulders with the flat of his hand. Giggling
away, he chanted: 'Buck, buck, how many fingers* have I
up?' This effort quietened Trimalchio for a time. He ordered a large bowl of wine to be served, and drinks to be
distributed to all the slaves sitting at our feet. He added this
proviso: 'If anyone refuses, pour it over his head. Harsh
discipline by day; now's the time for cheerful play.'

65   This show of kindness was followed by savouries; the very
recollection of them, believe me, makes me puke. In place
of thrushes, a whole fat chicken was brought round to each
guest, and hooded goose-eggs; Trimalchio pressingly begged
us to eat these, describing them as boneless chickens. As
we were engaged with them, an attendant rapped on the
dining-room doors, and a reveller clad in white,* followed by
a large entourage, made his way in. I was awed by his eminence, and thought that a praetor had arrived, so I struggled

to get up and put my bare feet on the ground. Agamemnon grinned at my panic, and said: 'Control yourself, you fathead. This is Habinnas, one of the college of priests, and a stone-mason to boot; apparently his tombstones are top-quality.'

This information reassured me, so I leaned back on my elbow, and eyed Habinnas' entry with considerable astonishment. He was already drunk. His arms rested on his wife's shoulders; he was weighed down by several garlands, and scented oil was trickling down over his forehead into his eyes. He settled himself in the place of honour,* and at once called for wine and hot water. Trimalchio was tickled by this show of party spirit; he too demanded a larger cup, and asked how Habinnas had been received. 'We got the whole treatment,' he replied, 'except that you weren't there; my favourite friends were here. But it was certainly a good party. Scissa laid on an elegant ninth-day memorial-feast* for the poor slave she declared free on his death-bed; I reckon she's going to have quite a heave-ho with the five-per-cent men,* for they claim that the dead man was worth fifty thousand. Still, it was a very nice do, even if we were forced to pour half our drinks over his poor bones.'

66   'So what did you have for supper?'*asked Trimalchio. 'I'll tell you,' he answered, 'if I can; my memory isn't what it was—I often forget my own name. The first course was pork topped with sausage, and on the side black puddings, beautifully cooked giblets, and beet of course, and pure wholemeal bread which I myself prefer to white, because it strengthens the constitution and saves you straining on the lavvy. The next dish was cold tart, with warm honey topped with a fine Spanish wine, so I had quite a helping of the tart, and I kept soaking up the honey. There were chickpeas and lupines, a range of nuts and an apple apiece—I actually lifted two; you can see I have them wrapped in my napkin, because if I don't take a wee gift to my little slave-boy, I'll get it in the neck. Oh yes, and my lady does well to remind me that we also had bear-steak on the menu. Scintilla casually swallowed a mouthful of it, and almost brought up her insides. But myself, I downed more than a pound, for

it tasted just like wild boar. What I say is, if a bear can eat us poor sods, we poor sods have the right to eat bear. To end up with, we had cream cheese soaked in new wine, and a snail apiece, and chunks of tripe, and little dishes of liver, hooded eggs, turnip, mustard, and plates of ragout—that'll do, Palamedes!* Pickled olives were also brought round in a dish; some people had the gall to remove three handfuls. As for the ham, we gave it the go-by.

67   'But do tell me, Gaius: why is Fortunata not reclining with us?'

'You know her,' answered Trimalchio. 'If she hasn't put away the silver, and divided the leavings among the slaves, she won't even have a drink of water.'

'In that case,' said Habinnas, 'if she doesn't take her place, I'm going to bugger off.' He began to get to his feet, but at a given signal Fortunata was summoned four or five times by the whole ménage in concert. So out she came, her dress hitched up with a yellow belt to show her cherry-coloured petticoat beneath, and coiled anklets and gilded slippers. At that moment she wiped her hands on the napkin at her neck, and took her place on the couch where Habinnas' wife Scintilla was reclining. Scintilla clapped her hands, and Fortunata kissed her, and said: 'Can it really be you?'

This interchange went so far that Fortunata tugged the bracelets off her great fat arms, and showed them to Scintilla's admiring gaze. In the end she even removed her anklets and her golden hairnet, which she said was pure gold. Trimalchio observed this, and ordered all the jewellery to be brought to him. 'These are women's fetters that you see,' said he. 'This is how we silly sods get rooked. She must be wearing six and a half pound's worth of the stuff. Mind you, I too have a bracelet weighing ten pounds, made out of the levy of the thousandth owed to Mercury.'* To crown everything, he even ordered scales to be brought in, to prove that he was not lying. The weight of the jewellery was attested by being passed round.

Scintilla was just as bad. From her neck she removed a little gold locket which she called her lucky box, and from it she produced twin earrings. She handed these in turn to Fortunata to examine, remarking: 'Thanks to my husband, no one owns a better pair than these.'

'That's not surprising,' said Habinnas, 'you really cleaned me out, just so that I could buy you a glass bean. I tell you, if I had a daughter, I'd cut her little ears off. If there were no women in the world, life would be dirt-cheap. But as things stand, what we piss out is hot, but what we drink down is cold.'*

Meanwhile the women were tipsily giggling at each other, and exchanging drunken kisses, as one boasted of her conscientious role as female head of the household, and the other complained of her husband's boy-favourite and neglect of her. While they were engaged with each other in this way, Habinnas quietly got to his feet, seized Fortunata by the legs, and threw her over the couch. 'Ouch, ouch!' she cried as her petticoat rose above her knees. She then took refuge in Scintilla's lap, and blushing rosy-red, hid her face in her napkin.

68   After a short respite Trimalchio gave the order for 'second tables',* at which all the servants replaced the tables with different ones, and sprinkled sawdust coloured with saffron, vermilion, and something I'd never seen before, powdered mica.* At once Trimalchio quipped: 'I could be quite happy with this as our next course, for you've got "second tables". But if you've anything nice, boy, bring it in.'

Meanwhile one of the Alexandrian slaves, who was providing the hot water, began to imitate nightingales, punctuated by shouts from Trimalchio of 'change the tune!'* Next came another diversion. The slave sitting at Habinnas' feet, prompted I imagine by his master, suddenly declaimed in a loud voice 'Meanwhile Aeneas reached mid-ocean with his fleet.'* No sound more excruciating ever struck my ears. Not only did his barbaric bawling rise and fall, but he also inserted Atellane verses, so that for the first time in my life even Virgil grated on me. When at last exhaustion compelled him to stop, Habinnas glossed the performance: 'He's never attended school, but I educated him by sending him to listen to the hawkers. So whether it's muleteers or hawkers he wants to imitate, there's no one to touch him. He's so hopelessly versatile: cobbler, cook, baker—he's a slave of all talents. But he has two faults, without which he would be the bee's knees: he's circumcised, and he snores. I'm not troubled by his squint; Venus looks the same way. It's turned out that he's never quiet, and his eyes are never stone-dead. He cost me three hundred *denarii*.'

69   Scintilla interrupted his flow. 'One thing's for sure; you're not revealing all the trickery of that villain of a slave. He's a pimp, and he'll be branded; I'll see to that.' Trimalchio laughed. 'I know a Cappadocian when I see one,' he said. 'He doesn't do himself down. By heaven, I've nothing but praise for him. You can't enjoy these things when you're dead. Now, Scintilla, don't be jealous. Believe me, we know what you women too get up to. Bless my soul, I myself used to have it off with my mistress, even incurring the suspicion of my master. It was for that reason that he banished me to become his steward away on the country estate. But "tongue, enough said; chew this bread."'

That most nefarious of slaves took this for a compliment. He produced a clay lamp from his clothing, and for a good half-hour gave imitations of trumpeters, while Habinnas mouthed an accompaniment, pulling down his lower lip with his fingers. Finally the boy went so far as to advance to the centre of the room, now using broken reeds to imitate flute-players, now wearing a cloak and brandishing a whip for a performance of *The Destiny of Muleteers*. Eventually Habinnas called him over, kissed him, and plied him with drink, saying: 'Bravo, Massa; you'll get a pair of boots for that.'

All this oppression would have been endless if the dessert had not been brought in. It consisted of pastry thrushes stuffed with raisins and nuts; quinces followed, with thorns implanted in them to make them resemble sea-urchins. So far we could put up with it, but then a much more preposterous dish appeared which made even death by starvation preferable. Placed before us was a fat goose surrounded by

fish and every kind of bird. Trimalchio then announced:
'My friends, all that you see before us here is made out of
a single body.' Being quick on the uptake I realized at once
what was going on. I looked over at Agamemnon, and said:
'I shouldn't be surprised if all these are made of wax, or at
any rate of clay. I've seen counterfeit dinners of this kind
served up at Rome during the Saturnalia.'*

70   The words were not out of my mouth when Trimalchio
said: 'As sure as I hope that my wealth and not my waistline
may swell, my cook has made all these out of pork. There
can't be a more valuable man anywhere. If you ask him,
he'll make fish out of tripe, a pigeon out of bacon, a turtle
out of ham, a chicken out of pork-knuckle. So I used my
brains to coin a suitable name for him; he's called Daedalus.*
I rewarded his talent by bringing him from Rome a gift of
steel knives made at Noricum.'*He at once ordered them to
be brought in, and having surveyed and admired them, he
allowed us to test the sharp edges on our cheeks.

Two slaves suddenly entered. They looked as if they had
been tilting at each other by the water-tank; at any rate, they
were still balancing water-jugs on their shoulders. Trimalchio
accordingly adjudicated between the disputants, but neither
accepted his decision; each bashed the other's jug with his
stick. We were taken aback at this outrageous behaviour of
the drunken pair, and stared as they grappled with each
other. Then we noticed oysters and scallops tumbling from
the pitchers; a slave gathered them, and carried them round
in a dish. That genius of a cook then matched this exhibition of refinement by bringing in snails on a silver gridiron,
singing as he did so in hideously wavering tones.

I am ashamed to recount the unprecedented performance that followed: long-haired boys brought liquid perfume
round in a silver dish, and bathed our feet as we reclined
there, first having festooned our legs and ankles with garlands of flowers. Then some of the same perfume was poured
into the wine-bowl,* and also into a lamp. By now Fortunata had shown signs of wanting to dance, and Scintilla
had abandoned her chat in favour of clapping her hands.

Trimalchio said: 'Philargyrus, despite your being a squalid supporter of the Greens,* I give you leave—and you can invite your partner Menophila as well—to recline at table.' Enough said; we were almost forced off the couches, for the household staff took over the entire dining-room. At any rate, I noticed the cook who had created the goose from pork reclining just above me, reeking of pickles and sauces. Not content with his mere presence at table, he at once began to imitate the tragic actor Ephesus, and then to challenge his master to pay up, if the charioteer of the Greens won the first prize at the next games.

71   This exchange made Trimalchio wax expansive. 'My friends,' he said, 'slaves too are men;* they have drunk their mother's milk like the rest of us, even if a malign fate has overtaken them. But so long as I'm spared, they will soon taste the water of freedom. In short, I intend to free them all in my will.* I'm also bequeathing a farm and his concubine to Philargyrus, and to Cario a block of flats, his manumission tax, and a bed complete with bedcovers. As for Fortunata, I'm making her my heiress, and commending her to all my friends. I'm making all these arrangements generally known, so that my household can show me now the affection due when I'm dead.'

They all began to express thanks for their master's generosity. He then abandoned all *badinage*, and ordered a copy of his will to be brought in.* He read out the entire document from beginning to end, to the accompaniment of lamentations from the household. He then looked over at Habinnas. 'Tell me, my dearest friend,' he said, 'will you order my tomb according to my instructions? My earnest request is that you set my little dog below my statue, and put in garlands, perfumes, and all the contests of Petraites,* so that through your kindness my life can continue after death. Build it a hundred feet wide at the front, and two hundred feet from front to rear. I'd like fruit trees of all kinds surrounding my ashes, and lots of vines; it's quite wrong for a man to have an elegant house in life, and not to give thought to our longer place of residence. So before all else I want an inscription with the words "This tomb must not pass to an heir."' I'll be careful to stipulate in my will that I come to no harm when dead; I'll appoint one of my freedmen to mount guard over my tomb, to ensure that people don't make a beeline to shit against it.

'I want you also to depict ships in full sail, and myself sitting on a dais wearing the toga with a purple stripe* and five gold rings, dispensing coins from a wallet to the people at large; you know that I laid on a dinner for them at two *denarii* a head. If you will, incorporate dining-halls as well, and all the citizens having a good time in them. On my right erect a statue of my Fortunata holding a dove, and leading along her puppy with its jacket on. Put in my boy-favourite, and some big winejars sealed with gypsum to ensure that the wine doesn't leak out. You can show one of the jars as broken, with a slave weeping over it. Put a sundial in the middle, so that whoever wants to know the time will read my name, whether he wants to or not. Oh yes, and give some thought to whether this inscription strikes you as suitable enough: "Here rests Gaius Pompeius Trimalchio of the household of Maecenas.* He was formally declared Priest of Augustus in his absence.* Though he could have claimed membership of every Roman guild, he refused. He was god-fearing, brave and faithful. He grew from small beginnings and left thirty million, without ever hearing a philosopher lecture.* Farewell, Trimalchio; and fare well, you who read this."'

72   As he uttered these words, Trimalchio began to weep copiously. Fortunata too wept, and so did Habinnas. In fact the whole household filled the dining-room with cries of grief, as though summoned to a funeral. By now even I had begun to blub, when Trimalchio said: 'So since we know that our death is in the offing, why don't we enjoy life? I want to see you in good spirits, so let's have a plunge into the bath. I'll guarantee you won't rue it; the water's as hot as hell."

'Good enough,' said Habinnas; 'nothing I like better than making two days out of one.' He put his bare feet on the floor, and began to pad after the beaming Trimalchio.

I looked over at Ascyltus, and said: 'What's your view on this? One look at the bath, and I'll perish on the spot.'

'Let's fall in with them,' he replied, 'and while they're making for the bath, we can slip away in the confusion.' This seemed a good idea. Giton preceded us through the colonnade until we came to the gate, where a dog on a chain greeted us with such a din that Ascyltus actually fell into the fish-pond. I was equally drunk, and earlier had recoiled at the sight even of the painted dog; so as I tried to lend help as he swam about I was pulled into the same pool. However, the doorman came to our rescue, both quietening the dog, and dragging us out shivering on to dry land. Giton had in fact already in the cleverest fashion bought off the dog;* he had thrown in front of the barking beast all the tit-bits from the dinner which he had got from us. The dog was distracted by the food, and had quietened down. We were shivering and soaking, and begged the doorman to let us out of the gate. But he responded: 'You're mistaken if you think that you can leave by the same entrance by which you came in. None of our guests is ever let out through the same gate; they come in one way, and go out another.'

73 What were we poor wretches to do, hemmed in as we were in this novel labyrinth? By now we had begun to long for that bath, so without prompting we asked the doorman to escort us to the bath-house. We threw off our clothes, which Giton began drying in the doorway as we went in. The bath-house was narrow,* shaped like a cold-water tank; Trimalchio was standing upright in it. Not even in these surroundings could we shrug off his disgusting boasting, for he kept saying that there was nothing better than taking a bath without being jostled, and that at one time there had been a bakehouse on that very site. Then he sat back as though exhausted, and enticed by the acoustics of the bath, he opened his drunken mouth as wide as the ceiling, and began to murder the songs of Menecrates*—or so those who could catch the words said. The other guests were chasing round the bath-tub, holding hands, tickling each other, and making a tremendous din; others with their hands tied behind them were trying to pick up rings from the floor, or

were on their knees bending their necks backward and touching the tips of their toes. While they were amusing themselves, we got down into the tub which was kept at the right temperature for Trimalchio.

Once we had dispelled our drunkenness, we were conducted into a second dining-room, in which Fortunata had laid out her prize ware . . . We noticed lamps cast with fishermen of bronze on them, tables of solid silver, and china cups inlaid with gold all around, and wine being openly strained°through a cloth. Then Trimalchio said: 'My friends, today a slave of mine has celebrated his first shave.° He's an honest lad, so help me, and careful with the money. So let's have a ball, and go on eating until daylight.'

74   As he was saying this, a cock crew.° This worried Trimalchio; he ordered wine to be sprinkled under the table, and the lamp too to be doused with neat wine. He even transferred his ring to his right hand, and remarked: 'That trumpeter has sounded his signal to some purpose. Either a fire is due to break out, or someone around here is going to snuff it. Pray heaven it's not me! So now the one who brings in that informer will get a bonus.' No sooner had he spoken than the cock was brought in. Trimalchio ordered it to be pot-roasted in wine; once that cook of prodigious learning, who shortly before had made birds and fish out of pork, had cut it up, it was thrown into a pot. Daedalus then drank the scalding gravy, and Fortunata ground the pepper in a box-wood mill.

After we disposed of this savoury-dish, Trimalchio turned to his serving-staff, and said: 'Why have you not had your meal yet? Off with you, and let others come on duty.' So then a second company of slaves appeared; the departing shift chorused 'Goodbye, Gaius', while the incomers cried 'Greetings, Gaius'. But now our enjoyment received its first jolt. What happened was that among the incoming servants was a quite handsome lad, and Trimalchio went bounding over and gave him a lingering kiss. This caused Fortunata to stand up for her just conjugal rights, and she began to rail at Trimalchio, calling him a shameful piece of garbage for failing to control his randy behaviour. As a final fling, she threw out: 'You dirty dog!'

Trimalchio took umbrage at this dressing-down, and countered by hurling a cup at Fortunata's face. She howled as though she had lost an eye, and put her trembling hands up to her face. Scintilla too was shell-shocked; she cradled her quivering friend in her breast, and a slave dutifully applied a cold jar to her cheek. Fortunata leaned her face over it, and began to moan and sob. Trimalchio's reaction was to remark: 'So does my flute-girl not recall that I rescued her from the slave-stand, and made her fit for human company? Yet here she is, puffing herself up like a frog, and giving herself airs. Thick as a plank she is—she's no woman. But if you're born in the shed outside, you don't aspire to the mansion. As I hope to keep my guardian spirit's favour, I'll surely tame that Cassandra in jackboots.* I could have married into ten million though I hadn't a penny to my name; you know I'm not telling fibs. Agatho in the perfume shop took me aside the other day, and said: "I do urge you not to let your line die out." But being a decent sort, not wanting to appear unfaithful, I've shot myself in the foot. Right, then, I'll make you go for me tooth and claw. To let you know here and now the harm you've done yourself: Habinnas, I won't have you put her statue on my tomb, so that at least when I'm dead I won't have any argy-bargy. In fact, to impress on her that I can do her a bad turn, don't let her kiss me when I'm dead.'

75   This thunderbolt led Habinnas to start begging Trimalchio to cool his temper. 'We all make mistakes,' he said. 'We're human, not gods.' Scintilla too spoke in the same vein through her tears; she called him Gaius, and started to implore him by his guardian spirit to relent. Trimalchio could restrain his tears no longer. 'As you hope to enjoy your nest-egg,* Habinnas,' he said, 'spit in my face if I've done anything wrong. I gave this model slave a kiss not because he's handsome, but because he applies himself so well. He knows his ten-times table, he can read at sight, he's bought himself a Thracian outfit* from his daily allowance,

and he's purchased an armchair and two goblets out of his own money. He's surely worthy to be the apple of my eye, but Fortunata says no. Is that how you see it, my lady in the high heels? My advice is to know what's good for you, you kite, and not to make me show my teeth, darling girl—otherwise you'll get a taste of my temper. You know me by now; once I get an idea into my head, it's embedded there with a six-inch nail.

'But what's done is done. Do enjoy yourselves, my friends. I too was once in the same boat as you, but thanks to my own merits I've reached where I am. It's the brain-box that's the making of people; the rest is disposable. "Buy well and sell well"—that's my motto. Other people will give you different advice, but I'm flushed with success.

'What's this, still whining, you sniffler? I'll soon see that you have something to whine about!

'As I was starting to explain, I reached this station in life through my own efforts. When I first arrived here from Asia, I was no bigger than that lampstand. To tell you the truth, I used to measure myself by it every day, and I'd grease my lips from the lamp to get some hair to grow round my gob more quickly. Still, at the age of fourteen* I was my master's favourite—there's no shame in doing your master's bidding. Mind you, I used to keep the mistress happy as well—know what I mean? I won't say more, for I'm not one to brag.

76 'It was by the gods' will; I became the supremo in the house, and completely won over my master's affections. No need to say more; he made me joint heir with Caesar,* and I came into the fortune of a senator.* But no one's ever content; I got the itch to go into business.* To cut a long story short, I had five ships built, loaded them with wine, which was worth its weight in gold*at the time, and sent them off to Rome. Every single one went to the bottom—truth is stranger than fiction; you'd have thought I'd given the nod.* On a single day Neptune swallowed down a cool thirty million. But do you think I lost heart? I swear the loss meant nothing to me; it was as if it had never happened. I had a second fleet built, bigger, better, and with a happier

outcome; no one could say that I lacked spunk. As you know, a big ship has a big heart. I loaded them up again with wine, bacon, beans, perfumes, slaves.

'It was then that Fortunata showed her devotion, for she sold all her gold and all her wardrobe, and put a hundred gold pieces in my hand. That was the leaven that made my fortune rise. The gods' will is soon accomplished. On a single voyage I cleared a cool ten million. There and then I cleared the debt on all the estates which had belonged to my patron. I built a house, put money into slaves and cattle; everything I touched grew like a honeycomb. Once I reached the stage of being richer than the whole community, I threw my hand in, and retired from commerce. I began employing freedmen as agents in money-lending.

'To tell the truth, I was loath to continue in business, but I was encouraged by an astrologer who chanced to come to our colony, a little Greek chap called Serapa,* even the gods seek his advice. He could tell me about events I'd forgotten, recounting them all to me in detail. The only thing he couldn't tell me was what I'd had for dinner the previous day. You'd have thought he'd been brought up in the same house.

77   'You can vouch for what he told me, Habinnas, for I think that you were there: "Those possessions of yours won for you your lady." "You are unfortunate in your friends." "No one ever pays you back as you deserve." "You own large estates." "You nurse a viper in your bosom." Another of his insights—I shouldn't tell you this—is that I now have thirty years, four months and two days of my life left. And I'm soon to enter on an inheritance, so my fortune foretells. If only I can extend my farms into Apulia,* that'll be far enough for my lifetime. Meantime, under Mercury's watchful eye* I've built this house. What was once a hovel is now a shrine. It has four dining-rooms, twenty bedrooms, two marble colonnades, a suite of small apartments upstairs, my own bedroom, the boudoir of this viper here, and a pleasant office for the doorman. The guest quarters can accommodate a hundred; in fact when Scaurus* comes here, there's nowhere

he would rather stay, even though he has the family lodge by the sea. The house has a lot of other amenities which I'll show you presently. Believe me, if you've only a ha'penny, you're ranked at a ha'penny; but if you have something behind you, you'll be thought to be someone. So that's the story of yours truly—once a frog, but now a king.

'While we're waiting, Stichus, bring out the shroud in which I'm to be buried. And bring the ointment and a drop of wine from that jar from which I've ordered my bones to be washed.'

78 Without delay Stichus brought the white winding-sheet, and also a toga with the purple stripe, into the dining-room ... Trimalchio told us to finger them to check that they were made of high-quality wool. Then with the ghost of a smile he said: 'Stichus, make sure that the mice and moths don't nibble these—otherwise I'll have you burnt alive. I want to be borne out to burial in style, to ensure that the whole community says a prayer for me.' At once he opened a jar of spikenard, applied some to all of us, and remarked: 'I do hope this pleases me as much in death as in life.' He even went so far as to order the bowl to be filled with wine, saying: 'Imagine you've been invited to my wake.''

It was enough to make you spew. Trimalchio, so earnest in his repulsive drunkenness, ordered trumpeters to be summoned to the dining-room as a new form of entertainment. Reclining on a mound of pillows, and stretching out along the length of the couch, he said: 'Imagine I'm dead. Play something nice.' In harmony the trumpeters blared out the dead march. One of them in particular (he was the slave of the undertaker, the most respectable man in the party) blew his trumpet so loudly that he roused the whole neighbourhood. The city sentinels, thinking that Trimalchio's house was on fire, suddenly kicked in the door, and began to cause their usual chaos with their hoses and axes. We seized this most opportune moment to give Agamemnon the slip, and we took to our heels as rapidly as if there really were a fire.

7

Giton spurns Encolpius for Ascyltus

79 We had no torch to aid us, to show us the way in our wandering, and as it was now midnight, all was silent, and there
was no likelihood of our encountering such a beacon. To
make matters worse, our drunkenness and ignorance of the
locality would have caused problems even in daylight. So for
almost an hour we dragged our bleeding feet over all the
jagged stones and jutting fragments of broken jars, until we
were finally rescued by Giton's resource. He had wisely put
chalk-marks on every post*and pillar for fear of going astray
even in daylight. These markings pierced the impenetrable
darkness, and their conspicuous whiteness pointed the way
for us as we wandered about. Yet even when we reached the
lodging we still had to sweat it out, for the old hag had been
sousing herself with liquor for quite a time in the company
of her lodgers, so that even if you had set her alight she
would have felt nothing. We might have had to spend the
night on the doorstep, but then Trimalchio's outrider turned
up . . . He didn't spend much time hallooing, but broke down
the door of the lodging, and let us in through it . . .

> Ye gods, ye goddesses! How sweet that night!
> On that soft couch we swapped our vagrant breath,*
> Sweating in close-knit passion, lips pressed tight,
> Forgetting mortal cares. Yet this spelt death.

For my self-congratulation proved unfounded. The wine had
caused me to relax and I had loosed my drunken embrace.
During the night Ascyltus, that contriver of all manner of
iniquity, removed the boy from my side, and transferred
him to his own bed. After sporting in considerable freedom
with this brother not his own—Giton remained unconscious,
or pretended to be—he fell asleep in this stolen embrace,

giving no thought to my just rights. When I awoke, I ran my
hand over my bed to find it stripped of its joy . . . and I fell
to wondering if any loyalty exists between lovers. I medit-
ated whether to run the pair of them through with the
sword, and to prolong their sleep in death. But then I
adopted the less hazardous course. With repeated blows I
roused Giton, and looked daggers at Ascyltus. 'With your
vile behaviour you have betrayed the trust and friendship
between us,' I said, 'so pack your belongings now, and find
some other place for your filthy habits.' He did not demur,
and we scrupulously shared out the loot. 'But now', he said,
'we must divide the boy as well.'

80   I thought that this was merely his parting quip, but
then with murderous intent he drew his sword, and said:
'You will not enjoy these spoils over which you gloat alone.
Since you spurn me, I must go even so far as to hack off my
share with the sword.' I took up the same stance facing him,
wrapped my cloak round my arm, and poised myself ready
for the conflict. While the wretched pair of us indulged in
this lunacy, that most unhappy boy tearfully clutched the
knees of us both, and in suppliant tones implored us not to
make that humble lodging witness a Theban duel, not to
defile the sacred nature of our most distinguished friendship by shedding each other's blood. 'But if at all events
you must commit an evil deed,' he cried, 'see, I bare my
throat. Direct your thrusts on me, press home your daggers; it is I who should die, for I have annulled your oath
of friendship.'

These pleas made us restrain our weapons, and Ascyltus
spoke first. 'I'll put an end to this disagreement. Let the boy
team up with the one of his choice, so that in selecting his
brother at any rate he can enjoy freedom.' I had no fears on
this account, for I thought that my long-standing intimacy
with Giton had become a bond of blood. Indeed, I latched
on to the proposal with headlong haste, and left the decision to the arbiter. He did not even pause to reflect, to show
signs of hesitation; no sooner were the words out of my
mouth than he got up and opted for Ascyltus to be his

brother. I was flabbergasted by this verdict, and collapsed in
a distraught state on the bed. The sentence imposed on me
would have led me to do violence to myself, but I begrudged
such a victory to my opponent. Ascyltus departed arrogantly
with his prize, thus abandoning on a foreign shore the
comrade who shortly before had been his dearest friend,
the mirror of his fortunes.

> Your claim to friendship's valid—while it pays;
>   You're fickle as the dice's doubtful throw.
> When Fortune smiles, you train your friendly gaze,
>   But when she quits, in shameful flight you go.

> A company mounts the stage, presents a play,   5
>   Taking the roles of rich man, father, son;
> But once these comic parts have had their say,
>   Our true selves reappear; the roles are gone.*

81   However, I did not let my tears flow for long. My fear was
that Menelaus,* the assistant at the school of rhetoric, might
compound my other misfortunes by finding me alone in the
lodging. So I packed my bags, and in the grip of melancholy
rented an isolated place close to the sea.* I shut myself in it
for three days, and as I reflected on being deserted and
humiliated, I thumped my grief-wracked breast and groaned
repeatedly from my heart's depths. I kept crying: 'Why could
I not have been engulfed by a landslide, or by the sea that
vents its rage even on the innocent? Did I evade justice,
cheat the arena, murder my host merely to lie here in spite
of these claims to daring, a beggar and an exile, a lonely
figure in this lodging in a Greek city?*And who has saddled
me with this solitude? A young scamp polluted with every
manner of lustful behaviour, who on his own admission
deserved the decree of banishment, a youth not merely free
but freeborn devoted to debauchery, his years spent in gam-
bling, hired as a girl even by the person who assumed him
to be a man! As for the other one, on the day for donning
the man's toga he put on a woman's dress instead, his mother
coaxed him to reject his manhood, he played the woman's

role in the slaves' quarters, and when he ran out of money he switched the direction of his sexual favours. He has renounced the claims of an old friendship; to his shame, he has behaved like a common whore, and sold his all in a one-night stand. So now they lie as lovers committed to each other all night long, no doubt jeering at my loneliness as they lie exhausted from their lustful duelling. But they will not get away with it. Either I am no man, no free citizen, or I will avenge my wrongs with their guilt-stained blood.'

82   At these words I buckled on my sword, and ate a lavish meal to build up my body's strength. Then I hurtled out of doors, and stalked like a madman round all the colonnades. Wearing a fierce and frenzied look, I thought of nothing but slaughter and bloodshed; I repeatedly slapped my sword-hilt on which I had uttered my vow. But then I drew the attention of a soldier—he may have been a trickster, or a mugger operating in the dark—who greeted me: 'Ho there, comrade! What's your legion, who's your sergeant-major?' I wore a brave face as I lied about the officer and the detachment. 'So tell me,' he said, 'in your army do the troops go round in soft shoes?' Both my expression and my agitation showed that I was lying. He ordered me to hand over my arms, and to keep out of harm's way. So not only was I robbed, but my plan for revenge was aborted. I made my way back to the lodging, and once my impulsive ardour cooled, I began to feel grateful to that impertinent ruffian.

*

Poor Tantalus, by longings sore oppressed!
Water eludes him, and the fruit o'erhead.
Likewise the magnate, dry-mouthed, stalked by dread,
All laid before him, hunger must digest.

*

'It is not advisable to put much trust in planning, for Fortune has her own rationale . . .'

8

Eumolpus in the Art Gallery

83 I walked into an art gallery, which had an astonishing range
of pictures. What I saw there included the handiwork of
Zeuxis, not as yet overcome by the ravages of time, and with
a kind of awe I scrutinized rough drawings by Protogenes
which vied in authenticity with Nature herself. As for the
painting by Apelles* which the Greeks call 'The Crippled
Goddess', I even bent the knee before it; for the outlines of
his figures were so skilfully clear-cut that you could imagine
that he had painted their souls as well. There was one picture in which an eagle aloft was bearing away the lad from
Mt. Ida; in another, the fair-skinned Hylas was trying to fend
off a persistent Naiad; a third depicted Apollo* cursing his
guilty hands and adorning his unstrung lyre with a newly
sprung blossom. As I stood surrounded by these portrayals
of lovers' expressions, in a spirit of desolation I cried out:
'So even the gods are pricked by love. Jupiter found no
object for his affection in heaven, and though he visited
earth to sin, he did violence to no one. The Nymph who
took Hylas as her prize would have repressed her feelings
had she believed that Hercules would appear to forbid the
deed. Apollo summoned back the departed shade of his boy
to turn him into a flower. All these stories, and not just the
pictures, have described embraces enjoyed without a rival;
but the person I hospitably befriended has turned out to be
more cruel than Lycurgus.'*

As I shared my disputation with the winds, a striking thing
occurred: a grizzled veteran* entered the gallery with a look
of concentration on his face which offered a hint of greatness. But his dress did not match his handsome appearance,
which made it perfectly clear that he was a man of letters,
such as the rich love to hate. This was the fellow, then, that
stood alongside me . . .

'I am a poet,' he said, 'a poet of not inconsiderable genius—that is, if one can lend any credence to those awards often bestowed by influence on men without talent. You will be asking: "So why this shabby outfit of yours?" The reason is simply this: devotion to the intellect never made anyone rich.

> Put trust in sea-trade, and your profits soar;
> Soldiers don arms of gold to go to war;
> Cheap crawlers loll on purple, crazed with gin;
> Seducers of young brides are paid for sin.
> Lone eloquence shivers in rags bone-stiff with frost;   5
> Impoverished tongue invoking arts now lost.

84 'The situation is undoubtedly this: if you confront all the vices, and start to tread an upright path in life, you first encounter hatred because your mode of life is different; for who has a good word for the man who tries to follow a different road? Secondly, those whose sole aim in life is piling up money, don't like the world at large to regard any philosophy as superior to their own. So they use every possible means to denigrate lovers of literature, trying to show that such people too are slaves to money . . . In some sense, poverty is sister to integrity of mind . . .

'I could only wish that the man who assails my honesty was sufficiently guilt-free for me to soften his attitude. But as things stand, he is an inveterate robber, more worldly wise than those very pimps . . .'

*

85* 'When I was taken to Asia as a paid assistant to the quaestor there, I was given accommodation at Pergamum.* I was pleased with the residence there, not just because the lodging was elegant, but also because my host had a most handsome son; and I devised a way of lulling his father's suspicions. Whenever the table-talk turned to the subject of sex with good-looking boys, I would seethe with such fury, and show such austere displeasure in refusing to have my ears outraged by foul gossip, that the boy's mother in particular regarded me as a real Stoic. So in no time I had started escorting the young fellow to the exercise ground, organizing his studies, acting as his tutor and moral adviser, and ensuring that no one set foot in the house on the hunt for sex.

'It so happened that a feast-day had allowed us to relax, and because our celebration went on quite late, we were dossing down in the dining-room. It must have been about midnight when I realized that the boy was awake. So very shyly I murmured a prayer: "Lady Venus," I said, "if I can kiss this boy without his realizing it, I'll present him with a pair of doves tomorrow." When the boy heard the payment on offer for the pleasure, he began to snore. So as he feigned sleep, I planted a few fond kisses on him. I was satisfied with this modest beginning; I got up early next morning and discharged my vow by putting a pair of choice doves in his expectant hands.

86 'Next night opportunity again offered, and I stepped up my prayer. "If I can run my roguish hands over him without his feeling a thing, I'll repay him for his trouble with a pair of really lively fighting-cocks." On hearing this the young lad snuggled up to me without prompting; I suppose he was beginning to fear that I had fallen off to sleep. So I relieved his anxiety, and immersed myself in the exploration of his whole body, but without indulging in the final pleasure. When daylight came, he was delighted with the gift of what I had promised.

'When a third night offered me the opportunity, I got up and spoke in his ear as he pretended to sleep. "Immortal gods," I said, "if I can gain the full pleasure I long for from this boy, in return for the joy, tomorrow I shall give him the finest Macedonian stallion, so long as he doesn't feel a thing." Never did that young fellow enjoy deeper repose. So first I curled my hands round his milk-white breasts, then I gave him a lingering kiss, and finally all my longings were concentrated in the single act. Next morning he seated himself on his bed, awaiting the customary routine. But you know how much easier it is to purchase doves and cocks than a stallion! And besides, I was afraid that a gift on that scale would make people eye my geniality with suspicion. So I took a stroll for a few hours, and on returning to the lodging all I gave the boy was a kiss. As he put his arms around my neck, his eyes wandered round, and he said: "Tell me, sir, where is the stallion?"

87   'By alienating him in this way, I had cut off the access which I had gained. But then I resumed my wanton behaviour, for after a few days' interval I began to press the youth for a reconciliation. I begged him to allow me to satisfy his needs, and used all the other arguments which oppressive lust dictates. He was quite incensed. All he said was: "Go to sleep or I'll tell my father." But unscrupulousness can climb every mountain. Even as he was saying "I'll wake my father", I crept in close, and took my pleasure against his feeble resistance. He was not displeased by my wanton behaviour. After a long rigmarole about his having been deceived and made a figure of fun and scorn among his schoolmates, to whom he had boasted of my wealth, he said: "But you'll see I'm not one of your kind. Have another go if you want." So all animosity laid aside, I was back in the boy's good books; and after exploiting his good will, I fell fast asleep. But he was now fully grown up, and at an age itching to play the partner; he was not content with a single repeat performance. So he roused me from my sleep, and asked: "Anything you want?" At this stage doing him a service was not tiresome, so with much panting and sweating I somehow wore him down, gave him what he wanted, and again fell asleep in contented exhaustion. Less than an hour elapsed when he began to poke me with his finger, saying: "Why don't we go at it?" Then I got really worked up at being wakened so often, and I answered him in his own words: "Go to sleep, or I'll tell your father."'

*

88   I was stimulated by this conversation, and began to tap his superior knowledge about the dating of the pictures and the themes of some of them which I found mysterious. At

the same time, I was trying to elicit the reason for our present decadence in which the noblest arts had died off, painting among them having left not the slightest trace.

His response was: 'It was lust for money* that induced this change. In the old days, when virtue unadorned was accepted, the noble arts flourished, and there was the fiercest competition between individuals to ensure that no benefit to posterity should lie undiscovered for long. So it was that Democritus squeezed out the juices of every plant, and devoted his life to experiments to ensure that the properties of stones and shrubs became known. Eudoxus grew old on the peak of the highest mountain, seeking to understand the movements of stars and firmament. Chrysippus* cleansed his mind three times with hellebore to prevent his ideas drying up. Lysippus died through poverty as he concentrated on the lines of a single statue; and Myron,* who almost caught in bronze the souls of men and wild beasts, has found no heir.

'But our generation is obsessed with wine and the women of the street. We don't presume to acquaint ourselves even with the most accessible arts. We censure the old ways, but teach and learn nothing but vices. What has happened to dialectic? And astronomy?* What is the most secure path to wisdom? Whoever sets foot in a temple, and solemnly vows thanksgiving if he attains eloquence, or gets to grips with the sources of philosophy? No one aspires even to mental or bodily health; even before stepping on the sacred threshold, one promises a gift if he can bury his rich neighbour, another if he uncovers buried treasure, a third if he can make thirty million unscathed. Why, even the senate, our mentor as regards good and right conduct, often promises a thousand pounds of gold for the Capitoline temple; so just in case anyone should hesitate to lust after money, the senate adorns Jupiter with his little pile. So you shouldn't wonder that painting is on the way out, when all gods and men alike regard a gold nugget as more beautiful than anything those crazy little Greeks Apelles and Phidias* have created.

89   'But I can see that you are wholly captivated by the picture which depicts the capture of Troy,* so I'll try to ex-
pound the subject in verses:

'Ten harvests now the Trojans had endured
In melancholy, poised 'midst anxious fears.
Black fear engulfed them; should they trust
In the seer Calchas' doubtful prophecy?
Now at Apollo's prompting, Ida's peaks   5
Are shorn of forests. Trunks are dragged below,
And the sawn logs assembled in a mass
To fashion a menacing horse. And deep within,
A spacious hollow, a cavern lies concealed
To house an army. Valour lies cloaked therein,   10
Its anger sharpened by ten warring years;
Crowding the corners, the oppressing Greeks
Lurk in the beast that they have vowed. Poor land!
We thought the thousand ships had been repelled,
That we had freed our native soil from war.   15
The inscription on the beast, and Sinon's role
In harmony with fate, and our own state of mind
With its capacity to seal our doom,
Strengthened our illusions.*

The crowd feels free; now unoppressed by war,   20
They hasten from the gates to pay their vows,
Cheeks wet with weeping; these are tears of joy,
Banished before by fear from troubled minds.
Neptune's Laocoon with hair unbound
Incites the mob to uproar. Then, spear poised,   25
He gashes the beast's belly. But the fates
Debilitate his hands; the spear strikes home,
But then recoils. Greek guile thus wins our trust.
Again the priest essays with feeble hand,
As with an axe he strikes that lofty flank.   30
The enclosed warriors growl angrily;
The wooden monster snorts with alien fears.
The youths who lay within our hands emerge;

And Troy falls under theirs. This is a war
Conducted with unprecedented guile.*   35

Fresh portents follow. Swollen waves rear high
Where Tenedos' high ridges span the sea.
The placid waters prised apart give place.
Over the silent night the plash of oars
Proclaims their distant message, as the ships   40
Pound the deep waters. The still surface groans
Under the burden of their wooden keels.
Our eyes are riveted. Twin coiling snakes
Are borne on ocean swell towards the rocks.
Their swollen breasts resemble lofty ships   45
Parting the sea-foam with their flanks; the deep
Echoes the impact of their tails; their crests
Range o'er the waters, conspiring with their eyes
Whose flashing gleam ignites the sea. The waves
Seethe with their hissing.
                         All are stupefied.   50
The priests adorned with headbands, and the twins,
Laocoon's pledges, in their Phrygian garb,
Stand in attendance. Then, quite suddenly,
The glistening snakes enfold them with their coils.
They raise their tiny hands up to their face,   55
Striving to free each other, not themselves,
In compact of devotion. Death itself
Destroys the wretches as they share their fear.
The father, feeble helper, spreads his frame
Over his children's corpses. But the snakes   60
Now gorged with death, attack the full-grown man,
Dragging his limbs down to the ground. The priest,
A sacrificial victim, strikes the earth,
Prostrate between the altars. Troy, its rites
First desecrated, doomed to imminent fall,   65
Surrenders the protection of its gods.*

Now the full moon has raised her radiant light,
Guiding the lesser stars with glowing torch.

While Priam's sons are buried in sleep and wine,
The Greeks unbar the door, disgorge their men.   70
Their leaders, fully armed, rehearse; just so
A steed, released from its Thessalian yoke,
Charges with tossing head and lofty mane.
They draw their swords, brandish their shields in front,
Inaugurating battle. While one slays   75
The Trojans heavy-eyed with wine,
Their sleep extended into ultimate death,
Another ignites torches from the altars,
Thus summoning the sacred Trojan rites
Against the very Trojans.'*   80

90   As he declaimed, some of the strollers in the colonnades
threw stones at Eumolpus. Acknowledging this hearty reception of his genius, he covered his head and bolted from the
temple. I feared that they would pin the label of poet on
myself as well, so I followed him in his flight down to the
sea-shore. As soon as we were out of the firing-line and
could relax, I said: 'Tell me, what will you do about this
disease of yours? You've been in my company for less than
two hours, and in that time you've spouted poetry more
often than talked like a human being. It doesn't surprise
me that people chase after you with bricks; I'll do the same
myself—stuff my pockets with stones, and give your head a
blood-letting whenever you threaten a take-off.' He nodded
his acknowledgement, and said: 'Young man, today is not
my first experience of this kind. In fact, whenever I step into
a theatre to deliver a recitation, the crowd treats me to this
kind of reception. However, to save brawling with you as
well, I'll go on a diet all day today.'

'Good enough,' I replied. 'If you forswear your madness
for the day, we'll dine together.'

*

I gave the porter at the lodging the job of laying on a modest
meal.

9

Reconciliation with Giton; Eumolpus as Rival

91 I caught sight of Giton leaning against the wall, holding towels and scrapers. He was downcast and disturbed; you could see that he was not enjoying his menial role. So to obtain proof of what my eyes told me . . .

He turned on me a face which dissolved in delight, and said: 'Dear brother, have pity on me. I can speak freely, away from the scene of battle. Deliver me from that blood-stained brigand; punish your repentant judge* as savagely as you like. I shall be sufficiently consoled in my misery if my downfall is at your wish.' I told him to stifle his lamentations, to ensure that no one should overhear our plans. I gave Eumolpus the slip, for he was declaiming in the baths; then I ushered Giton out through a dark and dirty exit, and sped on wings back to my lodging. There I barred the door, pressed his breast to mine in repeated embraces, and with my cheek rubbed his face which was suffused with tears. It was some time before either of us could find words, for the boy too was speechless, his lovable breast heaving with continual sobs. 'This is not as it should be,' I said. 'Though you deserted me, I still love you, and though the wound was deep, no scar remains on my heart. What excuse have you for having yielded to an outsider's love? Did I merit this injustice?' Once he realized that he retained my affection, he raised his gaze . . .

'I entrusted the judgement on my love to no arbiter but you. But I am no longer complaining, no longer harking back, if you are really and truly sorry.' As I poured out these words amidst groans and tears, he wiped his face with his cloak, and said: 'Now, Encolpius, I ask you honestly to cast your mind back: did I desert you, or did you betray me? I have to admit and openly confess that when I saw the two of you taking up arms, I took refuge with the stronger.' I kissed that breast so worldly-wise, and threw my arms around his neck. I wanted him to know clearly that I was reconciled to him, and that our friendship had taken on new life in perfect trust, so I hugged him unreservedly.

92   It was now pitch dark; the woman had carried out our instructions for dinner, when Eumolpus knocked on the door. I asked: 'How many of you are there?' Even as I spoke, I proceeded to take the most careful look through a chink in the door, to see whether Ascyltus had arrived as well. When I saw that Eumolpus was our sole guest, I at once let him in. He settled back on one of the beds, and his eyes lit on Giton, who was laying the table before us. He nodded approval, and said: 'Three cheers for Ganymede! This is going to be a good day.'

I didn't care for this attentive overture; I was afraid that my new associate was a second Ascyltus. Eumolpus persevered, and when the boy handed him his drink, he said: 'I'd rather take you than the whole bath-house!' He greedily drained his cup, and said that he'd never had a more disagreeable experience. 'There I was, washing myself,' he said, 'and just because I tried to recite a poem to those seated round the bath-tub, they almost gave me a hiding. I was driven out of the bath, and began to traipse round all the nooks and crannies, hailing Encolpius as loudly as I could. Over on the other side was a youth in the buff who had lost all his clothes. He was bawling equally angrily for some fellow Giton. The lads there were making fun of me, insolently mimicking me as if I were off my head. But a huge crowd engulfed Ascyltus; they clapped their hands in the humblest admiration, for his parts hung down with such massive weight that you'd have thought the chap himself was a mere appendage to his member. What a hard-working young man he must be! I bet he has to begin today to finish tomorrow. So it wasn't long before he got himself an aide; some Roman knight or other—with a dubious reputation, they say—covered him up with his own clothes as he wandered about, and bore him off home to exploit his good fortune unaccompanied. As for myself, I shouldn't have recovered even my own clothes from that busybody of an attendant if I hadn't taken someone along to vouch for me. It just shows that it's more profitable to exercise your balls than your brains.'

During this discourse of Eumolpus my expression kept switching from delight at my enemy's discomfiture to chagrin at his good fortune. However, I kept my mouth shut, pretending that the story meant nothing to me, and I laid out the contents of the dinner.

*

93 'What is lawful we hold cheap; our minds are enervated by sinning and embrace wrongdoing.

> 'Birds brought from Colchis
> Watered by the Phasis,
> And fowl shot in Afric wastes
> Cater for exotic tastes;*
> The humble goose, gleaming white,   5
> The duck renewed with feathers bright,
> Being such available birds,
> Are only meet for common herds.
> The wrasse, caught off distant shores,
> Wins a good deal of applause;   10
> Yields from seas round Syrtis' banks
> Netted by shipwreck,* gain our thanks.
> The mullet, frankly, is a bore.
> The wife's supplanted by a whore.
> The rose must cinnamon detest;   15
> The recherché is what seems best.'

'So this', I said, 'is how you keep your promise to spout no more verses today! For heaven's sake, spare the present company at least; we've never stoned you. If one of the topers in this building gets a whiff of the word poet, he'll rouse the whole neighbourhood, and because of this come

down on us like a ton of bricks. Spare us—just cast your
mind back to what happened at the gallery or at the baths.'

Giton, a boy who was the epitome of gentleness, rebuked
me for this criticism. He said I was wrong to speak discour-
teously to an older man, and that I was forgetting my duty
as host. These insults were taking the gilt off the spread
which I had so generously laid on. He went on at length
in this tolerant and modest strain, which so enhanced his
good looks.

94   'How blessed your mother is', said Eumolpus, 'to have a
son like you! That was well said. Beauty and wisdom are a
rare combination. Don't consider all your words wasted; in
me you have found a lover. I shall sing your praises in verses
in full measure. I shall walk behind you unsolicited as your
teacher and guardian. I won't be doing Encolpius an injustice, for he loves another.'

That soldier* who had relieved me of my sword did
Eumolpus a service as well as Ascyltus; otherwise I would
have focused the anger unleashed against Ascyltus to spill
Eumolpus' blood. Giton spotted this, so he left the room
on the pretext of bringing in some water. His tactful departure caused my rage to subside, so as my fierce indignation
cooled, I said: 'Eumolpus, I would rather have you even
spout poetry than entertain aspirations of this sort. I'm hotheaded, and you are randy; you must realize that the
two emotions are incompatible. Imagine that I have gone
off my head, give way before my madness, and clear off
quick!' Eumolpus was nonplussed by this declaration. Without questioning the reason for my anger, he at once left the
room, and suddenly slammed the door. He took me wholly
by surprise, shut me in,* swiftly removed the key, and ran
off in search of Giton.

In my prison I decided to hang myself and end my life.
I fastened a belt to the bed-frame which stood by the wall,
and I was just thrusting my neck into the noose when the
door was unbarred, and in walked Eumolpus with Giton,
restoring me to life when I was on course to death. Giton in
particular reacted first with distress, and then with hysteria;

he raised a cry, and with both hands pushed me headlong
on to the bed. 'You are mistaken, Encolpius,' he said, 'if you
imagine that your death can possibly precede mine. I took
the initiative in this, for I hunted for a sword in Ascyltus'
lodging. If I had not found you, I would have thrown myself
over a cliff. To make you realize that death is easily available
for those who seek it, you in your turn can witness what you
wished me to witness.'

Saying this, he grabbed a razor from Eumolpus' servant,
slashed at his throat repeatedly with it, and tumbled down
before our feet. I cried out in stupefaction, crouched over
him where he fell, and sought the path to death by use of
the same steel. But Giton was none the worse, with no suggestion of a wound, and for my part I experienced no pain,
for it was a practice-razor specially blunted; it had a sheath
fitted on it to give young apprentices confidence in its use.
This was why the servant had not panicked when the razor
was snatched, and Eumolpus had not tried to stop the staged
death-scene.

95   While this farce between lovers* was being enacted, the
porter provided a diversion by bringing in another course
of our modest dinner. He ran his eye over the squalid scene
as we rolled on the floor, and said: 'Tell me, are you drunk,
or runaways, or both? Who put that bed on its end? Why
this secret piling-up of the furniture? I'll swear that you've
planned to avoid paying rent for the room by making a run
for it during the night. But you won't get away with it. I'll
see that you realize that this block of flats doesn't belong to
some widow, but to Marcus Mannicius.'*

'What's this?' shouted Eumolpus. 'You threatening us as
well?' As he spoke, he gave the man a hefty smack on the
face with the palm of his hand. The porter had earlier shed
his inhibitions by knocking back the bottle with the lodgers;
he threw an earthenware jug at Eumolpus' head, and split
his forehead to stop his shouting. He then bolted out of the
room. Eumolpus wasn't putting up with this insult. He
grabbed a wooden candlestick, chased the porter out as he
retired, and took revenge for the damage to his forehead by

striking him repeatedly. The entire staff gathered round, followed by the crowd of drunken lodgers. I seized the opportunity for revenge, and closed the door on Eumolpus. So I turned the tables on the aggressor, and without a rival enjoyed sole use of the room and the darkness.

Meanwhile the cooks and the lodgers were battering Eumolpus outside the door. One held a spit crammed with sizzling meat which he thrust at his eyes; another had grabbed a long fork from a meat rack, and was taking up a duelling stance. In the van was an old hag with watering eyes, clad in an absolutely filthy dress and odd-sized wooden clogs, who was dragging along a massive hound on a chain, which she set on Eumolpus. But he defended himself from all danger with the candlestick.

96   We were watching the entire show through a hole in the door, opened up when the door-handle had been forced off shortly before. I cheered whenever Eumolpus got a belting. But Giton, mindful of his role as an angel of mercy, declared that we should open the door and lend aid to our beleaguered comrade. At this I could not restrain my hand, for my anger was unabated. With my clenched fist I struck the angel of mercy a sharp blow on the head. He began to cry, and sat back on the bed. I applied each of my eyes in turn to the hole in the door, gorging myself on the treatment meted out to Eumolpus as though it were a gourmet meal. I was all for the continuation of the process, but then Bargates, the block superintendent, whose dinner had been interrupted, was carried into the heart of the brawl by two litter-bearers; apart from anything else, he had bad feet. In impassioned and uncouth language he launched into a long rigmarole against drunkards and runaways, but then his eyes lit on Eumolpus. 'Most eloquent of poets,' he exclaimed, 'can this be you? Now why doesn't this rabble of slaves get out of here this minute, and stop this brawling . . . ?

'The woman I cohabit with is looking down her nose at me. Do me a favour, and compose a few lines of abuse about her, so that she shows me some respect.'

97   During this tête-à-tête between Eumolpus and Bargates, a crier followed by a municipal slave and a modest retinue

entered the lodging. He was brandishing a torch which gave off more smoke than light as he issued this proclamation:

'A slave has just gone missing at the baths. He is about sixteen years old, curly-haired, effeminate, good-looking. His name is Giton. There is a reward of a thousand sesterces to anyone willing to return him, or to indicate his whereabouts.'

Just behind the crier stood Ascyltus. He was wearing a multi-coloured shirt, and holding out a silver platter on which was a copy of the description and the promise of the reward. I gave the word to Giton to crawl smartly under the bed, to hook his feet and hands into the webbing which lashed the mattress to the bed-frame, and thus to elude prying hands, just as Ulysses of old clung to the ram's belly.* Giton jumped to it, and inserted his hands promptly in the webbing. He stretched out below the bed, outdoing Ulysses with almost identical guile. I didn't wish to leave any suspicious traces, so I covered the bed with clothes, and ordered them in the shape of a single person of my own size.

Meanwhile Ascyltus had accompanied the crier on a tour of all the rooms. When he reached mine, his hopes rose higher, because he found the doors more securely barred. The municipal slave pushed an axe between the door-joints, and prised out the close-fitting bars. I kowtowed before Ascyltus' knees; I begged him, in recollection of our friendship and our comradeship in misfortune, at least to reveal the whereabouts of my brother. To make my lying plea sound convincing, I went so far as to say: 'Ascyltus, I know that you are here to kill me; otherwise why have you come armed with axes? So you can glut your anger; here is my neck, shed my blood. This is what you sought in your pretended search.'

Ascyltus rebutted the charge of hatred, and said he was looking only for his runaway slave; he had no desire for the death of one who went on his knees before him, especially the man whom he held most dear following that deadly brawl.*

98 But the municipal slave did not show equal complaisance. He grabbed the manager's cane, and thrust it under the bed. He also looked closely at all the cracks in the walls.

Giton shrank from contact with the cane. He timorously held his breath, and even pressed his lips on the bed-bugs.

But the broken door of the room could not keep anyone out, and Eumolpus burst in. He was nettled, and said: 'The thousand sesterces are mine—I'll follow the crier on his way out, and betray you as you richly deserve by informing him that Giton is under your wing.' He stuck to his guns, so I grasped his knees, and begged him not to deliver the *coup de grâce* to the dying. 'Your indignation would be justifiable', I said, 'if you could produce the scoundrel. But as it is, he made off during the mêlée, and I haven't the faintest idea where he's gone. Do recover him, Eumolpus, I beg you; return him to Ascyltus, if you must.'

My persuasion was just winning his trust when Giton could no longer withstand the pressure of air on his nose, and he sneezed three times in rapid succession, so violently that the bed shook. Eumolpus greeted this explosion with the words 'Bless you, Giton!' He lifted off the mattress, and beheld a Ulysses whom even a hungry Cyclops would have spared. Then he turned on me, and said: 'You thieving blackguard, what's your game? You didn't presume to tell the truth even when caught in the act. If some god controlling human affairs hadn't forced the boy to give himself away in that precarious posture, you'd have made a fool of me, making me wander round the drinking-houses.'

Giton was far more accommodating than I. He first patched up the cut on Eumolpus' forehead with spider's web soaked in oil, and then he gave him a short tunic of his own to wear in place of his torn shirt. After softening him up in this way, he embraced him and planted kisses on him as soothing as poultices. 'Dearest father,' he said, 'we are in your hands. If you love your Giton, demonstrate your will to save us. I only wish that I could be trapped in some merciless fire, or that wintry billows could engulf me, because I am the substance and source of all these evil acts. My death would resolve the enmity between you.'

*

99 [Eumolpus speaking:] 'Always and everywhere I have lived
my life as though I were spending my last day, and would
not see another.'

                              *

I shed floods of tears, and begged and entreated him to be
reconciled to me as well. Mad jealousy, I said, lay beyond
the control of lovers, but I would ensure that I said or did
nothing further to cause him any possible offence. I asked
him only to efface all rancour from his heart, like the master of high principles that he was, leaving no scar behind.
'The snows cleave longer to rough and uncultivated country, whereas land made obedient and sleek with the plough
loses its light covering of frost even as one speaks. It is the
same with anger in the human heart; it clings to the barbaric mind, but melts away from the cultivated.'

     'To reassure you of the truth of those words,' said Eumol-
pus, 'come now, and I'll banish my anger with a kiss. So let's
live in hope. Pack your bags and follow me, or if you prefer,
lead the way.' Even as he spoke, there was a rap on the
door which creaked open, and on the threshold stood a
sailor with a shaggy beard.* 'You're holding us up, Eumolpus,' he said. 'You don't seem to appreciate the need for
haste.' We all rose at once. Eumolpus told his slave, who by
this stage was long asleep, to set out with the baggage. Giton
and I stacked our belongings in a rucksack, and with a
prayerful gesture to the heavens, we boarded the ship.

10

The Episode on Ship.
Enter Lichas and Tryphaena

100 'How irritating that our friend finds the boy attractive! Yet do we not all share nature's most glorious creations? The sun shines on all alike; the moon with its retinue of countless stars guides even wild beasts to their food. What lovelier thing can we instance than running waters? Yet they flow for everyone's use. So is love alone to be a stolen commodity rather than a prize to be won? It is, alas, true that the sole blessings which I long to possess are those envied by men at large. But a single companion, and one elderly at that, will not be an imposition. Even when he's inclined to force the pace, his laboured breathing will give him away.' Without much confidence I marshalled these reflections, and beguiled my sceptical mind. Covering my head with my shirt, I feigned sleep.

But suddenly my peace of mind, such as it was, was shattered by what seemed to be the hand of Fortune. A voice above deck said in aggrieved tones: 'So he's fooled me, has he?' It was a man's voice, one that my ears seemed to find familiar, and which made my heart thump. Then a woman, lashed by similar indignation, continued in this heated strain, and said: 'What a welcome I'd extend to my exiled Giton, if some God delivered him into my hands!' We both turned pale as ghosts when such unexpected words struck our ears. I was especially affected; I seemed to be experiencing the turmoil of a nightmare. It took me ages to find my voice, and with shaking hands I tugged at the hem of Eumolpus' cloak, just as he was dropping off to sleep. 'In God's name, father,' I said, 'to whom does this ship belong, and who are the passengers? Can you tell me?'

He was cross at being disturbed. 'Was this the reason why you decided that we should occupy this secluded spot below deck, to prevent our getting some rest? What difference does it make if I tell you that Lichas of Tarentum is master of the ship, and that he is ferrying Tryphaena' to Tarentum?'

101　　This thunderbolt left me gasping and all atremble. I bared my throat, and said: 'So at last, Fortune, your conquest is complete!' As for Giton, he was slumped across my chest, and long out for the count. We were both bathed in sweat, and this revived us. I clutched at Eumolpus' knees, and said: 'Have pity; we are as good as dead. Think of the studies we share, and come to our aid. Death is overtaking us; it will come as a welcome gift, unless you can prevent it.'

Eumolpus was at sea with the odium I had aroused. He swore by gods and goddesses that he had not been aware of those earlier happenings,' and that there had been no malicious guile in the plan he had laid; he had taken us aboard as his companions with the worthiest intentions and in genuine good faith. His decision to sail on the ship had been taken long before. 'But what ambush is there here?' he asked. 'Who is this Hannibal'we have aboard? Lichas of Tarentum is a highly respectable fellow, who not merely owns and runs this ship, but has several farms and a family business. He is carrying a cargo to deliver to market. So this is your Cyclops, your pirate-king to whom we are obliged for this passage; and besides him there is Tryphaena, the most beautiful of all women, who journeys to and fro in search of pleasure.'

Giton answered: 'But these are the very people we're escaping from!' He hastily explained why they hated us, and the danger which was overhanging us. Eumolpus was aghast. In his bewilderment and poverty of ideas, he urged each of us to suggest a way out. 'Imagine', he said, 'that we have entered the Cyclops' cave. We must devise some means of escape. Should we perhaps mount a shipwreck, and free ourselves from all danger?'

'No;' said Giton, 'persuade the helmsman to put into some harbour. I suppose we'll have to bribe him. Bluster it out

that your brother is seasick and in a bad way. You'll be able
to cloak the deception with troubled looks and tears, and
then the helmsman will be sympathetic, and grant your wish.'

Eumolpus turned this down as impracticable. 'Large ships',
he said, 'need enclosed bays in which to anchor. Also, the
story that my brother has fallen ill so soon after putting out
to sea will not be convincing. An additional problem would
be that Lichas will perhaps want to visit the sick person as
part of his duties. You can imagine how helpful it would be
to our cause if we took the initiative in summoning the
master to meet the runaways! But even supposing that the
ship can be diverted from its course on the high seas, and
that Lichas would not make a point of doing the rounds of
the sick—how can we quit the ship without being seen by
everybody? Are we to cover our heads, or go bare-headed?
If we cover them, all will want to lend a hand to the invalids;
leave them uncovered, and we might as well advertise our
identity.'

102 'Surely a better idea', I interjected, 'is to resort to bold
measures—slip down a rope into the ship's boat, cut the
painter, and leave the rest to Fortune. I'm not pressing
Eumolpus to embark on this hazard, for why should we load
an innocent man with other people's dangers? I'm happy
for the two of us to make the descent, and to leave it to
chance to aid us.'

'That wouldn't be a bad scheme', said Eumolpus, 'if you
could get away with it, but everyone will observe your departure, especially the helmsman. He has to stay awake all night,
and also observe the courses of the stars. Now if you were
seeking to make your escape off the ship at another point,
you could perhaps escape observation, even if he were wide
awake; but as it is, you would have to slide down at the stern,
right by the helm, where the rope is dangling. Also I'm surprised, Encolpius, that it hasn't occurred to you that there's
a sailor lying down there on watch day and night in the
ship's boat; your only way of getting rid of him is to kill him
or push him overboard. The two of you must reflect whether
you have the guts to achieve this. As for my accompanying
you, I shrink from no danger which brings some prospect of

safety, but I don't suppose that you'll be keen to squander your lives without justification as being of no account.

'See whether you favour this idea: I'll enclose you in two leather bales, fasten them up with straps, and store them as luggage with my clothing. Naturally I'll leave the ends open a little to allow you to breathe and take in food. I'll announce that my slaves have jumped into the sea during the night out of fear of harsher punishment. Then, when we reach harbour, I'll unload you as part of my baggage without arousing any suspicion.'

'Is that your plan?' I asked. 'To tie us up as though we're solid all the way through, as though our bowels won't do the dirty on us? Are we the sort of creatures who neither sneeze nor snore? Are you suggesting this merely because this kind of trick was successful once?* Even assuming that we can bear being tied up for a day, what happens if the wind drops, or bad weather comes on, and keeps us out at sea? What do we do then? Even clothes get creased and frayed if they're kept folded too long, and sheets of papyrus lose their shape if they're tied up. We are young fellows, not used to discomfort; will we be able to freeze like statues when we're wrapped round with cloths and tied up? . . .

'We must keep investigating some means of safety. Give thought to this plan that I have devised: Eumolpus, being a literary man, is sure to have some ink; let's use it as a means of changing our colour from head to foot. We'll look like slaves from inland Africa, waiting on you wreathed in smiles. By changing the colour of our skin, we'll put one over our enemies.'

'What a splendid notion,' said Giton. 'You can also circumcise us to make us look like Jews, pierce our ears to help us masquerade as Arabs, and plaster our faces with chalk to allow Gaul to claim us as her citizens! Do you really think that a change of colour alone can disguise our appearance? Many features must conspire to make the deception successful. Let's assume that the dye applied to our faces doesn't wear off for a bit; let's presume that a single drop of water won't leave its traces on our bodies, and that our clothes don't get stuck to the ink, as often happens without any

glue being applied; how can we fill out our lips, to give
them that unsightly swollen look? Can we curl our hair with
tongs? Or slash our foreheads to form scars? Or make ourselves bow-legged? Or turn our ankles over so that they touch
the ground? Or shape our beards to make them look foreign? Dye that's manufactured changes the body's colour,
but not its shape.

'Listen to the solution that my panic prompts. Let's bury
our heads in our clothes, and throw ourselves to the bottom
of the ocean.'

103   Eumolpus said: 'Neither gods nor men must permit you
to end your lives so ignominiously! Instead, you must follow
my instruction. My slave is a barber, as you gathered from
that razor of his.* He must at once shave off not just the hair
but also the eyebrows of you both. I shall follow on after him,
and mark your foreheads artistically to make it appear that
you have suffered the punishment of branding.* The letters
will simultaneously divert inquisitive suspicions and make
your faces unobtrusive under the shadow of the punishment.'

We did not postpone the deception, but crept over to the
ship's side, and presented our heads and eyebrows to the
barber for shaving. Eumolpus covered both our foreheads
with large letters, and generously emblazoned our faces right
across with the familiar mark tattooed on runaway slaves.
But it so happened that one of the passengers was very seasick, and was leaning over the ship's side vomiting. The
moonlight exposed to his eyes the barber intent on his un-
propitious duties. The man cursed this evil omen, since it
appeared to be the the final offering of shipwrecked mar-
iners, and then threw himself back on his bunk. We pretended not to have heard the cursing of the seasick man,
and we resumed our gloomy procedure. We then settled
ourselves in silence, and spent the remaining hours of the
night in troubled sleep.

*

104   [Lichas speaks:] 'In my sleep Priapus* seemed to be saying to
me: "As for Encolpius whom you are hunting down, you are

to realize that I have led him on to your boat."' Tryphaena shuddered as she replied: 'You would think that we had slept together, for I too received a message. It was from the statue of Neptune in the shrine adorned with four pillars at Baiae: "You will find Giton aboard Lichas' ship."' Eumolpus broke in: 'This will make you realize that Epicurus was a godlike man,* for he condemns risible experiences of this kind in the most witty fashion.' Lichas, however, on praying that Tryphaena's dream might turn out favourably, remarked: 'No one is preventing us from searching the ship. That way we shall not appear to disregard manifestations of the divine mind.'

Hesus, the man who had caught us wretchedly carrying out our deception in the hours of darkness, suddenly announced: 'So aren't these the men who were being shaved by moonlight during the night? I swear that's a dreadful example to set, for I'm told that no person on a ship must cut his nails or hair,* except when the wind and the sea are angry.'

105 Lichas was rattled by these words, and flared up. 'What?' he said. 'Has someone been cutting hair on the ship, and at dead of night? Let's have the guilty men out here at once. I want to see whose heads must be put on the block to ensure that the ship is purified.'

Eumolpus spoke up: 'I ordered this to be done. I was not imposing such an evil omen on myself, since I was to voyage on the same ship. But these men had long and disgusting hair, and in my anxiety not to be seen converting the ship into a prison, I ordered the gaolbirds to get spruced up. Besides, I didn't want those letters branded on their faces to be overshadowed by their hair, and so hidden from people's discerning eyes. Their misdeeds include wasting my money on a girlfriend they shared. They were both of them reeking with wine and perfume last night when I dragged them clear of her; to put it bluntly, they still stink through misappropriating the last pennies of my worldly wealth.'

*

So it was that to placate the guardian deity of the ship, it was
agreed to condemn us both to forty lashes. Without delay
some rabid sailors descended on us armed with ropes' ends,
and sought to appease that guardian spirit by shedding our
worthless blood. I myself endured three lashes with Spartan heroism, but Giton on receiving a single blow squealed
so loudly that his all too familiar tones rang loudly in
Tryphaena's ears. Not only was the lady herself affected, but
all her maids were drawn to the voice they knew so well, and
made a beeline for the suffering youth. Giton's remark-
able body had already disarmed the sailors; without even
opening his mouth, he had already begun to appeal to his
persecutors, when the maids as one cried out: 'It's Giton,
it's Giton! Take your savage hands off him! Mistress, come
and help! It's Giton.' Tryphaena had herself already reached
the same conclusion. She lent a ready ear to their cry, and
hastened over to the boy.

Lichas, who knew me in and out, also raced forward; it
was as if he had heard my voice as well. He didn't bother to
examine my hands or face, but trained his eyes directly on
my lower parts, extended a formal hand towards them, and
said: 'Greetings, Encolpius!' So should anyone be surprised
that Ulysses' nurse recognized his scar* as the mark of his
identity after twenty years, when this most sagacious fellow,
though confronted by the confusing evidence of my general
appearance, put his finger so unerringly on this single means
of identifying the runaway?

Tryphaena was shedding tears over us, for she was hood-
winked by those marks of punishment, and thought that the
tattoos on our foreheads were actual brandings made on
prisoners. In gentler tones she began to enquire about the
prison in which our wanderings had been interrupted, and
whose hands so harsh had steeled themselves to inflict such
punishment, though she conceded that runaways deserved
to undergo rough treatment when they turned with loathing against the blessings they enjoyed.

106   At this Lichas darted forward, hot with rage. 'What a naïve
woman you are', he said, 'to imagine that those letters trace

the line of scars inflicted by the branding-iron! I only wish
that such inscriptions on their foreheads had been caused
by their disfiguring themselves, for that at long last would
have brought us some consolation. But as things stand, they
have made us the target for tricks of the low stage, mocking
us with letters which have been painted on.'

Tryphaena was eager to show pity, for the pleasure she
had earlier experienced had not wholly died. But Lichas
still recalled the seduction of his wife, and the outrageous
treatment he had suffered in the colonnade of Hercules.
So he screwed up his face still more fiercely, and exclaimed:
'Tryphaena, I think you have come to realize that the immortal gods do order human affairs, for they have led these
men all unknowing on to our ship, and have kept us aware
of their movements in our two matching dreams. So consider: how can they win pardon, when the god himself
has consigned them to their punishment? I myself am not
vindictive, but I fear that any penalty remitted from them
may rebound on me.' This superstitious observation had
its effect on Tryphaena. She said that she was not opposed
to the punishment; indeed, she assented to this vengeance
as being wholly justified, for the insult she had endured
when her moral integrity was challenged in the presence
of a crowd was no less injurious than that which Lichas
had suffered.

*

107 [Eumolpus declaiming:] 'As a man of some repute in my
own modest estimation, I have been chosen by my friends
to speak on their behalf. They have begged me to heal the
breach between themselves and those who were once their
dearest friends. You surely cannot believe that the young
men came here unawares as into a snare; every traveller's
first concern is to investigate the reliability of the person to
whom he is entrusting himself. So relax your harsh attitude
towards them, which has already been softened by the repa-
ration they have made. Allow them to go free and without
harm to their journey's end. When runaways repent and

return to the fold, even harsh and unforgiving masters mitigate their cruel treatment; we spare even our enemies when they surrender. What further sanctions do you seek, what sterner punishment do you demand? These youths lie pleading before your eyes, freeborn and honourable, and what is more important than both these qualities, once closely bound to you in friendship. If they had embezzled your money, if they had betrayed your trust, you could still, heaven knows, feel sufficiently satisfied by the punishment which you yourselves witness; for you behold the marks of slavery on their foreheads, on those faces of freeborn men who are outlawed by a penalty which is self-imposed.'

Lichas interrupted this plea for mitigation. 'Stop confusing the issue,' he said. 'Limit yourself to one topic at a time. First and foremost, if they came aboard deliberately, why did they shave their heads? The man who disguises his appearance is planning deceit, not making amends. Secondly, if they were employing you as their envoy to win our favour, why did you take every precaution to keep your clients out of sight? Their behaviour makes it clear that they are guilty, and that they fell into this trap by chance; and now you have been seeking some means to divert the impact of our punishment. As for your hailing them as freeborn and honourable men so as to shift the odium on to us, see that you do not ruin your case by overbold assertion. What is an injured party to do, when malefactors hasten to embrace their own punishment? You may object that they were our friends; indeed they were, so they have merited a punishment all the more severe. For whereas one who assaults strangers gets the name of footpad, one who attacks his friends is little better than a murderer of kin.'

Eumolpus rebutted this utterly unfair harangue. 'I realize', he said, 'that the most damning charge against these unhappy young men is the fact that they shaved off their hair during the night, and this seems to indicate that they boarded the ship not deliberately but by chance. I should like the simple truth of what happened to be reflected in my frank address to your ears. They wanted to rid their

heads of their annoying and unnecessary burden before
embarkation, but then the wind freshened,*and caused them
to postpone their toilet. They did not think it mattered
where they set in train this clean-up they had planned,
because they were unaware of the omens and rules observed
by sea-travellers.'

'Why should petitioners shave their heads?' rejoined
Lichas. 'Is it perhaps that bald men usually excite greater
pity? But what is the point of our investigating the truth
through a go-between? You there, what have you to say for
yourself, you rascal? Did some salamander*scorch your eyebrows? To what god did you dedicate your locks? Speak up,
you gallows-bird!'

108   I was thunderstruck, and intimidated by the fear of execution. In my confusion I had nothing to say, for the case was
open and shut....

*

What with my repulsively cropped head and in addition
eyebrows as hairless as my forehead, my ugly appearance
made it seem inapposite to make any gesture or to say anything. Then, once a wet sponge was wiped over my woe-
begone countenance, and the ink running all over my face
enveloped my features in a murky cloud, their anger turned
to loathing...

Eumolpus said that he would refuse to allow anyone to
desecrate freeborn persons in defiance of what was morally
right and lawful, and he sought to prevent those threatening brutes from attacking us not merely by his words but
also by force. He was supported in this intervention by his
slave who stood by him, and also by one or two weaklings
among the passengers, who sympathized with his protests
rather than lent him physical support.

I myself offered no plea on my own behalf. I thrust my
fists into Tryphaena's face, and in clear and unrestrained
tones cried out that if that accursed woman, the only person
in the entire ship deserving of a hiding, did not refrain
from ill-treating Giton, I would resort to physical violence.

Lichas grew hot under the collar, blazing with rage at my impertinence. He was furious at my abandoning my own defence, and at my merely speaking on another's behalf. Tryphaena was equally incensed at the insult. Her reaction caused the entire company on the ship to split into opposing factions. On the one side, Eumolpus' slave distributed his shaving implements among us, keeping one for himself; on the other, Tryphaena's household bared their fists, and even her squawking maids joined her battle-line.

Only the helmsman stood off, and threatened to abandon the rudder if this madness induced by lustful criminals did not subside. Yet in spite of this the combatants joined battle with continuing fury. While the foe fought a war of vengeance, we battled for our lives. So many on both sides fell—though not in death; the greater number retreated, blood streaming from their wounds as in a regular battle, yet the anger of each and all raged undiminished. Then Giton with bravery supreme applied his razor threateningly to his manhood, and threatened to excise the root cause of all our troubles. Tryphaena restrained so monstrous a deed by the offer of an unconditional reprieve. I repeatedly set the barber's knife at my throat, but with no more intention of killing myself than had Giton of carrying through his threat. None the less, he played out his tragic role with greater assurance, because he knew that the razor in his hand was the one which he had earlier drawn at his throat.

Both lines stood their ground; clearly this was to be no casual engagement. But then the helmsman, not without difficulty, prevailed on Tryphaena to play the herald and to proclaim a truce. Guarantees were proffered and accepted, in accordance with ancestral custom. Tryphaena seized an olive-branch from the ship's figurehead. She held it out, and ventured to hold a parley with us, declaiming:

'What madness goads us to swap peace for war?
No deeds of ours deserved this! In our bark
No Trojan hero bears away the spouse
Of cuckolded Menelaus; no Medea,

Inflamed by brother's blood, resorts to arms.   5
Yet love rejected spawns its violence.
Who was it, then—that source of my lament—
That seized his arms, and summoned forth the fates
On these Italian waters? Does one death
Not satisfy him? Why outdo the sea,   10
And top the raging main with waves of blood?'*

109   As the woman uttered these lines in distressed tones, the
battle-line stood hesitant for a moment; our hands then
withdrew to embrace peace, and we suspended the war-
fare. Our leader Eumolpus exploited this opportunity for a
change of heart. Having first rebuked Lichas in words of
passion, he signed the articles of the treaty; the terms of
which were as follows:

'You, Tryphaena, do here express your determination not
to complain of any injury inflicted on you by Giton. If any
wrong has been committed against you before this day, you
will not hold it against him, nor take revenge for it, nor seek
satisfaction for it in any other way. You will not impose on
this boy against his will any embrace, kiss, or intimate sexual
behaviour, or you will disburse one hundred *denarii* for this
service.

'And you, Lichas, do here express your determination not
to prosecute Encolpius with any abusive word or look, and
not to enquire where he sleeps at night, or you will disburse
to him two hundred *denarii* cash down for each injurious
deed.'

These were the terms on which the treaty was struck. We
laid down our arms, and to ensure that no lingering anger
remained in our hearts even after we had sworn the oath,
we agreed to let bygones be bygones with an exchange of
kisses. As we all urged this course, the hatred subsided; the
feasting which had been postponed in the conflict conspired
to reinforce our genial mood. So the whole ship resounded
with singing. Because a sudden calm had halted the ship's
progress, one man tried to spear the leaping fish with a
harpoon, and another sought to haul in his resistant prize

on baited hooks. Then, would you believe it, seabirds perched
on the yardarm, and an experienced fowler brushed them
with a rod of interwoven rushes; they became attached to
his limed twigs, and were brought down into our hands.
The breeze caught up their soaring feathers, and the thin
spray sent them whirling over the surface of the sea.

By now reconciliation had set in between Lichas and
myself; Tryphaena was sprinkling the dregs of her drink
over Giton; Eumolpus too had loosed his tongue with drink,
and decided to fire off some words at men who were bald
and branded. But once his sadly laboured wit was exhausted,
he returned to his verse-composition, and began to declaim
a little poem in elegiacs:

'Proud locks, our body's solitary boast, have passed away;
    Grim winter has removed spring's foliage green.
Our greying temples, stripped of shade, lament their day;
    Our sun-scorched scalps bereft of hair are seen.

The gods beguile with nature's baleful law: 5
    First joys bestowed on youth they first withdraw!

                          *

    'Sad creature, once your hair did glow,
    More beauteous than the sun and moon,
    Now your head's smoother than worked bronze,
    Or garden mushroom, born in rain.
    You flee in fear from giggling girls.   5
    Why has your head's chief glory gone?
    To warn you of death's swift descent.'

110   I suspect that he would have liked to spout further lines
even more witless* than these. But now one of Tryphaena's
maids took Giton below deck, and adorned his head with
one of her mistress's wigs of curly hair. She also took from
a box some eyebrows, and by expertly following the lines of
his shaved hair, she totally restored his handsome features.
Tryphaena acknowledged her own true Giton; she was overwhelmed with tears, and for the first time kissed the lad with
real affection.

For my part, I was delighted to see the boy restored to his former beauty, but I repeatedly covered up my own face in the realization that I was so conspicuously hideous that Lichas did not consider me worth even addressing. But that same maid lifted my melancholy, for she summoned me away, and adorned me with equally fetching locks. In fact my features gleamed more attractively, because the wig was golden-haired.

*

Eumolpus, however, who was both the spokesman on our behalf when we were on trial and the architect of our present harmony, refused to allow the happy atmosphere to dissolve without some story-telling. So he launched a lengthy attack on women's fickleness, remarking on the readiness with which they fall in love, and the speed with which they cease to think even of their offspring, and claiming that no lady is so chaste that she cannot be driven even to distraction by lust for some outsider. He said that he was not thinking of those tragedies of old, nor of names familiar to earlier generations, but of an incident which occurred within his own recollection. He would recount it to us if we wished to hear it, so we all turned our eyes and ears towards him, and this is how he began:

111   'A married lady from Ephesus* had such a celebrated reputation for chastity that women even from neighbouring communities were drawn to gaze on her. This lady, then, had just buried her husband. But she was not satisfied merely to escort the body to burial, as most mourners do, with hair flowing free, beating her naked breast before the eyes of the assembled crowd: she also followed the dead man into his tomb, and when the body was laid in a subterranean vault after the Greek fashion, she proceeded to mount guard, weeping over it day and night. She remained there, abusing her body and courting death by self-starvation. Neither her parents nor her other relatives could induce her to leave; finally the magistrates after making the attempt were rejected and turned away. This lady, as she afforded

so unique an example, was the cause of grief to everyone as she dragged out five days without taking a bite to eat.

'As she pined away, her most trusted maid sat with her, and lent her tears to the grieving widow. She relit the lamp in the tomb whenever it went out. The whole city talked of nothing else; people of every social rank claimed that there shone out of her an authentic example of chastity and love.

'At about this time the governor of the province ordered some thieves to be crucified close to the cell in which the married lady was weeping over her late husband's corpse. The following night, a soldier guarding the crosses—he was to ensure that no one removed any of the bodies for burial—happened to notice a light gleaming quite brightly among the tombs, and he heard the groans of the grieving widow. The frailty endemic in the human race made him desirous of ascertaining who it was, and what the person was up to.

'So he went down into the tomb, where his eyes fell on this supremely beautiful woman. At first he was rocked on his heels, for in his confusion he imagined that she was some prodigy, some ghostly apparition from the world below. But then he noticed the corpse lying there, and spotted the woman's tears and scratch-marks of her nails on her face; the truth dawned on him that she could not bear the loss of her dead husband. So he brought his meagre supper into the tomb. He began to encourage her in her grief not to prolong her pointless sorrow, not to tear herself apart in unavailing lamentation. All of us, he told her, have to come to the same end, to the same final abode; and he added the other words of consolation by which inflamed minds are restored to normality.

'But the woman in her affliction had no thought for consolation. She tore at her breast more fiercely than before; she pulled out her hair, and laid it on the prostrate corpse. But the soldier did not withdraw. With the same words of encouragement, he tried to press some food on the wretched woman. Eventually the maid was seduced by the fragrance of the wine. She first extended her own defeated hand to receive the kind offer, and once she was restored by the food and drink, she began to lay successful siege to the obstinacy of her mistress. "What benefit will you gain", she asked, "if you faint away from hunger, if you bury yourself alive, if you breathe forth your innocent life before you are summoned by the Fates? 'Do you think the ashes or shades of the buried dead have a mind for such things?'* Why not return to the land of the living? Why not shake off this perverse way that women have, and enjoy life's blessings while you can? The very sight of your dead husband lying there should incite you to live."

'No one is reluctant to listen when pressed to take food or to remain alive. So it was that the woman, her mouth dry from several days' fasting, allowed her obstinacy to be broken down, and she stuffed herself with food no less greedily than the maid whose resistance had been overcome earlier.

112 'Now you know the temptation which often assails a person on a full stomach. The soldier mounted an attack on her virtue, exploiting that same coaxing which had succeeded in instilling in the lady a desire to live. The young fellow seemed quite presentable to look at, and articulate as well, in the eyes of the chaste widow, and the maid conspired to win her over by this constant refrain: "Will you strive to resist even a love that pleases?"*

'Need I labour the point? The woman did not hold back even from this invitation, and the soldier's persuasion was doubly successful. So they bedded down together not merely on that night's celebration of their union, but also on the next two days. The door of the tomb, we may imagine, was closed, so that any acquaintance or stranger visiting it would assume that this most chaste of wives had breathed her last over her husband's body.

'In his delight at both the lady's beauty and their hidden hideaway, the soldier would purchase such delicacies as he could afford, and as soon as darkness fell, he would take them into the tomb. So when the parents of one of the crucified thieves noticed that no watch was being kept, they hauled down the hanging corpse of their son during the night, and gave him the last rites. In this way they escaped the soldier's notice, while he was neglecting his duties, and next day he saw that the corpse was missing from one of the crosses. In his fear of execution, he told the woman what had happened. He said that he would not await the judge's verdict, but would impose sentence on himself with his own sword for neglect of duty. He asked only that she prepare a place for him before his death, and make the tomb the final resting-place for both her lover and her husband.

'But the woman's sense of pity matched her chastity. "The gods must not allow me", she said, "to gaze on the two corpses of the men I hold most dear. I would rather surrender the dead than put paid to the living." She followed up this declaration with an instruction to remove her husband's corpse from the coffin, and to have it fastened to the vacant cross. The soldier took advantage of the brainwave of this most thoughtful of women, and next day the locals speculated on how a dead man had managed to mount the cross.'

113   The sailors roared with laughter at this story. Tryphaena blushed to the roots of her hair, and leant her cheek affectionately on Giton's neck. But Lichas, far from laughing, shook his head angrily, and said: 'If the governor had done the right thing, he would have replaced the husband's body in the tomb, and strung the woman up on the cross.' Undoubtedly Hedyle was back in his mind, together with the plundering of the ship when she set out on her sexual adventure. But the terms of the treaty did not allow him to harp on these matters, and the general mood of gaiety allowed for no angry response.

Tryphaena by now was sitting in Giton's lap, alternately showering kisses on his breast and trying to improve his shorn appearance. I was depressed and upset at this new alliance. I took no food or drink, but watched them and gave them sideways piercing looks. Every kiss, every gesture of endearment which that randy woman conjured up was a dagger in my heart. I could not at that moment decide whether I was more angry with the boy for robbing me of my girlfriend, or with the girlfriend for seducing the boy. Both aspects were equally offensive to my eyes, and more painful than the arrest which I had just endured. What added to my depression was the fact that Tryphaena was not addressing me as the friend who had earlier been her favourite lover, while Giton did not think it worth his while even to raise his glass casually in my direction, or at the very least to draw me into the general conversation. I suppose he was afraid of reopening the newly healed wound, just when his relations with Tryphaena were beginning to be patched up. Tears born of resentment welled up over my heart, and the groans of anguish lurking beneath my sighs almost caused me to faint away.

*

He sought to be invited to share their pleasure, not assuming the arrogance of a master, but seeking the compliance of a friend . . .

*

[Tryphaena's maid to Encolpius:] 'If there is a drop of self-respecting blood in you, you will regard the nancy-boy as no better than a prostitute. If you're a real man, you won't go near the whore!'

*

Nothing embarrassed me more than the fear that Eumolpus realized what the game had been, and that with his ready tongue he might take his revenge by declaiming verses.

*

Eumolpus swore an oath in the most formal language . . .

*

114 In the course of our conversation about these and similar matters, the sea bristled threateningly, and storm-clouds gathered* from every side, shrouding the day in darkness. The sailors raced in alarm to their posts, and furled the sails before the storm. The wind did not lash the waves from any

one quarter, so that the helmsman did not know in which
direction to steer the ship's course. At one moment the
wind would drive us one way . . . but most often the north
wind, so dominant over the Italian coastline, would drive
the captive ship towards the shore of Sicily. More hazardous
than any storm was the fact that such impenetrable darkness suddenly blotted out the light that the helmsman could
not see even the full outline of the prow.

The storm was now clearly at its height. Lichas stretched
out imploring hands in panic towards me, and said: 'Encolpius, help us in our hour of danger. Restore to the ship the
sacred robe and rattle.' Show compassion to us, as always,
for the love of heaven!' Even as he cried out to me, the
wind swept him into the sea. He was claimed by the hostile
flood, and the storm whirled him round and sucked him
under. Tryphaena, almost unconscious, was grabbed by her
ever-devoted slaves, placed in the ship's boat with most of
her luggage, and rescued from certain death . . .

I hugged Giton close, and wept noisily. 'The gods have
granted us this boon,' I said; 'they have united us if only in
death. But cruel Fortune does not allow even this. You can
see how the waves will overturn the ship, how the angry sea
will prise apart the embraces of lovers. So if you ever loved
Encolpius truly, kiss me while you can, and snatch this joy
from the impatient Fates.' Giton laid aside his clothing; I
enclosed him in my shirt, and he raised his head for a kiss.
As we clung to each other in this way, he threw a belt round
the pair of us and fastened it, to ensure that some more
malevolent wave would not tear us apart. He said: 'We shall
be united for longer in death, at any rate, if in nothing else.
Or if the sea shows us mercy, and opts to cast us up on the
same shore, some passing traveller out of common decency
will erect a cairn over us, or the insentient sand will bury us
as the final legacy of the waves, angry though they are.' I let
him tie us together for the last time; like a person laid out
on a funeral-bier, I awaited the death which no longer
seemed an imposition.

Meanwhile the storm acceded to the demand of the Fates, and overcame the remains of the ship. Not a mast, not a rudder, not a rope or oar survived. She was like a length of rough, unshaped timber drifting on the waves.

*

Some fishermen equipped with light craft quickly put out to purloin the booty. But when they noticed that there were some survivors ready to defend their possessions, they abandoned their callous attitude, and lent help.

*

115 We heard a curious droning coming from below the master's cabin. It sounded like the plaintive utterance of a beast seeking to escape. When we tracked down the sound, we found Eumolpus sitting there, raining verses thick and fast on to a massive sheet of parchment. We showed some surprise at his leisurely composition of poetry when he was at death's threshold; we dragged him out shouting, and told him not to worry. But he flushed with rage at being disturbed, and said: 'Kindly allow me to formulate my thought. The poem is limping at its close.' I laid my hand on the lunatic, and bade Giton come to lend help, and to drag the bellowing poet ashore.

*

When this task was finally completed, we repaired in melancholy mood to one of the fishermen's huts. There we took some modest refreshment with food damaged in the shipwreck, and passed a dismal night.

Next day we were debating into which region we should venture our steps, when I suddenly caught sight of a human body swirling round in a gentle eddy as it was washed ashore. So I stopped short with feelings of sadness, and with tear-dimmed eyes I began to reflect on the treachery of the sea. 'It could be', I cried, 'that somewhere in the world a carefree wife awaits him, or perhaps a son with no knowledge of

the storm. Perhaps he has left a father behind, or at any
rate some person whom he kissed on his departure. These
are the designs, the aspirations in which men indulge, but
see how uncertain is man's floating destiny!'

I was still mourning the man as if he were a stranger,
when a wave turned his unmarked face towards the shore,
and I recognized Lichas, who shortly before had been so
fearsome and relentless a figure, cast up almost at my feet.
Then I could no longer contain my tears, and I even
pounded my breast repeatedly with my fists. I said: 'Where
is your foul temper and explosive rage now? Instead, you
are at the mercy of fishes and beasts. Not long ago you were
boasting of the powers of your command, but now in shipwreck there is not even a plank of that huge ship that you
own. So off you go, mortal men, and fill your minds with
ambitious designs! Off with you, careful souls, to order those
riches gained by fraud, which you think will last for a thousand years! Yesterday, no doubt, Lichas here was reviewing
his estate's accounts; doubtless he was clear in his mind
about the day when he would land back on home territory.
Ye gods and goddesses, how far from his destination he now
lies!

'But it is not just the seas which keep such brittle faith
with mortal men. The warrior in battle is let down by his
armour. A man paying his vows to the gods is buried when
his house collapses over him. An individual out riding in his
carriage slips off, and his life's breath is gone in a moment.
The glutton chokes on too much food, the abstemious man
dies through eating too little. If you reflect well on it, life is
a shipwreck everywhere.

'You may object that being drowned at sea is different,
because you get no burial. As if it makes any difference
whether a decomposing corpse is finished off by fire or
water or the lapse of time! Whatever your course of action,
it all ends up the same way. But you again object: beasts will
rend a corpse apart. Are you suggesting, then, that fire is a
kindlier host? Indeed, when our slaves infuriate us, we consider fire to be the grimmest punishment. What madness is

it, then, to do all in our power just to ensure that there is nothing left of us to bury?'

*

So the pyre that cremated Lichas was raised by his enemy's hands. Eumolpus gazed away into the distance, to summon the requisite thoughts as he composed an epitaph for the dead man.

*

11

The Journey to Croton

116 Once we had gladly discharged this duty, and decided on our route, we set out. Soon we were bathed in perspiration as we climbed a mountain. From the summit we saw a town lying within easy distance, and perched on a lofty height. We did not identify it in our wandering until we ascertained from a bailiff that it was the ancient city of Croton,* once the foremost in Italy. We then made more detailed enquiry about the natives of this celebrated site, and the particular nature of their business interests, now that their frequent wars had exhausted their resources.

'My friends,' said the bailiff, 'if you are businessmen, you must change your plans and seek out some other place to sustain you. On the other hand, if you are more sophisticated types and can play the role of perpetual liars, you are on the swift and direct road to profit. In this city, literary studies have no prestige, and eloquence no standing. The simple life and decent morals win no praise, and therefore no reward. Just realize that whatever men you clap eyes on belong to one of two groups, the money-hunters and the hunted.* In this city no one brings up children, for if a man has his own heirs, this disqualifies him from dinners and public entertainments. He gets none of the perks, and lives unknown as a social leper. But those who have never married and have no relatives not only attain the top positions, but are regarded as the only men of true valour and integrity. You are approaching a town', he added, 'that is a plague-ridden expanse, populated by nothing but corpses being pecked to pieces, and the crows at work pecking them.'

*

117 Eumolpus was more circumspect. He contemplated this unusual activity, and proclaimed that such a means of getting rich was quite attractive to him. I thought that the old man was being facetious, and was indulging in poetic banter. But he said: 'I just wish we had a larger stage to satisfy us, more civilized outfits, and a more sophisticated stage-apparatus to lend credibility to our imposture. I swear I wouldn't procrastinate, but advance you here and now to enormous riches. Even so, I promise . . .'

*

. . . whatever he asked for, as long as the outfit which I had worn for the burglary was good enough, as well as the loot which Lycurgus' country house had yielded when we broke in. As for money for our present use, the mother of the gods would provide it in accordance with her promise . . .

*

Eumolpus said: 'So why the delay in mounting this farce? Let me play the part of master, if you're happy about the business.' None of us presumed to pour cold water on the imposture, for we had nothing to lose from it. So to ensure that we all maintained the deceit securely, we swore an oath dictated by Eumolpus, by which we submitted to being branded, fettered, scourged, put to the sword, and such else as Eumolpus directed. We were like professional gladiators most solemnly committing bodies and souls to our master. Once we had sworn the oath, in our role as slaves we saluted our master.

We were all instructed that Eumolpus had earlier buried his son, a young man of great eloquence and high promise. For this reason the old man in his desolation had quitted his city as he did not wish to set eyes on his son's dependants and friends, nor on the tomb which daily moved him to tears. This sad state of affairs had been exacerbated by a recent shipwreck, in which he had lost more than two million sesterces. Not that the financial loss troubled him, but he was deprived of his retinue of slaves, so that he was

forfeiting the evidence of his high status. As an addition to
the fiction, he had thirty million sesterces secured in farms
and loans in Africa, where his establishment was scattered
widely over Numidian territories, and was massive enough
to storm even the city of Carthage.

This was to be his story, and to accord with it we instructed Eumolpus to cough incessantly, to have poor bowel-
control, and to grumble openly at any food set before him.
His talk was to be of gold and silver, of his farms not fulfill-
ing their promise, of the continuing barrenness of the soil.
Every day he was to sit reviewing his finances, and revising
the clauses in his will every month. To add the final touches
of the farce, whenever he sought to summon any of us, he
was to cite us by the wrong name, to make it obvious that
as master he was thinking of his slaves who were absent.

Once we had settled these details, we prayed to the gods
that everything would turn out happily and successfully, and
we set out on our way. But Giton wilted under his unaccustomed burden, and the servant Corax,* who always shirked
his duties, kept setting down his bundle and cursing us for
walking so quickly. He said that he would either dump the
luggage or make off with the load. 'Do you think I'm a
packhorse or a barge for transporting stones?' he asked.
'You hired me to do a man's job, not a horse's. I'm as free
an individual as you are, even if my father did leave me
impoverished.' He wasn't satisfied with cursing us; from time
to time he would lift his leg high, and fill the road with
disgusting noises and smells. Giton kept laughing at his
shameless behaviour; he would greet the sound of each fart
with a matching raspberry.

*

118 'Poetry, my young friends,' said Eumolpus, 'has beguiled
many*into believing that they have set foot on Mount Helicon* as soon as they have ordered their lines into feet, and
have woven their subtler thoughts into elaborate diction.
Thus men trained for the tasks of the bar often seek refuge
in the tranquillity of poetry as in some safe haven, in the

belief that a poem can more easily be crafted than a forensic declamation adorned with scintillating epigrams. But the nobler spirit has no time for empty words; the human mind cannot conceive or bring to birth its offspring unless it is first submerged in literature's vast flood. We must shun all that is coarse, so to say, in the sphere of language, and adopt words remote from common speech, taking as our motto "I hate the common mob," and keep it at arm's length."

'Moreover, we must ensure that epigrams are not detachable from the body of a work; their brilliance of colour should be interwoven in the garment itself. Evidence of this is provided by Homer, the lyric poets, Roman Virgil, and Horace with his studied but happy gift of expression. But the others have either not identified the true path to poetry, or having identified it are afraid to tread it. For example, the person who tries his hand at the lofty theme of the Civil War must be steeped in literature, or he will sink under the burden of the subject. Historical events are not to be treated in verses, for historians handle such material far better. The free spirit of genius should plunge headlong into oracular utterances, the succour lent by the gods, and the Procrustean control of lapidary phrases; the result should appear as prophetic frenzy rather than as a trustworthy, scrupulous account attested by witnesses.

'You may like to hear this foray of mine on the theme, though it has not received the final touches:

119   'By now the victorious Roman ruled the world,
     All seas and lands traversed by sun and moon,
     Yet hungered still for more. His laden ships
     Assailed the foaming deep. War was declared
     On bays remote, on lands which might discharge   5
     Their yellow gold. The Fates allowed grim battles,
     The search for wealth went on. Familiar joys,
     Pleasures well tried by common use, now palled.
     Soldiers on troopships praised Corinthian bronze;
     That metal's brightness vied with heliotrope.   10

Numidians yielded marble; unspun silk
Was China's offering; Arabs stripped their fields.

Yet further scourges scar and wound the peace.
Forests are combed for beasts for the Circus mob.
In darkest Africa, by Ammon's shrine,   15
The lion is hunted, for its sabre tooth
Is highly valued for inflicting death.
Our ships are weighted down with ravening beasts—
The padding tiger, shipped in gilded cage,
To drink men's blood before the applauding crowd.*   20

I shrink from words evoking future ruin.
From tender boys, adopting Persian ways,
We stole their manhood—the knife's cutting edge
Exploited for men's lust. Without success
Nature sought ways to encompass brief delay   25
Of years fast fleeting: hence all sought their joy
In harlots, in effeminates' mincing steps,
In flowing hair, in novel garb oft changed,
In all that captivates men's minds.
                              The citrus tree,
Uprooted from the soil of Africa,   30
Provides the table whose bright surface gleams,
Reflecting hordes of slaves, and purple drapes.
Its golden markings, costlier than gold,
Are there to attract the eye. Around this wood,
So barren, so low-born, a drunken mob   35
Reclines; soldiers of fortune, clutching arms,
Aspire to all choice produce of the world.
O, gluttony's so clever! See the wrasse,
Imported in Sicilian water, still alive;
Oysters dug up from Lucrine oyster-beds   40
To justify the dinner, whet the palate,
But at what cost! By now Phasis' broad stream,
Plundered of birds, its banks now silent, hears
Only the breezes rustling orphaned trees.*

The madness in our politics grows no less.   45
The citizens are bought, transfer their votes

To hope of plunder, parrot-cries of gain.
The commons is for sale, the senate too,
Their votes for auction. Even men of old
Had long abandoned meritorious liberty.   50
Their power had been corrupted by largess,
Their very majesty seduced by gold.

Cato was vanquished, humbled by the mob;
The unhappy victor felt the flush of shame
To have grabbed the rods of office from his hand.   55
Our shame and our corruption lay in this,
That such rejection was not of one man,
But of the power and glory of our race.
Rome, then, was fallen, for she sold herself,
Now ripe for plunder, and with no redeemer.   60

Foul usury and borrowed money spent
Submerged the people, and destroyed their lives.
No house stood safe, no person was unpledged.
The wasting sickness silently took hold,
Raging within them; cares barked loud outside.   65
Despair breeds violence. The comforts lost
In dissipation were recovered by the sword.
Boldness induced by poverty has nought to fear!
Since Rome was plunged in filth and heavy sleep,
No ways of sanity could now prevail;   70
Instead, rage, war, and lust roused by the sword.

120 Three generals, Crassus, Magnus and Julius,
All Fortune's sons, were buried by Enyo,
Death-dealing goddess, beneath their mounds of arms.
Parthia owns one, the Libyan shore another;   75
The third splashed Rome's ingratitude with his blood.
Three graves together the earth could not endure;
She split their ashes. Such is the meed of fame.*

Between the town of Naples and the fields
Óf famed Puteoli, there lurks a place   80
Deep down, concealed within a cloven chasm.
'Tis watered by the stream of Cocytus;

The wind which rages furiously without
Bears with it drops of that funereal spray.
There is no greenery in autumn there;   85
The fields are not luxuriant with herbs.
The yielding thickets hear no song in spring,
Nor chatter with the rival notes of birds.
All is disorder. Ugly boulders loom,
Formed of black pumice-stone, like burial mounds,   90
Sprouting forth cypress trees that presage death.

Ensconced in this abode, the lord of Hell,
Raising his head smoke-blackened from men's pyres,
And lightly flecked with hoary ashes, spoke,
Provoking winged Fortune with these words: 95
"O fickle arbiter of earth and heaven,
Setting your face against all power secure,
Forsaking, in your eagerness for change,
The seat of power which earlier you possessed,
Do you not see that you are overcome   100
By the dead weight of Rome, preventing you
From raising higher that edifice doomed to fall?
The Roman youth itself now loathes its strength,
Can scarce sustain the riches it has raised.
See the far-flung extravagance of its spoils,   105
The wealth which rages for its own destruction!
They build in gold, they raise piles to the heavens;
Sea-waters they repel with moles of rocks;
New seas begin to flow amid the fields;
Rebellious mortals now change Nature's face.   110
Why, even on my kingdom they encroach!
To sink their mad foundations they dig deep;
The earth yawns open. They ransack the mountains;
The caves beneath lament. As men commit
The marble to futile use, the shades below   115
Declare their hope of reaching upper realms.
So come now, Fortune, change your peaceful face
For war. Harass the Romans, and bestow
Their corpses on our kingdom. For too long

Our faces have been spattered with no blood;   120
Tisiphone has not bathed her thirsty limbs
Since Sulla's sword drank deep, and the unkempt earth
Raised to the heavens its harvest fed by blood.'"*

121   These were his words. Straining to take her hand,
He rent the surface of the earth asunder.   125
Fortune then answered from her fickle heart:
"Father, whom Cocytus' inmost depths obey,
If I may prophesy the truth unharmed,
Your prayers will soon be answered, for the rage
That seethes within my marrow matches yours,   130
Nor is the flame that burns my heart less fierce.
All that I once bestowed on Rome's proud heights
I loathe; I nurse aversion for my gifts.
The deity that raised those massive piles
Will bring them down. It's my ambition too   135
To burn those men and sate my lust with blood.
Already I foresee at Philippi
The corpses from twin battles strewn in death;
I see Thessalian pyres and Spanish burials;
The din of arms now strikes my eager ears.   140
In Egypt too I see Nile's barriers groan,
Apollo's darts infusing dread at Actium.
Unbar the thirsting kingdom of your realm,
Summon more souls. The ferryman in his bark
Will scarce contain those ghostly apparitions,   145
So hire a fleet! Bloodless Tisiphone,
Of widespread carnage you must have your fill,
Devour the severed flesh. The world is mauled;
Down to the Stygian shades all will be led.'"*

122   Hard on her words, the quivering clouds were rent   150
As lightning ripped them, vomiting forth its fire.
The father of the shades in fear sank back,
And closed earth's riven bosom after him;
He paled before his brother's lightning bolts.
At once divine-sent omens heralded   155
Disasters soon to visit the human race.

Titan looked hideous; his face bloodstained
He veiled in darkness. Already then he seemed
To witness civil strife. Across the sky
Cynthia's round orb was doused, as she withdrew   160
Her light from wicked deeds. The mountain-tops
Slipped downwards; shattered ridges thundered loud;
Meandering streams no longer hugged their banks.
Heaven raged with clash of arms; a quivering trumpet
Called Mars down from the skies; and Aetna's peak   165
Was now o'ertopped by unaccustomed flames,
Launching red fireballs into the upper air.
Amidst the tombs, and bones unburied there,
The infernal shades launched grim and hissing threats.
New stars escort a comet's blazing tail,   170
And Jupiter rains fresh-formed showers of blood.*

Without delay God made these portents plain,
For Caesar shrugged off all delay. Desire
For vengeance urged him on; abandoning
The war in Gaul, he embarked on civil strife.   175
Amidst the Alps' high peaks, where cliffs descend
(The Greek god trod them down, so men can pass),
There lies the sanctuary of Hercules, enclosed
By winter's frozen snow, its hoary peak
Out-jutting to the stars. From there the sky   180
Seems to have plunged below; no hot sun's rays,
No warming breeze of spring can soften it.
Ice and the wintry frost maintain their hold.
On its fierce shoulders the whole world can rest.

When Caesar with exultant forces trod   185
These heights, he chose this lofty mountain-peak
From which he could discern outspread below
The plains of Italy. Then to heaven above
He lifted up his hands and voice, and said:
"Almighty Jupiter, and Saturn's land   190
Which earlier acclaimed my arms and bore
My triumphs, I do solemnly attest:
Unwilling do I call Mars to this fight,

Unwilling are the hands I wield for war.
My wound compels me. Banished from my city,   195
E'en as I stained the river Rhine with blood,
And closed the Alpine routes against the Gauls
Who sought again to siege the Capitol,
These victories make my exile doubly sure.
My shedding Germans' blood, my countless triumphs, 200
Marked the beginning of my guilt. And yet
Who are these worthies frightened by my fame,
Idle spectators of our battles? Who else
But worthless hirelings, purchased at a price,
Adopted, no true sons of my dear Rome?   205
No cowards, methinks, will pinion my right arm
Unhurt, without fear of retaliation.
My comrades, passionate in victory, come,
Plead our case with the sword. We all are charged
With the one indictment, subject to one doom.   210
My thanks to you are due, for victory
Was not my doing alone. Since punishment
O'erhangs our trophies, since our conquests win
Nought but disgrace, the die must now be cast,
With Fortune as our arbiter. To war,   215
And prove your strength! My case is surely won;
Armed, with so many stalwarts, who can fail?"*

As he declaimed these words, the Delphic bird
Coursed through the air, a happy augury;
And on the left hand, from a gloomy grove   220
Strange voices sounded, with attendant flames.
Phoebus himself shone brighter than his norm;
His face was haloed in a golden glow.

123   Caesar was heartened by these favourable signs.
The standards were advanced, and he strode on,   225
Intent on ventures hitherto unknown.
At first the ice, and hoary, frost-bound earth
Made no resistance, kept a rigid peace.
But once the cavalry pierced the rain-turned-ice
(The horses' hooves shattered its frozen bonds),   230

The snows turned liquid. New-formed torrents poured
Down from the lofty mountains, then held fast
As though they had been bidden; the waters froze,
The streams stopped, hypnotized. What was before
A foul cascade, could now resist the axe.   235
The ground was treacherous earlier, but now
Refused a foothold, and deceived their steps.
Horses and men together, with their arms,
Lay piled and jumbled in despairing heaps.

Then suddenly, assailed by freezing blasts,   240
The clouds discharged their burden; there burst forth
A whirlwind; swollen hail fractured the sky.
The cloudburst thundered on the soldiers' arms;
Masses of ice like sea-waves showered down.
The earth was conquered by deep snow. The stars   245
Were blotted out in heaven; and the streams
Froze to their banks, admitting their defeat.
But Caesar was not worsted; a tall spear
Sustained him, as with fearless step he trod
The rugged fields. Just so, Amphitryon's son   250
Strode quickly down from Caucasus' high peaks,
His head held high. So, glowering Jupiter,
Descending from the summit of Olympus,
Disarmed the hostile Giants doomed to die.*

While angry Caesar trod the swollen peaks,   255
Swift Rumour, startled, flapped her wings and flew
To the tall ridges of the Palatine.
She impressed on all the statues of the gods
Tidings of thunder soon to threaten Rome:
The ships already afloat upon the sea,   260
The seething cavalry soaked in German blood.
Before all eyes flit arms and gore and slaughter,
Arson and war's whole panoply. Men's hearts
Are shaken with confusion, racked with fear,
And riven between the two conflicting causes.   265
Some opt to flee by land, others by sea,
A safer prospect than their native soil;

Yet others intend to have recourse to arms,
To follow through the dictates of Fate's bidding.
In these conflicting currents, sad to see,   270
The city-folk abandon Rome, to go
Where stricken hearts lead them. Rome is glad to flee,
Its citizens overwhelmed by Rumour's voice.
They quit their grieving houses. One holds fast
His offspring in his trembling arms; another   275
Secretes his household gods close to his heart,
And mourns the threshold that he leaves. In prayer
He summons death upon the absent foe.
Some clasp their fond wives to their sorrowing breasts;
Men in their prime lead out their aged fathers;   280
Unused to burdens they take nothing else
Save what they fear to lose. Only the fool
Takes with him all he has as loot to war.
They act as when a southern gale at sea
Rages, and makes the driven waves rear high;   285
Rigging nor steering can avail the crew.
One man secures with ropes the vessel's sails;
Another seeks safe harbour and calm shore;
A third commits his sails to flight, and leaves
All things to Chance.
                            Why dwell on petty plaints?   290
Magnus—the scourge of Pontus, the discoverer
Of fierce Hydaspes, who became the rock
On which the pirates foundered, who triumphed
Three times of late (why, even Jupiter
Regarded him with awe!), whom the Black Sea,   295
Its waters overcome, and Bosporus
With waves submissive, worshipped—that same man,
Together with both consuls, took to flight,
Abandoning his claim to high position.
Thus fickle Fortune, by his shameful deed,   300
Beheld no less a man than Pompey flee.*

124   This monstrous bane vanquished the very gods,
      Since heaven's fear assented to the flight.

Over all the earth the gentler deities
En masse forsook with loathing this mad world.   305
Peace led the way, her snow-white arms outraged;
Her helmet hid her vanquished head; from earth
To the relentless realm of Dis she fled.
Submissive Faith as her companion went,
And Justice, hair unbound; Concord in tears   310
Had torn her garment. Facing them, the hall
Of Erebus, forced open, yawning wide,
Disgorged Dis' broad array—grim Erinys,
The truculent Bellona, Megaera
Torches in hand, Destruction, Ambush, Death   315
—This last a pallid ghost. Among them all
Ranged Madness, like a steed with broken reins.
He tossed his bloodstained head from side to side,
His face, already scarred by myriad wounds,
He covered with a helmet streaked with gore.   320
In his left hand he gripped the shield of Mars,
Well-worn and weighed down with innumerable darts,
While in his right he bore a blazing brand,
Carrying his threatening fire through all the world.

Earth felt the presence of the gods. The stars   325
Experienced change, and sought their former poise;
The sky's whole palace parted, and collapsed.
The first to plot her Caesar's course was Dione;
Then Pallas joined her, and the god of war,
Waving his massive spear. On Pompey's side   330
Were Phoebus with his sister; Cyllene's son;
The Tirynthian, aping him in all he did.*

The trumpet's trembling din went forth. Discord,
With hair dishevelled, raised her Stygian head
To heaven. The blood had clotted on her face,   335
And tears welled from her black and bruised eyes.
Her brazen fangs were foul with rusty scales;
Her tongue was dripping with disease, her face
Beset with snakes. Beneath her tattered dress
Her breasts heaved. In her quivering hand she waved 340

A blood-red torch. Emerging from the depths
Of pitch-black Cocytus, the realm of Hell,
She marched towards the lofty Apennine hills,
To gaze from there on all the lands and shores,
On all the armies streaming through the world.   345
These words erupted from her maddened breast:
"Seize now your weapons, nations; fire your hearts!
Seize them, put torches to the hearts of cities!
The one who lurks inactive will be lost.
No woman must withdraw, no child, no man   350
Consumed with age. The earth itself must shake;
Even the shattered houses must revolt.
Marcellus, uphold the law! And Curio,
Arouse the common mob! You, Lentulus,
Seek not to put an end to valiant war.   355
And you too, divine Caesar, in your arms
Why play the laggard? Why not storm the gates,
Deprive the cities of their walls, and grab
Their treasures? Magnus, can you not defend
Rome's citadels? Then seek the foreign walls   360
Of Epidamnus, dye Thessalian bays
With human blood."
Discord's commands were all fulfilled on earth."*

12

The Encounter with Circe

We finally entered Croton, once Eumolpus had poured out
his monstrous deluge of words.* There we gained admission
to a modest lodging-house, and next day we searched for a
more imposing residence. We met a gang of fortune-hunters; they asked us what branch of business we belonged to,
and where we hailed from. So in accordance with the scheme
which we had jointly laid, we informed them of our origin
and identity, laying it on thick with a welter of words. There
was no doubt that they believed us. They at once vied fever-
ishly in pressing on Eumolpus offers of financial help
. . . these fortune-hunters were all competing to win Eumolpus' favour . . .

125   This went on at Croton for quite a while . . . Eumolpus
was ecstatic with his success, and so far forgot his earlier
parlous state as to boast to his cronies that no one at Croton
could resist his charm, that through the good offices of his
friends, his dependants could get away scot-free with any
wrongdoing. I myself, however, kept harking back to my
usual misfortunes rather than to the matter in hand. It was
true that every day I was stuffing and fattening myself on
an ever-increasing abundance of luxuries, and I was beginning to think that Fortune had stopped observing me with
her beady eye. None the less, I said to myself: 'What if
some devious fortune-hunter sends a man over to Africa to
investigate, and finds out that we've been lying? Suppose
Eumolpus' slave becomes restive with our pleasant life here,
gives the nod to these friends, and betrays our whole imposture in a fit of spiteful treachery? We'll surely have to take
to our heels again; we shall have to revert to the poverty
which we've overcome after all this time, and start begging

again. Ye gods and goddesses, how grim it is for outlaws, always anticipating their deserts!'

         *

126 [Circe's maid addressing Polyaenus:]* 'Because you are conscious of your own sexual attractions, you play hard to get, and you sell your favours rather than offering them freely. What other motive have you in your curling your hair with the comb, plastering your face with make-up, giving that melting come-hither look with your eyes, walking with that carefully composed tread so that not a step is out of place, except to advertise that handsome body of yours for sale? You see what I'm like; I know nothing of fortune-telling, and I'm not in the habit of studying the stars as the astrologers do, but I can tell what men are like by the expressions on their faces, and I've only got to watch how a man walks to know what's on his mind. So if you're selling what I'm after, you've found a buyer; or if you do the decent thing and offer it for free, let me be in your debt. As for your admission that you're a slave with no pretensions, that's precisely why you fire my lady's passion, and she's on heat. The fact is that scum rouses some women; they don't feel randy unless their eyes are on slaves* or public employees with their tunics hitched up. Some get excited at the arena, or it could be with a grimy muleteer, or with someone disgracing himself as an actor, making an exhibition of himself on the stage. My mistress is one like that; she vaults over the first fourteen rows* in front of the orchestra, and looks for a lover from the dregs of society.'

    At this I turned up the charm to the full with my reply. 'So are you the one who's keen on me?' The maid laughed her head off at this crude ploy. 'Don't sound so pleased with yourself,' she said. 'I've never knuckled under to a slave yet. Heaven forbid that I should ever see any intimate of mine strung up! Slaves are a job for the married women; *they* go in for kissing the traces of the whip. I'm just a lady's maid, but the only ones I climb on to are knights.'

I was struck with amazement at this paradox in sexual pre-
ferences; the maid showed the hauteur of the matron, and
the matron the base inclinations of the maid.

This badinage continued for quite a while, and then
I asked the girl to bring her mistress over into a glade
shaded by plane trees. She approved the idea; hitching up
her skirts, she turned aside into a laurel grove which bor-
dered on the path. A moment or two later she escorted the
woman from her hiding-place, and settled her at my side.
No statue could match her perfection, no words could do
justice to her beauty; any description of mine would be an
understatement. Her hair fell in natural waves all over her
shoulders; from her narrow forehead her hairline receded in
curls; her eyebrows extended to the edge of her cheekbones,
and almost met close to her eyes. Those eyes were brighter
than the stars which twinkle beyond the range of the moon's
light; her nose was delicately curved; her diminutive mouth
was like that which Praxiteles envisaged for Diana.* And what
a chin, and neck, and hands—and her gleaming foot circled with a slender golden band! Parian marble* by comparison lost its sheen. So now for the very first time my erstwhile
love-partner Doris sank low in my estimation.

'Why, Jupiter, discard your arms, and why
Amongst the gods so indolently lie?
Why is the scandal muted? Surely now
Fresh horns should sprout forth from your lowering brow!
Swan's feathers should disguise your hoary head;   5
Here is a genuine Danaë to bed.
A mere exploratory touch inspires
Your limbs to tingle with inflamed desires.'*

127   She was charmed by this, and her smile was so enticing
that it was like the moon revealing her full face from behind
a cloud. Then she let the movement of her fingers guide her
words. 'Young man, if you do not despise a lady of means,
one who up to this year had no association with any man,
I am offering you a sister. Admittedly you already have a
brother (I was not ashamed to make enquiries about this),

but what is there to prevent your adopting a sister as well? My approach to you is on the same terms as his. Merely deign at your pleasure to acknowledge a kiss from me as well.'

'But the boot is on the other foot,' I replied. 'It is I who must beg you by that beauty of yours not to disdain to accept this foreigner among your votaries. You will find me a devout follower, if you permit me to prostrate myself before you. And so that you may not think that I set foot in this shrine empty-handed, I award my brother to you as a gift.'

'Are you saying', she asked, 'that you are bestowing on me that boy who is your very life, the boy on whose kisses you hang, the boy whom you love as much as I want you to love me?' As she uttered these words, her voice exuded such charm, and so sweet a sound caressed the enraptured air that you would have imagined that the Sirens' harmonious song was borne on the breezes. So I was lost in wonder; the whole dome of heaven seemed in some way to shine more brightly on me. I took the liberty of asking the goddess's name.

'So did my maid not inform you that my name is Circe?' she replied. 'Not that I am the daughter of the Sun,* or that my mother at will ever held back the course of the smoothly gliding firmament. But if the Fates unite the two of us, I shall be in heaven's debt. Indeed, God's silent purpose is already achieving some end. Not without cause does Circe love Polyaenus, for between these names a mighty torch of passion is always set ablaze. So come to my embrace, if such is your pleasure. You need fear no prying eye, for your brother is far from here.'

These were the words Circe spoke. She enfolded me in arms softer than feathers, and bore me to the ground, which was decked with a coloured array of blossoms:

Such flowers as mother Earth on Ida's summit laid,
Roses and violets aglow, and the soft galingale,
And smiling lilies glistening from green meadows,
When Jupiter obtained the love that Juno gave
And felt his heart ablaze, engulfed in passionate fire.   5

Such was the turf and its soft grass that beckoned venery;
The day dawned brighter to enhance our secret love.*

128   *

[Circe to Polyaenus:] 'So what is the problem?'* she asked.
'Does my kissing grate on you? Am I lacking in vigour for
want of food? Have I not remedied the perspiration below
my arms? If it is none of these, does fear of Giton haunt
you?' My embarrassment was obvious, and what little strength
I had ebbed away. My whole body felt limp, and I said:
'Princess, do not compound my misery. Witchcraft has got
the better of me.'

                                 *

[Circe to her maid:] 'Be honest with me, Chrysis; am I
unattractive? Do I look dishevelled? Does some blemish of
nature cast a cloud over my beauty? Don't deceive your
mistress; somehow or other I have slipped up.' She then
snatched a mirror from the maid, who had nothing to say.
Circe rehearsed all the facial expressions which usually
awake geniality between lovers, and having shaken out the
creases from her dress caused by lying on the ground, she
bolted into the shrine of Venus. By contrast I stood there,
a condemned figure, like a person horror-struck at the
sight of a ghost. I began to ask myself whether the pleasure
of which I had been robbed was a true experience after
all:

> As in our nightly slumber, vivid dreams
> Beguile our errant eyes, when from the soil
> The spade in broad daylight uncovers gold.*
> Our greedy hands massage the stolen treasure;
> The sweat pours down our faces, and deep fear   5
> Pervades our minds, lest unseen witnesses
> Be privy to the hidden gold, lest they
> May then abstract it from our laden breasts.
> But once deceptive joys have fled our minds,
> Reality returns. Our hearts aspire   10

To the lost treasure, totally absorbed
In phantoms now behind us...

*

[Giton to Encolpius:] 'So on this count I thank you for
loving me as honourably as Socrates. Alcibiades*was not so
unscathed as I am, when he lay on his mentor's couch.'

*

129 [Encolpius to Giton:] 'My brother, you must believe me. I
have no awareness or feeling that I am a man. That part of
my body which once made me an Achilles*has been laid to
rest.'

*

The boy feared that if he were found sequestered with me,
people would start talking, so he wrenched himself away,
and fled into the heart of the house.

*

Chrysis made her way into my room, and handed me a
letter*from her mistress, which read as follows:

'Dear Polyaenus,
   If I were the randy sort, I would complain that you had
let me down. But as things stand, I am thankful for your
lack of urgency. For too long I have sported in pleasure's
shadow. I am writing to inquire about your health, and to
ask whether you were able to arrive home on your own two
feet. Doctors say that people who lose their sexual powers
are unable to walk. I warn you, young man: you may become
a paralytic. No sick person I have ever set eyes on is in such
grave danger. I swear that already you are as good as dead.
If the same chill gets to your knees and hands, you can send
for the funeral-pipers. So what must you do? Though you
have mortally insulted me, when a man is down I do not
begrudge him the remedy. If you wish to get better, you
must beg Giton for a break. If you sleep for three days

without him, you will recover your strength. As for myself, I have no fear of encountering any man who will find me less attractive than you do. After all, my mirror and my reputation do not lie.

Keep fit, if you can!

Circe'

When Chrysis saw that I had reached the end of this reproving letter, she said: 'Yours is a common state of affairs, and especially in this town, where women can even draw down the moon from the sky. So a remedy will be devised for your difficulty, as for the others. Merely reply to my mistress with some flattery; restore her spirits with ingenuous kindness. I have to say that she has not been herself since she was subjected to your affront.'

I obeyed the maid with alacrity, and put pen to paper like this:

130 'Dear Circe,

I confess, dear lady, my frequent faults, for after all I am human, and still in my youth. But never before this day has my wrongdoing incurred death. I admit my guilt to you, and deserve whatever punishment you impose. I am a traitor, a murderer, one who has profaned your shrine; devise a penalty for these crimes. If your verdict is to be execution, I shall come to you with my sword; if you are satisfied with a whipping, I shall hasten to my mistress unclothed. Only remember that the fault lay not in my person, but in my equipment. I myself was ready to campaign, but was bereft of arms. Who was responsible for this débâcle, I do not know. Perhaps my body was dilatory, and my desire outstripped it. Perhaps my longing for complete fulfilment caused me to wait too long, and so exhausted the pleasure—I cannot account for what happened. You bid me beware of the onset of paralysis—as if the malady which robbed me of the possibility of possessing you could intensify! This is the burden of my apology. If you will allow me to expiate my guilt, I will render you satisfaction . . .'

Once I had sent Chrysis off with such promises as these, I paid particular care to my body which had caused such offence. I dispensed with a bath, but rubbed myself down with a little perfumed oil, and had a filling meal of onions and snails' heads without gravy, accompanied by a modest glass of wine. I then settled myself for sleep with the gentlest of perambulations. I retired to my bedroom without Giton, for in my anxiety to appease the lady, I feared that my brother would impair my strength.

131   Next day I arose, sound in limb and mind, and made my way down to the same grove of plane trees, in spite of my being chary of that place of ill-augury. I hung about there among the trees, waiting for Chrysis to lead the way. After strolling about for a little while, I settled in the place where I had sat the previous day. Then Chrysis turned up, with a little old woman in tow. She greeted me with the words 'Well now, mister Disdainful, has sanity begun to take over?'

The old woman then produced from her pocket a twisted coil of different-coloured threads, and bound it round my neck. Then she mixed some dust with her saliva, dipped her middle finger in it, and signed my forehead as I tried to disengage from her.

*

After reciting this spell, the hag told me to spit three times, and then to drop pebbles three times down my shirt, after she had pronounced a spell over them and covered them with purple cloth. She then placed her hands on my member to test its virility. The sinews responded to her command more quickly than I can describe, and with a prodigious leap filled the old woman's hands. She was overjoyed, and said: 'Chrysis, my dear, just look at this hare that I've raised for others to hunt down!'

*

The waving plane tree spread its summer shade;
Daphne was wreathed with berries, cypresses swayed;
Shorn pines, their tops atremble, on every side

Enclosed us. Threading the trees a foaming brook
Sported with errant waters, and dislodged   5
Its pebbles with its splashing, grumbling course.
How apt a place for love! The nightingale,
A woodland bird, and Procne, city-bred,
Dotted the grass and gentle violets around.
They hymned their rustic dwelling in glad song.*   10

*

Circe lay languidly there, her marble neck resting on a
golden couch. She was fanning the still air with a myrtle-
branch. When she caught sight of me, the recollection of
the previous day's rebuff brought a momentary blush to her
cheeks. Then all her attendants were dismissed, and at her
invitation I took my place beside her. She laid the myrtle-
branch over my eyes, and once this partition, so to say, had
been set between us, her confidence grew. 'How is it with
you, my paralytic?' she asked. 'Have you come today in full
working order?'

    'Is that a question rather than an invitation?' I retorted. I
locked my whole body in her embrace, and enjoyed her kisses
to the full without the preliminaries of beneficent spells.

132   The very beauty of her body drew me into love-making.
Our lips joined noisily in kiss after kiss; our hands inter-
twined explored all the variations of love; and our bodies
closely joined to each other effected also the union of souls.*

*

The lady was wounded by such blatant affronts, and finally
resorted to revenge. She summoned her attendants, and
ordered me to be hoisted up and flogged. Still not satisfied
with inflicting this humiliating treatment, she summoned
all her seamstresses and the dregs of her household, and
ordered them to spit on me. I covered my eyes with my
hands, and made no plea for pardon, for I knew what I had
deserved. So after being whipped and spat upon, I was
hustled out of doors. Proselenus was likewise ejected, and
Chrysis got the strap. The whole household was down in the

mouth, grumbling to each other, and asking who had disturbed their mistress's composure.

*

So after weighing the pros and cons, I took a more positive attitude. I skilfully hid the signs of the whipping so that my ill-treatment would not amuse Eumolpus or depress Giton. The only thing I could do to save face was to pretend that I was exhausted. I tucked myself up in bed, and turned the entire fire of my anger on the cause of all my troubles.

Though thrice my hand took up the fearsome, two-edged
    steel,
Thrice did my body sudden enervation feel.
With less strength than a cabbage-stalk, I feebly banned
The weapon cruelly servicing my trembling hand.
No longer could I execute my earlier will.   5
My fearful member, colder than the winter's chill,
Shrank to my belly, within a thousand wrinkles hidden;
Its head could not be raised for punishment, though bidden.
Thus did the blackguard's mortal fear ensure frustration;
Words of abuse were more effective castigation.   10

So I raised myself on one elbow, and assailed my wanton parts with a speech on these lines: 'What have you to say for yourself, you living reproach to all men and gods alike? Even to cite your name in worthy conversation would be sacrilegious! Did I deserve this of you, that you should exalt me to heaven, and then drag me down to hell? That you should betray my green years in the flower of their early vigour, and harness me with the enervation of extreme senility? Come on, then; offer me the conventional defence.'

As I angrily poured out these words,

She looked away, and kept her eyes fixed on the ground.
Her face was no more softened by these opening words
Than pliant willow, or poppy with its drooping head.*

Once I had delivered this disgusting reproach, I too began to feel ashamed at my outburst, and feelings of shame flooded my heart for having forgotten my natural modesty, for having

exchanged words with that part of the body which men of
more austere stamp do not even acknowledge. But then,
after scratching my brow for some little time, I remarked:
'But what's wrong with my relieving my resentment with
reproaches that come naturally? Don't we regularly curse
other parts of our human frame—belly, or throat, and even
the head when it aches from time to time? And didn't Ulysses
have words with his heart, didn't figures of tragedy rebuke
their eyes as if they had ears?* Men who suffer from gout
curse their feet, and people with arthritis grumble at their
hands. Those with rheumy eyes berate them, and when
people stub their toes they blame the pain on their feet.

> 'You Catos, why do you wear that frosty look?
> Why slate my new and unpretentious book?
> The language is refined, the smile not grave,
> My honest tongue recounts how men behave.
> For mating and love's pleasures all will vouch;   5
> Who vetoes love's hot passion on warm couch?
> Hear Epicurus, father of truth, proclaim:
> "Wise men must love, for love is life's true aim!"'*

*

'Nothing rings so false as stupid prejudice; nothing is so
absurd as hypocritical morality . . .'

*

133 At the close of this declamation I summoned Giton. 'Tell
me,' I said, 'dear brother, and be honest about it. That
night when Ascyltus stole you from me, did he remain awake
to rape you, or was he satisfied to spend the night chastely
apart from you?' The boy touched his eyes, and in the most
solemn tones swore that Ascyltus had not taken him by
force . . .

*

I genuflected at the threshold, and made this entreaty to
the hostile deity:*

'Companion to the nymphs, and Bacchus' friend,
Assigned as guardian god by beauteous Dione
To roam rich forests; Lesbos of fair fame
And verdant Thasos hearken to your words;
All Lydia athwart its seven streams   5
Offers unceasing worship, and has raised
A temple in your town of Hypaepa.
Guardian of Bacchus, Dryads' true delight,
Come close, and hearken to my diffident prayer.
My hands are not awash with sombre blood,   10
Nor as a hostile foe have I profaned
Temples with violence.
                         Without resource,
Exhausted and impoverished, I have sinned,
But not with my whole person. He who errs
when left resourceless, surely bears less guilt.   15
This is my prayer: relieve my burdened mind,
Pardon this lesser sin, and when, in time,
Dame Fortune deigns to smile on me again,
Your glory I shall not neglect unsung,
But to your altar, holy one, shall come   20
The father of the flock, a hornèd goat.
With it the offspring of a plaintive sow,
A sacrificial suckling will be yours.
Within the bowls the year's new wine will foam;
Three times around your shrine with joyous steps   25
Our youth will circle, merry in their cups."

While I was reciting these lines, and keeping a careful eye
on my offering, the old hag entered the shrine, presenting an
ugly appearance with her dishevelled hair and black clothing.
She laid me hand on me, and led me out of the porch . . .

*

134 [The hag Proselenus to Encolpius:] 'What demonic owls
    have gnawed your nerve-ends? Or did you step on some shit
    or on a corpse at the crossroads after dark? You could not
    prove yourself even with a boy; what an effeminate, tired

weakling you are, puffing like a hack on a hill, toiling and
sweating to no purpose! Not satisfied with sinning yourself,
you have roused the anger of the gods against me . . .'

*

Again she led me unprotesting into the room of the priestess. There she pushed me on the bed, grabbed a cane from
the door, and beat me; again I offered no show of resistance. The cane splintered at the first stroke, and thus less-
ened the force of the blows; otherwise she might even have
split my head and broken my arms. This flagellation caused
me particular distress. I wept buckets, covered my head with
my right arm, and cowered back upon the pillow. She was
equally upset, and shed tears; she settled at the foot of the
bed, and began to utter trembling reproaches at her old
age for lingering in life too long. Then the arrival of the
priestess interrupted her.

'Whatever are the pair of you doing in my room?' she
asked. 'You're behaving as though you're at the grave of
one lately deceased! And this on a holiday, when even
mourners can afford a smile!'

'Oenothea,'* replied the hag, 'the young man whom
you see here was born under an evil star. He can sell his
goods to neither boy nor girl. You never set eyes on such
an unhappy creature. He has a wet washleather for a sexual organ. Put it like this: what sort of man do you think
would leave Circe's bed without having had a good time?'

On hearing this, Oenothea sat down between us, shaking
her head for some little time. 'I am the only person', she
said, 'who knows how to cure this illness. Don't either of
you imagine that my treatment is complicated. I want the
young fellow to spend a night with me . . . See if I don't
make it as stiff as a horn!

> All in the world before you does my will.
> At my behest the blossoming earth grows idle,
> Barren and withered, for its sap dries up.
> At my behest it lavishes its riches;

Crags and rough rocks spew water like the Nile. 5
For me the ocean makes its waves stand still,
Before my feet the winds restrain their blasts.
Rivers perform my bidding; at my command
Hyrcanian tigresses and snakes lie still.
Why speak of lesser things? The very moon, 10
Drawn by my spells, descends to earth; in fear
Phoebus perforce turns round his fiery steeds,
His course reversed. Such is the power of spells.
A maiden's rites could quench the flaming rage
Of bulls; Circe, descended from the Sun, 15
By magic spells transformed Odysseus' men;
Proteus is wont to take new shapes at will.
I too, one practised in such skills, will plant
Shrubs rooted on Mount Ida in the sea,
And streams in turn set on its lofty peak.* 20

135 I shuddered in panic at hearing promises which were the
stuff of legend, and I began to take a closer look at the old
woman . . .

*

'So do as I tell you,' screamed Oenothea . . . She carefully wiped her hands, leaned over the bed, and kissed me
repeatedly.

*

Oenothea set up an old table at the centre of the altar, and
covered it with burning coals. On it she warmed some pitch,
and patched up a cup which had cracked with age. When
she took down the wooden cup, the nail on which it hung
had fallen out with it, so she hammered it back into the
smoke-begrimed wall. She then slipped on a square-shaped
apron, and placed a massive kettle on the hearth. At the
same time she took up a long fork, and with it she lifted
from the kitchen rack a bag containing beans stored there
for cooking, and a mouldy scrag-end of pig's cheek slashed
in a thousand places. She loosened the string of the bag,
poured some of the beans out on to the table, and told me

to shell them carefully. I did as I was told, conscientiously
separating the beans from their grimy shells. But the woman
impatiently snatched them up, grumbling at my slow progress, and with a single movement tore off the shells with
her teeth and spat them out on the ground, where they lay
like dead flies.

*

For my part, I was admiring the ingenuity bred by poverty,
and a sort of artistry evident in each object:

No Indian ivory set in gold shone here;
No marble pavement gleamed beneath our feet,
Beguiling the earth-floor with its gift; instead,
A willow bed-frame topped with straw . . .
Cups moulded by a cheap wheel's easy turn;   5
Soft limewood drinking-bowls, and wooden plates
Made from the pliant osier-tree; and jars
Stained by the dregs of wine. The walls around,
Packed with light straw and random mud applied,
Were lined with rustic nails, from which there hung   10
A broom of slim reeds, tied with rushes green.
That lowly cottage guarded other wealth
Dangling from smoke-stained beams; soft service-berries,
Dried Cretan thyme, and clustered raisins hung,
Entwined amidst fragrant wreaths . . .   15

Such was the hostess Hecale of old,
Who dwelt on Attic soil, and merited
Commemorative rites. With wondrous tongue
The Muse of him who dwelt in Battus' town
Portrayed her, in the years of eloquence.*   20

*

136 While the old hag was sampling a scrap of the meat as
well, . . . and was then replacing the pig's cheek, which was
as old as she was, in the meat-safe by using the long fork,
the rickety chair, which had lent her extra height, collapsed
under her. Her own weight brought her down, and she was

thrown on to the hearth. The result was that the neck of the kettle broke, and the water put out the fire which was just gaining hold. Her elbow came into painful contact with a burning brand, and her entire face was coated with the ash that was thrown up. I jumped to my feet in alarm, and with a quiet grin hauled the old woman up . . . She at once dashed off to the neighbours to get the fire rekindled, so that nothing should delay the sacrifice.

*

So I made my way to the tiny entrance to the cottage . . .

*

Suddenly three sacred geese—I suppose they were used to demanding their daily rations from the old woman at midday—launched an attack on me. As I stood there trembling, they surrounded me with the most unholy and frenzied cackling. One of them ripped my shirt, and the second loosened the laces of my sandals and made off with them; the third, the leader and master of the savage onslaught, had no hesitation even in going for my leg with its jagged bill. So forgetful of the niceties, I wrenched a leg off the little table, and began to belt that most aggressive creature with the weapon in my hand. Not content with a perfunctory blow, I took my revenge by finishing off the goose:*

> So, to my thinking, the Stymphalian birds
> Were, through the skill of Hercules, constrained
> To head off skywards. So, too, Harpies*fled,
> Putrid with filth, once they had fouled the feast
> Of Phineus with their poison. The air above   5
> Shuddered and trembled at such novel cries;
> Heaven's court was plunged in disarray . . .

*

By now the two remaining geese had gathered up the beans, which were scattered here and there where they had rolled all over the floor. I imagine that the birds felt deprived of their leader, and had made their way back to the shrine.

I was elated both by my booty and by the revenge I had exacted. I threw the goose that I had killed behind the bed, and applied vinegar to the shallow wound on my leg.

Then I made plans to quit, for I feared that I would get a dressing-down. I gathered my belongings, and started to leave the place, but I was not yet clear of the doorway of the hovel when I saw Oenothea approaching, carrying an earthenware pot full of live coals. So I retraced my steps, threw my bundle of clothing down, and stood at the entrance as if I were waiting for her tardy return.

She set the live coals close to each other, enclosed them in some hollow reeds, and piled more fuel on top in the shape of sticks. She began to apologize for having been so slow in returning, saying that her lady friend had not allowed her to leave until she had downed the statutory three glasses. 'So what did you do', she asked, 'while I was away? And where are the beans?'

My presumption was that my action was praiseworthy, so I recounted the entire battle from beginning to end. Then, so that it would not continue to upset her, I produced the goose to atone for the loss. When the old hag clapped eyes on it, she raised such an outcry that you would have thought that the geese were back in the cottage again. So in my confusion and surprise that my exploit was branded as a new form of crime, I asked why she had flared up, and why she showed more feeling for the goose than for me.

137   She clapped her hands in annoyance. 'You villain!' she said. 'Do you dare even to ask? You do not realize the enormity of the crime you have committed. You have killed the favourite of Priapus, the goose on which all the married women dote. Let me free you of the delusion that your deed was innocent: if the magistrates get to hear of it, you'll be strung up. You have defiled my dwelling with blood; until today it has never been polluted. Your action will allow any enemy of mine with the inclination to have me stripped of my priesthood.'

*

'Please don't raise such an outcry,' I begged. 'I'll give you an ostrich to make up for the goose.'

*

As I stood there open-mouthed, she seated herself on the bed, and bewailed the goose's death. Meanwhile Proselenus turned up with the purchases for the sacrifice. When her eyes lit on the slaughtered goose, she asked what happened. Then she too started to keen still more loudly, expressing her grief on my behalf as if I'd killed my own father and not the town goose. I found it all so cloying and exhausting that I said: 'Look, let me purify my hands by paying for the bird . . . if I'd annoyed you, or even if I'd murdered someone. Here are two gold pieces for you to purchase geese and gods as well.'

When Oenothea saw the coins, she said: 'Young man, do forgive me. I am worried on your behalf, and this is a mark of affection, not of ill-will. So we'll make sure that no one hears of this. You must merely entreat the gods to pardon you for what you have done.

> 'If you have money, you can sail at ease;
> Your ship is driven by a wholesome breeze.
> Take Danaë to bed, and you'll persuade
> The girl, and father too, that she was laid
> By Jupiter. Money can help you be   5
> A poet, orator, one wholly free
> To snap your fingers at the world, outdo
> All comers in the courts—and Cato too!
> As jurist, "guilty" or "not guilty" show,
> Become a second Servius, or Labeo.   10
> No need for so much talk: if money's there,
> Just pray for what you want; it will appear!
> Your money-box holds Jupiter within;
> His presence there ensures that you will win."

She set a bowl of wine below my hands, parted each of my fingers over it, and cleaned them with leeks and parsley. She dropped hazelnuts into the wine, uttering a prayer as she did so. According as they floated back to the surface or settled at the bottom, she uttered auguries for the future, but I did not fail to notice that the hollow nuts stayed on the surface, while those heavy with the full nut inside were borne to the bottom.

*

She opened up the breast of the goose, and drew out its sturdy liver, and foretold my future from it. Moreover, to ensure that no trace of my crime remained, she slashed the goose across, and pinned the pieces on spits. She prepared quite an elegant meal for me, in spite of her claim just previously that I was doomed to die.

*

In the course of this, cups of neat wine were rapidly circulating . . .

*

138 Oenothea produced a leather phallus, sprinkled it with oil, ground pepper, and crushed nettle-seeds, and proceeded to insert it by degrees up my backside.

*

The sadistic old hag then sprayed my thighs with the stuff . . .

*

She mixed the nasturtium-juice with southernwood, and soaked my parts in it. Then she took up a bunch of green nettles, and with measured strokes began to whip all my body below the navel . . .

*

Though the pathetic old creatures were fuzzy with wine and sexual arousal, they followed the same route and chased me along several streets as I fled, shouting: 'Grab that thief!' But I made my escape. All my toes were oozing blood in my headlong flight . . .

*

'Chrysis abominated your previous career, but intends to follow you in your new life, even if it involves personal danger . . .'

*

'What was Ariadne's or Leda's beauty, compared with hers? How could Helen or Venus match her? Why, if Paris himself, who acted as arbiter between the competing goddesses, had run his wanton eyes over her and compared her with them, he would have passed over the goddesses and Helen too in her favour.* At any rate, if only I were allowed to steal a kiss, if only I could press that heavenly, godlike bosom to my own, perhaps my body would regain its strength, and my parts, which I suspect lie dormant through witchcraft, would return to their senses. The abuse she heaped on me does not damp my ardour; the floggings I have expunged from my mind; my summary ejection I count as mere sport. I pray only that I may regain her favour.'

*

139 The bed creaked as I tossed and turned, seeking to embrace the fugitive ghost of my loved one . . .

*

> That will divine, the unappeasable Fate,
> Seeks victims other than myself alone.
> Was Tiryns' son not driven from the shore
> Of Argos, made to bear the weight of heaven?
> Laomedon, for sacrilegious sin,   5
> Sated the anger of twin deities.
> Juno afflicted Pelias, and Telephus
> Was smitten by the angry Dionysus;
> Odysseus trembled at Neptune's domain.
> I too, o'er lands and hoary Nereus' seas,   10
> Am hounded by the heavy wrath of Priapus,
> Who haunts the region of the Hellespont.*

*

I proceeded to ask my Giton if anyone had sought me out. 'Not today,' he replied, 'but yesterday a quite elegant woman came in. She chatted with me for quite a time, and kept drawing me out till I was exhausted. Finally she claimed that you had incurred guilt, and that you would suffer a slave's punishment if the person you have wronged persisted in the complaint . . .'

*

I had not finished when Chrysis interrupted, and hugged me in a most fervid embrace. 'You are in my arms,' she said, 'the partner I hoped for and longed for, the joy of my life. The only way in which you will put out this fire of mine is if you quench it with my blood.'

*

One of the apprentice-slaves suddenly bustled up, and told me in no uncertain terms that my master was furious with me for having absented myself from duty for the past two days. He added that the advisable course for me was to devise some plausible excuse, as it seemed most unlikely that his furious rage would abate without my getting the whip.

*

13

Eumolpus and the Legacy-hunters

140   There was a married lady of outstanding respectability called
Philomela. She had often exploited the services of her
youthful body to wring out numerous legacies, but she was
now old, and her beauty's bloom had withered. So she would
foist her son and daughter on childless old men, and thus
continue to practise her profession by keeping it in the
family. For this reason she approached Eumolpus, saying
that she wished to entrust her children to his sage coun-
sel and upright nature ... She was putting herself and her
aspirations in his hands; he was the only person in the entire
world who could give the young ones a good grounding by
teaching them sound principles every day. In short, she was
leaving the children in Eumolpus' residence to listen to his
discourse; this was the only legacy which she could pass on
to her young charges.

She was as good as her word. She left her stunningly
beautiful daughter and the girl's adolescent brother in
Eumolpus' apartment, on the pretence that she was off to
the temple to recite her vows. Eumolpus, a man of such
chaste disposition that he regarded even myself as a likely
lad, did not delay in inviting the girl to some sacral sodomy.
But he had told everyone that he was gout-ridden and suffering from enervation in his loins, and he was in danger of
undermining the entire dramatic performance if he failed
to keep the pretence intact.

So to maintain the plausibility of the deception, he entreated the girl to sit on his 'upright nature', and bade
Corax crawl under the bed in which he lay, to do press-ups
on the floor, and thus keep his master mobile by push-
ing upwards with his loins. The slave obeyed the instruction
in slow measure, alternating his movements with the girl's

practised technique. Then, when things were reaching their
climax, Eumolpus loudly urged Corax to speed up the service. Between the slave and the girlfriend the old fellow
seemed to be riding up and down on a see-saw. Eumolpus
repeated the exercise a number of times, causing gales of
laughter in which he himself joined.

I did not wish to get out of practice, so while the brother
was watching his sister's performance through the keyhole,
I too made my approach to see if he would submit to my
advances. The boy was well schooled, and did not demur,
but on this occasion too that hostile deity searched me out . . .

*

'There are gods with greater power who have restored me
to full health; for Mercury, whose regular role is to escort
souls in both directions, has by his kindness restored to me
what an angry hand had removed. So you can realize that
I am more favoured than Protesilaus or any other of the
ancients.' With these words I lifted up my shirt, and fully
demonstrated the point to Eumolpus. To begin with, he
started back in consternation, but then to give full credence
to what he saw, he fondled the kindness of the gods with
both hands.

*

'Socrates, the cynosure of gods and men, used to boast that
he had never poked his head into a tavern, or lent his eyes
to any assembly where there was a large crowd. The moral
of this is that nothing is more profitable than perpetually
communing with wisdom . . .'

*

'All that you say', I agreed, 'is true. No class of men deserves
to fall more quickly into ill-fortune than the covetous. But
how would impostors and pickpockets gain a livelihood, if
they didn't bait their hooks by throwing wallets or jingling
moneybags among the crowd? We entice dumb animals with
titbits, and people are just the same—they would never be

inveigled if there was no gain in prospect for them to nibble
at . . .'

*

141 'The ship from Africa which you promised was bringing
your money and slaves has not arrived. The legacy-hunters
are now bled dry, and are cutting back on their generosity.
So if I'm not mistaken, the usual parlous state that we share
has begun to make its regrettable reappearance . . .'

*

'All those who are left legacies in my will, with the exception of my freedmen, will obtain my bequests only on one
condition, that they cut my body in pieces and eat it before
the eyes of the citizens . . .

'We know that there are certain nations which still observe the custom by which the bodies of the dead are consumed by their relatives. In fact the sick are often rebuked
for allowing their bodies to deteriorate. In view of this, I
urge my friends not to disregard my instructions, but to
devour my flesh with the same enthusiasm with which they
have prayed for my life's end . . .'

*

The pervasive rumour of his wealth blinded the poor fools
in their eyes and minds. Gorgias was quite ready to carry out
the instructions . . .

*

'I have no fear that your stomach will regurgitate me.
It must surely obey your command, if you promise it the
recompense of many delicacies, in return for the repug-
nance of a single hour. You must merely shield your eyes,
and imagine that what you have swallowed is not human
entrails but ten million sesterces. Then too we shall devise
some seasoning to disguise the taste. No flesh tastes good
on its own; it has to be artfully spiced to win over a reluctant stomach. If you wish to have my plan approved by the

additional justification of precedents, the Saguntines when overthrown by Hannibal ate human flesh, and they had no legacy to look forward to. The Petelians did the same when sorely beset by hunger; they too got nothing out of the feast except relief from starvation. When Numantia' was captured by Scipio, some mothers were found clutching the half-eaten corpses of their children to their breasts . . .'

Fragments, Testimonies, Poems

1 Servius on Virgil, *Aeneid* 3. 57, *auri sacra fames: sacra* here means 'accursed'; the word is taken over from Gallic custom. Whenever the Massilians were in the toils of a plague, one of their poor people would volunteer to be fed at public expense for a whole year on foods of ritual purity. He would then be decked out in foliage and sacred robes, and led round the whole city as the recipient of curses, so that the ills of the entire state could descend on him. He would then be cast out. This account appears in Petronius.*

2 Servius on Virgil, *Aeneid* 12. 159, on nouns of feminine gender ending in *-tor*: But if not derived from a verb, they are common in gender, both masculines and feminines ending similarly in *-tor*. For example, *senator* = 'male or female senator', *balneator* = 'male or female bath-attendant'. Mind you, Petronius arbitrarily uses *balneatrix*...

3 Pseudacro on Horace, *Epodes* 5. 48: 'Canidia biting her thumb'. He has depicted the behaviour and feelings of Canidia in a rage. Petronius in seeking to depict a person in a fury speaks of him 'biting his thumb to the quick'.

4 Sidonius Apollinaris, *Poem* 23:

> Why must I sing of you
> As founts of Latin eloquence,
> Sons of Arpinum, Padua,
> And Mantua? Or you,
> The Arbiter, and peer of Priapus   5
> God of the Hellespont?
> You settled in Massilian gardens,
> Where stands that hallowed trunk.*

5a Priscian, *Inst.* 8. 16, 11. 29, citing examples of past participles of deponents used in the passive sense: Petronius: 'the soul embraced within our breast'.

5*b* Boethius, *Commentary on Porphyry's Eisagoge in Victorinus'
translation*, 2. 32: 'Since, in Petronius' words, the sun has
now smiled on the housetops, let us suspend our discussion . . .'

6 Fulgentius, *Mythol.* 1: 'You do not realize . . . how much
married women stand in fear of satire. Before women's tide
of words advocates may yield, schoolmasters may cease to
burble, rhetoricians may be struck dumb, and heralds may
silence their cries. Satire alone can put a stop to their rav-
ing, even that of an Albucia* in heat in Petronius.'

7* Fulgentius, *Mythol.* 3. 8, explaining that essence of myrrh
is very strong: Petronius Arbiter too recounts that he drank
a cup of myrrh to excite his lust.

8 Fulgentius, *Expos. Virg. Cont.*: so too Petronius inveighs
against Euscius* as 'the advocate who was the Cerberus of
the courts'.

9 Fulgentius, *Expos. Serm. Antiq.* 42: *ferculum* means 'meat-
course'. So Petronius too says 'When the *ferculum* was brought
in'.

10 *Ibid.* 46: *valgia** denotes the twistings of the lips when
vomiting. So Petronius likewise says 'With lips twisted in
vomiting'.

11* *Ibid.* 52: *alucinare* means 'to have false dreams'. It is
derived from *alucitae*, the word equivalent to our 'mosquitoes'. Petronius Arbiter says: 'For the mosquitoes were
afflicting my bed-companion.'

12 *Ibid.* 60: *manubies* means 'royal adornments'. Hence
Petronius Arbiter likewise says: 'These numerous royal
adornments found in the possession of a runaway.'

13 *Ibid.* 61: *aumatium* means 'a corner in a public place',
such as theatres or the Circus. So Petronius Arbiter likewise
says: 'I launched myself into a hidden corner.'

14 Isidore, *Orig.* 5. 26: *dolus* means a deceiver's mental
cunning, for he does one thing while pretending to do
another. Petronius takes another view in these words: 'Gen-
tlemen of the jury, what does *dolus* mean? It surely applies
to an action prejudicial to (*quod . . . dolet*) the law. So much
for *dolus*; now what *malum* means . . .'

15 Glossary of St Dionysius: *petaurus* is a sort of game. Petronius has: 'Now rising higher at the urging of the trampoline.'

16 *Ibid.*: Petronius writes: 'So it was quite clear that they usually passed through the tunnel at Naples only by crouching low.'

19 Terentianus Maurus, *On metres*:

> The verse of Horace, as we see,
> Is of this metre wholly free.
> But Arbiter, with eloquent pen,
> Employs it time and time again.
> No doubt you readily recall   5
> The chant familiar to us all:
> 'Maidens of Memphis,* all arrayed
> To attend the sacred gods' parade;
> A boy as dusky as the night;
> His hands depict the sacred rite.   10

Marius Victorinus, 3. 17: We know that lyric poets inserted some lines with this rhythm and shape in their compositions. We also find them in the Arbiter; for example,

> Maidens of Memphis, all arrayed
> To attend the sacred gods' parade;
> A boy as dusky as the night
> Depicts the Egyptians' choral rite.

20 Terentianus Maurus, *On metres*:

> This arrangement, now to be reported,
> Will reveal the metre which Anacreon
> Used, so they say, for his delightful verses.
> Petronius also used this very metre
> In recording that the same lyric poet   5
> Sang out words which accommodate the Muses.
> So did several others. Let me now state
> How the caesura is incorporated.
> *Iuuerunt segetes meum laborem*
> ['Thus did the harvest delight my body's labour']:

Here *iuuerunt* launches a hexameter;
Then what's left, *segetes meum laborem,*
Scans just like *triplici uides ut orto*
              Triviae rotetur ignis,
              Volucrique Phoebus axe   15
              Rapidum pererret orbem.
          ['You see how Trivia,
          From her triple rising,
          Rotates her star, and how
          Phoebus' flying chariot   20
          Traverses its swift circle']

Marius Victorinus 4. 1: The metre will be Anacreontic, so
called because Anacreon used it so often, but so did several
of our Latin poets, among them Arbiter in his *Satyricon,* who
writes *triplici . . . orbem* (as above).

21* Diomedes, *On grammar* 3: Hence the caesura employed
by Arbiter as follows:

              Anus recoctus uino
              Trementibus labellis
          ['An old hag, wine-soaked,
          Lips all atremble']

22 Servius, *On the Grammar of Donatus:* Then too he uses
Quirites only in the plural. But in Horace we read *hunc
Quiritem* ['this citizen'], so that in this instance there is the
nominative *Quiris.* Horace also writes *Quis te Quiritem?* ['Who
has restored you as citizen?']. The nominative in this instance
will be *Quirites,* a form used by Petronius.

   Pompeius, in his commentary on the Grammar of Donatus:
No one says *hic Quirites* ['this citizen'] but *hi Quirites* ['these
citizens'], though we have seen the former written. Read
Petronius, and you will find this usage of the nominative
singular, for Petronius writes *hic Quirites.*

23 A grammarian on nouns of doubtful gender: *fretum*
['strait'] is neuter, and its plural is *freta.* Petronius has *freta
Nereidum* ['straits of the Nereids'].

24 Jerome, *Ep.* 130. 19: a virgin should avoid like the plague

boys who have curled and wavy hair, and whose skins smell
like musk-rats, for they are a pernicious threat to chastity.
Arbiter is referring to them when he says that the man who
always gives off pleasant odours is malodorous.

25* Fulgentius, *Mythol.* 2. 6 on Prometheus: but Nicagorus
records that Prometheus was the first to have embodied the
image. His yielding his liver to a vulture depicts a metaphor
for envy. So too Petronius Arbiter writes:

> That vulture which probes the liver deep within us
> Extracting our heart and our inmost sinews,
> Is no bird, as our witty poets call it,
> But lust and envy, the canker of our being.

26 By laying eggs at harvest-time, the crow
    Flies in the face of Nature's well-known law.
    The she-bear licks her cub to shape its girth;
    Fish need no joys of love to bring to birth.
    Apollo's tortoise shuns Lucina's harm,   5
    Hatching its eggs with breath from nostrils warm.
    Bees that with valiant troops their camp-ground fill,
    Roused from their waxen hives, are virgin still.
    To stereotype her ways Nature is loth;
    She loves to ring the changes in her growth.   10

27* Fear was the gods' begetter in this world,
    When from high heaven lightning-bolts crashed down
    And towns were shattered in the flames. Athos
    Was struck, and glowed with fire. Then Phoebus' orb
    Ducked down below the earth it had traversed,   5
    To rise again; the moon waned, then regained
    Its glory; spangled stars then decked the heavens;
    The year was marked out by the changing months.
    That falsehood flourished, that unfounded flaw
    Impelled the farmers to offer their first fruits   10
    To Ceres, to bind Bacchus' brow with leaves
    Of palm-trees, and shepherds to give delight
    To Pales with their handiwork. In their turn
    Neptune demands allegiance in the deep

From voyagers, Pallas from those on land   15
Dwelling in hostelries. The man forsworn,
And he who'd sell the whole world for a price,
Each manufactures gods for his own use,
In greedy competition.

28 People would rather nurse flames in their mouths
Than keep a secret. Suppose that you divulge
Some scandal in a courtyard; out it flows,
Striking with sudden rumours distant towns.
It's not enough to violate a trust;   5
The betrayal spawns additions, and works hard
To make the story still more grievous. When
That slave was burning to reveal the deed,
He fearfully dug a hole into the ground,
Entrusting there the secret of the king*   10
Who'd sprouted ass's ears. The earth absorbed
His whisperings, and chattering reeds betrayed
The informer's secret words of Midas' plight.

29* Eyes are deceivers, and our erring senses
Downgrade our reason, and project their falsehoods.
That tower close by, with its four-square structure,
Seems round from far off, rubs away its corners.
Taste-buds when overstuffed spurn Hyblean honey;   5
Often our nostrils loathe the scent of casia.
One thing could not seem better than another,
If our senses were not locked in disputes,
With doubtful outcome warring on each other.

30* Our dreams with fleeting shadows mock our minds.
They do not emanate from shrines of gods,
Nor do divinities launch them from the sky;
We each compose our own, for when our limbs
Are overcome in sleep, and quiet reigns,   5
Our disembodied minds enjoy their sport,
Rehearsing in the night their daytime thoughts.
The man who causes towns to shake in war,
And levels wretched cities with fierce flames,

Beholds in sleep war-weapons, routed lines,   10
The deaths of kings, and plains awash with blood.
The lawyers, who routinely plead a case,
Envisage laws and court-scenes—and dismayed
They see the daïs ringed with armèd men.
The miser hoards his wealth, or lights on gold   15
Extracted from the earth. The huntsman dreams
Of flushing out the woodland with his hounds.
The sailor saves his vessel from the waves,
Or grabs its upturned keel, confronting death.
The mistress pens a letter to her gallant,   20
The adulteress bestows on hers a gift.
The sleeping dog scents traces of the hare
And barks . . .

(Numeration of these fragments follows that of Bücheler's
1862 edition, subsequently followed by Müller, whom I follow in excluding 17–18, 31–53 as being non-Petronian or as
being irrelevant to the *Satyricon.*)

Explanatory Notes

1. At the School of Rhetoric

In this first extant scene, Petronius casts a satirical eye over the Roman system of higher education; the Elder Seneca, Quintilian, and Tacitus in his *Dialogus* provide damning evidence of its remoteness from the real world. See S. F. Bonner, *Roman Declamation* (Liverpool, 1949); M. L. Clarke, *Rhetoric at Rome* (London, 1953), ch. 8. Scholarly opinions vary on whether Petronius seriously identifies himself with the criticisms expressed by Encolpius and Agamemnon. I take the view that Encolpius' contribution is a *mélange* of banal clichés and dubious judgements which make him a walking parody of the *scholasticus* as represented on the mimic stage; see G. Sandy, *TAPA* (1974), 329 ff., and the notes below. Encolpius himself stigmatizes his utterance as a declamation (§ 3).

§ 1 *nothing but verbal gob-stoppers*: the declamations took the form of *controuersiae*, or discussions of hypothetical cases at law, or *suasoriae*, advice offered to historical or mythological characters on momentous occasions. The examples cited here of the themes, and earlier of the style of the utterances, are no exaggeration.

2 *Sophocles . . . Demosthenes*: the references to the giants of Greek literature are banalities. 'Pindar and the nine lyric poets' (Alcman, Stesichorus, Sappho, Alcaeus, Ibycus, Anacreon, Simonides, Bacchylides; Pindar himself is conventionally the ninth!) 'shied from Homeric measures' by composing in lyric metres rather than in heroic hexameters. Plato and Demosthenes are the pre-eminent stylists in Greek philosophical writing and in oratory respectively.

from Asia to Athens: condemnation of the florid Asianic style is a conventional feature of rhetorical criticism (see e.g. Cicero, *Brutus* 325 ff.).

Thucydides or Hyperides: Thucydides was justly celebrated as historian, but even his admirer Dionysius is critical of his style (*De Thuc.* 51); he was scarcely a model for the aspiring orator. Hyperides, pupil of Plato and of Isocrates, was for ancient critics 'the pentathlete among orators, second only to Demosthenes as an all-round speaker' (so G. A. Kennedy, *CHCL* i. 525). The pairing is a further anomaly in the tirade.

Painting . . . pursuit: the wild generalization (it is not clear to which tradition Encolpius refers) further undercuts any temptation to take Encolpius' lecture seriously.

3 *Agamemnon*: the derisive name for the teacher recalls the formulaic 'Lord of the host' in Homer; his assistant is called Menelaus (§§ 27, 81). Kennedy (*AJP* (1978), 171 ff.) suggests that because Agamemnon has vacated the hall, he is a visitor rather than the resident teacher, but this is implicitly refuted in § 48; it is hardly likely that the town boasts two schools of rhetoric.

in Cicero's words: cf. *Pro Caelio* 41.

4 *score out with ruthless pen*: I retain the reading *atroci* against Müller's *Attico*.

the . . . utterances of a Lucilius: at first sight the connection between this reference and what precedes is obscure. But Lucilius, the father of Roman satire (died 102/1 BC) was mildly criticized by Horace (*Sat.* 1. 10. 56 ff.) for over-rapid composition and lack of polish. Agamemnon may be hinting at these weaknesses in his regard.

5 *insolent palace . . . dinners of intemperate hosts . . . sit . . . before the stage*: it is tempting to construe this as Petronian irony on two levels: more obviously, Agamemnon offers hypo-critical advice as a future parasite at Trimalchio's table, but perhaps also Petronius is ridiculing his own role as *arbiter elegantiae* at the court of Nero, who was an enthusiastic performer on the public stage; see Tacitus, *Annals* 14. 21.

Whether the smiling citadel: in the Latin, the metre switches at this point from the scazon to the dactylic hexameter; the change of measure in the English signals the end of the 'Lucilian' sequence.

armed Tritonis . . . the Spartan immigrant . . . the Sirens: 'Armed Tritonis' (line 13) is Athena, regularly represented in her cult-statues as armed because of her functions in war. 'The

Spartan immigrant' (line 14) lives at Tarentum, originally
a Spartan colony. The Sirens (line 15) are associated with
Surrentum on the western coast of Italy. Thus the verses
encourage both Athenian and Italian students to follow
the curriculum which ensues.

the pool Maeonian . . . Socrates' school . . . Demosthenes' armoury:
education in the Roman secondary school began with
Homer; 'Maeonian' (line 18) means 'Homeric', because
both Smyrna and Colophon in 'Maeonia' (= Lydia) claimed
to be Homer's birthplace. For Plato ('Socrates' school', line
19) and Demosthenes (line 21) as admired models, see
§ 2 above.

Roman poets: by the age of Nero, successful Roman poets
(especially Virgil, Horace and Ovid) were studied in the
schools; see H. I. Marrou, *A History of Education in Antiquity*
(London, 1956), 277.

Proclaiming Fortune . . . feasts . . . war's harsh blasts: it is not
clear whether lines 27–9 are a prescription for a student's
reading or writing; more probably, they advocate written
exercises on historical and dramatic themes.

2. *Dubious Encounters in the Town*

6 *Agamemnon's set piece of persuasion*: for the *suasoria*, see § 1
above. Presumably the teacher had provided a model for
the student to follow.

I had failed to take careful note of the route: the trio are recent
arrivals in the town (see § 11), which scholars identify vari-
ously as Naples, Cumae, Misenum, Formiae, Minturno, and
even Capua. The most favoured location is Puteoli, but the
evidence is inconclusive.

7 *I'd been brought to a brothel*: this passage offers one of the
most detailed descriptions of a Roman brothel; see F.
Henriques, *Prostitution and Society* (London, 1962), 124 ff.

8 *the whole town had been downing aphrodisiacs*: Encolpius is
reflecting on his and Ascyltus' recent experiences. His
friend's recent escort, or more probably another towns-
man, has been making further sexual advances. On the
aphrodisiac, see Pliny, *NH* 26. 10.

3. Jealousy at the Lodging

In this scene Encolpius appears as the typical jealous man of mime and of Roman Comedy; cf. K. Preston, *CP* (1915), 165 f.

> 9 *Giton*: this is the first appearance of the comely slave in the extant sections of the novel. For a fuller description of him, see § 97; on his character, P. George, *Arion* (1966), 338 ff.
>
> *If you are Lucretia*: for the celebrated story of the rape of Lucretia, see Livy 1. 58; for the mimic presentation of the incident here, see Walsh, *Roman Novel*, 87.
>
> *saved by the midday Circus crowd*: for the reading, *quem meridiana harena dimisit*, see *CR* (1967), 137. Seneca, *Ep.* 7. 3, explains that at the midday session in the arena, murderers were disposed of by confronting an unarmed man with one armed.
>
> 10 *our scholarly status*: *scholasticus* in the Elder Seneca means 'a declamation-buff', an enthusiastic amateur who frequents the lecture-halls without being an enrolled student; see Kennedy, *AJP* (1978), 171 ff.

4. An Episode in the Market

As P. Corbett, *Petronius* (New York, 1970), 49, comments, this episode would provide a characteristic plot for a mime or an Atellane farce. Pomponius wrote a *fabula Atellana* called *Rusticus*, and there was a *fabula palliata* (Roman adaptation of New Comedy) called *Tunicularia*. The *Aulularia* of Plautus contains similarities of plot.

> 12 *the stolen cloak*: the trio must have stolen it in a lost episode set in the countryside, where Encolpius had deposited his shirt.
>
> 13 *our treasure still intact*: this money may have been rifled from the house of Lycurgus which the hero later (§ 117) confesses that he had burgled.
>
> *a most foul suspicion*: Ascyltus must have accused Encolpius of appropriating the money.
>
> 14 *the very Cynics who scorn modern ways*: the Cynic sect, founded by Diogenes of Sinope in the fourth century BC,

preached a doctrine of happiness by satisfaction of needs in the cheapest, most natural, and most shameless way; hence their name, which means 'doglike'. The sect made a striking revival in the early Empire; Demetrius, a notable Cynic, was praised by Seneca for his castigation of wealth and luxury. See A. A. Long, *Hellenistic Philosophy* (London, 1974), 234.

The knights who sit empanelled: jurors in criminal trials and judges in civil law were in Petronius' day drawn from three equestrian panels or *decuriae*; see A. N. Sherwin-White on Pliny, *Ep.* 4. 29. 1, with bibliography.

apart from one shekel and some counterfeit coins: (Reading *unum sicel lupinosque quibus* . . . ; cf. now G. Schmeling, *Mnem.* (1992), 531 ff.) The *sicel* (Hebrew *sekel*) circulated widely in the cosmopolitan area of the Bay of Naples. Lupine seeds were used as counterfeit money, notably on the stage (cf. Plautus, *Poenulus* 597 ff.; Horace, *Ep.* 1. 7. 22 f.).

the dealers: these *cociones* appear in the mimes of Laberius (see *OLD*); the description of one of them in § 15 encourages us to regard him as a mimic figure.

15 *suddenly*: I adopt Müller's earlier emendation, *repente*, which he later rejects.

security men on the evening shift: a rather free rendering of *aduocati nocturni*, who had a quasi-legal standing as assistants to the magistrates. They play a venal role in Plautus, *Poenulus* 515 ff.

trustees: disputed property was lodged with these officials (*sequestri*) when a court case was anticipated. See Plautus, *Rudens* 1004; *Vidularia* 95.

as we thought: the reservation hints at a complication; perhaps worthless coins had been substituted for the gold.

To sate . . . on a plate: this verse-fragment may be misplaced. The language suggests an erotic context; it would more aptly appear before § 11.

5. *Enter Quartilla, the Priapic Priestess*

16 In this second encounter with a disreputable figure of the age (Agamemnon is the first), Petronius directs his irony

at Roman religious ritual. In an earlier lost scene, the trio
have illicitly witnessed an orgiastic ceremony in the shrine
of Priapus. Since so much of the action of the novel is
parody of epic, it is tempting to conclude that the anger of
Priapus is a dominant theme, like that of Poseidon in the
Odyssey, and of Juno in the *Aeneid.* Certainly the motif of
the anger of Priapus is sustained (see §§ 104, 128, 137,
139), but some critics regard the references as too scattered to maintain the thesis (see, e.g., B. Baldwin, *CP* (1973),
294 ff.; M. Coffey, *Roman Satire* (London, 1976), 185). What
is clear is that this episode bears similarity to the action of
the low stage. Augustine (*Civ. Dei* 6. 7) mentions a Priapus-
mime, and the characters and incidents recall mimic con-
texts, as the notes below confirm. For a full discussion, see
C. Panayotakis, *Mnem.* (1994), 319 ff.; Slater, *Reading
Petronius,* ch. 3.

17 *easier to find a god here*: Quartilla's nymphomania is anticipated here.

barely a thousand mortals: Müller and Sullivan accept Nisbet's
emendation of *mille* to *tres,* but the paradoxically high figure
may point to the priestess's libidinous behaviour.

19 *with the laughter of the low stage*: this is one of several
pointers to the mimic nature of the scene.

At that moment of bewilderment: the heroes are presumably
disconcerted by the arrival of the rest of Quartilla's retinue, who supervise the sexual humiliation of the trio, and
later lay on the banquet.

22 *painted his torso*: reading *latera* for *labra* in Müller.

two Syrians: for the ill-repute of Syrians, see, e.g., Cicero,
De Or. 2. 265. The slapstick that follows further underlines
the mimic nature of the scene.

23 *in came a catamite*: it is not clear if this is the same character who appeared in § 21; the description that follows suggests he is a different person. For the *cinaedus* as a mimic
character, see Sandy, *TAPA* (1974), 340 n. 25. The indecent
song that follows is a feature of mimic performances; see
Quintilian 1. 2. 8 for such songs sung at the dinner-table.

the Delian's knife: the allusion is to the healing god Apollo, who
'personally performs the operation so that the patients shall

not suffer' (so E. Courtney, *The Poems of Petronius* (Atlanta, 1991), 19, citing Ovid, *Amores* 2. 3. 3). Courtney also suggests taking *molles ueteres* as 'effeminates of long standing'.

24 *a tumbler to have in bed*: the Greek word *embasicoetas* means both a drinking cup and a person who lies down; Encolpius was expecting to get a sleeping-draught, but Quartilla exposes his *naïveté*.

25 *demanded a wedding*: the mock-marriage may have had its inspiration in mime; Laberius wrote a mime entitled *Nuptiae*; cf. also the Elder Seneca, *Controv.* 2. 4. 5. Quartilla and Encolpius are the audience, so to say, for the performance.

Juno strike me down: the Latin speaks of 'my Juno's anger', Juno being to a woman what *genius* or native spirit is to a man. As the goddess's particular function is concerned with a woman's sexual life, the oath is apt.

6. *Dinner at Trimalchio's*

For the suggestion that the entire episode is the narrative equivalent of a mimic performance, see Sandy, *TAPA* (1974), 331 ff. ('A nine-scene skit . . . with a startling, eye-catching entrance . . . concluded by the noisy, precipitate departure of Encolpius, Giton, and Ascyltus . . .').

26 *the free dinner*: as Smith points out in his Commentary (p. 51), this cannot refer to Trimalchio's dinner, since the heroes were regarding 'the free dinner' with apprehension, whereas the news of Trimalchio's dinner comes as a relief. *Libera cena* is the technical phrase for the preliminary meal offered to men who are to confront the wild beasts in the arena, the ancient equivalent of the condemned criminal's hearty breakfast. The 'free dinner' was perhaps to be provided by Quartilla's ménage prior to the climax of the orgiastic ceremonies.

Trimalchio: he is the third contemporary type in the extant sections of the novel to be selected for satirical portraiture. For the characterization, see the Introduction, p. xxvii ff.

27 *thrown in the course of the game*: for the various ball games played by the Romans (this may be the game known as *lusus trigo*) see Balsdon (see list of Abbreviations), 163 ff.

Menelaus: Agamemnon's assistant (cf. § 81) at the school of rhetoric.

28 *we had raised a sweat . . . cold plunge*: the guests pass from the sauna (*laconicum*) to the cold bath (*frigidarium*). For the various divisions of the bath, see Balsdon, 29.

commemorating him: Trimalchio says this with a broad grin. The brawl enacts, so to say, the gladiatorial contest at funeral-games, and the spilt wine is the funeral-libation.

four bemedalled runners: this is the first of several striking parallels between Trimalchio and the appearance and entourage of the emperor Nero (see Suetonius, *Nero* 30). Trimalchio is not being presented as a comic Nero, for such a comparison between the youthful emperor and the ageing buffoon would be ludicrous; rather, Trimalchio is given the status of a posturing *princeps*.

his boy-favourite: this is Croesus, soon to reappear at the dinner (§ 64).

a dappled magpie: for the magpie which greets guests as they enter, one of many touches in the novel drawn from contemporary life, see Pliny, *NH* 10. 78. Petronius clearly regards it as the essence of vulgarity.

29 *a massive dog*: there are several such representations of dogs in mosaic at Pompeii, a further demonstration of the vulgarity of the age.

holding a herald's wand; Minerva was escorting him: the herald's wand is the symbol of Mercury, god of commerce and Trimalchio's favourite deity. Minerva, as the god of skilled craftsmen (cf. § 43), is a flattering escort as he enters Rome, perhaps to be sold there.

Trimalchio's beard was stored: the *depositio barbae*, marking the transition to manhood, was a solemn occasion for Romans, but not for an ex-slave from Asia. It seems all the more likely that Petronius as earlier is drawing a parallel with Nero, whose first shaving-hairs were likewise enclosed in a golden casket (Suetonius, *Nero* 12).

Laenas' Gladiatorial Games: Laenas is probably a local magnate and magistrate who has financed a show. Trimalchio's vulgarity extends to his undiscriminating mingling of epic themes.

30 *a bundle of rods and axes*: the pretentiousness of the host knows no bounds; these are the consular insignia. The bronze beak on display as a trophy would indicate an admiral's success in a naval battle. Trimalchio's priesthood was a petty office held by wealthy freedmen supervising the emperor's cult in a provincial town.

the moon . . . seven planets: Petronius here offers a preliminary indication of another strand in Trimalchio's characterization, superstition and morbidity; see the Introduction, p.xxxii.

Right feet first: this is further evidence of Trimalchio's superstition. The Romans considered it propitious to set out on a journey with the right foot.

a slave stripped for flogging: it is the mark of Trimalchio's grandiose establishment that as in the imperial house the higher echelon of slaves have their own attendants.

the steward's clothes . . . at the baths had been stolen: this was a familiar hazard. Compare the comic story in Apuleius, 9. 21. 6; other passages are cited by Smith (see Abbreviations).

no more than ten thousand sesterces: Smith defends this reading of *L* (the parent of several MSS breaking off at § 37) against 'ten sesterces' in *H* (the sole MS of the entire *Cena*). This is an indication of the extravagance rife in the establishment. See Martial 4. 61. 4 f. for a cloak costing ten thousand sesterces.

They were Tyrian . . . but . . . laundered once: connections with Nero are perhaps again visible here. The emperor reputedly imposed a prohibition on the wearing of luxurious garments of Tyrian purple; he himself was said never to wear the same garment twice (Suetonius, *Nero* 30, 32).

31 *master's wine . . . gift*: a homespun proverb; cf. M. Hadas, *AJP* (1929), 378 ff.

Alexandrian slave-boys: 'Alexandrian' in Roman eyes connoted eastern degeneracy; cf. Quintilian 1. 2. 7, etc.

a dancer's supporting-group: the *pantomimus* was a ballet-performer acting out a mythological or literary role to the accompaniment of singers or instrumentalists; see Balsdon, 274 ff.

a top place: the Latin, *locus primus*, refers to the top place
on any of the three couches in the diagram below. The
place of honour, *imus in medio*, was reserved for Trimalchio's
friend Habinnas the stonemason. The host at dinner normally reclined *summus in imo*. One side of the table was left
open for service. Unusually at this dinner each guest has
his own small table (see § 34).

PLACINGS AT TABLE

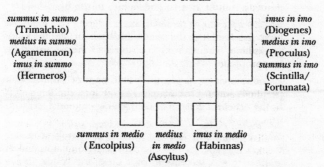

summus in summo
(Trimalchio)
medius in summo
(Agamemnon)
imus in summo
(Hermeros)

imus in imo
(Diogenes)
medius in imo
(Proculus)
summus in imo
(Scintilla/
Fortunata)

summus in medio
(Encolpius)

medius
in medio
(Ascyltus)

imus in medio
(Habinnas)

32 *a napkin with a broad purple stripe*: Trimalchio invests himself with the dignity of a curule magistrate, whose toga was
similarly decorated.

*a huge gilt ring . . . a smaller one . . . solid gold . . . studded with
iron stars*: rings were a popular affectation among the
wealthy (see Seneca, *NQ* 7. 31). Only equestrians of free
birth were allowed to wear gold rings (Pliny, *NH* 33. 32).
So Trimalchio's most prominent ring is gilt, and the other
of pure gold is hidden by iron stars, which make it an
amulet, another mark of his superstition.

a golden bracelet: another feature shared with the emperor
Nero (Suetonius, *Nero* 6).

33 *the game*: perhaps this was *ludus duodecim scriptorum*
(Balsdon, 156).

terebinth wood: the wood of the turpentine-tree was frequently used in costly furnishing.

gold and silver denarii: a gold *denarius* was worth twenty-
five silver *denarii*, each of which was worth sixteen asses. A

legionary in the late first century AD was paid seventy-five silver *denarii* a year.

this tableau: the word (*scaena*) is suggestive of a stage set. Throughout the dinner there is a series of such scenes, in many of which Trimalchio engineers unexpected effects against the background of musical performance.

34 *loudly authorized*: a mark of the boorish host.

long-haired Ethiopians: like the Alexandrian slaves, they impart a hint of eastern degeneracy to the household.

who sprinkle water on the sand: this rendering (cf. Smith, ad loc.) is preferable to the usual translation, 'scatter the sand' (so Sullivan's translation), for which a wineskin would be inappropriate.

poured wine on our hands: this would be wine thinned with perfumed water. Cf. Plutarch, *Phocion* 20, a condemnation by the Athenian general of the washing of guests' feet with wine and aromatic herbs.

those stinking slaves: it is the mark of the arrogant master to treat his slaves at one moment with contempt, and at another to wax sententious over them; see Walsh, *Roman Novel*, 129 f.

Falernian wine of Opimian vintage: Trimalchio vainly tries to hoodwink his guests with spurious labels. Opimius was consul in 121 BC; wine of that date would be undrinkable, but 'Opimian' is sometimes used for any venerable vintage (Martial 1. 26. 7). Wine was not bottled in glass so early, and the phrase *diligenter gypsatae* reflects Encolpius' suspicions. For other views of the fraud, see P. Bicknell, *AJP* (1968), 347 ff.; B. Baldwin, *AJP* (1967), 173 ff.

let us drink and be merry: the reading *tangomenas* is uncertain, and the rendering speculative.

a skeleton of silver: it was a diversion at dinner parties to introduce a skeleton, but Petronius develops the motif to underline Trimalchio's morbidity. See M. Coffey, *Roman Satire*, 188, 268 n. 50; N. Horsfall, *G&R* (1989), 199. The mediocre verses that follow unite in the Latin a hexameter with an elegiac couplet, a demonstration of Trimalchio's comic incompetence as *littérateur*. Orcus, god of the underworld, frequently represents the personification of death.

35 *plate . . . honeycomb on it*: the dish indicates Trimalchio's
     superstitious addiction to astrology. The associations of the
     various foodstuffs with the signs on which they are placed
     are mostly self-explanatory. There was a type of pea known
     as 'ram's head' (Pliny, *NH* 18. 124); a crown (rather than a
     garland) was placed on the Crab because the monarch
     Trimalchio was born under this sign (see § 39); the African
     fig has geographical connections with the lion. There is
     controversy over *oclopetam*, here rendered by 'crow'—it may
     mean 'eye-seeker' because the crow attacks a corpse's eyes,
     or it may mean a fish with staring eyes like an archer's tar-
     get; the lobster's claws resemble the goat's horns; the goose
     presages rain. The turf in the centre represents the earth,
     as Trimalchio explains in his idiosyncratic interpretations
     of the signs in § 39.

     a mime-song from The Silphium Gatherer: the mime is other-
     wise unknown. The mimic motif may have arisen from
     earlier discussion of the Zodiac dish, for Laberius wrote
     several mimes with titles such as *Aries, Cancer, Gemelli.*

     the dinner menu: Trimalchio makes one of his execrable
     puns; *ius cenae* can mean 'the rule for dinner' or 'the sauce
     for dinner'.

36 *a veritable Pegasus*: Pegasus was the winged horse which when
     tamed by Bellerophon assisted him to prevail over the
     Chimaera and other foes; see *OCD.*

     Marsyas . . . the channel: the satyr Marsyas challenged Apollo
     to a musical contest, and when worsted was flayed alive. He
     is represented in statuary with a wineskin over his shoulder
     (cf. Horace, *Sat.* 1. 6. 120). The fish are in a channel run-
     ning round the edge of the tray, and are thus separated
     from the meats; the first meaning of Euripus is the chan-
     nel between Attica and Euboea.

     a charioteer engaging to the music of a water-organist: the
     essedarius frequently competed at gladiatorial shows. Water-
     organs were as old as the third century BC; Nero showed
     great interest in them (Pliny, *NH* 7. 125; Suetonius, *Nero*
     41).

     Carve 'er, Carver: Lowe's witty rendering of *Carpe, carpe* in his
     edition of the *Cena.*

the man reclining next to me: this is Hermeros, whose criticism of the boorishness of Ascyltus and Giton extends through §§ 57–8; he is cited by name in § 59.

37   *all the gossip*: the conversation of the freedmen here and in §§ 41 ff. 'comes closer to our modern conception of realistic presentation than anything else that has come down to us from antiquity' (E. Auerbach, *Mimesis* (Princeton 1953), 30 ff.).

a real magpie of the couch: the phrase suggests chattering and back-biting.

he can box and bury: literally, 'he will consign to a rue-leaf'.

38   *from Tarentum*: this was a celebrated area for agricultural produce, and especially wool. See Varro, *RR* 2. 2. 18; Horace, *Odes* 2. 6. 10, etc.

mushroom-spawn . . . from India: a part of the joke may be that mushrooms were thought to require no cultivation; see Pliny, *NH* 22. 94.

he's worth 800,000: the size of the fortune can be estimated from the fact that qualification for the equestrian order was 400,000 sesterces (Pliny, *NH* 33. 32).

grabbed a gnome's cap: the origin of this proverbial saying was that Incubo (a gnome or demon identified by Augustine, *Civ. Dei* 15. 23, with Silvanus/Pan) guarded a treasure which could be acquired by stealing his cap.

his upper room . . . a house: a *cenaculum* was an upper room in a house with its own entrance, frequently let to lodgers (see Varro, *LL* 5. 162); a *domus* was a much grander affair. Diogenes has moved into the ranks of the wealthy bourgeoisie.

the freedman's place: this was *medius in imo*, where Proculus reclined.

39   *'Is this the Ulysses . . . ?'*: Trimalchio quotes from Virgil, *Aen.* 2. 44, where Laocoon warns the Trojans that the apparent departure of the Greeks is a trick; likewise Trimalchio's concealment of more substantial fare.

The sky above: for discussion of the Zodiac dish, and the comic interpretations of the signs, see J. G. W. M. de Vreese, *Petron 39 und die Astrologie* (Amsterdam, 1927); K. F.

C. Rose and J. P. Sullivan, *CQ* (1968), 180 ff. Many of the interpretations are too witty for a simpleton, and the satirical portrayal of Trimalchio is accordingly undercut. So, for example, the comments on the *scholastici* ('shameless front . . . sharp horn') allude to the thefts and sexual behaviour of Encolpius and his confrères; and those under the Bull who 'provide their own dinners' are not parasites like Agamemnon and Encolpius.

woman-chasers, runaways, and slaves in chains: reading *mulierosi* for *mulieres*. As Astraea, Virgo fled from the earth (Juvenal 6. 19), and virgins in general flee from their pursuers. On depictions of the Zodiac, Virgo appears to be bound by the knots which indicate the cardinal points.

teachers of rhetoric: they are under Pisces because they fish for pupils; see § 3 above.

40 *Hipparchus and Aratus*: both were celebrated astronomers. Aratus (*c*.315–*c*.240 BC) wrote an extant poem, *Phaenomena*, which gained praise from literary men including Callimachus, but was criticized for its errors, especially by Hipparchus (*c*.190–*c*.120 BC) whose commentary on the *Phaenomena* survives.

nets . . . the chase: see C. P. Jones, 'Dinner Theater', in *Dining in a Classical Context* (ed. W. J. Slater, Ann Arbor, 1991), 186 f.

Spartan dogs: they were famous as hunting dogs; see Varro, *RR* 2. 9. 5.

wearing the cap of freedom: see § 41n.

gifts to take away: see § 56n.

41 *Dionysus, now be Liber*: Trimalchio utters yet another of his atrocious puns. Liber is both the Latin for 'free' and the name of the Italian god of fertility and wine who is identified with the Greek Dionysus. When Trimalchio adds 'My father is Liber', the feeble joke lies in the fact that his father was not a free citizen; the host's drinking habits make him a son of Bacchus.

Dama spoke up first: in this splendidly patterned conversation of trivialities, Dama (the name of a slave in Horace) begins with a report on the weather and his drinking habits; Seleucus (the name betraying his eastern provenance) informs the company about a recent funeral, adding sententious comment on the frailty of the human condition; Phileros (whose name, 'Amorous', suggests a sunnier role) injects a more optimistic note; the fourth speaker Ganymede (the name of Zeus' catamite) is the arch-moralizer, whose longing for the good old days is in turn balanced by Echion's vigorous attack on such a Jeremiah. On the linguistic peculiarities of these speeches, see B. Boyce, *The Language of the Freedmen in Petronius' Cena Trimalchionis* (Leiden, 1991).

42   *The doctors killed him off*: Jerome's celebrated *mot, ubi medici, ibi multae mortes*, echoes many such cynical criticisms; see Balsdon, 132 f.

he'd freed several slaves: slaves were often declared free in the will of their owner, which induced them to appear as mourners at his funeral. Legal restrictions were placed on the number which could be manumitted; see Balsdon, 113 f.

43   *I'm a Cynic with a dog's tongue*: this is one of several possible interpretations of *linguam caninam comedi*; see Smith's Commentary.

if you give credit: there is a play on the double sense of *credit*, 'trusts' and 'lends'.

44   *To hell with the aediles*: these magistrates were in charge of the corn supply, and regulated the price of bread.

If the best Sicilian flour: reading *si simila Siciliae inferior erat* (J. H. Simon).

play morra: this game, by which the first of a pair throws up a number of fingers, challenging his partner to guess correctly the number, is still played in rural parts of Italy.

his thousand gold pieces: 1,000 gold *denarii* (= 100,000 sesterces) was the property qualification required to become a city councillor. See Pliny, *Ep.* 1. 19. 2 with Sherwin-White's n.

the gods wrap their feet in wool: the meaning of this phrase is clear enough (expressive of divine displeasure), but the ancient explanations offered (see Smith's Commentary) are speculative.

45   *a lot of freedmen*: these were doubtless men who had earned their freedom after service as gladiators; see Balsdon, 289 ff.

Mammaea is going to lay on a banquet: probably a guild dinner for the town's clothiers. See R. Duncan-Jones, *BSA* (1965), 210 ff.

Norbanus: see § 46 below. The two men are rival candidates for a magistracy.

matched with the wild beasts: the *bestiarii* were usually criminals, untrained and therefore easy victims for the lions or other beasts; see Balsdon, 308 ff.

came off table-lamps: the picturesque phrase denotes the diminutive stature of the horsemen. Lamps with gladiator figures upon them are frequent features of grave-finds.

the reserve: the *tertiarius* was held back to take on the earlier victor; see Pliny, *Ep.* 8. 14. 21; Seneca, *Ep.* 7. 4.

one Thracian: 'Thracian' gladiators performed with a sword and small shield, and were often matched against the heavier-armed 'Samnites'. These names may have originally denoted the provenance of enslaved captives committed to the arena.

46 *the weasel ate them*: there is evidence that weasels were kept in some households as the equivalent of the modern cat, to cope with rodents (Pliny, *NH* 29. 60).

He knows his stuff: reading *scit quidem litteras* (Blümner).

47 *my stomach has not responded*: Trimalchio apes Theophrastus' disgusting man in *Char.* 20. 6 in this account of his constipation. The mopping of his brow on his return indicates the protracted struggle.

having to hold it in: Suetonius (*Claudius* 32) reports that Claudius considered issuing an edict permitting guests to belch and break wind at table. The ensuing remark that this is one thing that Jupiter can't forbid may obliquely refer to the deification of Claudius and Seneca's guying of it in the *Apocolocyntosis*.

the spokesman: the *nomenculator* was a slave who attended his master and acquainted him with the names of persons greeting him outside or at the daily *salutatio*. In the diningroom the slave had other duties, ushering guests to their places and making announcements such as this.

'Which company do you belong to?': slaves were divided into companies of ten. By contrast with the norm of twenty

slaves possessed by Hermeros (§ 57), Trimalchio's retinue runs into hundreds if not thousands.

in the will of Pansa: Trimalchio is implicitly compared to a Roman emperor, for it was a frequent custom to bequeath slaves to an emperor in one's will.

48 *Tarracina and Tarentum*: since the first is north of Naples on the west coast, and the second lies in the heel of Italy, the estate covers most of southern Italy.

have you any . . . pincers?: the labours of Hercules was a particularly hackneyed theme. The Cyclops' twisting off Ulysses' thumb is a comic confusion of the scene in the *Odyssey* when Odysseus/Ulysses plunges a stake into the Cyclops' sole eye.

suspended in a bottle: Trimalchio implies that he has read about the Sibyl not in Virgil's *Aeneid*, but in Homer. This extract was used as prefatory quotation by T. S. Eliot in *The Waste Land*, to indicate the sense of a world stale, flat and unprofitable. The Sibyl was said to live to an advanced age, and after her death the mummy was exhibited.

50 *At the capture of Troy . . . Hannibal*: here Trimalchio confuses the capture of Troy with Hannibal's seizure of Saguntum in Spain in 219; neither, of course, has any connection with Corinthian ware.

no smell comes off it: the characteristic smell given off by Corinthian ware attested its genuineness; cf. Martial 9. 59. 11, Pliny, *Ep.* 3. 6. 1.

51 *a glass goblet which was unbreakable*: this anecdote of the invention of unbreakable glass has an extended history. Various versions of it were current in antiquity (Pliny, *NH* 36. 195; Cassius Dio 57. 21). The story was transmitted into the Middle Ages by Isidore of Seville, *Etym.* 16. 16. 6, and John of Salisbury, *Policraticus* 4. 5 (citing Petronius). The emperor is cited as Tiberius by Pliny, Dio, and Isidore.

52 *something like a hundred*: reading *plus minus <centum>* (Wehle).

Cassandra . . . Minos . . . Daedalus: Trimalchio, in this further exhibition of his mythological learning, confuses Cassandra with Medea, and Niobe in the Trojan horse with Pasiphaë in the wooden cow. The reading *patrono meo rex*

Minos is Müller's ingenious emendation; the claim further demonstrates Trimalchio's learning.

Hermeros and Petraites: the bizarre combination of these gladiators with the preceding mythological motifs recalls the wall-paintings at § 29. The first name appears on a first-century lamp found at Puteoli, the second on several commemorative cups speculatively dated to the Neronian period (see H. T. Rowell, *TAPA* (1958), 12 ff.).

the cordax: this indecent dance (cf. Athenaeus 14. 631d) is said by Theophrastus (*Char*. 6. 3) to be danced by the shameless man when drunk.

Madeia, perimadeia: various emendations and explanations have been offered for this chorus, which may possibly have originated with the names of the witches Medea and Perimedea; the connection between witches and drunkenness is often made in Roman literature.

53 *the equivalent of the city gazette*: in this section Trimalchio is again characterized as posturing *princeps*. From 59 BC a daily communiqué was issued at Rome (cf. Suetonius, *Iul*. 20. 1), containing such statistical detail as is found here (see G. Boissier, *Tacitus and Other Roman Studies* (London, 1906), 197 ff.).

thirty boys and forty girls; five hundred thousand pecks of wheat: 'On the present U.K. birthrate, Trimalchio's Cumaean estate would have had a population of one and a half millions, and Friedländer calculates that the grain listed would feed 10,000 people for a year' (Smith).

the aediles' edicts: the city aediles were responsible for public order; Trimalchio's estates are so large that his security guards are modelled on them.

disinheriting Trimalchio: a mark of the master's magnanimity, implicitly contrasted with the behaviour of Caligula, who forced subjects to include him in their bequests (Suetonius, *Cal*. 38. 2).

a hall porter exiled to Baiae: Trimalchio once again plays the emperor, but absurdly, because Baiae was a desirable watering-place to which to be relegated.

comic performers . . . perform in Latin: dinners were often the occasions for refined recitations from New Comedy.

Trimalchio has the talented declaimers performing Atellane farces, which were crude Italian shows portraying provincial life. It is not clear whether the host's instruction to the flute-player to perform in Latin is as absurd as it sounds, since he sometimes accompanied singers.

54 *the boy tumbled down*: in this episode Petronius may have merged reminiscence of an incident in life with a passage of a celebrated literary forbear. Suetonius (*Nero* 12) reports that an actor playing Icarus fell 'and sprinkled Nero with his blood'. More sustained is the reminiscence of Horace, *Sat.* 2. 8, in which the boorish host, Nasidienus, is devastated by the fall of an awning over the dinner-table, and is ironically comforted by his guests, who rail at the iniquity of Fortune. See Sullivan, *The Satyricon*, 126 ff.; Walsh, *Roman Novel*, 38 ff.

55 *Just when you're off your guard*: Trimalchio's masterly epigram probably consisted of a mixture of a hexameter and an elegiac couplet (this is on the assumption that words have fallen out of the first two lines); alternatively, the master versifier has composed hexameters with only five feet.

Mopsus of Thrace: some absurdity lies behind the cryptic reference; perhaps, as Smith suggests, it is a misnomer for Orpheus.

Cicero . . . Publilius: the contrast between the most eminent of orators and the composer of mimes (Publilius Syrus' *floruit* was in the age of Julius Caesar), and the verses attributed to Publilius that follow, have probably been inserted by Petronius to guy Seneca, who was fond of citing the mimographer to underline his moral teaching. There is an obvious irony in Trimalchio's recommendation of simplicity of diet and lifestyle. The verses are to be attributed to Petronius himself rather than to Publilius; see Courtney, *Poems of Petronius*, 20 ff.

56 *cattle . . . and sheep*: apart from the Irishism (bread from cattle), the comedy of Trimalchio's patter lies in the banality of the utterances. For the lament of men's ingratitude towards cattle and sheep, cf. Ovid, *Met.* 15. 116 ff. For bees as heaven-sent creatures, Virgil, *Georgics* 4. For the proverb of bitter-sweet, Plato, *Philebus* 46c.

gifts to be taken away: Suetonius (*Aug.* 35) states that Augustus was fond of punning descriptions of such gifts. This seems to be another example of the characterization of Trimalchio as posturing *princeps*. Some of the puns here are impossible to reproduce in English. The Latin for 'accursed' (*sceleratum*) puns on the Greek word for ham, the vinegar-bottle presumably being of silver; *contumelia* ('given the stick') puns on apple and stick (*contus cum malo*); the Latin for leek and peach (*porrum sectivum* and *persica*) suggests the cut of a whip and the incision of a knife; sparrows (*passeres*) puns on *uvam passam* (raisins); lamprey (*muraena*) puns on *mus* and *rana* (mouse and frog), and beet puns on the Greek letter beta.

57 *you're a Roman knight? Well, and I'm a king's son:* Hermeros speaks in tones of heavy irony; see the further autobiographical details later, and the doubts he casts on Ascyltus' equestrian ring in § 58.

preferring to be a Roman citizen: a person could enter the service of a Roman, with the prospect of later award of the citizenship, rather than continue paying taxes as a provincial; see J. A. Crook, *Law and Life of Rome* (London, 1967), 59 f.

without subscription as one of the six priests: for the priesthood, see § 30 above. The usual levy on attainment of the office was 2,000 sesterces, but the payment was sometimes waived; see Smith's Commentary, ad loc.

58 *the Saturnalia:* from 17 December there was a three-day cessation of business, in the time of the early Empire. After religious festivities on the first day, there were parties and games on the 18th and 19th, during which slaves were waited on and treated as equals; see W. Warde-Fowler, *Roman Festivals* (London, 1899), 271 ff.

pay your five per cent: this was the tax levied on manumission, so that the phrase came to mean 'obtain your freedom'.

a golden beard: this would be an indication of divinity; see e.g. Suetonius, *Cal.* 52.

what am I?: Hermeros doesn't provide the answers to this and the following two riddles; Petronius presumably regarded them as self-evident. The likeliest answers are respectively the foot, the eye and the hair. Such riddles at table characterize the company as uncouth and unlearned; cf. Plutarch, *Moralia* 988a.

boxwood rings: Hermeros is suggesting that the rings are not of genuine gold which would be an indication of equestrian rank; see § 32n.

with my black cap on: literally, 'with the toga reversed', the garb of the presiding judge at a trial (Seneca, *De Ira* 1. 16. 5).

59 *the story they're dealing with*: Trimalchio's garbled version (*a*) substitutes Diomedes and Ganymede for Helen's brothers Castor and Pollux (and probably for the Greek leaders Agamemnon and Menelaus); (*b*) makes Agamemnon, not Paris, carry off Helen; (*c*) makes Agamemnon, rather than divine agency, substitute the hind for Iphigenia; (*d*) replaces Greeks with Tarentines; (*e*) makes Agamemnon present Iphigenia as bride to Achilles after the war, rather than pretend to offer her to him at Aulis before the war; (*f*) makes Ajax go mad at losing Iphigenia to Achilles, whereas the traditional story was that his frenzy resulted from the award of the arms of Achilles to Odysseus.

Ajax . . . finished off the beast: this was in imitation of the madness of the Homeric hero, who slaughtered cattle which he mistook for Greek leaders.

60 *suddenly the panels parted*: ceiling panels on swivels were a feature of some Neronian houses (Seneca, *Ep.* 90. 15). Nero's dining-rooms had such ceilings, from which flowers and perfumes descended on the guests (Suetonius, *Nero* 31).

steeped in such a sacred preparation: saffron featured in sacrifices; when the dried pistils were placed on glowing embers, the crackling sound was regarded as a good omen. See Ovid, *Fasti* 1. 76, 1. 342 ff.

Health to Augustus: this regular feature at dinners (cf. Dio 51. 19. 7), like the British toast to the queen, came usually at the tail-end of the meal, not in the middle. The traditional address 'Augusto' was to the reigning emperor; the title *patri patriae* appears on Neronian coins (M. T. Griffin, *Nero* (London, 1984), 59).

with medals round their necks: when a freeborn child received the *toga virilis*, the amulet received at birth was dedicated to the household gods.

Gods, have mercy: this prayer normally followed the main course (Servius, *Ad Aen.* 1. 730.)

a living likeness of Trimalchio: in the lost section of the text immediately before this, a group of statues, including that of Trimalchio, has been brought in. The deities are those which dominate the host's life; obeisance of his own statue is part of the strand characterizing him as quasi-emperor.

61 *these were the words he uttered*: for this cliché in introducing a story, cf. Virgil, *Aen.* 2. 790 with the note in R. G. Austin's edition.

he embarked upon this tale: the werewolf story has attracted wide scholarly discussion, much of it devoted to parallels with similar anecdotes; see K. F. Smith, *PMLA* (1894), 1 ff.; A. Rini, *CW* (1929), 83 ff.; M. Schuster, *WS* (1930), 149 ff.; G. Sandy, *TAPA* (1970), 468 f.; T. Pàroli in *Semiotica della novella latina* (ed. L. Pepe, Rome 1986), 281 ff.; N. Horsfall, *G&R* (1989), 196 f.

This girl's partner died: perhaps referring to an earlier liaison with a fellow slave, prior to her marriage to Terentius, whose name indicates a free man.

62 *passed between the tombs*: the graveyard would be outside the city gate on each side of the road.

the early-morning shadows: reading *matutinas umbras* (Heinsius).

63 *a hair-raising incident*: see Schuster, *WS*, for this story, which characterizes Trimalchio as credulous and superstitious.

the donkey on the roof: for anecdotes of animals raising a commotion by sudden appearance on top of blocks of flats, see e.g. Livy 21. 62. 3, 36. 37. 2.

as the Chians do: the Chians were proverbial for their degenerate habits.

64 *Apelles*: a famous tragic actor in the reign of Caligula (Suetonius, *Cal.* 33); the joke is that Plocamus' histrionic accomplishments hardly extend to tragedy.

Scylax, 'the guardian of home and household': the hulking animal is given the comic name 'Puppy'. This is one of many evocations of Theophrastus' *Characters*, whose Boor (*Char.* 3. 5) summons his dog and utters these identical words.

Buck, buck, how many fingers: the game resembles *morra* (see § 44n.).

65 *a reveller clad in white*: the late arrival of this tipsy guest recalls Alcibiades' entry in Plato's *Symposium* (212 D–E; cf. A. Cameron, *CQ* (1969), 367 ff.).

the place of honour: the 'praetorian place' (*imus in medio*) has been reserved for Habinnas the local dignitary.

ninth-day memorial-feast: this was a regular custom; see e.g. Tacitus, *Ann.* 6. 5.

the five-per-cent men: for the tax on liberated slaves, see § 58n.

66 *what did you have for supper?*: Theophrastus' garrulous man (*Char.* 3) is condemned for recounting the supper menu; Habinnas thus stigmatizes the manners of Trimalchio's boorish circle.

that'll do, Palamedes: the phrase *pax, Palamedes*, may indicate the desire to end a lengthy rigmarole (so Bendz, *Eranos* (1941), 44 ff.). It derives from that Greek hero's laments at Troy (Hyginus, *Fab.* 105). For other possible interpretations, see B. Baldwin, *CP* (1974), 293 f.

67 *the levy of the thousandth owed to Mercury*: presumably Trimalchio has vowed this sum from his profits to the patron god of commerce, and has had it converted into a gold bracelet stored in the shrine in the house.

out is hot . . . down is cold: that is, we lose more than we gain.

68 *'second tables'*: *secundae mensae* is the Latin phrase for dessert, but the servants pretend to misunderstand to allow Trimalchio to make his hackneyed joke.

sawdust coloured . . . mica: such brightly coloured sawdust was a feature in the Circus under Caligula (Suet. *Cal.* 18; cf. H. H. Davis, *CJ* (1957), 361 f.).

'change the tune': there was a wide range of such nightingale-songs; cf. Pliny, *NH* 10. 81 f.

Meanwhile Aeneas . . . fleet: Virgil, *Aen.* 5. 1.

Venus looks the same way: on Venus' attractive squint, see Ovid, *AA* 2. 659, Varro, *Men.* 344.

69 *I know a Cappadocian*: Cappadocians were proverbial for their crude strength, applied allegedly to sexual services; see Apuleius, *Met.* 8. 24, etc.

The Destiny of Muleteers: this sounds like the title of a mime.

during the Saturnalia: see § 58n.

70 *he's called Daedalus*: this is the name of the artist and inventor who created the Cretan labyrinth to house the Minotaur, and the two pairs of wings to permit his son Icarus and himself to escape. The name was a hackneyed one for a slave.

made at Noricum: for the town as the ancient equivalent of Sheffield, see Horace, *Odes* 1. 16. 9 with Nisbet-Hubbard's n.; Ovid, *Met.* 14. 712, etc.

into the wine-bowl: a barbaric practice, according to Pliny, *NH* 13. 25.

supporter of the Greens: there were four factions of charioteers in the Circus, sporting green, blue, red and white colours; see Balsdon, 314.

71 *slaves too are men*: in this sententious utterance, Petronius appears to be parodying Seneca on the equality of mankind; cf. *Ep.* 47. 10; Sullivan, *The Satyricon,* 132 ff. and *ANRW* 2/32.3, 1682. Such sentiments were also a feature of mime; cf. Seneca, *Ep.* 47. 14.

so long as I'm spared . . . I intend to free them all in my will: apart from the comic Irishism, there were restrictions on the number of slaves which could be freed in this way; see Balsdon, 113 f.

ordered a copy of his will to be brought in: in this final maudlin scene, the characterization of Trimalchio as the superstitious and morbid man is completed.

the contests of Petraites: § 52n.

wearing the toga with a purple stripe: this would depict him as a member of the college of Augustan priests.

of the household of Maecenas: Maecenas was the famous patron of Virgil and Horace; Trimalchio may be claiming not so much a connection with his household, as a kindred role as lover of literature. The portrayal of Trimalchio's appearance resembles that of Maecenas in Seneca, *Ep.* 114.

in his absence: the implication is that like some high state-official he has been engaged on important duties abroad.

without ever hearing a philosopher lecture: this echoes the traditional Roman distrust of philosophy (see e.g. Tacitus, *Agricola* 4. 3), but it may also sardonically suggest that the path to riches skirts the grove of Academe.

72 *let's have a plunge . . . as hot as hell*: the dangers of taking a bath after a gargantuan meal are underlined by Juvenal 1. 144 ('hinc subitae mortes atque intestata senectus'). A hot bath is especially dangerous; cf. Pliny, *NH* 29. 26.

Giton . . . bought off the dog: Petronius evokes Virgil here; when Aeneas journeyed to the realms below, Cerberus was likewise quietened by Aeneas, who fed the beast a honey-cake as soporific (*Aen.* 6. 419 ff.).

73 *The bath-house was narrow*: this is a surprising feature in an otherwise luxurious establishment. Perhaps it is a mark of inverted snobbery to have a small bath-house like that of Scipio Africanus as described by Seneca (*Ep.* 86. 4), which ensures that the owner can bathe alone.

began to murder the songs of Menecrates: Suetonius (*Nero* 30) states that a harpist of that name was rewarded by Nero; this is one of the evidences of a Neronian date for the novel. Singing in the bath, according to Theophrastus (*Char.* 4. 13), is the mark of the boorish man.

wine being openly strained: a further sign of ill-breeding. Good wine would suffer if strained in this way (Horace, *Sat.* 2. 4. 53 f.); Trimalchio is keeping the rough wine till the last.

celebrated his first shave: see § 29n.

74 *a cock crew*: in this section, the characterization of Tri-malchio stresses his superstition. For the ominous import of an early cock-crow, see Pliny, *NH* 10. 49. If it portended a fire, water was poured under the table (Pliny, *NH* 28. 26), but Trimalchio goes one better and sprinkles wine. A sput-tering lamp was a good omen, so Trimalchio creates one. For the superstitious transfer of a ring from left to right hand, see Pliny, *NH* 28. 57.

that Cassandra in jackboots: Cassandra prophesied the fall of Troy. Fortunata is so depicted because she is a nagging woman looking on the dark side.

75 *your nest-egg*: Habinnas, like Trimalchio, is an ex-slave. Slaves were allowed to accumulate money (*peculium*) to set themselves up when freed.

a Thracian outfit: on the gladiators known as 'Thracians', § 45n. Since the slave is a young boy, he will have bought a model set of armour, much as children nowadays buy football strips modelled on those of professional teams.

at the age of fourteen: the usual rendering, 'for fourteen years', seems improbable; I assume the ellipse of *natus* after *annos XIV*. See M. D. Reeve, *Phoenix* (1985), 378 f.

76 *he made me joint heir with Caesar*: rich individuals often did this to ensure the benevolence of the emperor towards their heirs; Nero is said to have encouraged the practice (Suetonius, *Nero* 32. 2). The ploy was not always successful; witness the fate of Boudicca and her children, named joint heirs with Nero by her husband Prasutagus (Tacitus, *Ann.* 14. 31).

the fortune of a senator: the property qualification for senatorial rank was a million sesterces (Tacitus, *Ann.* 1. 75); the phrase does not mean that Trimalchio actually entered the senate.

the itch to go into business: the sketch of Trimalchio's career that follows reflects Petronius' sardonic awareness of the source of wealth of the *nouveaux riches* in Italian society.

worth its weight in gold: over-production of wine later became a problem in the Flavian era (Suetonius, *Domitian* 7. 2). If a Neronian date is accepted for the *Satyricon*, Trimalchio may be describing the economic situation under Claudius, assuming that the astrologer's forecast of thirty years to live sets him in late middle age.

you'd have thought I'd given the nod: there is a hint here that Trimalchio alludes to a bogus insurance claim. The emperor Claudius guaranteed shipowners security against loss in storms (Suetonius, *Claudius* 18. 2), though Trimalchio does not appear to have benefited.

an astrologer . . . Serapa: Trimalchio's credulous trust in these vapid prophecies is a further indication of his superstitious attitude to life.

77 *extend my farms into Apulia*: at § 48 his properties extend from Tarentum in the south to Tarracina in the west; Apulia would take in areas in the south-east.

under Mercury's watchful eye: Mercury was the god of traders —and of thieves!

Scaurus: Petronius has incorporated elsewhere real-life figures; it is possible that this is Umbricius Scaurus, a sauce manufacturer from Pompeii.

78 *Imagine you've been invited to my wake*: in this splendid epilogue to the *Cena*, Petronius depicts Trimalchio as a prey to morbidity. Similar mock-funerals are attested in contemporary life; Seneca, for example, documents two figures, Pacuvius and Turannius, indulging themselves in such morbid behaviour (*Ep.* 12. 8; *Brev. Vit.* 20. 3). The festival of the Parentalia ('my wake') took place annually in February, but the expression may be used loosely here for the *novendiale*, the funeral banquet celebrated nine days after interment.

7. *Giton spurns Encolpius for Ascyltus*

79 *chalk-marks on every post*: the literary texture is evident in the resumption of the imagery of the labyrinth from § 73; 'Giton plays Ariadne to Encolpius' Theseus' (Slater).

our vagrant breath: Petronius, here at his most literary, imitates the Platonist notion found in the epigram at *Anth. Pal.* 5. 78 ('As I kissed Agathon, I held my soul back on my lips, for it was keen, poor thing, to cross over'). Our author was struck by the image, for it appears again in § 132.

80 *with murderous intent he drew his sword*: the whole of this scene, like the earlier confrontation between Encolpius and Ascyltus in § 9, is a melodramatic comedy redolent of the mimic stage. The language is absurdly stilted.

a Theban duet: the hackneyed literary reference, characteristic of mimic performances, evokes the conflict between Eteocles and Polyneices in Aeschylus' *Seven Against Thebes*.

Encolpius and Ascyltus are brothers in the less decorous sense.

A company . . . roles are gone: most commentators assume that this epigram (unlike the preceding four lines in which Encolpius bitterly reflects on his being betrayed by his friends) is misplaced here. But it can be connected with what precedes, for the scene just enacted is a mimic presentation; Encolpius may be suggesting that the play is over, that he is now faced with the cruel reality of Giton's desertion.

81 *Menelaus*: see § 27 above.

rented an isolated place close to the sea: Encolpius here becomes a second Achilles, resentful at the loss of the slave-girl Briseis to Agamemnon. Achilles too mopes by the sea (*Iliad* 1. 348 ff.).

Did I . . . a Greek city: Encolpius refers to a previous escapade in a lost section of the novel; there is a passing reference to it in § 9.

82 *like a madman*: he now becomes a second Aeneas (cf. Virgil, *Aen.* 2. 671 ff.); the language in this sustained parody of epic becomes notably Virgilian.

Poor . . . must digest: the context on which this epigram reflects is lost.

8. *Eumolpus in the Art Gallery*

83 *Zeuxis . . . Protogenes . . . Apelles*: for these outstanding painters, see Pliny, *NH* 35. 61 ff., 79 ff. Zeuxis is the oldest of the three, having travelled from his native Lucania to Athens at the time of the Peloponnesian War; hence 'the ravages of time' here. The others were contemporaries a century later. Protogenes was famous for his slow and painstaking workmanship, at which Encolpius' comment hints. Apelles was the most celebrated painter of his era; he attended the court of Alexander the Great. The reference to the Crippled Goddess may be to his celebrated *Aphrodite Rising From the Foam*, which when damaged in its lower part no painter presumed to restore (Pliny, *NH* 35. 91). The conventional judgements here characterize Encolpius as the brash poseur. In addition, Petronius adds

to the comedy by making feeble puns on their names. Zeuxis ('Yoked') is not 'subdued' by the ravages of time; Protogenes ('First-born') is represented by 'first-born' sketches; the painting of Apelles, which they call (*appellant*) 'The One-legged', renders Encolpius one-legged as he genuflects before it.

the lad from Mt. Ida . . . Hylas . . . Apollo: appropriately to the context, Encolpius as he mourns the loss of Giton surveys a sequence of homosexual motifs. The lad from Mt. Ida is Ganymede, borne up to heaven to become the cup-bearer of Jupiter. Hylas, the page of Hercules, was kidnapped by nymphs when voyaging on the Argo, and Hercules then searched for him. Hyacinth was killed when his lover Apollo accidentally killed him when throwing the discus; the corpse was transformed into a flower.

more cruel than Lycurgus: this man, with whom Ascyltus is being compared, figured in a lost episode earlier. The further reference to him in § 117, and Encolpius' admission that he committed murder in § 81, suggest that the hero had lodged with him, and after ill-treatment had killed him and plundered his house.

a grizzled veteran: enter Eumolpus, the manic and hypocritical poetaster, a further figure in the sequence of disreputable characters encountered by the anti-hero.

85 This Milesian tale of the boy at Pergamum has the purpose of pricking the bubble of Eumolpus' self-advertised probity, and of pointing forward to his attempted liaison with Giton.

the quaestor . . . at Pergamum: the quaestor was the man charged with financial supervision of the province. Though Ephesus was the outstanding city in the province of Asia, Pergamum was its official capital.

88 *lust for money*: this claim, that cultural decline was linked with a decline in morality, is a hoary theme in Roman letters which Petronius satirizes.

Democritus . . . Eudoxus . . . Chrysippus: in this catalogue of great philosophers, Eumolpus' confident judgements mask his ignorance. The atomist Democritus of Abdera (born *c*.460) was not celebrated as botanist or geologist; Eumolpus may be confusing him with Aristotle. Eudoxus of Cnidus (born *c*.390) was certainly interested in astronomy, but personal observation was never his strong point. The eminent Stoic Chrysippus (born *c*.280) was said to have taken hellebore three times, but as a cure for madness, not to promote fluency of thought (he wrote no fewer than seventy-five books!).

Lysippus . . . Myron: Eumolpus shows similar ignorance about the plastic arts. Lysippus of Sicyon (*floruit c*.328), so far from being a slow worker and dying in poverty, sculpted 1,500 pieces of statuary and died a rich man. Myron of Eleutherae (mid-fifth century) was notorious for *not* catching the souls of his subjects (see Pliny, *NH* 34. 37 and 58).

dialectic . . . astronomy: in the seven liberal arts, the staple of ancient education, the three most important (the *trivium*) were grammar, rhetoric and logic/dialectic, this last inculcating logical thought through disputation. Astronomy, together with arithmetic, geometry and music, formed the *quadrivium*.

Apelles and Phidias: for Apelles, see n. on § 83. Phidias (born *c*.490), the greatest of all sculptors, was the creator of the famous statue of Athena in the Parthenon, and of the statue of the seated Zeus at Olympia; he designed the sculptures of the Parthenon.

89 *the capture of Troy*: Eumolpus demonstrates his literary versatility by composing this piece after the manner of Seneca, the content being adapted from some mythological version, but with echoes of Virgil's account in *Aeneid* 2; for the differences from Virgil, see Walsh, *Roman Novel*, 46.

Ten . . . illusions: Calchas, the Greek seer, had prophesied that the war would last ten years. In the tenth year, Apollo inspired him to persuade the Greeks to build the wooden horse; they constructed it from trees felled from Mt. Ida overlooking the city. The Greek Sinon, pretending to be a deserter, urged the Trojans to accept the horse within the city, claiming that Calchas had prophesied Trojan conquest of the Greeks if this were done. Virgil emphasizes Trojan complacency as contributory to the success of the ruse.

The crowd . . . guile: the priest of Neptune, Laocoon, warned the Trojans not to trust the Greeks. He hurled his spear at the horse, but failed to pierce it. His suspicions of the Greeks were overridden by the crowd, who admitted the horse into the city.

Fresh . . . gods: the Greeks had hidden their forces behind Tenedos, an island off the coast. From there twin snakes (symbolizing the cunning and violence of the Greeks) cross to the mainland. They destroy Laocoon, who had implacably opposed the reception of the horse, together with his children—a theme immortalized in sculpture by the famous Laocoon-group in the Vatican, found near the Baths of Titus in 1506.

Now . . . Trojans: the Greeks concealed in the horse are released (in Virgil by Sinon). The memorable phrase 'buried in sleep and wine' is Virgil's.

9. *Reconciliation with Giton; Eumolpus as Rival*

91 *your repentant judge*: in § 80 above, Giton had been appointed as judge by Ascyltus and Encolpius to settle the issue of the ownership of the slave. In this melodramatic reconciliation, the language is as stilted as in the previous encounters.

93 *Birds . . . exotic tastes*: the theme is similar to that of the verses in § 55, perhaps here a comic comment on the pedestrian fare provided by the host. Petronius may also be waxing ironical at this condemnation of exotic objects of desire by Eumolpus, even as he ingratiates himself with Giton. Colchis, on the river Phasis at the eastern end of the Black Sea, was the destination of the Argo in the expedition for the golden fleece; it has therefore an exotic ring.

Syrtis' banks . . . shipwreck: these notorious shallows off the north-African coast were frequently a graveyard for ships, so the fishing there was hazardous.

94 *That soldier*: see § 82 above.

shut me in: a reversal of the locked-out lover theme (*exclusus amator*), so popular in Augustan love-elegy.

95 *this farce between lovers*: repeatedly Petronius presents the action as the narrative equivalent of the low stage. The

attempted hanging, the practice-razor, and the slapstick that ensues all convey this impression of low farce.

Marcus Mannicius: the name suggests a connection with *manicae* (handcuffs).

97 *as Ulysses of old clung to the ram's belly*: the banal reference to the Homeric episode in the Cyclops' cave (*Od.* 9. 431 ff.) is characteristic of mimic performances.

following that deadly brawl: this is usually interpreted as referring to the recent quarrel over Giton, but 'brawl' (*rixa*) implies something more physical, and more probably refers to the earlier struggle with Lycurgus (§ 83n.) which was 'deadly'.

98 *spider's web soaked in oil*: for this application to close a wound, compare the medical treatise of Celsus 5. 2: 'If a wound is slight, even cobwebs will close it up.'

99 *a sailor with a shaggy beard*: apparently a *deus ex machina* to advance the plot to the next episode on board ship. But it is possible that Eumolpus in a lost passage made reference to his forthcoming journey. See § 101, 'his decision to sail on the ship had been taken long before'.

10. *The Episode on Ship. Enter Lichas and Tryphaena*

100 *the hand of Fortune*: this is a repeated motif in the romance; see §§ 101, 114, 125. It lends support to the thesis that Petronius burlesques the action of the Greek love-romances, in which Fortune invariably takes a hand; see Walsh, *Roman Novel*, 78 f.

Lichas . . . Tryphaena: 'Captain Harshman' and 'Madame Luxury' differ in morals but present a united front in their superstitious outlook upon the world.

101 *had not been aware of those earlier happenings*: it becomes clear in §§ 105–6, 113, that Encolpius in earlier lost episodes had seriously wronged Lichas, even so far as seducing his wife Hedyle, and had enjoyed a sexual romp with Tryphaena, in the course of which he had spirited away her slave Giton.

this Hannibal: the Carthaginian invader of Italy in the Second Punic War was popularly regarded as the epitome of cruelty and deceit.

102 *into the ship's boat*: ancient ships towed a lifeboat from the stern; see C. Torr, *Ancient Ships* (Cambridge, 1895), 103.

this kind of trick was successful once: the celebrated precedent was Cleopatra's secret entry to Julius Caesar wrapped in a carpet; cf. Plutarch, *Caesar* 49.

103 *that razor of his*: see § 94 above.

the punishment of branding: the motif appears in a well-known mime of Herodas (5; see C. P. Jones, *JRS* (1987), 139 f.).

104 *Priapus*: see § 16n.

Epicurus was a godlike man: the followers of Epicurus of Samos (341–271 BC) frequently grant him a godlike status; see e.g. Lucretius 5. 8. Some scholars claim that Petronius was an adherent of the school, but the evidence of the romance hardly supports this. So far as the present passage is concerned, Epicurus taught that dreams offer true sense-data, but that our opinions may intervene to delude us about them. Eumolpus' assertion that Epicurus wittily disparages them is misleading; it again characterizes the poet as one who offers confident opinions based on hazy knowledge.

no person . . . must cut his nails or hair: this was a widespread superstition; see J. G. Frazer, *The Golden Bough* (London, 1900), i. 378.

105 *Ulysses' nurse recognized his scar*: the nurse Eurycleia identified Ulysses after his twenty years' absence by the scar which he had sustained on the hunting-field; see Homer, *Odyssey*, 19. 467 ff.

106 *the colonnade of Hercules*: scholars speculatively place this location at Baiae, where Tryphaena saw the statue of Neptune (§ 104).

107 *the wind freshened*: Eumolpus is suggesting that the captain gave orders to exploit the freshening wind by setting sail at once.

some salamander: this newt-like amphibian was popularly supposed to emit a substance which removed hair; cf. Martial 2. 66. 7.

108 *What madness . . . of blood*: throughout this section, Petronius has comically dignified the scuffle with the high-

flown language of historical narrative. As climax, Tryphaena now declaims these verses in a pastiche of Virgil, Propertius, and above all Lucan 1. 8 ('quis furor, o cives . . . ?'). The hackneyed references are to Paris's abduction of Helen, which caused the Trojan war, and to Medea's murder of her brother Apsyrtus when she was escaping with Jason from Colchis.

109 *the articles of the treaty*: Petronius' literary versatility extends to parody of the formula of a peace treaty.

110 *lines even more witless*: it is important to note the repeated 'put-downs' of Eumolpus' verses. Some critics are inclined to take Petronius' facility as a versifier more seriously than does the author himself or his anti-hero.

111 *A married lady from Ephesus*: this Milesian tale of the widow of Ephesus has fascinated many in subsequent ages; the story is rightly analysed as narrative theatre by Slater, 108 ff. Ephesus was the largest and most celebrated city in the Roman province of Asia. A vivid picture of the social life there at this period is found in *The Acts of the Apostles*, ch. 19.

Do you think . . . such things: The literate maid slightly misquotes Anna's advice to Dido at Virgil, *Aen.* 4. 34.

112 *Will you strive . . . that pleases?*: the Virgilian evocation is sustained here; the maid cites Anna's words to Dido at *Aen.* 4. 38.

113 *Hedyle was back in his mind*: see § 101n.

114 *storm-clouds gathered*: here the Virgilian storm at *Aen.* 1. 88 ff. is evoked. The shipwreck is a frequent feature of the Greek sentimental romance (e.g., Achilles Tatius 3. 1 ff.), so that this scene furnishes a further argument for parody of them.

the sacred robe and rattle: Lichas must be referring to the plundering of the ship mentioned in § 113. Encolpius made off with the sacred objects associated with the Egyptian goddess Isis when he seduced Hedyle.

115 *food damaged in the shipwreck*: the evocation of Aeneas cast up on the African shore continues; cf. *Aen.* 1. 177. The following sentence ('we were debating into which region . . .') echoes *Aen.* 1. 306 ff.

As if it makes . . . of time: on the Epicurean sentiment, cf. Lucretius 3. 888 ff.

11. *The Journey to Croton*

116 *the ancient city of Croton*: this town, situated on the toe of Italy, was an Achaean foundation dating from the eighth century BC, and reached the height of its glory in the late sixth and fifth centuries, though the claim to have been the foremost in Italy is an exaggeration. Later it declined, in spite of being designated as a Roman colony in 194, and by Cicero's time it was a mere place of passage to Greece. Petronius exploits the run-down place to symbolize its degenerate manners. The bailiff who responds to the request for information is the prosaic equivalent of Venus in the first book of the *Aeneid.*

the money-hunters and the hunted: we are being introduced here to a frequent butt of Roman satire, the legacy-hunters, to whom Horace allots a celebrated satire (2. 5), and whom Juvenal also pillories (5. 131 ff., 12. 93, etc.).

117 *Lycurgus' country house*: see § 83n.

Corax: the name means 'Crow' in Greek, an apposite title in the context of § 116.

118 *Poetry, my young friends, . . . has beguiled many*: there is some dispute about the correct interpretation of this piece of literary criticism. Sullivan in his notes to the translation argues that 'it gives us a very good idea of Petronius' views on literature. He is a traditionalist . . .'. But scholars are increasingly disposed to evaluate it within the characterization of Eumolpus as the pompous traditionalist, mouthing 'politically correct' notions of what true poetry should be.

Mount Helicon: the abode of the Muses, situated in Boeotia.

I hate the common mob: a quotation from Horace, *Odes* 3. 1. 1.

the lofty theme of the Civil War: in what follows there is implicit criticism of the epic of the poet Lucan, a contemporary of Petronius. His was a 'godless' poem on the civil war fought between Julius Caesar and Pompey as leader of the senatorial party. Lucan follows Livy's outline of the course of the war, interspersing it with highly rhetorical adornment. Eumolpus' criticism is closely addressed to this approach, which is censured as too historical and non-traditional.

119 *By now the victorious Roman ruled the world*: the poem opens with a general introduction on Rome's abuse of world-dominance, which made civil war inevitable (1–84). Next, the powers of evil in Hades conspire to cause war, and omens presage it (85–171). The extract then centres on Julius Caesar, and the effect of his arrival in Italy on the senatorial forces (172–301). The gods become involved, and battle commences (302–63). The poem evokes Virgil most of all; echoes of Lucan are also evident, together with a few phrases derived from Seneca, Horace and Ovid.

By . . . crowd: Eumolpus begins with the hackneyed theme of Rome's plundering the world's resources; compare especially Virgil, *Georgics* 2. 463 ff., 503 ff.; Pliny, *NH* 12. 1. 2. 'Numidians yielded marble' (line 11) adopts the likely emendation *crustas* for the corrupt *accusatius*; Numidian marble was a luxury import (see Juvenal 7. 182, etc.), as were Chinese silk (visualized by Virgil as fleeces gathered from trees; *Georgics* 2. 120 f.) and Arabian perfumes and incense (see Tibullus 2. 2. 3 f.). The Roman fondness for shows with wild beasts (lines 14 ff.) was frequently condemned by sensitive souls like Cicero (*Ad Fam.* 7. 1. 3) and especially Seneca (*Epp.* 90. 45, 95. 33). The Egyptian God Ammon (line 15), whose shrine was at Siwa on the borders of Egypt and Cyrenaica, is frequently mentioned in Greek and Roman literature.

1 . . . trees: Eumolpus next reflects on how these imports have led to moral degeneration at Rome. 'Adopting Persian ways' (line 22) echoes the proverbial condemnation of Persian luxury, with particular reference to castration of young boys; the Persian name Bagoas stands for 'eunuch' at Ovid, *Amores* 2. 2. 1, etc. Tables made of citrus-wood (lines 29 ff.) fetched huge prices at Rome; Cicero is said to have paid a million sesterces for one; the markings determined the value (cf. Pliny, *NH* 13. 29 f.). The oyster-beds in the Lucrine lake (line 40), near Baiae on the Bay of Naples, were celebrated (cf. Seneca, *Ep.* 78. 23; Martial 13.

82). The river Phasis (line 42) is the modern Rion flowing into the Black Sea at its eastern end; it was famous for pheasants thronging its banks. With this section compare Lucan 4. 373 ff., 10. 155 ff.

120 *The . . . fame*: political corruption follows. Cato (line 53) became the patron saint of Republicanism, and the nearest approximation to a hero in Lucan's epic. He was defeated in the contest for the praetorship through Pompey's opposition, and for the consulship in 51 through the joint opposition of Caesar and Pompey. But 'the flush of shame' of his successful opponent (whether Vatinius as praetor or Claudius Marcellus as consul) is *post hoc* romanticism. 'Foul usury and borrowed money' (line 61) recalls the analysis of Sallust's *Catiline*, in which violence and anarchy are visualized as the outcome of profligacy and greed. Crassus (line 72) was killed in 53 at Carrhae when warring on Parthia; Pompey was assassinated at Pelusium on the coast of Egypt while fleeing after his defeat at Pharsalus in 48 (compare Lucan 8. 698 ff.); Caesar was murdered on the Ides of March 44.

Between . . . blood: we are on the Bay of Naples between that city (called Parthenope in the Latin because it was said to stand on the tomb of the Siren of that name) and Puteoli (its legendary founder was Dicarchus; hence its name in the Latin). The region between (80 ff.) is the Phlegraean Fields, the area from which Aeneas made his descent into Hades in *Aeneid* 6. Cocytus (line 82), which means 'Wailing' in Greek, is one of the rivers of Hades. Dis, the lord of Hell (line 92) urges Fortune (the capricious deity who exalts men to bring them low) to turn her attention to Rome. 'They build in gold' (line 107) may have reference to Nero's Golden House. Tisiphone (line 121) was one of the three avenging Furies, with Allecto and Megaera. Sulla's sword 'drank deep' (line 122) in 82 BC, when he massacred the supporters of Marius; the blood-bath between the two leaders was regarded as the prelude to the Great Civil War, and in Lucan's epic they rise from Hades to warn of the impending struggle.

121 *These . . . led*: in her reply, Fortune prophesies that Mars ('the deity' in line 134) will humble Rome. She foresees

'twin battles at Philippi'; Roman poets with fine disregard for geography frequently conflate the battlefields of Pharsalus in Thessaly (the scene of Caesar's victory over Pompey in 48) and Philippi in Macedonia (where Mark Antony defeated Brutus and Cassius in 42). 'Spanish burials' (line 139) refers especially to Caesar's final victory at Munda in Spain in 45, and 'Nile's barriers groan' (line 141) to Caesar's campaigns in Egypt following Pharsalus in 48–7. At the Battle of Actium (line 142), Octavian defeated Mark Antony in 31, in the final round of the Civil Wars; Virgil's depiction of the prophetic shield of Aeneas has Apollo wielding his bow above the conflict (*Aen.* 8. 704 f.). The ferryman (line 144) is Charon.

122 *Hard . . . blood*: dread omens now prefigure future disaster, as in Lucan 1. 522 ff. 'His brother' (line 154) is Jupiter the sky-god; 'Titan' (line 157) is the sun, for the older sun-god Hyperion was a Titan; 'Cynthia' (line 160) is the moon, also named Diana, who was born on Mt. Cynthus in Delos. 'Aetna' (line 165) is Europe's highest volcanic mountain, overlooking Catana in Sicily.

Without . . . fail: Caesar had been engaged in his Gallic campaigns since 59, and his senatorial enemies refused to extend his command, seeking his political extinction on his return to Rome. The Civil War technically began with the crossing of the Rubicon, the small river separating Cisalpine Gaul from Italy; the poem substitutes the Alps for the Rubicon. The claim that Caesar could see the plains of Italy from the Graian Alps (lines 187 f.) is fantasy. The speech inserted here was actually made at Ravenna (Caesar, *B.C.* 1. 7). The claim that he embarked on the war unwillingly (line 193) was Caesar's constant cry. The suggestion that his Gallic campaign was aimed at preventing the Gauls descending again on Rome as in 387–6 (lines 197 f.) is fantasy. The 'worthless hirelings' (line 204) must be the troops recruited from the east by Pompey (cf. Caesar, *B.C.* 3. 4). 'The die must now be cast' (line 214) is an echo of Caesar's celebrated 'iacta alea est' (Suetonius, *Iul.* 32) when he crossed the Rubicon. Caesar's superstitious belief in Fortune was famous; with line 215 compare Lucan 1. 226 f.

123 *As he . . . die*: the 'Delphic bird' (line 218) is the raven (cf.
Ovid, *Met.* 2. 544 ff.) or less probably the falcon (Homer,
Od. 15. 525 f.). The 'gloomy grove' (line 220) is out of
place in the eternal snows, evidence of hasty composition.
The 'left hand' (line 220) is for the Romans the favourable side in omens. 'Phoebus' (line 222) is the sun. The
description of the terrain, and of the arctic weather following, evokes Livy's account of Hannibal's crossing of
the Alps and Apennines (21. 36. 6 ff., 21. 58. 3 ff.).
'Amphitryon's son' (line 250) was Hercules, who liberated
Prometheus from his chains in the mountains of the Caucasus. Jupiter threw down the Giants (lines 252 ff.) when
they sought to scale heaven (Apollodorus 1. 6. 1).

While . . . flee: Rumour (*Fama*, line 256) plays a constant
role in Roman epics after Virgil, *Aen.* 4. 173 ff. The Palatine (line 257) was the chief of Rome's seven hills, and
here stands for the city as a whole. With the account of the
evacuation of Rome (lines 271 ff.) compare the evacuation
of Troy (Virgil, *Aen.* 2. 486 ff.) and the dismantling of Alba
Longa in Livy 1. 29; in general, the panic at Rome is evocative of Lucan 1. 466 ff., where there is likewise the storm
simile (1. 498 ff.). Pompey ('Magnus') was 'the scourge of
Pontus' (line 291) when he defeated Mithridates, King of
Pontus, in the Third Mithridatic War; the claim that he
discovered the river Hydaspes in India is wild exaggeration, conflating him with Alexander the Great (Pompey
halted at the Euphrates). He was 'the rock on which the
pirates foundered' (lines 292 f.) when he swept them off
the seas in 67 BC. His three triumphs (lines 293 f.) were for
victories in Africa over Iarbas, in Spain over Sertorius, and
in Asia over Mithridates. His 'claim to high position' refers
to his appointment as commander of the Roman forces in
50 BC.

124 *This . . . he did*: Erebus (line 312) is another name for Hades.
Erinys (line 313) is one of the Furies; Bellona is the goddess of war; for Megaera, see n. on line 121. The symbolic
deities that follow (line 315) recall the personifications in
Virgil, *Aen.* 6. 273 ff. Madness (*Furor*, line 317) is a key-word
in the *Aeneid* and then in later epic for irrational violence.
Dione (line 328), properly the mother of Venus, is often
used of Venus herself, from whom Caesar claimed descent;

hence '*her* Caesar's course'. Pallas (line 329) is Athene/
Minerva. I take Mavortius ('the god of war', line 329) to
refer to Mars rather than to Romulus. 'Phoebus' sister'
(line 331) is Diana; 'Cyllene's son' refers to Mercury who
was born on Mt. Cyllene in Arcadia; 'The Tirynthian' (line
332) is Hercules, born at Tiryns; Pliny, *NH* 7. 27 also makes
the parallel with Pompey, for both travelled widely in their
struggles.

The . . . earth: Claudius Marcellus and Cornelius Lentulus
Crus (lines 353 f.) were consuls at the outbreak of the Civil
War in 49; they precipitated the conflict by proposing the
senatus consultum ultimum and by refusing to negotiate with
Caesar. Scribonius Curio, who as tribune in 50 had been
active on Caesar's behalf, fled to join him when the senatorial decree was passed. 'Divine Caesar' (line 356) is a
proleptic address; he was deified after his death (Suetonius,
Iul. 88). Epidamnus (line 361) was the Greek name for
Dyrrhachium in Epirus, where Pompey established his base
after fleeing from Italy. 'Dye Thessalian bays' (line 361)
refers to the slaughter at the battle of Pharsalus in 48. The
parallel with Lucan 7. 473 is notable.

12. *The Encounter with Circe*

his monstrous deluge of words: such regular criticism of
Eumolpus' poetic efforts encourages the reader to take
them as they are presented—as impromptu declamations
of a banal kind.

126 *Circe's maid addressing Polyaenus*: the hero Encolpius now
becomes entangled with a promiscuous lady called Circe. In
this, Petronius resumes his presentation of his anti-hero
as a comic version of epic hero. Here Encolpius takes on
the persona of Odysseus/Ulysses, who tarried for a whole
year with Circe on the island of Aeaea. The name Polyaenus
echoes Homer's epithet attached to Odysseus, *poluainos*
(probably 'much-praised'; *Od.* 12. 184), an ironical label in
view of what follows. Presumably this is the name Encolpius
adopts in his simulated role as slave of Eumolpus.

unless their eyes are on slaves: for the predilection of some
matrons for slaves, cf. §§ 69, 75 above. For the connection
with the mime, see Walsh, *Roman Novel*, 26.

the first fourteen rows: these seats at the front of the theatre were reserved for the knights.

like that which Praxiteles envisaged for Diana: the famed Athenian (*floruit* mid-fourth century) sculpted several statues of Artemis/Diana in bronze and marble.

Parian marble: the island of Paros in the Cyclades was famous for its gleaming white marble; Ovid, *Amores* 1. 7. 51 f. makes a similar comparison with female beauty.

Why, Jupiter, discard . . . desires: in this extempore composition Encolpius suggests that Circe is worthy of a visit from Jupiter. In love-elegy, courtship is often depicted in terms of military campaigning; hence 'why discard your arms?' Jupiter seduced Europa by taking the form of a bull (hence 'fresh horns'), and Leda by appearing as a swan (so 'swan's feathers'). He won over Danaë by becoming a golden shower. See among other testimonies Ovid, *Met.* 6. 103 ff.

127 *Circe . . . the daughter of the Sun*: the enchantress Circe was the daughter of Helios and Perse (Homer, *Od.* 10. 137 f.). The description of this earthy Circe resembles those of women in the Greek romances (e.g. Chariton, 2. 2. 2; Xenophon, 1. 2. 6; Longus 1. 17. 3).

Such flowers . . . our secret love: the verses recall that during the Trojan war Hera/Juno distracted her husband from the fighting by inviting him to a love-liaison on Mt. Ida. The passage of Homer describing this (*Il.* 14. 347) catalogues the flowers on which they lay; Encolpius here cites a different selection. Jupiter's inflamed response recalls the love-scene between Vulcan and Venus at Virgil, *Aen.* 8. 388 ff. (cf. also *Aen.* 7. 356).

128 *So what is the problem?*: the theme of Encolpius' sexual enervation evokes Ovid's indelicate poem, *Amores* 3. 7.

The spade . . . uncovers gold: some have taken this to be a reference to the famous spoof in 65 AD when Caesellius Bassus claimed to have uncovered the treasures of Dido in Africa (Tacitus, *Ann.* 16. 1). But allusions to buried treasure are too frequent in ancient literature to justify the assumption.

Socrates . . . Alcibiades: in Plato's *Symposium* 218C–19C, Alcibiades describes how he inveigled Socrates into sleeping with him, and how Socrates resisted his approaches.

129 *which once made me an Achilles*: Achilles' fame as archetypal hero extended to sexual liaisons, heterosexual and homosexual; see the *OCD*, s.v. Achilles.

handed me a letter: for such letters in the Greek romances, see Chariton, 4. 4; Xenophon, 2. 5, etc.

130 *I am a traitor, a murderer*: the self-accusations are often interpreted as referring to lost episodes in the novel, but more probably they are metaphorical, recalling his betrayal of Circe and the profanation of her shrine through loss of his virility.

131 *A little old woman*: this is Proselenus (see § 132 below), whose name 'Before the moon' indicates her role as witch.

The waving plane . . . song: (I read *mobilis* for *nobilis* in Müller). Daphne is the bay-tree, into which the girl was transformed when escaping Apollo's clutches (Ovid, *Met.* 1. 548 f.). 'Procne, city-bred' is the house-martin which nests in the roofs of houses; Procne was transformed into a bird when she fled from the vengeance of Tereus after serving up their son Itys to him in an Irish stew (Ovid, *Met.* 6. 668).

132 *the union of souls*: see § 79n. above. As Sullivan remarks, the gloss in the MSS heading this section, 'Encolpius de Endymione puero', seems to be an intrusion.

She looked . . . head: the literary evocation, which softens the crudity of the theme, here continues with pastiche of Virgil. Encolpius' errant *mentula* is compared with Dido in her confrontation with Aeneas in Hades. The first two lines directly cite *Aen.* 6. 469–70; in place of 471 ('than if she were unmoving flint or Marpesian marble') Petronius comically and more aptly compares his member with a weeping willow or drooping poppy (cf. *Ecl.* 5. 16, *Aen.* 9. 436).

didn't Ulysses . . . had ears?: for Ulysses' self-communion, see Homer, *Od.* 20. 18 ff. The obvious tragic figure in Encolpius' thoughts is Oedipus (Sophocles, *OT* 1271 ff.); perhaps also Philoctetes (Sophocles, *Phil.* 1354).

You Catos . . . aim!: these lines are often cited as Petronius'
apologia for the *Satyricon* as a whole; certainly *opus nouae
simplicitatis* is apposite, since Tacitus states that *simplicitas*
was regarded as a feature of his character (*Ann.* 16. 18. 1).
But recent commentators insist that the lines are to be
ascribed to Encolpius in the immediate context (F. Zeitlin,
TAPA (1971), 676; R. Beck, *Phoenix* (1973), 51 ff.). For the
activities of old Cato, stern regulator of Roman morals, in
his censorship, see Livy 39. 42. 5 ff. The final line describes
the debased interpretation of Epicureanism as pilloried by
Cicero and others rather than the actual teaching of the
founder.

133 *the hostile deity*: this is Priapus: see the introductory note to
§ 16 for the recurrent motif of the god's anger, which comically evokes that of Poseidon in the *Odyssey* and that of Juno
in the *Aeneid*. The address to the god in elegiac couplets
has a whiff of similar prayers in Tibullus and Lygdamus
(Tib. 2. 5, 3. 6); the former actually addresses a poem to
Priapus (1. 4), though there is no connection with this.

Companion . . . in their cups: in these verses the invocation to
Priapus reflects the syncretism which attended the god
as his cult spread from Lampsacus successively to Asia,
Greece and Italy. Originally worshipped as the son of
Dionysus and Aphrodite, he takes on features of Pan/
Faunus. 'Companion to the nymphs' seems to evoke
Horace's hymn to Faunus (*Odes* 3. 18); 'beauteous Dione',
originally the mother of Venus, is frequently used of Venus
herself as here. There are no surviving traces of worship
of Priapus at Lesbos (except for conjectural coin-figures)
or at Thasos; and Hypaepa is associated rather with Pan
(cf. Ovid, *Met.* 11. 152). The Dryads are nymphs of the
woodland.

134 *Oenothea*: the name means 'wine goddess'; she is an alco-
holic witch in the tradition of Ovid's Dipsas ('Drunkard')
in *Amores* 1. 8.

All in . . . lofty peak: Petronius puts in the mouth of the
priestess a parody of such expressions of magical powers as
appear in Ovid, *Amores* 1. 8 and Lucan 6. 461 ff. 'At my
behest' . . . 'At my behest' is an echo of Ovid's *cum uoluit
. . . cum uoluit* (1. 8. 9 f.). 'Hyrcanian' (= Caucasian) as

applied to wild animals is a literary cliché. For snakes
stopped in their tracks, cf. Tibullus 1. 8. 20, Seneca, *Medea*
684. The combination of the moon drawn down from
heaven and Circe's transformation of Odysseus's men into
beasts is in Virgil, *Ecl.* 8. 69 f. 'A maiden's rites' (line 14)
were those of Medea (Ovid, *Met.* 7. 29 ff.); for Proteus' ability
to 'take new shapes' (line 17), see especially Virgil, *Georgics*
4. 440 ff. Most scholars assume that lines 10 and following
are spurious, in view of some repetitions and infelicities,
but that is to ascribe too lofty a status to the composition,
which should be read against the ludicrously inept performance of the witch which follows.

135 *Oenothea set up . . . of eloquence*: in the passage in prose and
verse that follows, Petronius extends the range of parody
to evoke the classic description of the pauper's hut, which
appears in Ovid's account of the visitation by Jupiter and
Mercury to the humble dwelling of Philemon and Baucis
(*Met.* 8. 628 ff.). The long fork, the willow bed-frame (line
4), the wooden cups, and (later) a goose are all in evidence in Ovid, who had drawn upon a poem of Callimachus.
This Greek poem celebrated the hospitality given by the
aged Hecale to Theseus when he slew the bull of Marathon;
'him who dwelt in Battus' town' (line 19) is Callimachus,
who came from Cyrene, the legendary founder of which
was Battus. This comparison of Oenothea with Hecale is of
course derisive.

136 *By finishing off the goose*: Petronius here may be extending
his sustained evocation of the *Odyssey*, for the slaughter of
the goose recalls the slaying of the sacred cattle of Helios
(*Od.* 12. 343 ff.).

the Stymphalian birds . . . Harpies: Stymphalus, a region in
Arcadia, was infested by man-eating birds which Hercules
disposed of (Hyginus, *Fab.* 30. 6). The Harpies were grisly
winged creatures employed by Jupiter to punish the seer
Phineus for revealing divine secrets. They snatched or polluted his food (Hyginus 19.1; for their flight, see Virgil,
Aen. 3. 242 ff.)

the statutory three glasses: this was the 'law' of the celebratory
party; see, e.g., Horace, *Odes* 3. 18. 15 f.; Ausonius 15. 1
(Green).

137 *If you have . . . will win*: Danaë (line 3) was the daughter of
the Argive king Acrisius. An oracle declared that she would
bear a son who would kill him; he accordingly enclosed
her in a tower, but Jupiter gained access to her in the
guise of a golden shower, and fathered Perseus. The myth
became proverbial for the power of money over virtue (see
Ovid, *Amores* 3. 8. 29 ff.). Cato (line 8) is Cato the Censor,
a legendary performer in the courts as well as the symbol
of incorruptible virtue (§ 132n., 'You Catos . . .'). Servius
Sulpicius Rufus (line 10) was a friend of Cicero and a
celebrated jurist; Antistius Labeo was a similarly famous
lawyer of the Augustan age.

138 *Ariadne's . . . in her favour*: Ariadne delivered Theseus
from the Cretan labyrinth (cf. Catullus 64. 52 ff.). Leda's
beauty attracted Jupiter, who visited her in the form of a
swan, as a result of which (in some versions) she hatched
out Helen, and Castor and Pollux. Priam's son Paris was
the arbiter of the beauty contest in which he chose
Aphrodite in preference to Hera and Athene, and was
rewarded with Helen.

139 *That will . . . Hellespont*: Tiryns' son (line 3) was Hercules, who
in the course of his labours imposed by Eurystheus at the
instigation of Juno took Atlas's place and bore the sky on
his shoulders. Laomedon (line 5), king of Troy and father
of Priam, cheated Apollo and Neptune of their reward for
building the walls of Troy; for the punishment, cf. Ovid,
Met. 11. 207 ff. Pelias (line 7), king of Iolchos in Thessaly,
neglected the cult of Hera/Juno, and Medea caused his
destruction (Ovid, *Met.* 7. 297 ff.). Telephus, King of Mysia,
was wounded by Achilles at the instigation of Dionysus when
the Greeks were *en route* to Troy. Odysseus (line 9) was
hounded by Poseidon/Neptune in his lengthy return from
Troy. Nereus (line 10) is the sea-god who fathered the
Nereids. For the pervasive motif of the anger of Priapus
(line 11), see § 16n.

13. *Eumolpus and the Legacy-hunters*

140 *to listen to his discourse*: Eumolpus in this final scene is cast
in the role of a dissolute Socrates whose education of the
young proceeds on different lines.

Mercury ... to escort souls: it was one of the functions of Hermes/Mercury to guide souls to Hades (Homer, *Od.* 24. 1 ff.). He was also the god of commerce and of thieves; in this latter role, he serves here as the comic counterpart of the deities of the Greek romances who deliver the pious lovers from their misfortunes; Encolpius is delivered from his sexual enervation.

more favoured than Protesilaus: once again Encolpius is depicted (or depicts himself) as a latter-day epic hero. Protesilaus was the first Greek killed at Troy (Homer, *Il.* 2. 695 ff.); Encolpius is more favoured because Protesilaus was restored to life for three hours only, to be with his wife Laodamia.

141 *Gorgias*: Petronius may have exploited the name of the famous sophist of Leontini to extend the portrayal of Eumolpus as a dissolute Socrates in dialogue with a philosophical adversary.

the Saguntines ... the Petelians ... Numantia: Eumolpus continues to the bitter end to parade his meretricious learning without substance. In the examples of earlier cannibalism, he cites the fall of Saguntum to Hannibal in 219, that of Petelia in Bruttium to the Carthaginians in 216, and that of Numantia to Scipio Aemilianus in 133; in none of these cases do the sober historians (cf. Livy 21. 7 ff., 23. 30, *Per.* 59) make any mention of such cannibalism, though the influence of the schools of rhetoric is seen in foisting it on the Saguntines (cf. Augustine, *CD* 3. 20).

It remains an open question whether this scene marked the close of the novel. It is clear that Eumolpus' demand that the legacy-hunters devour his corpse is a ruse to impel them to lose interest before they discover that he is an impostor, thus permitting the nefarious trio to make good their escape. It has been well remarked that a picaresque work of fiction such as this required no formal close; the novel could have ended with the heroes embarking on another disorderly adventure.

Fragments, Testimonies, Poems

The purpose of appending these passages is twofold. First, they collectively indicate how widely known the *Satyricon* was in the period of late antiquity from the fourth to the sixth centuries AD, from which the bulk of the testimonies come, and secondly, they afford evidence of lost sections of the novel.

1 *This account appears in Petronius*: scholars speculatively suggest that Encolpius volunteered to be the scapegoat, and that the novel begins with such an episode in Marseilles, where the hero brought on his head the wrath of Priapus (see fr. 4 below, and Sullivan, *The Satyricon*, 40 ff.).

4 *peer of Priapus . . . hallowed trunk*: (Note that Sidonius Apollinaris in this youthful composition joins Petronius with Cicero, Livy and Virgil as one of the masters of Latin eloquence.) Here Petronius is mistakenly identified with his hero Encolpius in this allusion to the first episode of the *Satyricon*. One scholar (Cichorius) interprets 'peer of Priapus' as intimating that Encolpius impersonated the statue of Priapus ('that hallowed trunk') during a ladies' orgiastic outing.

6 *Albucia*: she does not appear in the extant parts of the novel; the description here suggests that she is a second Quartilla or Circe in a lost episode.

7 A late interpolator appends to this passage in Fulgentius the remark: 'In Book 14, where Quartilla . . . says: "What? Has Encolpius drunk all the aphrodisiac?"' Cf. § 20, and for the citation of the book number, the Introduction, p. xvi.

8 *Euscius*: He could have appeared in the episode at Marseilles, if we assume that Encolpius was indicted there, or at Baiae.

10 *valgia*: this expression may have appeared in the description of the vomiting traveller in § 103.

11–12 These fragments must refer to Giton and Encolpius respectively where short sections have fallen out of the surviving text.

19 *Maidens of Memphis*: Memphis in Egypt (hence 'dusky boy' in line 9) was a celebrated centre of Isiac worship. One speculative suggestion is that a later episode was centred in Egypt.

21 This citation could have appeared in the Circe episode.

25 Lucretius' rationalization of the Tityus myth is evoked here (3. 978 ff.).

26 *Apollo's tortoise*: because Apollo is the god of music, and the lyre is made of tortoise-shell. The rest of the line has suffered corruption, and is only approximately rendered. rendered.

27 The inspiration here was Lucretius 5. 1161 ff. (though Lucretius, in line with Epicurean epistemology, accepts the existence of gods which we envisage). Athos (line 3) is the mountain on the peninsula of Acte in the Thracian Chalcidice; for the literary evocation here, see Virgil, *Georgics* 1. 332. Lines 14–15 hazard the general sense of the corrupt Latin.

28 *the secret of the king* (line 10): Ovid, *Met.* 11. 146 ff. recounts how Midas challenged the judgement that Apollo's music-making was superior to Pan's. Apollo punished the king by encumbering him with ass's ears, which Midas hid under a turban. His barber became privy to the secret, and confided it to the earth, but his confidence was betrayed by whispering reeds. The satirist Persius is said to have inveighed against Nero by depicting him as 'King Midas with ass's ears'; see Suetonius' *Life of Persius*.

29 This poem is an evocation of Lucretius, who in Book 4 of the *De Rerum Natura* outlines Epicurean notions of sense-perception, and at 353 ff. incorporates the image of the tower found here. The Epicureans believed that all objects give off film-like images of themselves which strike the senses, but that in their passage through the air they become distorted. Hyblean honey (line 5) from Hybla in Sicily was a delicacy, and casia or cinnamon (line 6) was proverbial for its exquisite scent.

30 Here again Lucretius is the inspiration, for at 4. 962 ff. he explains dreams with a similar sequence of advocate, soldier, seaman, and huntsman.

Index and Glossary of Names

The
Oxford
World's
Classics
Website

www.worldsclassics.co.uk

- Browse the full range of Oxford World's Classics online

- Sign up for our monthly e-alert to receive information on new titles

- Read extracts from the Introductions

- Listen to our editors and translators talk about the world's greatest literature with our Oxford World's Classics audio guides

- Join the conversation, follow us on Twitter at OWC_Oxford

- Teachers and lecturers can order inspection copies quickly and simply via our website

www.worldsclassics.co.uk

MORE ABOUT **OXFORD WORLD'S CLASSICS**

American Literature

British and Irish Literature

Children's Literature

Classics and Ancient Literature

Colonial Literature

Eastern Literature

European Literature

Gothic Literature

History

Medieval Literature

Oxford English Drama

Poetry

Philosophy

Politics

Religion

The Oxford Shakespeare

A complete list of Oxford World's Classics, including Authors in Context, Oxford English Drama, and the Oxford Shakespeare, is available in the UK from the Marketing Services Department, Oxford University Press, Great Clarendon Street, Oxford OX2 6DP, or visit the website at www.oup.com/uk/worldsclassics.

In the USA, visit www.oup.com/us/owc for a complete title list.

Oxford World's Classics are available from all good bookshops. In case of difficulty, customers in the UK should contact Oxford University Press Bookshop, 116 High Street, Oxford OX1 4BR.